Galaxy at War:

A Prophecy Fulfilled

Written by Trey Deibel

2022 Global Book Award Winner for Self-Published
Authors for Sci-Fi / Space Exploration

Book 3

I met the wind head on, greeting it as a welcome friend. That seemed to be the only greeting I would get. Only seconds after I touched down, I heard yelling from the left. I turned to see new creatures unlike any I'd ever laid eyes on, but my gut told me they were amphibians. Each had dark purple eyes as big as a softball, with a gathered tangle of flexible tentacle-tresses extending from their heads and long enough to reach halfway down their backs. They were alarmed, hands waving and pointing past me. Their words were lost over the thick winds. Then came the alarms, blaring over and over.

The creatures pulled up weapons! But not at us. They fired past us. I turned my attention to that direction. Out of a forest of darkened gray trees, dripping of black goo, came creatures almost as large as maelkii. The creatures shrieked and trampled the ground as they stampeded for us all.

Table of Contents:

Milky Way Galaxy System Map:

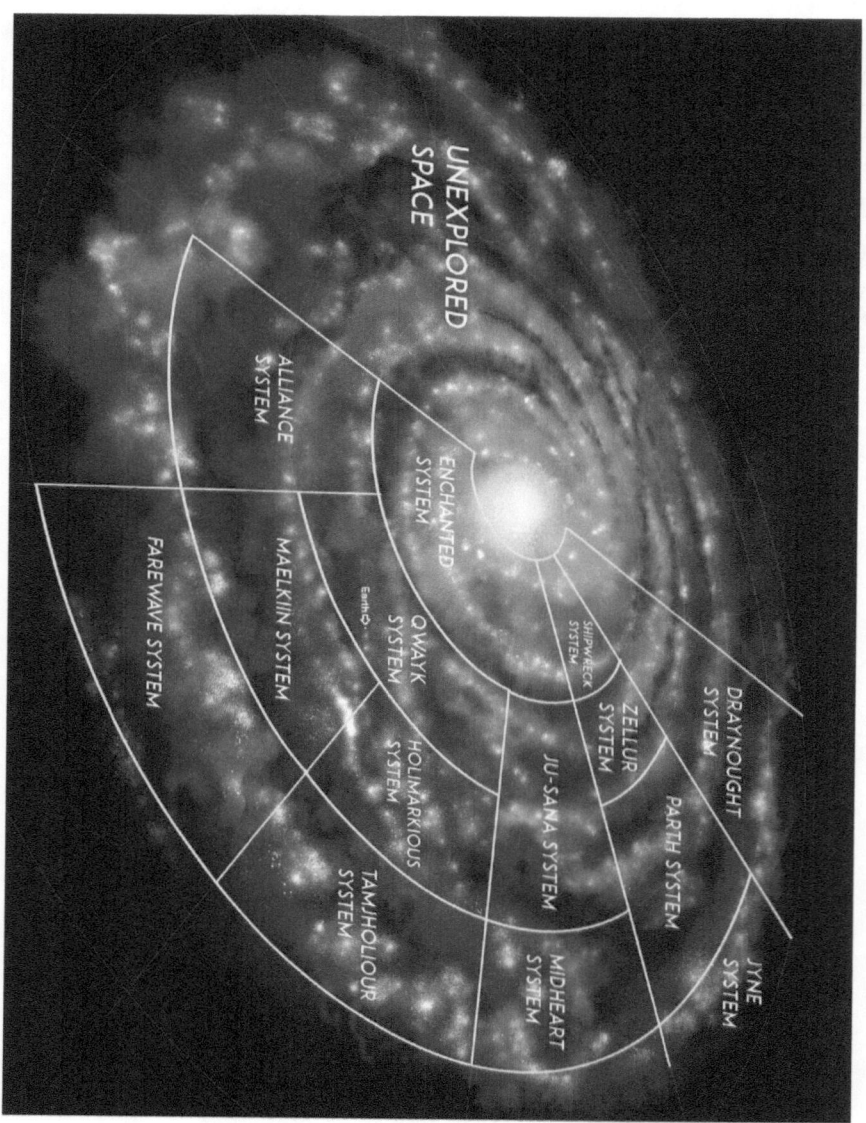

Concept Art:

"DOR'O"

" MAELKII "

"QWAYK"

"DYTRIC"

"KORKYRA"

"LYCARGAN"

"OMELIC"

Mentioned Alien Species:

Alliance of Republic Worlds (ARW):
- Dor'o
- Humans
- Maelkii
- Qwayks

Wersillian Legion:
- Dytircs
- Korkyras
- Lycargans

ARW Supporters:
- Laburtles
- O'garks
- Plowsu
- Valistares

Species Loyal/Colonized by the Wersillian Legion:
- Gatero
- Plauranians
- Smokmorjoroks

Neutral:
- Allsungs
- Corelinns
- Jenjarians
- Mordazuls
- Omelics
- Yuerr

Extinct:
- Devisors
- Precursors

Chapter 1: The Prophecy
February 31, 2041

Sunfire

The call was made. And Sunfire was here to answer it. Using a refractor field, Sunfire, a steadfast knight of the Brotherhood of Relics, entered the tent of the caller. Located on a planet close to the center of the galaxy and within a settlement still at least a hundred years from reaching space traveling technology, Sunfire didn't expect this trip to be worthwhile, but she had been wrong before.

Sunfire slipped underneath a line of hanging beads into the main lounge of a hut. The space was both vibrant in color and cluttered with antiques looming around the perimeter. Making no sound, she waited, masking her breathing and keeping her scent to herself. A lady of the corelinn species came from the back room.

As a knight of the Brotherhood of Relics, Sunfire has seen many intelligent species through the galaxy. Even among the intelligent amphibian types, the corelinns didn't stand out to her. As a species, they were not particularly tall, strong, or smart. A sole benefit she saw of them was their strong resilience out of water over other amphibious species of the galaxy.

The corelinn lady hadn't turned toward Sunfire's direction yet. Her years were young, and she was near motionless. Skin colored such a deep purple, she could almost hide in the shadows. Dressed in a splash of colorful clothes, she had no care of style, or sense of it.

The lady took a quick look in Sunfire's direction. And her eyes were not like that of her species. Sunfire could see this particular corelinn wasn't like the others of her kind. She was unique, different, like Sunfire was among her own species. This woman's eyes were a night sky full of stars.

Then the mystery woman smiled at Sunfire. No, this lady couldn't see her, could she? Not with her refractive field active. That would be improbable.

"Hello, Sunfire," the woman spoke while taking a seat on a chair next to a desk.

Chapter 1

Sunfire, stunned, contemplated her next move. She shifted forward, deactivated the refractive field around her, and looked the affable woman over for a few seconds. "You know my name without me telling you. Seems this journey here may be worth my time."

"Please, sit." She gestured to a chair in the middle of the room, resting on multiple mats and rugs. "Don't worry. Nobody will bother us today. And my words are truth."

"I don't know you. I'll stand."

"Be my guest." She took a breath. "Members of your organization weren't easy to find. You're secretive and, apparently, cautious as well. I respect that."

Sunfire took a nibble at her lower lip. "And you're quite an interest. When one of my undercover bishops told me that someone from this planet, a planet without space travel, not only made him out as a Brotherhood of Relics member but also addressed him by name, I didn't believe it. After he relayed your message for me, I just had to investigate this myself. Now, tell me why you've called me here."

"Relax, Sunfire. You are not alone. For I am Anighta Yin'Dahen, and I, too, am like you."

"Tell me in what way you are like me." Sunfire's head tilted up in intrigue.

"You have powers that defy natural laws. I'm similar to you in that respect."

"Given your eyes, I had a hunch. Though, I'm sure you've come to see that these powers of ours come wrapped in a mystery. I have only had these powers for five years, and, as far as I can tell, I'm the only omelic with abilities," Sunfire responded.

"Time has an interesting way of shining light on unanswered questions. For you are the first ever. I am the third. And more enhanced beings like us will be born in the years to follow. And my words are truth," said Anighta.

Sunfire's eyebrow spiked. *Raises the question as to who is the second?*

Anighta continued. "You will go to sleep - a long sleep. And when you awaken, this very galaxy will be under a dark shadow of war. You will be the light to cast the away the shadow. For this is my gift, my prophecy to you. Now go. For you have a life to live before falling to slumber. Then when the time is right, fulfill this prophecy. My words are truth."

Sunfire smirked. "Very vague with your predictions. Never had a taste for that."

"We all have our limits."

"Do we?" Sunfire spoke the question as if it were a statement.

"Some more than others," Anighta reaffirmed.

Sunfire stared at the seer for a moment. "It is the job of the Brotherhood of Relics to protect this galaxy. I above the rest have the will to carry such a burden. And based on what you had to say to me, I now see clearly just where my place is, and I thank you for that."

"No thanks needed. And my words are truth." Anighta gave a small bow for respect.

"This has been enlightening. But I must leave you now. As you said yourself, it's time for me to live my life, and I have much to do." Sunfire turned her back to the stranger, ready to leave.

"Before you depart, I give you one last thing." Anighta came up to Sunfire and handed her a small device. Sunfire opened her hand to see that it was no bigger than her palm, shaped like a long triangle, and not made with technology available to Anighta or her species. Made Sunfire wonder how she got access to such a device.

Sunfire looked back at Anighta, and before she could say something, Anighta spoke. "Keep this with you and go. You will know what you need to do when the time comes."

Sunfire gave her one last head tilt before she departed from this planet.

Chapter 2: Station 51
January 14, 2112

Kalvin Keefe

Information is power, but if misused, it can be catastrophic. And that is what makes information a misunderstood asset. Those who would have leverage yet flaunt it outward like an avaricious child will only incite friction and animosity from others. It is all but guaranteed that those results end bloody and pugnaciously. Only foolish wise men fall for such disaster. However, the right information used under the right circumstances guarantees fortune to the handler. Such information has been the weapon of choice for Kalvin Keefe throughout his long life. He learned early on he was never meant to be a man who fights with fists or physical brawn. That was a game for the less elegant. Only by admitting what we are can we gain what we want. That is why Kalvin was a man who never fought, because he would have already won before ever meeting opponents face to face.

Kalvin rested comfortably in his desk chair, in thought, with his eyes glued to the desk in his private quarters. This was his official place of business, the place he went to when he needed to run the Order of Aegis to its fullest capabilities. A place of legend and lore where its true purpose is known only to distinguished members of the Order of Aegis and ARW military. A place known as Station 51.

Before him were the latest results on his study of Steion and the nano-bugs he had been fascinated by for some time. After all, the Wersillian Legion tried to destroy his findings a while back. Based on these findings, those same nano-bugs were found in Steion's brain as well as the countless other dytircs and lycargans they studied. A result that only added questions to his already overworked mind. Kalvin theorized the nano-bugs had something to do with the warlords' influence over lesser dytircs and lycargans. However, finding some in the warlord Steion seemed to be discredit that hypothesis. Maybe it all links back to that head warlord he had heard about recently, Airra. Or even a different, still unknown warlord. So many unanswered questions connected to this one little thread.

He slid open his drawer and pulled out a bottle of brown pills and took his daily medicine. He then placed it back where it belonged.

There was a knock on his office door.

"Enter," Kalvin called.

One of his assistants entered. "Sir. Chief Admiral Day-Bringer is orbiting the station."

Why would she be here?

Right now, Day-Bringer most certainty was not one of his favorite people, and he, forthrightly, did not want anything to do with her. This emotion had nothing to do with her as a person. It was the mere fact that she remained the only chief admiral he had little useful information about. It was not due to a lack of trying. Because of this unfortunate situation, Day-Bringer remained one of the few who could defy his charisma. Which she often did. And she customarily led in ways a bit unorthodox compared to the other three chief admirals, which aggravated Kalvin.

"Tell her she does not have authorization to enter," Kalvin responded.

"Sir. I told her, and she's insisting that I put her through to you."

Kalvin sighed. "Fine. Put her through to my channel." Once she was through, Kalvin began. "Day—"

"Shut up, Kalvin. I don't have time for your power games. I need to meet with you *this* moment."

"This is a privately owned facility, and, honestly, under our laws I am not obligated to let you in."

Day-Bringer raised her voice. "Either you let me in now, or I come back with a few star cruisers and let myself in. I leave the choice to you."

Damn upstart always trying to overreach, Kalvin thought to himself. He let out a breath of stress. "Have it your way." He swiped a sequence on his cyberwatch, and the main hatch began to open. With this, Kalvin began his walk to the hangar to meet his very stubborn guest.

Kalvin traveled through the long corridors of Station 51, followed by some of his guards. Kalvin dragged his hand down the dark ashen walls, each made of a concrete-like compound more expensive and durable than the aforementioned material and strengthened with a fair sum of veridium-dipped rebar.

Chapter 2

Station 51, his home away from home, was the most fortified and enormous station owned by the Order of Aegis. It was constructed almost completely inside a remarkably dense asteroid that took a decade to carve out. Due to Station 51's high durability and scale, it served two purposes: It housed the most safeguarded projects, and it housed the projects too colossal to be conducted in any other station.

Kalvin arrived at the control room overlooking the hangar. A few Aegis employees manned the operations from the corner. Kalvin stepped to the hard-glass that overlooked the hangar. There she was, Day-Bringer's starship; fast and armored, fit for a chief admiral.

Day-Bringer stepped off her ship. And she looked up to the glass. It was one-sided, so she would not be able to see him.

"Escort her up here," Kalvin told a guard.

He nodded and opened the door leading down to the hangar. Kalvin waited the minutes until she walked through that same door herself, not once looking away from the glass until she was out of view.

She started, "I'm glad you could see things my way." As per usual, Day-Bringer's presence seemed to brighten the room. Kalvin always attributed this strange phenomenon to her elegant style of leadership. Or perhaps it was her unusually bright-red skin for a dor'o.

"I see that you enjoy finding ways around the rules of the game. I admire your ingenuity," Kalvin teased.

"Still as sharp as ever, Kalvin," Day-Bringer responded, without hesitation.

"Are you referring to my suit, or my intelligence?"

"Does it have to be just one?"

"Well, we do all have our talents after all." He tilted his head.

"Some more than most." Day-Bringer's sharp eyebrows and smirk indicated she was referring to herself.

Kalvin began to lead them down the hall. "In that case, surely a chief admiral such as yourself must have more important matters to attend to." His statement attempted to appeal to her superiority complex.

Day-Bringer walked to Kalvin's direct right. "Don't sell yourself short, Kalvin. What is a chief admiral compared to the man himself, the big director of the Order of Aegis?" Day-Bringer paused for a brief moment and then stopped. "As chief admiral, I have standards that I'm held to. There are rules in my world. So, it must be nice to operate *without* being restrained by such pesky irritations." Now standing next to him, Day-Bringer placed her hand over Kalvin's back.

Kalvin looked to her arm, then down to her face. He was not going to let himself be fooled by such a noticeable attempt at playing his friend. He knew better. "I would not know," Kalvin responded.

She let her hand go. "If that's the case, why keep this ah--" she gazed around, "--surprisingly marvelous facility hidden from public eye?"

"I am a purveyor of both confidentiality and innovation. In my line of work, I find both to be equally important."

"Although, what some could call innovation, others may not. While I'm sure the public and military find many of the products the Order of Aegis so kindly puts out to be inventive, they don't quite see the full picture, do they?"

"And you do?"

"I have it from a good source that the Order of Aegis dabbles in many... projects, and not all see the light of day. Take Project Ace, for example--"

Kalvin interrupted. "Project Ace has trained valuable assets with great success for military use. You are welcome."

"Oh, I wasn't talking about *that* Project Ace. I am referring to the old Project Ace, the one focused on taking one ace, James Stone, and making more. Must've been difficult for you to acquire subjects willing to undergo such dangerous testing procedures. Or maybe it was easier to snatch unwilling subjects instead."

Kalvin raised an eyebrow, slightly tilting his head. "Strictly speaking, such a thing would not be in accordance with the law."

"*Strictly speaking,* of course," Day-Bringer quoted him.

Kalvin flinched his lip. "Tell me, Day-Bringer, how does one such as yourself come out of nowhere and end up in one of the most powerful positions among our alliance? I have often wondered."

"Strange for you to wonder such a thing. I'm sure it's as easy as looking in a mirror and asking yourself for the answer," Day-Bringer shot back.

Kalvin's quick tongue nearly caught on itself. He knew there was no way she would know such a buried secret. There was no way she could know, he was the only one left alive to know, so he had to continue to play cool.

Day-Bringer gazed back up to Kalvin and smiled. "Of course, I'm joking," she teased. "I like to think we have the same goal, Kalvin. So let me put this forward: I know that the Order of Aegis hides certain projects behind closed doors and uses less than ethical methods for the sake of progress. I'm certainly against this practice. But the ARW needs to win this war. I wholeheartedly agree with this fact, because our galaxy depends on it. And to win, we need you, Kalvin, and the Order of Aegis. So I can often look the other way for the sake of the galaxy. Are we at an understanding?"

"We are."

Day-Bringer brightened the room. "Pleasant." There was that strange verbal tic of hers again.

"Now that we have laid it on the table, I would like to know what your purpose is for being here."

"I'm sure you would, Kalvin. In fact, I do only seek one project in particular - Project Aurum."

Kalvin snickered.

Day-Bringer squinted her eyes. "Does that amuse you?"

"*Amuse* is not the right word. I actually find it quite sardonic, yet not at all unbefitting your entitlement. I say this because it was only just recently that you - what is the word - mishandled a few of my aces."

"Your aces? You speak to me as if those people are your property."

"Hmm." Kalvin raised an eyebrow. "You dodged the point."

"And who's dodging right now?" Day-Bringer mirrored Kalvin's expression. "We both know that we could do this all day. Instead, I propose that you take me to what I want to see."

"It would save time." Kalvin led the way, and Day-Bringer followed his lead down a long hallway. "Now what is your intention with Project Aurum?"

"I came upon a report by you, actually. And in that report, it stated that you believe that this project will be part of what wins us the war. Then again, you've made that deduction over many projects in the past years, so--" Day-Bringer shrugged. "That being said, I do have the perfect test run in mind."

"Test run? You mean a field test, do you not?"

"I do."

"That is something I am not about to sanction."

"Excuse me?" Day-Bringer halted. "If I recall correctly, most of these individuals are active members of the ARW military, and you are merely being allowed access to them on loan. Remember who is the chief admiral here."

"Trust me, you would not let me forget edgewise. So let me bring this forward: I was the one who found every one of these individuals--"

"I'm sure that means so much to them--" Day-Bringer tried to interrupt.

"I wasn't finished! I also convinced most of them to enlist. You are welcome for that. And after you lost James Stone, Jay Bridges, and both the Bruising Brothers, I will be damned before I let you take these aces away, too."

"No, that's not it. You intended on using them yourself. It's the only reason I can think of for your overheated reaction."

"I have no idea what you mean."

"I'll tell you what: I'll let you know what I have planned for them." Day-Bringer pulled up a disturbing image of sharp bones piercing a dozen soldiers. Blood and guts poured all over the control center of a star cruiser. One man had his head spiked clean through by bones shaped almost like a spear. Another was torn apart, with bones sticking out of his stomach, arms, and face like a porcupine. And those two got off easier than the rest.

"What, dare I ask, happened to them?!" Kalvin finally asked.

"I wish I knew." Day-Bringer cleared her throat. "We lost contact with this ship - the Madame Galactic - for days. When we finally got a recon unit to investigate, this was only one of many images they sent back."

"Did you have the bones tested?"

"No, I never thought of that." Her sarcastic tone was apparent. Kalvin frowned. "Be serious."

"Yes, we had the bones along with a few deposits of organic material tested, and our computers came up with nothing that would link us to any known species. Whatever these bones belonged to, it isn't in our database. But the most unpleasant news... the bones are more dense and durable than any other bone makeup we have on record."

"Quite a discovery. What does this have to do with my aces?" Kalvin crossed his arms.

"This wasn't a single case. Over this last month, we have had units ambushed, and the Madame Galactic was the first of three star cruisers we lost! I think we have a new threat."

"And you want my aces to figure out what it is?"

"Yes, and I want them to take out the threat at all costs," Day-Bringer said, "Whatever or however many of them exists."

"I appreciate the guilelessness. So allow me to reciprocate, I was planning on using them to retrieve the lost aces."

Her apprehension showed. "For one, we don't know if they are alive. And two, we have no way of knowing where they are."

"Are you so certain?" Kalvin chuckled.

"I'm not following." Day-Bringer held a confused expression.

"Let me let you in on another secret. I know someone who may know of such information, and, before you arrived, I was planning on summoning him today."

"*Summoning?*" Day-Bringer gave Kalvin a dubious stare.

"Follow me." Kalvin gestured down the hall.

And down they went - down the halls of Station 51. Kalvin formed a grin on his face. It had been years, but he was finally going to see him again; the man more mysterious than anyone he had ever encountered, a man he called The Broker.

Chapter 3: Aces of the ARW I - Project Aurum
January 14, 2112

Night-Shade

Night-Shade was the newest ace to hit the age of eighteen, which had happened only a few months ago. Eighteen is a big number, too. It's the minimum age required to be in the service of the ARW military. Even though, as a dor'o, adulthood is traditionally the age of sixteen; rules were rules.

A mixed bag of emotion filled her rose-red chest. War was scary to her, like a looming shadow in the darkness. All the horror stories were enough to make her skin crawl. That didn't stop her from feeling a sense of pride that she could help win against those savage enemies she had heard so much about.

She knew it was her duty as an ace to play her part. Kalvin Keefe had told her such.

Despite it all, the feeling putting the most amount of pressure on her chest was unease. Up until a couple weeks ago, she was still part of Project Ace - a project that helped her learn and master her abilities. Now she was put into a new project known as Project Aurum. To her knowledge, she wasn't completely sure what Project Aurum was intended to do or why it required banding all aces of the ARW together. She knew it had something to do with winning the war, but as to how it would accomplish that implausible goal, she did not know. As a whole, the idea was Kalvin's, just another one of many so-called golden bullets.

She had only arrived on Station 51 hours ago and was only briefed on Project Aurum less than one hour ago. It was a lot to take in, and now she was in the presence of strangers. Although, she did know that each of the other three individuals in her sight were aces of the ARW.

Night-Shade sat quietly on a limestone block with one earbud in her left ear playing rock music. To the beat her head banged only slightly, and her left hand tapped her knee to the tempo of the current song playing. She knew she should give her full attention to the current mission about to commence, but she always felt that she did better with a song playing. Plus, it helped ease her trembling mind.

The mission, though, was quite unorthodox, and the target was beyond this galaxy. Literally, the target was not from the Milky Way, making the briefing she had an hour prior to this moment insanely interesting. But that is how things roll sometimes, and she liked to roll with it. After all, how threatening can a being who called himself The Broker and traded wishes for souls be?

Exactly, very dangerous. She shivered.

At least the setting was unique. Currently, she was in a testing room decorated and prepared for one singular purpose. At the center of the room was a coffin, decorated in Egyptian hieroglyphs, and it rested at the center of a trapezoid-shaped platform. Stairs lined all four sides and led straight up to the coffin. At each of the four corners, limestone columns stood taller than the coffin with torches on top. Limestone blocks and columns were brought straight from the original location of the coffin into this testing room. They were stacked many meters tall against the walls and scattered seemingly randomly around the room.

She was furthest to the right, and when she looked left, she saw one of the other aces making his way over to her with eager strides. A qwayk male; fair skin the color of snow and hair just as white, he was short yet confident. He wore light-weight, technology-driven armor not uncommon for a qwayk. Two daggers were strapped to his hip, along with a line of pouches attached over his butt.

As the qwayk male neared Night-Shade, he didn't come in to shake her hand or make conversation like she expected. He came in, arms extended, and gave her a hug. Night-Shade didn't move and blinked several times from discomfort.

The qwayk eased away and faced her. "My name is Ayeko Madoryia."

"You're friendly." Night-Shade was still motionless.

"Nice to meet you." Ayeko tilted his head and leaned forward, waiting for her name.

"Oh. I'm Night-Shade," she said, seeming to slip from her trance. She took out her earphone and rolled it up neatly.

"You must be the newest ARW ace," he jubilated. "Tell me, tell me, what are your abilities? Where are you from? How old are you?"

Chapter 3

"Oh. I umm--" Night-Shade started. Her eyes darted from his, and she felt her body close off a bit at the rush of questions.

Ayeko flipped over his hand. "Wait... I'm sorry. You must be overwhelmed. Here I am, jumping right into your life when you would probably rather know a bit more about us first. That way, you can feel more comfortable. Am I right, friend?"

Night-Shade nodded. "I haven't been here even a day, so I wasn't briefed much on the people I'm supposed to work with, just on the situation."

"Yeah, ain't that something? The Broker." His eyebrows rose. "Scary, right? Shoot, I'm getting off topic, though. I'll start with me. I'm twenty years of age, I became aware of my ace abilities five years ago. I'm from a polygamous household with one parasibling - a sister, and--" Ayeko stopped.

Night-Shade stared with narrowed eyes at the strange word.

"I lost you, didn't I?"

She nodded. "I'm not sure what all that means."

"Well, here is the summary of it. Qwayks are beings of pleasure and science. It's not uncommon for qwayks to find multiple life partners and form households with them. And me... I was born into one. I have two mothers and three fathers, and I have one sister. She isn't blood related, but she was born into the household, which is why she is my parasister. Make sense?"

"I'm sorry." Night-Shade shook her head no.

"It's fine. I know it is a lot to take in if you've never seen our qwayk worlds first-hand. *I know!* Let's get to know you a little bit." Ayeko smiled. "I noticed you listening to music earlier. What kind was it?"

"Metal."

"Metal?"

Night-Shade shifted a bit uncomfortably. "Oh, it's ah... just an old genre of human music. I usually listen to hard rock, punk rock, and some grunge. But those metal genres are nowhere near as popular now as they were in their heyday."

"So why rock? Why not something more modern?"

"There is a lot of pain in the galaxy. For me, metal bands seem to capture that emotion the best."

"Seems too depressing for my taste, no offense." He smiled, showing he wasn't trying to judge her. "So when you were in Project Ace, what were you told about us anyway? Which of course, I assume you were in Project Ace... well, because all aces were--" He stopped, realizing he was rambling on too long.

"Kalvin told me there were more of you than I see in this room."

"You didn't hear? A few aces went MIA."

"Who?"

Ayeko gazed around the room before speaking. "James Stone, Geariic and Alabon Zserin, and Jay Bridges AKA Frost; all MIA after some top-level mission. And Kalvin's pretty pissed about it."

"I've heard of James before. Who hasn't heard of the first ace in the ARW? But I'm not familiar with the others."

Ayeko lit up. "I guess you wouldn't be familiar, being the new ace on the block and all. So let me give you a quick breakdown. James was the first ace, currently twenty-four, developed his powers almost twelve years ago. Geariic and Alabon were discovered by Kalvin three years later, each having developed their abilities only a few months prior to being discovered. Funny enough, they are actually older than James, but ace abilities seem to develop during the puberty stages of the host. This can happen early on or later, of course. And maelkii already have the longest frame of time that puberty can take place. Now back on track... Frost developed his powers six years ago." Ayeko motioned his head toward the only maelkii in the room. "See her?"

The maelkii was female; deep orange skin and taller than average. Unlike what is traditional of a maelkii to wear during times of war, this female warrior wore tight-fitted cloth covered with a looser fabric instead of dense, heavy armor. The cloth covered her upper chest and around her shoulders, along with her waist to her knees. Her exposed skin carried purple inked tattoos that extended from the tips of her fingers up her arms and all the way to her lower back, vining out like a tree. She had one weapon, and it wasn't the tradition forcidion-metal shield used by maelkii or one of their hand-covering plasma cannons. Her weapon of choice was a large broadsword, as tall as a full-grown human man, shaped like a butcher knife and pearlescent purple in color. The blade itself had one small notch to allow a strap to be wrapped around the weapon, making it easier for the user to carry. It's extremely long handle was made for two-handed grip.

"Yeah, I see her," Night-Shade responded.

"She's known as Drayvan Pryde. She entered Project Ace almost a year after Frost." Ayeko was grinning like a little kid. "And she's said to be the ARW's most powerful ace. The sharpest tool in the shed... so to speak," he whispered with excitement.

"Really?" Night-Shade eyes were full of wonder.

"Oh, yeah. Word has it that she took on both the Bruising Brothers and ran through them like it was nothing."

"What's her abilities like?"

"She hasn't told me yet. But I do know this: She's from the Escanorinn House. And that house has a bit of a reputation among the maelkii. Honor to them... isn't the same as what most houses consider honorable. Honor to the Escanorinn House is superiority and glory, a belief in oneself above all other things. In their Book of Ancient Prophets, God, to them, gave them the gift of themselves, and it is upon themselves to cherish that gift from their first day until their last day."

"Sounds hard core," Night-Shade concluded.

"They're definitely different, for sure. Anyway, I entered Project Ace less than a year after her, followed closely by a human girl named Makayla Katakurry."

"Where is she?"

"Don't know. But next was Xavier 'Tank' Brockman over there." Ayeko pointed to the last of the aces in the room. "He got the nickname Tank from his unit that he used to run with and it just stuck. Oh... he also only developed his powers a few months ago."

"Strange. I've had my powers longer than him."

"Just before he gained his powers, he hit a massive growth spurt, so maybe he had a late puberty."

"How old is he?" Night-Shade asked.

"Nineteen."

Night-Shade studied him. He was human, but whatever ace ability he had transformed him. Near the peak of height for a human, Tank was broad and well-defined. Night-Shade wondered if that was how he naturally was or if his ability had something to do with it. What was truly bizarre was his violet skin tone with a wavy texture that seemed to layer on each other somewhat like scales but still carried a fleshy texture. He still had much of the same human attributes, such as two arms, two legs, two eyes, a head, and whatnot, except for a strange rock-like object attached to his back like a shell. The rock pillar was more symmetrical than to be expected of a rock and carried an obsidian tint with various purple lines decorating it.

"He seems preoccupied," she observed.

"He's not doing so hot. Poor buddy got dumped by his fiancé after he began to change. On top of that, he seems to have lost his ability to speak."

Night-Shade's words were lost to her upon hearing such a tragedy. In her empathy for him, she noticed her lower lip quivering slightly. She'd never been in love, but she knew the venom of rejection very well.

The only door to this room hissed open. "Seems we'll have to continue this chat later." Ayeko trotted back to the place he was before talking to her. Night-Shade gazed behind her and saw Kalvin enter the room, followed by Chief Admiral Day-Bringer and a few escorts. Both were in conversation.

Night-Shade put back in an earbud but eventually began to overhear what was being said. "--and he calls himself The Broker," Kalvin told Day-Bringer with his lips half-closed as he smiled on her.

"If a being such as this existed, then you would've used his gifts to your benefit much more than once. So why lie?" countered Day-Bringer, with a ceased brow.

"I am not. The answer is reasonably simple: He can only be summoned with the correct ingredients. And I have only recently located another ancient mask like the one I used once before, which leads me to the belief that he will make an appearance today."

"Okay, then. Let's meet this charlatan, this shadow man." Day-Bringer was skeptical. A feeling Night-Shade shared to an extent.

Kalvin nodded to his assistant, who then communicated the 'all clear' signal. It was now a matter of waiting. The assistant headed from the back of the room and up the stairs leading to the coffin. After a dozen or so steps, he slid the coffin lid half-open and began the summoning ritual.

From a bag, the assistant placed a wooden mask in the coffin, followed by the skull of a jackal. He then took two containers - one full of gold dust and another full of dirt - and poured it inside. Lastly, he took a blade to his palm and sliced. The man winced as the blade drew qwayk blood, and he squeezed so the blood would come.

With the ritual done, a deep humming sound resonated through the room, sounding almost like a steady bass. Little rings carved into the coffin glowed a black light. "I have come to make a deal - a bond unbreakable," the assistant spoke. Through the render chip in Night-Shade's ears, the words were clear as day. However, she knew it was spoken in a language she would never know.

The assistant finally pressed the square hieroglyph that was now emerging from the front of the coffin. The room vibrated for a few seconds before a sudden surge of power, followed by a thunderous clap, knocked out the power. The room went black, and the torches blew out. The glowing and humming were no more. Darkness had engulfed every inch of the room. Even the music stopped playing in Night-Shade's earbud, so she removed it.

Some of the station's lights turned back on, followed by a low and slow alarm. The room was blinking red from the emergency lights stationed about.

Night-Shade looked backward.

"Seems the reaction set off an EMP of some sort - an electromagnetic pulse," a guard told Kalvin. "We are on backup power right now."

"We all know what EMP stands for." Kalvin looked down at the man. "Now go apprise everybody in the control station to restart our emergency systems." He looked to Day-Bringer. "The automated advanced circuit rejuvenating systems should restore things any moment."

On the timing of his words, the main lights flipped back on, and the siren shut down. Everything was back to normal. That was until Night-Shade turned back to look at the coffin. It was now closed, and the assistance was now at the bottom of the stairs, looking at his hands with a quizzical expression.

What started as tiny black particles formed into a full person. Legs relaxed over the edge of the coffin with his arms resting atop, he immediately squeezed his fist together, and the coffin rearranged its shape into a throne. Through his mask, his eyes moved from person to person until he had seen everyone in the room. Night-Shade couldn't believe how humanoid and fit he looked. Not exactly the proportions of a human, omelic, or qwayk, but there was an uncanny resemblance to those species. Noticeably different were his longer arms and fingers, and the nails at his fingertips were sharp and resembled a werewolf more than a human. Just like she heard during the briefing, he wore a kilt with wrapping covering the main parts of his body. However, his signature black spiral-patterned mask that focused and spiraled around the eyeholes had been replaced. Presently, he wore new mask instead of the one that she was told about. Patterned in symbols, a sharp gold and raisin black, this new mask highlighted his eyes and assorted jewelry.

"My, my. I have an audience." The Broker spoke with a smoky accent.

Night-Shade's eyes immediately jumped back to Day-Bringer and Kalvin. Day-Bringer was utterly wide-eyed, not a common expression shown by her, by any means. Kalvin didn't share that look; his eyes had a hint of a thrill at seeing Day-Bringer at an actual loss for words.

Kalvin called up to The Broker, "Hello, old acquaintance. Do you remember me?"

Night-Shade's eyes were back to the foreigner.

"I remember all my customers. And how could I forget the man who convinced another man to forfeit his soul for his own benefit? It seems you used the information I gave you after all. Glad I was able to satisfy another customer." The Broker nodded indifferent to Kalvin.

Kalvin sounded a bit thrown off by The Broker's words. "Umm, how do you know whether or not I heeded your advice?"

"I anticipated that I would someday meet you again should you take my advice. And here we are."

Day-Bringer jumped in before any more words could be spoken. "Is what Kalvin said about you true? Are you actually from another galaxy?"

"If you mean to ask whether or not I was born in your galaxy, then no. I was not."

"I don't believe you."

The Broker shrugged. "And I don't care. I'm not here to prove anything to anyone."

"So if I asked you for proof, would you provide it?" Day-Bringer continued her questioning.

"No."

"I thought not. What a shame, really. I was really hoping to understand just what you are."

"Most of my past customers want to jump right into their own desired wishes. They don't care much for who I am as long as I can provide them with what they desire. But I get the sense you aren't most."

"I just find all this a bit unfitting. To hear about this mystic man who grants wishes seems all too convenient."

"Or maybe you just don't want to believe that there exists things in this universe that you don't have the answers to," The Broker gleamed. "So tell me, Day-Bringer, what is it you desire?"

"You really just want to jump right to it, don't you?"

"I'm a businessman." He gave a carefree shrug.

"Too bad I'm not in the market to trade away my soul."

"And yet, we are in a room full of individuals." The Broker gazed around. He pointed his finger toward Ayeko, then to two different guards, and finally to Kalvin's assistant, who was now back to their side. "Four qwayks." He then lifted his finger again and pointed to Tank, then to Kalvin, plus the last guard. "Three humans." Drayvan was next. "One maelkii." His finger stopped at Night-Shade. "One dor'o and--" his finger then lingered on Day-Bringer, "--well, two dor'o." He inhaled. "So much potential in this crowd. I am so... humbled to finally meet many of this galaxy's enhanced beings." His gazed fixated on Night-Shade for a few seconds. "I choose you. What is it you desire?"

Night-Shade perked up, though her words were unsure. "It's umm... it's common courtesy to introduce yourself first."

"I'm who you want me to be."

"Aren't deals supposed to be built on trust? And in my culture, names are as important as our very lives. But you sit there pretending to be a man with no name... a man who is nobody."

"I'm nothing more than a guide meant to help others gain what they want," The Broker voiced, his tone calm. "I'll tell you what. I'm in the mood to make a deal with someone in this room today, so I'll go along with this if one of you can guarantee that a trade is made."

"No offense, buddy, but ah... I don't think anyone is going to trade their soul. We were taught better," Ayeko added.

"Who said anything about souls?"

"Isn't that, like, your entire role?"

"While I do have a preference towards that type of currency, I do barter in other things. I'll be honest with you, I don't really need many more souls anymore," The Broker snickered.

"So what, then, do *you* desire?" Kalvin asked, with a twinge of mockery towards The Broker.

Ayeko giggled at the remark.

The Broker was unfazed by the humor. "I need a specialist of sorts. This person would have to be the kind of person with knowledge capable of setting up civilizations."

The room was silent. Everyone stared at The Broker, waiting for more.

Kalvin jumped back in. "That would be easy to arrange."

The Broker clinched his fist. "Uh, this is... maybe a bit awkward, but here's the issue, Kalvin: I can only make a deal with someone once. That means, Kalvin, our business is over. On the bright side, you have a person just to your left able to make such arrangements."

"Day-Bringer?" Kalvin mumbled the question.

Day-Bringer smiled at Kalvin with the intent to put him down. "Well, of course I can make such an arrangement, too. But how long would you require the assistance of this specialist?"

"Indefinitely."

"What?! How can I ask someone to walk away from their lives indefinitely?"

"That person would be treated well. I guarantee it." The Broker chuckled.

"That isn't the issue."

Kalvin stuck up his finger. "Allow me to chime in. Day-Bringer, I can produce those arrangements for you. You just consent to the deal."

"It's not that simple, Kalvin. We are talking about a person here."

"Sure it is. I will simply produce a proposal that somebody desperate cannot refuse, such as lifetime support for their family and every future generation of their family. Easy as that." Kalvin grinned.

The Broker pointed his finger up to Kalvin, looking at the group of aces. "I like that man there."

Day-Bringer was ill at ease. "How about we discuss this outside some more?"

Kalvin nodded, then looked back to the group of aces. "I should not be long." He headed out the door, with Day-Bringer just behind.

Ayeko got up from his seat. He headed closer to The Broker and stopped at the base of the stairs. "So Mr. Broker... how 'bout we talk while the bosses are out?"

"I don't mind the silence," The Broker responded.

Ayeko smiled and let out a hint of a laugh. He waved his finger in humor. "You're definitely something else."

"Something else. If you mean to imply that I'm not of your species, then you are correct."

Ayeko's humorous grin did not subside. "No, no, buddy. I was simply talking about the way you conduct yourself. I like it. I do. You-you got that, ah... mystery thing going well for you. But I've been doing my research."

The Broker waited in silence.

Ayeko continued. "Our buddy, Kalvin, had us all briefed on anything and everything he could find out about you based solely on your little chat with him all those years ago. And there is a common theme I picked up on."

The Broker did not speak.

"Rumpelstiltskin. That was a name you used when you first meet Kalvin. You've been called that, no?"

"I have indeed."

"Any human will recognize that name as an imp who likes to make deals, although not exactly for souls. And most humans don't realize that the original story can be traced back four *thousand* years ago in human history. Given you told him that you last visited this galaxy a few centuries ago, the facts line up."

"A rough estimate," The Broker acknowledged.

"You also mentioned Sinnerman. Another name of yours?"

"Indeed, it is."

"Not one to talk much." Ayeko laughed. "That's fine. I'll carry the conversation for the two of us. Now back to the fancy name of Sinnerman. Well, it sure has a ring to it, I'll give you that. But even more interestingly, there is an old tale not well known in maelkii history of The Sinnerman. It's just your basic children's story following a main character who sells his soul to a *fleshy male being* for riches - a sin of greed. He gets his weight in gold but, over time, loses his virtue to corruption. He is eventually shunned and banished. And the moral of the story was to not give in to inner sins. I find it a bit funny that the *fleshy male being,* as described in the story, was just an afterthought, and not the main focus." He took a breath. "And you'd think that was all... but no. Qwayks have a folk tale song that dates back many centuries about a magical man who makes deals named Jyruckal. In every story, it's almost as if you don't really care much to stick around." Ayeko praised that last line as if to challenge The Broker.

"You speak of stories many centuries old created in times of lesser-minded individuals."

"So what?" Ayeko asked.

"It may come as a shock to you, then, that I'm not exactly as such works of fiction portray."

"No, I don't think it is as you say. I can read people pretty well... it's a gift, really. And you strike me as a man with a wall."

"A wall? What a curious metaphor." The Broker tapped his finger to his knee.

"You mask your face from view, care little for your own identity, and charade around like nothing more than a simple businessman. All of it is meant to build a wall to hide away who you really are. You aren't making deals for the sole reason of helping others like you claim. You commonly make exchanges for souls, and everyone else here seems to miss that point. There *must* be a reason you are collecting souls."

"I am just as everyone else. I have my own motivations."

Ayeko chuckled. "Hard to imagine what motivates a man to go from planet to planet making deals over and over again. I guess life could be worse."

Chapter 3

"Could it?" The Broker asked. Night-Shade could've sworn his tone had a sliver of pain in it.

Night-Shade chimed in, raising her head upward. "You reek of loneliness. I've been there before."

"What makes you think he is lonely?" Ayeko asked Night-Shade.

"He is always alone in those stories." She looked back to The Broker. "I've been alone before."

The Broker took a moment before responding, staring at Night-Shade with his golden eyes. She couldn't get a read on him. His expressions remained hidden. "Loneliness," he scoffed. "You would not know the meaning of the word loneliness had I not wrote the book on it eons ago."

"Then let's talk about it," Ayeko pleaded. "Let's talk about you."

The Broker nodded and flicked his chin towards both Drayvan and Tank, both near each other. "Doesn't seem everyone shares your enthusiasm."

Night-Shade could see the gloomy look in Tank's depressed eyes. She knew The Broker was right about him. He was in too much heartache to really care about the situation. Drayvan, on the other hand, was different. Her gaze had been locked on The Broker since the first second. Despite being lower to the ground than The Broker, she still seemed to stare down at him like he was just an ant. Night-Shade was glad to not be on the receiving side of that glare.

"Oh, please," Ayeko shrugged it off. He pointed to Tank. "He can't talk at all, and Drayvan... she doesn't speak much anyway. So don't let them fool you. Both would like to know more, as I would."

"Maybe we can start with you and the other... enhanced beings here. I must admit, I've often wondered what the best of this galaxy can do."

"I'm surprised you don't already know," Night-Shade jumped in.

"No mortal can know everything," The Broker informed. He stretched his long arms outward. "You seem eager to speak. What's your story?"

"Do you really want to know?" Her body shifted away.

"Let's say yes," he nodded.

"Come on, Night-Shade, do take forever now," Ayeko added with sarcasm.

Night-Shade sighed. "I'm afraid I'm pretty boring. I never stood out in any way growing up. I kept to myself, drew sometimes, listened to rock music, and never had a rebellious phase; just a typical teenager."

"And you're unique gift as an enhanced?" The Broker dipped his head.

"Nothing special either. It boils down to this: I can project myself out-of-body and walk about without risk of being seen or hurt. I can only go so far from my body though." That was not all she could do, however. Much of the limits of her ability was still mysterious to her, and she seemed to discover something new about it each time she used it.

"And how does the world look through spiritual eyes?" he asked.

"Everything is shades of gray."

The Broker flinched. "Very interesting indeed--"

Ayeko was bubbling with enthusiasm and couldn't hold on any longer. Despite The Broker looking as if he had some more to say, Ayeko jumped right in. "My friends call me Doctor Time. You won't guess how I got that name--"

"Because you're a doctor," Night-Shade teased.

Ayeko frowned. "Ah, yes... that. But I'm still in training. However, don't let my over-eager personality overshadow what I can do. It's awesome, really. I can create a nonphysical sphere near me, and within it, I'm a master of time itself."

"You control time?" The Broker blinked.

"Only in the sphere, and I cannot jump forward or backward in time. I merely slow it down."

"And that allows you to save lives, I presume." The Broker spoke as if he already knew the answer.

"Now, if you don't mind, I can tell you about Tank if you would like. I mean, he won't tell you himself anyway, so--"

"Speak if that is your desire." The Broker gestured him onward with an open palm.

"Well, Tank is the strangest one of the bunch. Not that the dude is strange or anything. It's his ability. See he is the newest one of us, and well-- Have you ever heard of an old comic featuring a kid who gains, like... spider-based powers?"

"I am unfamiliar."

"Tank is in a similar situation. He was a normal human male, but somehow his ace ability, whatever it is - 'cause we don't really know much about how it works and whatnot – it, ah... kind of began to partially transform him into a mordazul - you know, the species."

"A human who has blended himself with a mordazul? Unwilling or otherwise, that has potential." The Broker showed his respect with his tone.

"Granted, he is a bit more powerful than that ancient species, even though they are pretty strong already," Ayeko added.

The Broker's eyes closed in on Drayvan's and met hers. It was a staring match for a few moments before The Broker started to speak. "This one's been staring down on me from the moment I showed myself. I must say, I'm curious as to what goes through your mind."

Drayvan stopped leaning against a hieroglyphic column. Her stance was straight as a line, chest out, arms to her side. "How presumptions of you. To think you are worthy of my thoughts," her orotund voice taunted.

For the first time, The Broker let out a hint of hilarity.

Ayeko started. "Don't mind Drayvan--"

His mouth stopped moving the moment Drayvan placed her hand on his shoulder. She stared down at him with burning eyes, then nodded toward the door. Kalvin and Day-Bringer had just returned.

Kalvin spoke. "I apologize for the delay. That was longer than anticipated. Nonetheless, I shall make it worth your while since I bring splendid news, Broker. Day-Bringer and I have reached an agreement on what to do."

The Broker leaned back on his throne as he waited.

Kalvin turned to Ayeko. "Move forward with Code C."

Night-Shade's heart thumped faster.

Ayeko sighed. "Damnit. Sorry, buddy." He extended his arm, and a golden sphere formed around The Broker, meters in radius and hazy, with pinches of smoke flowing off the surface. "I've distorted time around both of your legs, body, and arms by one-ten-thousandth the speed. The only thing you will be able to move is your head."

The Broker expressed an initial shock but didn't seem overall phased. Though, his expressions hid behind a mask, so he was difficult to read.

"And just as we were getting to know each other." The Broker shook his head to Ayeko, his smoky tone just as calm as his movements.

"I know, buddy. I wish I didn't have to."

Kalvin had stepped forward. "Alright, Broker, we expect a few favors from you and in return you will be granted your freedom. Understand?"

"I understand my situation," The Broker said, only he seemed not to be answering Kalvin with his remark.

Kalvin entered the sphere and moved toward The Broker.

"If you're wondering why Kalvin seems unaffected by the time distortion, it's simple. I can choose how time affects different matter in the sphere. It didn't come without a lot of practice, however." Ayeko chuckled to himself.

Kalvin was now in front of The Broker. "I desire three favors from you. Favor one: I want the whereabouts of James Stone." Kalvin laid out a map of the galaxy. "Favor two: I want to pinpoint the location of the threat that caused this." Kalvin pulled out an image showcasing the disturbing leftovers of many men butchered and shredded apart by what seemed to be bones. "And favor three: Tell me precisely who and what you are."

The Broker began laughing. "I've thought I've seen everything." He let out a breath of fresh air. "This moment... it feels so fresh... so new. You have no idea how miserable I've been these last few millennia. All of you have breathed new life into me. You have shown me that there are still many surprises left in this existence. And I thank you."

"Thank us by making the deal," Kalvin urged.

"That is simply out of my hands."

"Explain," he commanded.

"Rules. I'm bound by rules given to me by-- Let's just say my gift for making deals is a borrowed talent."

"That tells us nothing," Day-Bringer shouted from the back.

"I assure you the process of making these deals is more complex than you can handle."

Chapter 3

Kalvin had fire in his breath. "Enough of this. Ayeko, give me a dagger."

Ayeko did as requested.

Kalvin held the blade over the knee of The Broker. "I will start here and work my way around until we get what we want."

"The heart of a desperate man." The Broker did not stir in his chair. But he did give Kalvin a long, judging look.

Night-Shade's pulse was beating like a drum. Her skin felt cold, and her eyes were glued to the blade. It stabbed downward right into The Broker's knee. Night-Shade's heart nearly jumped from her chest as she waited for the cry of pain.

There wasn't any. No sound. In fact, the stab wound wasn't even bleeding. Wait. Night-Shade's eyes focused around the wound. There was no cut either. The blade was very much inside his knee, but it seemed to pass through, not slice through.

Kalvin pulled it back up, staring down at The Broker's knee in complete bewilderment. Their eyes met.

"Shocked? Not what you were expecting?" The Broker's eyes had a menace to them as he looked down at Kalvin.

The Broker stood up! And that is in spite of the fact that he shouldn't've been able to move in Ayeko's bubble.

He pointed to Ayeko but spoke to Kalvin, "You should teach your pets not to speak so carelessly about what they can do. To someone like me, information is a weapon to use against those who would wish me harm."

Kalvin stepped back with rapid steps. "Someone restrain him! Now!"

Night-Shade sat still; she was no good in a close fight. Ayeko pulled out his other dagger and ran at The Broker. He didn't flinch. Yet his body seemed to break apart into black particles.

"Over there!" Kalvin's voice rang.

Night-Shade looked over to see The Broker was now a meter behind Drayvan Pryde. She turned rather nonchalantly. She then crossed her arms as she looked down at him.

"Brave of you to step forward to *me*, only to forfeit your insignificant life," her voice issued a challenge.

"I know what everyone here is capable of except for you," The Broker breathed, "and that knowledge is of interest to me."

"I invite you to try and find out." Drayvan Pryde didn't even reach for the sword over her back.

The Broker didn't move forth.

"Tank! Remember what we spoke about? Get in there and do something!" Kalvin commanded.

Tank had already put away the ring. Now he stood tall and reached back with one hand and touched the pillar attached to his back. It took only a slight touch of his fingers, and the giant thing spun right off his back. He soon maneuvered it in front of him. That same second, he leaped toward The Broker and slammed the bottom end of that pillar to the ground! The very foundation popped upward in front of the pillar and shards of the floor below The Broker fragmented everywhere. And a shockwave of sound erupted through the room!

It was to no avail! The Broker didn't move, his body unharmed. Everything just phased right through him. Drayvan was not impressed yet stood there as a spectator.

The Broker raised his hands to the air. "I yield."

What?! Night-Shade thought she had just imagined the words he had just said.

"You yield?" Ayeko, still in his bubble, shouted.

"I'm afraid I don't care for fighting. Each of you can throw all the attacks you want at me if you desire... but sooner or later... my time will run out, and you won't see me again for a long time. Neither of us would get what we want."

"So what, then?" Day-Bringer had joined the group. She was almost a meter away from the dealmaker.

"You and I make that deal you promised. Kalvin seems to want three things, but what do you want?" He turned to face her.

"Day-Bringer--" Kalvin started.

She turned her head to him. "I've got this!" She directed her words to The Broker. "And no exchanging of my soul?"

"I never go back on a deal."

"Pleasant. Then I want you to tell me where we will be able to find the threat responsible for this." She held up the same picture of the massacre Kalvin did earlier.

"Day-Bringer!" Kalvin was livid. "We need him to find James and Jay!"

"Back off! I know what I'm doing," she insisted.

The Broker spoke. "I cannot tell you where that threat is this very moment. Whatever it is seems very good in the art of shrouding itself. Though I can tell you of a place that will prove to be of great use to you in finding it. Do you desire this deal?"

"The deal is to my pleasure."

"Excellent. Meet me a kilometer south of this facility, in the forest that surrounds it, at midnight in your ARW time. Come only with the specialist whom you will be exchanging for that information." His gaze fixed on Kalvin, who was barely containing his anger. "As a past customer of mine, I grant you this: James will not be lost to you forever. May that ease your mind."

Night-Shade could hear the steam of anger expel from Kalvin's head as he let out a long breath. Everyone seemed to gaze his way. She almost missed The Broker glance Tank's way before evaporating into particles again.

Chapter 4: Otherworldly Visitors
December 6, 2111

Jeremiah

The last human survivor of an unfortunate event had returned to a city nicknamed the Treasured City after more than a month away; his pocket now full with the item he sought. This man, the last survivor, was named Jeremiah. A man of the cloth, Jeremiah was well-studied in the subject of religion, having two specializations in all.

Now within the walls of his residence, Jeremiah rested his bottom against the loose, soft sand of his sand-chair on his pink patterned, porch floor; his gaze was fixed over the legendary gate of the legendary Treasured City not too far in the distance. What he saw wasn't quite the spectacle of most structures on the planet. Instead, he saw a haunted forest filled with creatures of a nightmare not too far off from those gates; always there, always a threat to this city's walls. Black smog could be seen emitting from below the low hanging trees and thick brush. In-between the forest line and gate was a massive patch of barren and coarse sand. One of the two suns was high in the sky, casting low shadows.

He had enough of that. He stood up and rested his arms onto the railing enclosing his porch. Far down below, his eyes were pulled like a magnet to the waterpark close to the city's edge. Children of the corelinn species played with joyous wonder and excitement. Some of the guardians of these children watched from a distance, while others played with their kids. It was an innocent and pure sight if ever there was one. They were all the children of God.

This had become a calling of sorts for Jeremiah - guiding and observing. Over his many years, life seemed to grow more beautiful every day. It was a gift, and he loved to watch the beauty of life pass through time. Guiding and observing, after all, felt like what he was created to do - the purpose he had while he lived.

At first, when he was still young, observing was all he thought he was supposed to do. Be a watchful eye. Never did he expect to hear the word of God. Never did he expect to be called to teach. At that early age, he thought he was unworthy to speak, too young to be taken seriously. God assured him then it wouldn't be a hindrance and not to be intimidated by others.

That day he was made a fortified city, an iron pillar and bronze wall to stand against a whole land.

That was so long ago, back on Earth. That day and age, his mission was more testing than he ever imagined. He was tasked with reforming the ways of sinners. Standing among many other priests, he was the only one preaching darkness and destruction. And he did it faithfully and loyally for God, all to a land that had turned away from God like an unfaithful wife. If they didn't give up their sinful ways, they would face death, capture, or worse.

A hard lesson was learned early on. Jeremiah found out through experience that people were unable to change their nature, just as a leopard cannot change its spots. People then were so consumed with their desires over their intellect, and for that reason they couldn't change their evil ways until they experienced a change of heart. This change couldn't happen on its own. It happened only with the influence of God. Reform can occur only through cooperation with God, and God can act on human hearts only when they recognize their need for it. But he always had hope.

Jeremiah heard the soft knocks at his door. His curious mind forced his body over to see the person who awaited him. He opened the door and recognized the lady at first glance: Witnamerrys Kekay'Hegar - the prime keeper of this great city.

"I greet you, Prime Keeper Witnamerrys," said Jeremiah.

"No need for the formalities, dear friend. You know you can just call me Witna."

He gestured her inside. The living quarters was the room adjacent to his porch. The room was filled with ankle-high water. Waves, shallow and soft, swooshed to a slow tempo against the walls. It was accompanied by the noise of a thin waterfall flowing from the ceiling. The setting was tranquil, and to the corelinn species, a room such as this was standard. They call this spiritual room a majaray. Witnamerrys sat down in the water, with the waterfall flowing over her shoulders. She looked almost in mediation and relaxed beyond comfort. Alternatively, Jeremiah decided to take a seat above the water line.

"My council informed me you had arrived back into our city," she said. Her oval teal eyes greeted him gently, and her skin was the color of God's blue ocean.

He gave her a nod and smile. "A long but fruitful journey."

She continued. "Anighta has made a prediction in your absence. We are to be visited by aliens who will save our world."

"I've not lost hope in our own citizens."

"That may be, but we simply aren't strong enough to do what is necessary to survive the threat." She gave pause. "It's been more than twenty years since the last otherworldly visitors arrived. Of course that was a complete disaster. No one knows better than you."

Jeremiah remembered his traveling companions like it was only yesterday. "They didn't last the week. We should've listened to your warning."

"I'm glad you lived through it. You're kind and compassionate and would've been a great corelinn had you not be born a human."

Jeremiah gave a humble nod.

She continued. "The question remains, when will more come? Anighta assures me it is soon."

Without the luxury of slip space technology themselves, the species of corelinns remained at the mercy of not knowing what was going on beyond the ecosystems of their own planet. Such technology for them was most likely decades away, and most of the fault could be placed on their ingressiveness. In the mind of Jeremiah, this was a gift rarely seen in the galaxy. However, other political minds of their time call this quality a curse. Their species is the type to show generosity and selflessness instead of being adversarial. Often, they can be seen giving and helping as opposed to falling into selfish desires. Thus, war has mostly remained a faraway concept to them. Rare is it that the corelinns engage in such turmoil and conflict.

While the upsides of a world in peace may be apparent, the downsides are less considered. War accelerates the rate of technological achievement, and without it, development seems to drag on slowly, like a wounded, slimy snail.

"Anighta is more often correct than wrong," Jeremiah reassured. He trusted her opinion. Her seeing ability is quite rare, and an asset to have.

A sonic boom whipped them out of their conversation, and they shot up and ran to the edge of the porch to see what the source was, kicking water up everywhere. They saw a light in the sky, burning with flames and increasing in size. It was falling!

"Is it a meteor?" Witnamerrys wondered.

The flames intensified, and Jeremiah began to say a prayer as he realized the object was falling beyond the city's walls. He knew exactly what it was and what species that escape pod belonged to. His eyes stayed glued to the falling object as it neared the sand beyond the gates.

"This isn't good! Noise attracts the nightmare from the forest!" Witnamerrys's eyes darted to Jeremiah.

The object came shrieking towards the surface, but there was not a collision. At least not when there should've been. Then hissing overtook the shrieking. The object made contact with the surface, only with a much softer sound than expected. It had landed.

"Aliens," Jeremiah whispered.

Chapter 5: First Encounter
December 6, 2111

James Stone

My unit was somewhat naked as we traveled in our escape pod down to the unknown planet below. That was the feeling I felt after using most of my ammunitions and equipment during our last battle. Since none of us had the luxury of resupplying, we all were low on ammo, save Brad Swift.

Having the right sense of mind to remove his power armor while we were stranded, Brad's suit of armor had juice to spare. Knowing him, he probably even had a spare power source tucked away, too. Having taken substantial attacks from Ghost, it was bruised up. Shortly after our battle with Airra in Garatopia, Brad's cyberwatch was damaged as well. To that end, he was able to repair his cyberwatch with parts around our starship. As far as I know, that was the extent of wear and tear Brad had collected.

Jay Bridges, better known as Frost, still held on to his swagger for clothes. With the exception of some dirt and mud on his pants, his outfit was still fit for use. He even managed to hang on to his fedora through it all, which was a feat in and of itself.

Valiic and Shadow-Walker were not as lucky. Valiic's armor had various dents, and both had stains covering their respective outfits like a pattern. They managed to hang on to their gear, though; Shadow-Walker had his custom scout rifle, and Valiic had his handy-dandy shield.

Worst of all was me. I no longer carried the weapons I had originally brought to Idor all that time ago. My current weapons were barrowed, though I doubt I'd be able to return them. While my stasis shield was undamaged, it was low on power. None of that even holds a candle to my clothes; rips, tears, and holes a plenty. I no longer had my upper armor vest, and my military pants were falling apart. Only a black tank top filled with holes covered my torso, and that thread was barely hanging on.

My torso, head, and arms alike shook like a tree in an earthquake. It had nothing to do with fear or anxiety. I shook for one reason alone: Our escape pod had just entered the atmosphere. And I could hear the raging fires roaring outside the pod like a lion. Every one of us could. All of us, so snug together. A bond with your squad runs deep. Only, I never expected I'd have my face rubbing against Valiic's side with each bump. But that's what happens when five people are forced into an escape pod made for four.

As for our situation, it was a matter of zero choice. All of us were lost in space with our location unknown to the ARW. We were MIA and had no way to call for help. When our food and water rations had run dry, I made the decision to escape from the dropship, hoping to find aid on the planet below us. And it was coming in on us fast.

"How are you handling yourself down there, James?" Valiic looked down to me. Valiic Bessile was my closest friend, one I've known all the way through legionnaire training, and my unit's lieutenant.

"I'm as good as any man can be with my cheekbone this close to your ass. And you?"

"The broken seat has found its way between my armor and is pinching my side." Though Valiic answered the question, he didn't give me the answer I was looking for. With him being apart from his soulmate, Narrisa, this long, I know it's eating him away. And he may be avoiding the topic through his answer.

"Yo, this, ah... this is kind of awkward, but I gotta piss," Shadow-Walker, just behind me, called out. He is my unit's engineer, sniper, and self-designated spirits-lifter. In other words, among his talents as a soldier, he loves to crack jokes. As a male of the dor'o species, Shadow-Walker has his fair share of charm.

"If you don't hold that shivf, I'll cut your damn balls off!" I cursed, but in jest.

"I second that, uzzo!" Frost, across the pod, added. "For real, though, you should've handled your business before we abandoned the ship."

"Yeah, well... shivf, I was bored and decided to look at the stars alone in the cockpit and--"

"And you had a date with Peachy Palm and her five daughters, shivf we get it," I teased.

"It is called a cockpit after all," Shadow-Walker laughed.

There was a responding eek of disapproval.

"Now hold your bones, Shadow, I was only joking. You saying you actually milked the eel?"

I saw him give a sly smile, and he shrugged. "We've been away from the Whispering Dragon for nearly a month." He laughed. "At least in our first drought, I had Erryn to fall back on."

"Mother of God, I knew she didn't want to see you for a *strategy meeting.*" I shook my head.

"And if you thought that was my idea, you'd bet wrong," he added, with seconds of laughter.

And Frost and I joined in, catching the disease of a good laugh.

Valiic shifted uncomfortably. "I knew that woman was too coquettish for her own good."

"Look at my li'l uzzo here," Frost teased. Though this man is not a part of my legionnaire unit, he has become close to us all the same. I was only introduced to Frost about a month ago by Kalvin Keefe. Recently, I have made peace with Kalvin, the man whose hand was partially responsible for my traumatic past, and have come to accept Frost as part of my family. Like me, he is an ace - the name for us supernatural folk. Furthermore, he carries energy in battle and brains everywhere else. Even though he is Kalvin's apprentice, he holds his own liquor as a soldier.

Wiping away a joyful tear, I caught it. I saw Valiic's expression. Though his eyes peered through the hard-glass barrier at the fire around our pod, I could still see it. Shadow's words sent his mind to thoughts of the love of his life, Narrisa. With no way for them to contact each other, I knew this must've been torture on his poor soul.

The moment was interrupted by the escape pod's thrusters suddenly blasting. The ship's momentum was brought slowly to a halt as the measures designed to give us a soft descent took place. There was a thud. We had landed.

Out the window, I could see a forest of gray leaves and thicket so impenetrable, I couldn't even glance meters beyond the wall of the forest line. Between the trees and us was an ocean of sand mixed with mud.

The escape pod door depressurized and opened.

"On me, boys." As captain and the leader of my unit, I took the brave first jump out of the escape pod.

I met the wind head on, greeting it as a welcome friend. That seemed to be the only greeting I would get. Only seconds after I touched down, I heard yelling from the left. I turned to see new creatures unlike any I'd ever laid eyes on, but my gut told me they were amphibians. Each had dark purple eyes as big as a softball, with a gathered tangle of flexible tentacle-tresses extending from their heads and long enough to reach halfway down their backs. They were alarmed, hands waving and pointing past me. Their words were lost over the thick winds. Then came the alarms, blaring over and over.

The creatures pulled up weapons! But not at us. They fired past us. I turned my attention to that direction. Out of a forest of darkened gray trees, dripping of black goo, came creatures almost as large as maelkii. The creatures shrieked and trampled the ground as they stampeded for us all. They didn't seem to have a face, just a jumbled mess of vein-like stems around where a face would have been. Shadow-gray with a violet accent, the creatures, looking metallic and robotic in nature, gained speed with their powerful legs oozing with putrid goo. And while one arm was as thin and weak as a twig, its other arm was disproportionately big for its body. It had a pillar-like claw where its hand should be, and its shoulder extended over its head, like armor. Needless to say, this beast of a machine was not something I wished to do the hard tangle with.

Not itching to meet these things face-to-face, I pulled my weapon off its mag lock and fired my get-the-hell-away bullets, hoping the thing would get the message.

"Enemies coming in hot!" I warned my unit, who was already popping off rounds at the dozens of creatures as they neared us.

The rounds hit and shrieks, loud and ear-piercing, rattled me to the bone.

"James, they aren't dying! Why... why are they not dying?!" Shadow-Walker called. And he was right. Every bullet fired, every plasma burst, laser, and even the shock rounds from our various arsenal of weaponry only delayed them. Sure, it took chucks off their robotic bodies, but more metal was produced to replace what was lost, and they kept pushing toward their prey - us!

"Hot damn! These things made of iron or something?" Frost hollered.

I felt a tap on my shoulder and looked back to see an amphibian creature from before handing me a pistol-like weapon. Teal-blue, glowing, and it looked like some kind of endothermic weapon. I fired my new gift multiple times at the creatures and shells of crystalized water exploded on their skin, drenching them and, to my surprise, melting holes in them like acid until they were nothing more than a gooey grave. I kept firing, backing up with the new crowd of allies. If it weren't for the looming threat, I would've given them a firm hug right there. Our new allies were leading us to their gates, on top of which sentries fired weapons to cover us from above.

The thirty meter tall gates opened, and a couple soldiers came towards us, pushing what looked like wheelbarrows with a turret of some kind on top. They passed us and planted the wheelbarrows into the mud, activating them. Then those machines started firing a hailstorm of endothermic projectiles at the crowd of enemies coming at us from the trees. When the deed was done, the guards rounded up with us as we entered the gates. Once clear of the archway, the gates slowly closed us inside the walls of this unknown place.

Shadow-Walker collapsed to his ass, then lay down completely, with his custom weapon over his chest. His stomach ballooned with each of his rapid breaths. "Frak, I'm getting old."

The rest of us stood there, looking from eye to eye at the dozens of guards around us. Each of them stared with the ever so expected glances of curiosity, but with no fear in their expressions. A surprise given strangers just strolled in through their gates, and rather loudly I might add. Some even seemed to be quite cheerful, like we were long lost buddies.

We were surrounded by two rows of houses, one on each side of us, inside a tightly laced base camp. Over us was a fabric-woven net that shaded the small camp and blurred out the towers beyond the net. Stoned-carved refresh stations flowed through the camp with much more water than I sure expected.

Before I finished taking in the embrace of our new surroundings, one of the guards came up to me. He bore the valor of a few more stripes on his cloth than any other guard I saw. "Who's in charge here?" he asked me.

I pointed at myself, and he nodded.

"What's your name?" the guard asked.

"James Stone," I responded.

His friendly expression clouded with hints of confusion. "Why did you come here?"

"Well shivf, as choices go, we had a large number of just one. Our dropship was subject to a major technological screw up of its nav-systems. We were unwillingly warped over this planet... which, by the way, what is this planet anyway? And why do we get no intergalactic service on our cyberwatches here?"

The guard looked at me with a long, wordless face. He stared as if he understood nothing. But that, of course, would be impossible unless--

He finally spoke. "You can understand me, correct?"

I nodded with a smile and thumbs up for extra emphasis. "I do."

"To us, you speak gibberish. I'm not quite sure why that is, so I would like you to wait by the visitation barracks over there." He pointed to the building. "I'll be back later." He then wandered off.

I waved my hand toward the barracks, and my crew followed my order. As we made our way over, I was still in my head about the strangeness of everything.

We entered a single room full of a few bunk beds. Waterfalls rushed from the sides above the beds and poured over them like a fountain. No mattress; just water over sand. And the floor and walls alike seemed to be built of some oddly teal and patterned stone. Such a room sure wasn't my keg of beer, and I sure as hell had not a hint of interest in staying in this room for a night.

"Ain't dis some shit," Brad clicked his tongue. "Shit if Imma 'bout tah stay in dis bitch," He shook his helmet in disapproval. "I'll catch yah outside if yah need me." He marched back out of the house and waited by the door.

Shadow-Walker headed to the wall in-between the bunks. A waterfall was coming from the wall and collecting in a bowl-shaped cauldron, which seemed to be flowing down a drain at the back. Shadow unzipped his leather armored pants and added some water of his own to the fountain. "Does it strike you guys as weird that they didn't take our weapons from us?" he asked over his shoulder.

I leaned against the frame of one of the beds. "And they couldn't catch the words I was throwing them either."

Frost pushed together some sand and sat on it, with his back against a wall. Valiic joined in-between me and Frost.

"I must ask, did any of you recognize them?" Valiic asked.

"No, but not recognizing other species is fairly standard with me. As you remember, traveling the galaxy was off the table when I was still finding my way into adulthood," I admitted.

"Never seen them in my life," Shadow added. Which surprised me, given his years of experience traveling the stars as a mercenary. We waited for Frost to respond.

His gaze was toward the bottom-right; he was thinking. "They didn't recognize us and we don't recognize them. Uzzos, I think there's a monster-sized pickle on the table and we've stumbled onto it."

Valiic tensed.

"How big of a pickle are you talking here? Shadow-sized, or James-sized pickled?" Shadow joked.

I laughed. "I'll whip this enormous cucumber out right now and put you to shame, Shadow."

He chuckled. "Sure. Whip it out in the company of men. You'd feel at home."

"Really, uzzos. Pisser jokes. That's like the knock-off brand of humor. I thought your two were better." Frost sported a teasing grin.

"Now you're just being a gray sprinkle on a rainbow cupcake," I shot back, with a laugh.

Valiic jumped in. "I agree with Frost, you guys have had your jokes." He had a point. Of the group, Shadow and I had a tendency to get carried away and came off crude at times. Chalk it up to life as soldier or twisted up wiring in our heads.

Shadow fired back, "Hold still, Valiic. I'm trying to imagine you with a sense of humor."

He didn't laugh at Shadow's friendly poke.

After a moment, Frost continued. "The point I was trying to get at is this: I believe we are on a planet that has yet to achieve slip space tech."

Valiic agreed, with a nod. "It would explain why they didn't understand us. They wouldn't have render chip as we do."

"And without knowing what language they speak, we can't communicate with them!" Shadow-Walker realized.

Frost looked to me. "You realize what this means, too, right?"

I sighed. "We are technically breaking a pretty hard-set law by being here."

"Law? What law?" Shadow-Walker asked.

"Since the beginning of the ARW, it has been against the law to intrude on the development of species without slip space technology. Though the law is official in the ARW, it reaches beyond our alliance. It is an unspoken understanding that relatively all species in the galaxy abide by, even to the point that our enemies in the Wersillian Legion respect this," Valiic informed.

Frost squinted with skepticism and a smile. "Most of the time," he added.

Shadow-Walker gave himself to wry amusement. "You know what sucks? This whole breaking laws and orders thing is becoming a theme with us."

"Just another day tittering on the edge of a cliff, I suppose," I chuckled.

There was a moment of silence as we each took in a few breaths.

"Well, then, what's the game plan, uzzo?" Frost asked.

"Sit on our asses until that soldier comes back," I shrugged. *What else was there to do?*

Shadow-Walker stopped slouching. "I hate waiting." He was shifting around quite a bit. Looking from here to there and there to here. Getting all squirrelly, I wondered what was going on in his head. Seems I wasn't the only one to pick up on it. After a moment of silence, he started, "I, uh... I've been thinking. Been really, uh... really mulling over a thought over the last few days. It's... It's just there's been a lot of *it* lately. A lot of--" Shadow's jaw and eyes winced, and he circled his wrist repeatedly, "--shivf happening to us lately. When it was just Clover, Bremco, and me, before all the major integration in our militaries, we did our share of missions. But that was it. Nothing spectacular. Lately... lately there's just so-*so much*. You know?" Shadow expressed, with visible confusion.

"Death. You mean death?" Valiic mumbled, trying to add reason to Shadow-Walker's ramble.

"Yes. Yeah," he said, softer. "That... a fair share of that and more." He forced a wry laugh. "The thing is, most squads spend years without ever seeing a warlord. Not us. No, we've had the displeasure fighting off multiple. And it's a lot. I just feel... I feel like a lot has been put on us lately. And I wonder, luck be on our side, if this place-- Could this place be right for us? Could we maybe just stay here and let whatever happens out there happen?" He gestured to space.

I felt the weight of his words. Weighed heavily under truth, the words he spoke carried logic. And really, who was I to say it was a bad idea? At some point or another, I knew I had those thoughts - thoughts of just leaving it all behind. There was no way I was the only other one who had thought that before.

Frost finally spoke, with words calmer than usual. "I can't, uzzo. I got a girl to go back to. A mother, a mentor."

Shadow brushed it off, swatting his hand towards Frost. "No, you're right. Never mind me and my dumbass rambling."

"You alright, Shadow-Walker?" Valiic asked.

He was silent a moment. "Well, you guys... you all have something, someone to go back to. As Frost said, he's got people. Valiic, you have your cohinla, and James has that scrawny kid... that--" Shadow-Walker snapped his fingers repeatedly, "--Ben-something."

"Ben Cross," I said. Fond memories of hanging out with him during boot camp training and before a few missions crept back to my mind.

"Yes. Your friend, Ben Cross."

"You always have us. We'd never turn you away because you're family."

Shadow-Walker turned his head. "You're real embarrassing sometimes. You know that, James?"

I went over to him and gave him a bear hug with a few shakes. "You better believe it. You better fraken believe it." I caught the laughter from the others.

I let him go. Shadow-Walker put his hand to his face. "Makes me wonder, still, if we'll ever see home again."

I could hear Valiic sniff and sob. It was on those thoughts and sounds that we sat, waiting for the soldier to return.

Chapter 6: Aces of the ARW II - In Desperation
January 14, 2112

Night-Shade

Meditating on her bed, Night-Shade allowed herself to give in to her ability. Using the relaxation to fuel the transition, she pulled herself from her body, astral projecting herself within her quarters. She knew she wasn't supposed to, but she had the urge to explore the highly guarded Station 51. After all, who wouldn't?

In that very moment, she could feel a sensation she had never felt while using her ability. There was a presence, very faint and far away from her. She looked in that direction but saw nothing beyond the walls of her room. Strange as it was, she didn't desire to investigate it any further. Her curiosity was already taken by what lay beneath her, by what lay within Station 51.

She then let her astral body fall through the floor for a few seconds. She stopped on a brightly lit hallway. The first door down on this lower level was off to the near right. She pushed her body through the door with no effort, phasing through it like a ghost.

Men and women were in the process of putting together ships, none of which looked like any she'd seen previously used in the ARW.

Must be new models, Night-Shade thought.

As there wasn't much of anything of interest to her in the works, she left the room and moved on. The next few doors also had some experimental starships inside. She figured that was what this floor was used for.

Leave it to me to find the boring floor, she thought, with a sigh.

On that, Night-Shade decided to let her body phase down a few dozen floors and see what happened. So she did, closing her eyes to anticipate the surprise.

She forced herself to stop falling through floors and, with a small inhale, opened her eyes to a dark room. She was unable to see anything at all. She was blessed with the ability to spy on anything she wanted, completely undetectable, but apparently being able to see in the dark was too much to ask.

Not knowing where to go, she decided to walk forward until she could see something. After phasing through what seemed to be a wall, she could see again, but not that well. The room was dark, with a cubicle in one corner, opposite an elevator, and next to a reinforced door complete with a security panel.

By the elevator was a sign that read, *"Sublevel 44: Unknown Beings Catalogue."*

Not sure exactly what to make of it, Night-Shade decided to take a look in the cubicle. Curiosity had her pulse rate up, and she took half a peak around the wall, almost fearing being seen despite knowing that would be impossible.

Nothing, nobody. The cubicle was empty except for a holographic monitor over a one-person desk. She frowned, disappointed from the reveal. That very emotion was what then drove her past the door leading into a new hallway full of mystery. Like the previous room, this was just as dimly lit.

Night-Shade approached the first door, and the sign read, *"The Broker,"* in quotation marks.

The Broker? Night-Shade perked up at the thought. *I wonder what's inside.*

She ventured in to see a chalkboard at the back, with a meeting table in the center of the room and chairs surrounding it. Nobody was present, and the lights were also dim. Night-Shade started to think this level was not in use at the moment.

She ventured over to the chalkboard, which was covered with words and pictures with string lines attached to them, creating a web. The center picture was of an ancient room of Egyptian origin. Night-Shade had no idea where that would be. Two pictures showed masks of jackals. At the top left was a list of names:

The Broker
Jyruckal
Sinnerman
Rumpelstiltskin
Swallower of Millions
Reality

Chapter 6

Undertaker

The list went on to the bottom with at least twenty names. Next to that was a list of Egyptian prophets, rulers, pharaohs, and even biblical names. At least that's what Night-Shade speculated, as she was unsure herself. That was only one of many lists. Nonetheless, she began to understand this room had the sole purpose of identifying who and what The Broker was. At the top right, the word *"human?"* with a question mark was displayed over a list of projects:

Project Gravebeyond
Project Pyramid
Project Zoxza
Project SAR II

Each of the projects connected into chains of string leading to pictures. There were so many, she knew she wouldn't have time to look at them all. But one did catch her eye. A picture of The Broker from a distance. It was blurry and forced Night-Shade to take a closer look.

It was definitely him; mask, kilt, and everything. He seemed to be striking a deal with a bearded human male. The location was secluded, near trees and a fence. To the back right, she could vaguely see the outline of a shed made of rotting wood and covered with vines.

Peering closer, she froze when she noticed a distorted spot next to the shed. In shades of gray, it looked to be an outline of The Broker, but only his upper chest and mask were visible. The shock of it all was that this couldn't be The Broker. He was near the man. It must be a camera glitch.

Once she realized what she was seeing, her mouth twisted. The picture didn't make sense. The Broker claimed he hadn't been on Earth for centuries before meeting Kalvin. Yet this picture looked to be of Earth, maybe a hundred or two hundred years ago. Could The Broker have lied? Then again, the black and white image could be a simple result of not being able to see in color while out of her body, and it stood to reason this location could still be around in spite of the now seldom used type of construction used to create the barn. One thing she knew for sure, The Broker was a lot more than he claimed to be.

Her heart jumped to her mouth at the sound of a knock. She relaxed some when she realized it wasn't from this room. Which meant it must've been on the door to her quarters where her motionless physical body was resting.

Night-Shade closed her eyes and thought about her body and its location, and in no time at all her metaphysical form returned to its origin. She opened her eyes and could feel her back against the mattress and the sheets up to her chest. She searched for her lamp with a free hand and pulled down on a string to turn it on. Her eyes adjusted as she got up from her bed and headed to the door, still in her sleeping attire. She pushed a button to the side of the door, and it slid open.

Standing in front of her was Ayeko. "Your bed is unmade. Were you asleep?" he asked.

"It's two hours from midnight," Night-Shade responded, still rubbing her eyes.

"Yet it's still daytime outside. Funny how that works. Also, I'm somewhat sure that the asteroid this station resides on rotates around this sun at the same speed that it rotates on its own axis. Which, ah... I think that's how Earth's moon, Independence, is too."

"You talk too much," Night-Shade tittered, her vision still foggy.

"So I've been told." Both his eyes and nose crinkled.

"So--" Night-Shade egged him on with her hand.

"So?"

"So what brings you here?" she asked.

He hit his head with his palm. "Right. Ah... so Tank Brockman beat up some guards and left through the front door. Soooo... that's, like, a whole situation."

"What?! Does Kalvin know?"

"Duh! Of course he knows. Weren't you listening? He beat up guards on the way out. Plus, this is, like, a super high-tech facility--"

"Yeah, I get it. But what are you telling me for?"

"Kalvin has a least a hundred guards out looking for Tank, but this asteroid is completely covered with trees, so he wants us to look, too."

Chapter 6

"Show me the way." She grabbed her shoes by the door and put them on. Not long after following Ayeko, Night-Shade positioned herself by his side. "Why do you think Tank would do that anyway?"

"I don't know Tank on personally level... 'cause of the whole he-can't-talk thing. All I know is what I've heard from others. So I can't say what his motivations might be."

"And what about what Kalvin said to him? Think that has something to do with it?" she asked, with big eyes.

Ayeko was quizzical. "Not sure what you mean? What did he say?"

"Well, uh... remember when Kalvin wanted to detain The Broker? He said something to Tank - something along the lines of *remember what we spoke about*. He said that to Tank before commanding him attack The Broker."

Ayeko gave it a moment. "To be completely honest, I really don't know what he meant by that. But Kalvin-- Knowing him, he probably has something on Tank. That... or he made him a deal of some kind. Same kind of thing happened to me when I was discovered with an ace ability."

"Kalvin made you a deal?"

"He did. He sure did."

Now that Ayeko mentions it, Kalvin did promise Night-Shade quite a lot when he first spoke to her. But what she cared about most was that Kalvin generously offered to help provide for her community back home. In a sense, it was a deal disguised as generosity.

Ayeko continued. "Most people don't see what that man goes through. Kalvin, above anything, is driven. He yearns to win this war and practically kills himself to find a way beat our enemy. The guy barely sleeps... always going here and there and all over the galactic systems as needed. This project, the great Project Aurum, is just another idea of his to win. Did he ever tell you the purpose he has for putting all the aces under one roof?"

"He didn't," Night-Shade said.

"He means to put us together and train us. We are meant to be the team to kill the warlords, which Kalvin believes will destabilize the Wersillian Legion and make them easier to defeat. And as far as I know, he plans of bring James Stone, Geariic, and Alabon into this project with Drayvan and James taking the lead."

Night-Shade had no idea.

Ayeko gave her a shrug. "Anyway, that all is likely still a whiles away. Don't let that stuff get into your head right now. We have something more important to worry about."

They had finished their walk from her quarters to the already open main gate. In spite of seeing it before, she was still surprised at its scale; the size of a basketball court and thicker than a tree trunk. When they arrived, the guards let them outside.

Rain poured down, and lightning lit up the sky every so often. Dark clouds swirled over the sky. Night-Shade knew of few asteroids with atmospheres such as this one. With terraforming technology, it is possible to create more, albeit time consuming and expensive.

"I thought you said it was daytime here?" Reluctantly, Night-Shade stepped into the freezing drops of water with a pouting expression. She regretted not changing out of her sleepwear.

"It is, but I guess the clouds are blocking out the sun," Ayeko said. He didn't seem to mind the rain as much as Night-Shade.

A perimeter fence lined the outside of the gate, with a few guard towers within the walls. Thick, tall, and metallic, the fence buzzed with and an electrical current. Behind Night-Shade, a near vertical mountainside shot straight up for hundreds of meters, and many turrets were built into it.

They neared the gate of the perimeter fence just as some more guards were leaving to find Tank. They had a few tracking dogs with them and some handheld devices unfamiliar to her.

"That stuff won't do them any good," Ayeko motioned to the device.

"What are they?"

"Multi-purpose tracking pads. They can detect motion, scan for footprints and disturbances in the brush, and can even identify the path that the target went down."

"Impressive."

"Sure... for pretty much anything except for mordazuls."

Ayeko and Night-Shade passed through the gate and entered the endless forest that spanned in all directions. The brush wasn't thick by any means, so they could see far in every direction. Though it wouldn't make it any easier to find just one person among the woodlands.

Ayeko and Night-Shade took their first steps into the slick, wet mud covered with fallen leaves and sticks.

"So what's different about a mordazul?" she asked.

They both stopped to talk by a tree hanging over a rock, roots expanding over a small ravine below them. They were not far from the station entrance.

"They are notoriously known to be evasive and elusive--"

"Evasive and elusive mean the same thing." Night-Shade laughed.

"Well, whatever." He smiled. "You get my point. But I'm sure you want to know why they are so stealthy."

"Sure."

"They have a way with sound and vibration manipulation. The palms, backs, and feet of a mordazul are very responsive to vibrations of all kinds. Did you notice that totem that Tank had over his back?"

Night-Shade nodded.

"All mordazuls grow them. Kind of like how turtles grow a shell. Just as your vertebrae grows as you near adulthood, so does a mordazul totem. And that is their focal point of vibration and sound manipulation. When a mordazul touch their palm, back, or feet to it, they can use the totem to do various things involving sound and vibrations. A few such perks are moving without creating any sound, feeling every distinct vibration as they move through the forest... which allows them to replace anything they disturb perfectly and avoid breaking anything such as sticks--"

"What about tracks?" Night-Shade asked.

"Ah, yes... as they moved, they can release vibrations through the soles of their feet, which prevent tracks from forming."

Night-Shade's nose crunched up, and her eyes focus on him. She could tell Ayeko gathered her disbelief from her expression. "That sounds too farfetched to believe."

"Okay, well... maybe I did over exaggerate the extent that mordazuls can do all that stuff," Ayeko admitted, "but even if they can't completely cover their tracks, they are easily good enough to fool those sensors."

"That doesn't bode well for us, then." Night-Shade took a seat on the rock. "Might as well just sit here and wait. There is no way we can find him."

"What's that thing about a needle in a haystack?" Ayeko asked rhetorically. "Still... better to try than sit here wasting space. Why don't you astral project or something and scout around?"

"Honestly, that form isn't any faster than my physical body. It really only helps when I need to search places I can't enter on my own or places that may cause me harm."

"How's that work anyway?" Ayeko sat beside Night-Shade.

"What do you mean?"

"I mean, if someone were to shoot you while you were astral projecting, would it hurt?"

"Nobody would be able to see me."

"But if by some chance a bullet came at you--"

"It would just go through me as if I were air."

Ayeko pondered on the thought for a moment, his eyes up and his hand to his jawline. *"Go through you.* You mean just like our friend, The Broker, when Kalvin stabbed his knee."

Night-Shade was silent for a moment. "I hadn't thought of that, but yeah, exactly just like that. Even still, he couldn't have been taking a metaphysical form, because we could see him. And he could interact with objects. I can't do any of that."

"So there are differences, obviously. But maybe there are similarities, too. Did you notice anything when using your powers?" Ayeko fiddled with a small leaf.

"I never used them near The Broker. But--" Her thoughts wandered away from the conversation and back to earlier.

"But what?"

"But I was in my metaphysical form before you knocked on my door and--"

"And what?!" Ayeko pushed, with excitement in his voice. His hands were rubbing together, and the pace only got faster.

"There was something different. I could feel something in the distance, and I'm not sure how to describe it."

Chapter 6

"Well, damn! I think it's about time you try again. Wouldn't you say?" His eyes begged her.

Night-Shade nodded and closed her eyes. She entered her metaphysical form, and there it was. That feeling from earlier was still there. She turned her head to the direction, and it was somewhere deep past the trees. She left that form and returned to her body.

Night-Shade pointed down the tree line. "It came from that direction."

"Then let's go!" Ayeko jumped to his feet instantly and headed off through the trees as fast as his feet would carry him. His steps were quick, and Night-Shade was a bit annoyed at having to keep pace with him. Mud sloughing up her legs and rain water pouring down her body, she was not in her element.

"Ever since we met The Broker, something about him bothers me," Night-Shade let her inner thoughts creep out loud.

"What do you mean?"

"I mean, his talk of souls like... like they are undeniably real. If that were the case, wouldn't that confirm the existence of an afterlife?"

"Actually, Kalvin did mention something about this during the briefing he had with Drayvan, Tank, and me. Hmm... I remember him mentioning that every person carries energy, which I think he said has been proven by the Order of Aegis long ago. Kalvin mentioned no afterlife but did say dying bodies are believed to release energy upon death, which, in a way, can be seen as a soul leaving the body. I mean, it could make sense if The Broker had some way of collecting that energy. But really, all the complex details are out of my field of expertise."

Night-Shade scowled to herself. "I don't know. I always believed in scientifically provable things, not magic or fairy tales."

"I'm a thousand percent with you on that. But one thing I know for sure... The Broker trades for something. That I know. He doesn't seem the type to go away empty-handed."

They went silent for a while, letting their pace pick back up. Over a river they passed, around dozens of trees, sliding in the mud more than once. It even seemed like they weren't going anywhere at some points. Every minute that passed made Night-Shade itch more and more to turn back, afraid that she wouldn't find Tank. Afraid that her sense of whatever was in the distance was actually nothing at all.

She was wrong.

There he was! Many meters further into the forest stood Tank Brockman. Standing there, his gaze was fixed on a row of trees and shrubs. That's when Night-Shade saw those same greeneries move and out stepped The Broker.

She had a hunch that's why Tank left. After all, why else would he. Even still, she couldn't help feeling uncomfortable.

"Come on. We need to back up our teammate just in case." Ayeko ran towards the two, followed by Night-Shade.

Tank noticed and frowned as they approached. Then his expression darkened with aggressive intent. Ayeko, who was a couple meters ahead of Night-Shade, slid to the ground just as Tank spun his totem off his back and swung at Ayeko. Luck had it that he missed.

Now behind Tank, Ayeko held up his hands. He pleaded, "Tank, calm it down, buddy. We're here to help."

Tank wasn't listening and started the motion of slamming his totem to the ground - an attack that had devastating results earlier.

Ayeko yelled, "Damn you!" He created a golden bubble around Tank and drastically slowed Tank's attack to a point that he looked motionless.

The Broker, amused by the whole situation, walked up to Ayeko from behind. He placed his long fingers over Ayeko's shoulder. "No need for all this unnecessary violence. I expected that Tank would seek me out."

"Why would he?" Ayeko asked.

"Let him loose, and we shall find out together." The Broker stepped back and formed a chair for himself from the ground with almost no effort.

"Fine. But he better not cause any more shivf."

Ayeko released the bubble. As he did, Tank's motion was set free and he nearly completed the slam he started beforehand. But he stopped himself short. His eyes met each of the aces for a moment as he put the totem on his back. And when his eyes met Night-Shade, she could see despair and desperation.

"Tank, please don't do something you'll regret," she begged.

He ignored her and marched past Ayeko, standing in front of The Broker. Ayeko and Night-Shade watched from the sidelines, not knowing what to do.

"Speak your mind in any way you can, I will understand your words," The Broker assured.

There was silence for almost a minute. Ayeko looked back to Night-Shade, asking with his expression what they were supposed to do.

The Broker smiled. "Your fellow enhanced has spoken to me."

"How?" Ayeko asked.

"He spoke in a way only a mordazul could understand."

"And you, apparently," Ayeko added. "What did he want?"

Tank nodded to The Broker, giving him approval.

The Broker informed, "Tank wished for me to take away his ability as an enhanced, thus returning him to how he was before he transformed into a *monster...* as he put it."

"Damn it, Tank! You can't be serious!" Ayeko shouted.

Tank turned to face him. His skin seemed to be making small motions like tiny waves. His eyes were red, and tears were falling.

The Broker spoke. "Tank claims he must. Everything went to ruin when he transformed. He lost his fiancé. His friends and family didn't recognize him. He said they called him a fiend."

Tank looked over at The Broker with painful eyes.

"And he's not happy with me for not speaking each of his sulking words exactly as he wished," The Broker snickered.

That mockery lit a spark in Night-Shade. "Is something funny about that? Do you find his pain amusing?"

"Beings of this galaxy carry so much emotion." His tone was uncaring.

"And that means nothing to you? He has lost everything, and you react to his suffering by finding it funny."

The Broker disappeared! Night-Shade felt fingers reach over her right shoulder, and from her left side, The Broker's mask was inches from her ears. She was frozen with shock and panic. The others stared at the scene, stunned and at a loss of words.

The Broker spoke in her ear loud enough for everyone to hear. "Let me tell you all something about suffering. The strong look to suffering with open arms, for suffering produces perseverance, and perseverance is what fuels accomplishment. Only the weak dwell on the sufferings of their past and let themselves be burdened by it." The presence of The Broker disappeared once more, and he reappeared in his chair. "I know you want to strip yourself of these powers, but in this I cannot help you," he said to Tank.

Tank slammed his fist to the ground. But only seconds later, he fell to his knees in tears. He hands now in the dirt, he was hunched over.

The Broker ignored Tank. Instead, he directed his stare at Ayeko. "Ayeko. Tell me what you know of the origin of your abilities."

Ayeko's eyes were on Tank, but he answered nonetheless. "I know only what Kalvin has discovered. Our abilities have something to do with some 2nd Big Bang and are linked to our genetics."

"There is some truth to that, but the picture is far greater. Ace abilities are not only tied to genetics, they are engrained in one's soul. And an ace's soul is incomprehensibly more complex than a standard soul... such is the reason I cannot help Tank. It's beyond my capability."

"And why should we believe such a ridiculous claim?" Night-Shade asked.

"Ask Kalvin why he was never able to create more aces. Science only got him so far. Take it from the being who has brokered deals for souls since before any of you ever existed." He paused and looked over the three once more. "This was interesting, but I must bid you farewell. I have a meeting with the divine Day-Bringer to prepare for."

The Broker left them no time to react as he evaporated into effervescent particles. He was gone, leaving Tank an emotional catastrophe and both Night-Shade and Ayeko without words.

Chapter 7: One Hand Washes the Other
December 6, 2111

James Stone

We did it again - rebels breaking ARW law. Never had I had the intentions of putting myself in a position to intrude on an underdeveloped species' home world. With that realization, I can't describe how much my gut and bones alike jittered at the thought of being caught by the ARW under these circumstances. Maybe they would understand the fact that our ship decided to blast us into orbit around this planet with no way to leave. Then again, with my already sketchy track record, this instance could be the last puff of air that burst the balloon. In either case, I hoped to keep those thoughts a fantasy, wishing I'd never have to find out. Despite it all, I must keep the little mouse powering my brain active on the present, not the future.

I let the thoughts fade and headed out of the visitation barracks. On the porch, Brad lay over a bench to my right. Still wearing his helmet, his head was against one armrest, while his legs were over the other. Behind him was the wall that separated this camp from the beasts that attacked us earlier, and our barracks was built right against it.

"Anything happen out here worth a mention?" I asked Brad.

"Hell nah. Borin' azz place," he replied.

I turned back to what was in front of me. The same line of buildings faced back, almost like looking at a mirror of our side of the camp. And the camp was fitted with guards. I noted a few training in a field further from the wall. That same field was close to a much smaller stone wall, which I assumed led out of the base camp. Other guards switched posts with their peers, going up a riser that led up to the top of the wall. Just a plain base similar to what I experienced in my earlier years as a solider. There was both fond and dreadful feelings in those memories.

I heard a minor commotion back towards the fields. I saw a small crowd of guards by the smaller wall, in conversation. That commotion then traveled its way towards me soon enough.

Out of the crowd, the same man I talked with before led the pack with another by his side.

"They are the aliens I spoke of," the man said.

The one by his side was slimmer and curvier by nature, likely female. "My name is Witnamerrys Kekay'Hegar. Many just call me Witna, and I'm the prime keeper of this city." Her voice was higher pitched. With so many species in the galaxy, guessing who was female and male by their frame and voice pitch wasn't an exact science. However, I had confidence my hunch about her being a female was likely spot on.

City? I thought. *I don't see a city.* "They call me James Stone. I'm the captain of the rug rats you've graciously allowed inside your walls."

"Rug rats?" she asked. "I don't understand."

"Oh, it's just-- Wait! You can understand me!" I shouted louder than I meant to.

"I do. But that's a long story... best told over dinner."

My stomach growled at the thought of food.

Witna rubbed at her nose. "But first - and not to be rude - you reek. We have a bathhouse nearby. You can clean up there, and I'll have someone wash those clothes of yours."

I put my hand to the back of my neck and turned with slight shame. "The ship we came had some nice tech but wasn't made for long-term living. See, we were stranded in it for some time, waiting for rescue that never came. We had to bite the bullet and choose to conserve the water for drinking instead of showering. Food and water eventually ran dry, and that situation eventually forced us here, but we intend to leave as soon as fate allows."

"I see. Even more reason to take my offer."

With so much unknown, I could never feel comfortable giving in to trust alone. For all I knew, that bathhouse could be a trap used to murder us while our pants are down, literally. Some species in the galaxy wouldn't hesitate to commit such an act. The question of the day, though, was would this species be one? Or are their intentions good? Up to this point, they haven't made a threating move towards us. So maybe these fishheads can be trusted.

"Your generosity has no limit, ma'am. I hope we can pay you back for it."

"We'll get to that. I just want to see to it that you are well taken care of. After you're done, we can meet for dinner. I'm sure there will be a lot to discuss on both ends." She smiled and waved me on. "Come now, I'll show you the way."

I tapped on the door to our barracks. Shadow-Walker opened. "Yo?"

"Grab our shivf. It's time to put our asses in motion."

"Righty." He closed the door and reemerged shortly with the rest of the squad and the gear we brought.

We followed Witna, who lead us through the door of the smaller wall surrounding the base.

As I stepped through, my eyes could now see the city she mentioned earlier, and I did not want to tear them away. It seems that base was just a tiny bug compared to the vastness this place offered. Towers, towers, and more towers stood tall, some taller than the bordering wall, and each was so close to each other that they were nearly hugging. Streets only made big enough for walking pathed all through the city, made of tiled-stone. Waterfalls flowed down so many of the city's buildings, which was only the beginning. More streams of water channeled down artificially created channels that spun through an entire network, and the streets had its share of water to dip your feet into.

So much water, I started to think, *probably has something to do with these beings amphibian-like appearance.*

As far as aesthetics go, the buildings seemed to be made of stone that consisted of tiny ridges along their surface, which seemed to make the water bounce away. Almost as if the water were repelled to the building like a bug to bug spray. Triangle-shaped, colorful tarps hung high in the sky, connected by wires to many of the buildings. With so many of them, most of the inner streets were shaded.

Most breathtaking of all, a beam every so often shot out from the center of the city into the sky and disappeared. It was a sight to marvel at and certainly something not often seen.

My squad behind me stepped past the gate and took notice as well.

"I must say, I'm surprised to see this much water," Valiic observed.

"It's to help us stay hydrated in the intense temperature. Our species doesn't do so well in direct sunlight for long periods of time," Witna admitted.

"All I know is that stone is out of this world," Frost hyped.

"If it's *out of this world,* how do they have it?" Shadow-Walker asked rhetorically, teasing Frost.

Witna explained, "We call it deepstone. It's found in underwater caverns and does not decay from water corrosion. Quite useful for us, of course."

"Cool and all for the exterior, but all that water on the interior just ain't my bag," said Frost.

"I agree, Frost. It isn't for me either," I added.

We strolled through a main street, behind Witna. Busy plazas full of shops, food stands, tents, trade stands, and local restaurants filled the edges of the streets. Some were tucked into the towers, and others were independent. This place was a genuine commercial boardwalk. Civilians and salesmen alike roamed free throughout. Essentially, this was an area for families and leisure for locals all around this planet and was especially vibrant with life today.

Brad jabbed my shoulder, and his visor directed my attention to a building we just passed. "My azz iz headed tah dat smithhouse."

"You don't want to get cleaned up?" I asked.

"My gear comez first. I'll catch up wit yah lata, Stonewall."

I glanced to Witna, who gave me a nod of approval. I turned back to him. "We'll keep you updated." On that, he split off from the group.

As we continued to walk through the boardwalk, we got our share of looks. None seemed to be of fear, but more of interest. Those who neared us showed with their expressions that we were malodourous. But that wasn't our fault.

We came to the bathhouse near the end of this main street. Chiseled with tile siding, this building was wide and at the bottom of a moderate sized tower.

Witna took us to the front desk after we entered. The man at the front asked, "How may I help you, Prime Keeper?" though his gaze was on my unit.

Witna waved to get his attention. "See that these guests to our planet are treated to a private wash room and that their attire is properly cleaned. It's all on me."

He didn't speak for a moment. "Uh, sure. I'll have someone show them to room four. It's vacant."

Chapter 7

"Thanks."

The attendant gestured to the hallway behind him, and someone else appeared. Of course she was taken aback by our presence. However, Witna nodded to her, giving her assurance.

"Right this way, please," the employee said.

We followed her through a hallway to a room marked with a sign written in their native language. We entered behind her into a tiled room with stalls on each side and a bench in the middle. Water flowed from a few walls and emptied into a drain under the bench.

"Each changing station has a towel to cover yourself before entering the wash room, which is through the far glass door." She pointed. "Leave your clothes in the stations, and someone will be by to collect and wash them... if you can understand what I'm saying anyway." She mumbled that last part mostly to herself and left us to ourselves.

"Take your time, boys. Lord knows the grime stuck to our skin is no quick wash away," I said before heading to my station.

"See y'all uzzos in the tub." Frost chuckled as he entered another stall.

The stall was stone and tile, a close cousin in design to the material used to construct many of the structures here. I entered through a blurred glass door and noticed my towel neatly folded on a bench to my right. It was a two-part station, and I stepped over a small stone step into an empty space with a reflective mirror.

The light was dim, but I could see my filthy self well enough. And boy, did I look like horseshivf. My face bared smudges of dirt, mud, and blood; war's chaotic stew. My beard and hair, once a handsome orange, looked to have brown and black highlights and was clumped in random places.

First, I tossed my gear and weapons to the side. Then I pulled off the black tank top lent to me by Frost after my armor was destroyed on Idor. I tossed the shirt riddled with holes in the corner. Just like my face, my torso bore the same mess. I brushed some of the dried mud off the right side of my chest, revealing a circular scar the size of a coin. And I remember that exact moment my old man decided to use me as an ash tray for his cigar, forever leaving its mark. I turned a bit and was able to see a long scar going vertically down part of my back from the time my father pushed me into the side of a counter. Even though that bastard was dead, those scars were reminders of just how awful he was to me and my mom. A perk of my ace abilities was having no new scars, only the ones I received before I got my regenerative powers.

For a moment, I stood there, running my hand on the vertical scar. I was thinking up and down over my life up to this point. Maybe it was this place, maybe it was the reflection of my soul staring back at me through glass like a window. With all that has happened to me, I couldn't help feeling I've lived three lifetimes already.

Next, I shed my padded military pants. I followed that with my boots and boxers. Staring back at me was a soldier's body, decorated by war. Given that this was about to be my first complete dunk under water since our mission on Idor, I gave myself only one choice. I was going in that water with just the suit God graced me with.

Bare ass and all, I snatched up the towel and headed out to the water, towel wrapped around my waist.

I pushed through the glass and was welcomed to two separate containers of crystal-clear water. The bathing room was private, separated by dressed stone and a roof. Steam emitted straight up to the vents, and spring water poured into the baths.

Shadow-Walker and Frost were already in the same spring, on opposite sides.

"Still looking as shredded as ever, uzzo," Frost observed, with a quick laugh.

I tossed the towel to the edge of the water and jumped in without waiting. Now under the water, eyes closed, I took a moment to enjoy the magic. The water lifted all the shivf glued to me, and I felt like a heavy invisible weight was unstrapped from my back.

I can't imagine any water feeling better than this, I thought, *it's like fraken angel tears.*

My head emerged from the water, and I let in the lightest breath of air I'd had in weeks. I pushed the water from my hair, eyes, and beard.

"You good, uzzo?" I heard Frost ask. "After all the shivf we'd been through, I'd hate for you to drown."

I rubbed the last of the water from my eyes.

"Imagine that headline on his gravestone." Shadow had a laugh.

Chapter 7

I inched over to the closet corner of the bath and rested my arms over both sides, letting myself relax.

"God's mercy, this is heaven's heaven," I said.

Valiic was the last to enter the water. He eased in, and the water nearly breached over the top due to his size.

"You look like a completely different dude without all that armor on," said Shadow-Walker.

"I feel much lighter, too." He gave half a smile. He was trying his best to hide it, but his eyes gave it away. He missed Narrisa, and every moment that he remained out of contact with her, he grew worse for wear. If this goes on too much longer, I fear for his state of mind.

"Speaking of maelkii armor, I've always wondered why you big, badass warriors still use what you use," said Frost.

"Armor has always been a traditional wear for a warrior. It's taxing and heavy, not just for durability, but for the resolve the armor gives your spirit. It forces your body to adapt and get stronger to bare it, producing better warriors."

"I get that, uzzo. Trust me, big dog, I understand the drive maelkii have. What I meant was, why not use forcidion to create armor instead of shields. Wouldn't it have made for better use that way?"

"Forcidion may be the most durable metal in the galaxy, but it's also one of the most dense and heaviest. Most don't realize that most maelkii shields used this day and age are not completely forcidion. Most shields use the alloy, durrinium, to make the core with forcidion layered over it. It would take melting down two or three shields to make a full set of armor which would be too heavy for maelkii to wear in the first place."

"Yours is like that, too?" I asked.

"My shield is pure forcidion, passed down in my family for generations. I was lucky."

"Maelkii are so cool, man. I wish dor'o had half the history and depth of your species." Shadow-Walker let out a few laughs.

"You're too harsh. Every species was given their own unique qualities and gifts. You'd never find a maelkii as athletic or agile as a dor'o."

"Or one who loves mountains as much," Frost chuckled.

Our conversations and state of relaxation continued through a few hours until we were ready to meet Witna for the meal she humbly offered.

*****

Our attire had been cleaned and dried. They went as far as to stitch our tears back together. Brad was still off doing his lone wolf thing, but the rest of us entered into a fancy diner behind one of Witna's little helpers.

I was the first to push through the bejeweled beads of the main archway. The inside was par for the course in terms of material and the water atmosphere. Though the sources that water flowed from had been touched up by fancy's wand, and the walls and ceiling had been hand carved with designs. Artwork was a big part of the setting, too. Both of which took heavy inspiration of seas and oceans, capturing their natural beauty.

As we entered past the tables, I noticed each one was empty. After taking a longer look around, I came to realize Witna must be one influential fish. After all, it seems the place had been booked out with just us and her to fill the place.

Witna was at a long table, with her knees on a towel and sitting upright.

"What a terrible way to sit for a meal," Shadow-Walker whispered in my ear.

I took a knee at a towel placed next to a table which was waist high. By the expressions shared by my team, I wasn't the lone man with a distaste for this custom these people seem to have when it comes to eating. Witna could see our concern. "What's the matter?"

I picked a smile from my collection in an effort not to come off impolite. "I mean, not to come off as a rude redhead, but would you mind bringing out something to rest our asses on and a table with more height to compensate?"

"Oh... do you dislike our customs?" Her smile turned to concern.

Valiic stepped in. "Ma'am." He gestured to his thick, bulky legs and knees. "This is just not a comfortable position for someone of my stature and anatomy."

"I see. No problem." She waved her hand over to some waiters and whispered in their ears. The whole time, their interest stuck to us like cobbler's wax. Soon, the waiters brought a second and third table to stack over ours, raising the height. They carried in two benches from the outside of the restaurant and placed them to the sides of the tables. We all sat, and even Witna joined in.

"Sorry for the inconvenience," one waiter started. "Can I offer you all beverages or nourishment to start with?"

Witna looked to me. "Would you like a menu?"

Shadow jolted. "Nope. Get me some rum, I'm starving."

I was with Shadow on that. "Right now, there's one thing my taste bugs are begging for, and that one thing is beer. Do you have it?" I asked the waitress.

Her glazed face told me all she heard was folderol. She looked to Witna, who repeated my statement. She then responded, "We do."

"We'll take your best beer. And any appetizer will do. Just get some grub out here," I said politely. Witna translated.

"Coming right up." The waitress capered like had she just received delightful news.

"So... here we are. When we speak, you don't hear bunk, so where's the answers to follow those string of questions?" I asked.

She tipped her finger toward myself and Frost. "This isn't the first time we've been visited by your kind." She let her glance rest on Valiic, then Shadow-Walker. "But your two friends are new to me."

The news came as a bit of a surprise to me. "That can't be true." Though in my head, I thought, *It's against the law to visit planets like this. So how is it others came before us? And how many?* I couldn't tell her that, at the risk of word spreading.

"I assure you it happened. When they first arrived, they told me they were here for investigative purposes only."

"Investigating what?" Valiic adjusted himself in the bench.

"Something to do with *strange energy* in the *Enchanted System* - I believe those were the words used."

"Enchanted System," said Frost. "Is that where this planet is located?"

"It would make sense given what the lead researcher told me."

"Hold on, and excuse my ignorance, as astronomy was a subject that knocked me sound asleep. Where's the Enchanted System?" I asked.

"The closest known system to the center of the Milky Way Galaxy," Valiic answered. "The ARW hasn't mapped that much in the Enchanted System. For reference, the omelic home planet of Omulice is within the Enchanted System. If I had to make a guess, this planet must be deeper towards the center of the galaxy." Valiic interest rose as he turned back to Witnamerrys.

If all this is true, then that would explain why she can understand us. Whoever came first must've brought render chips, and she must have one. Because some of the others couldn't understand my words, there mustn't have been enough render chips to go around.

The waitress returned with drinks and two plates full of bite-sized fish and a thick red sauce. I took a sip of the bubbly and slightly bitter brew and enjoyed the hell out of it. The fish dipped in the sauce slid down my throat just as pleasantly. And it seemed my crew was just happy to have real food and drinks grace their stomachs after so long.

Before leaving, Witna whispered in the waitress's ear and sent her off.

Frost cleared his throat. "I might've an answer to all this. In 2095, the Order of Aegis launched an exploration project called Project Outreach in an attempt to set up research colonies on inhabitable planets within the Enchanted System. From what I remember hearing, it was due to strange energy detected around this system. Kalvin thought it worth the time to start studying this energy."

"What happened?"

"In most cases, Project Outreach succeeded in further mapping out the galaxy, just not so much with the energy. In some cases, ships never returned. This must've been the case here. Unfortunately, before Kalvin could put more resources into Project Outreach, the Wersillian War began to take shape, and the project was put on hold. That's all my egghead can remember about it, anyway."

"Sounds to me like just some more Order of Aegis bullshivf," I sighed.

Frost gazed at Witna. "Do you know what happened to our people?"

"The same fate that falls on anyone who goes to the Blood Forest."

"Blood Forest?" Shadow shivered.

"Officially, our ancestors named the forest Qurangmaar, and it's the forest you saw when you landed outside our Treasured City."

"Yeah, about that. In what sinister, hellish factory did those crazy machines come from?" I asked.

"They are the reason we have walls separating that side of the city from that forest. And there are many of them, called shjarrs. You had a peek yourself when you landed, but those were just the simple ones. From the legends, some can take out an army. As luck had it, our ocean-rivers seem to hurt and kill them, so they won't ever venture into the water. Your people... they did not listen to our stories...said they wanted to study the strange energy in the Blood Forest."

"Why?" Valiic threw two fish down his throat at the same time.

"According to them, it was strongest up there."

"Guessing that their stupidity led to disastrous results," I said but figured I knew the answer.

"All of them were slain by the monsters of the forest... all except one." She held a doleful mien.

"One?" Valiic held up his finger. "What happened to the one left?"

"He stayed on this planet."

"Why would anyone want to stay here?" Shadow-Walker bumped me in the shoulder. He glanced quickly at Witna. "No disrespect to your planet, of course. I'm just saying, why not want to be with your own?"

"None taken," Witnamerrys shrugged. Her eyes looked past us, and she waved. We looked back, and through the doorway stepped a human! "Why don't you meet him yourself?"

The man found his way to the edge of our table. He was male, dirt-brown hair and wearing near circular glasses. Lean build and not much in the height department. Dressed in the holy cloth, he looked to be pastor.

"Pleased to meet you bunch. I go by Jeremiah, servant of the lord and savior."

"Biblical name for a biblical man," I observed. "I'm James Stone, captain of this unit."

"James is a biblical name just as mine," he winked.

"Is it?"

"Haven't read the holy book, have you?"

"No. But that thick book isn't exactly a page turner," I joked. Jeremiah was kind enough to join in my laughter.

"In fact, as many as six different men in the Bible are named James. Jesus, our savior, even had two apostles named James: James, the son of Zebedee, and James, the son of Alphaeus."

Valiic jumped in. "Have you ever read the Book of Ancient Prophets?"

"It was a spiritual journey, I found. I took a particular interest in the story of Raylic the Bright, son of Juuklon. *Raylic, warrior of light, inscribed life and death, light and darkness, hope and despair. The divide was created, and on that day, the sons and daughters of twilight were let free to roam the world, free. Joanmurla 202:34-35.*"

"*It is on thou self to seek the truth of the universe and achieve enlightenment, Obitan 6:20.* You know your verses," Valiic held a joyous smile.

"I can see you are a man of wisdom," Jeremiah complimented.

Valiic nodded graciously. "And you as well."

"I hate to interrupt whatever it is that is going on here, but what are you doing here, Jeremiah?" Shadow-Walker asked.

"Only what I was created to do - preach to all that will listen," he replied.

"Frivolous work, if you ask me," I added.

"James. What the man does isn't a journey taken by the weak of heart," Valiic countered.

I held up my hands with apologetic intent.

"It's a thankless task," Frost said to Jeremiah. "I don't envy you, uzzo."

Chapter 7

Jeremiah blinked at that word, not seeming to catch the meaning. Hell, it wasn't long ago that I learned what I meant. But who can keep up with the crazy slang kids use today?

Witna tipped up her hand. "I'm sure you will have plenty of time to chat later. I brought him here for a reason." She let out a breath. "Our planet will have a problem in the near future. And we need some way to face it."

"What problem?" Valiic asked.

"A monster of the forest will bring destruction to this planet, or so it has been foretold. We believe the problem will be brought on by a very deadly shjarr from the Blood Forest. And if this city falls, this planet falls!"

We stared at her in silence.

She continued. "A tower of ancient origin lies in the city. You saw those beams from earlier blasting into the sky?"

We nodded.

"It came from that tower - its purpose is to control our planet's weather. And thus, if no prime hand is alive and present to operate the tower, our planet's weather will be uncontrollable... disasters after disasters. For centuries we have defended this tower, even when the shjarrs started to show up decades ago."

"So what does that have to do with us?" Shadow asked.

"Simple. You want to leave this planet. We have the means to send out a long distance communication to your allies. But we need you to retrieve a weapon to use against the shjarr monster predicted to wipe us out."

"One hand washes the other, then." I nodded.

"Exactly," Witna said.

"So where and how do we get this great weapon?"

"The weapon lies in a cavern not made by corelinns. But a bit of a warning. That cave will be dangerous, and you will face challenges like you never have before, and it's guarded by shjarrs."

"Fantastic." Shadow rolled his eyes.

"But that's why I brought Jeremiah here. He is informed and will help your achieve your goal. He will guide you in the cave--"

I interrupted. "Look, I'm not married to the idea of charging headfirst into a cave of dangers without any sort of light to guide our way, but you seriously think Jeremiah can be that light? You really think it's a good idea to take a priest with no battle experience into such a place?"

"He is the best guide you can ask for. I insist you take him."

I was ill at ease with this proposal. Though I felt I had little choice in the matter. "Very well. You've got a deal. We'll scoop up this weapon for you, kill the monster, and in turn you provide us a means to contact rescue." I stood up, slouched a bit over the table, and reached across, holding out my hand. She stared at my hand with an etched face.

"What are you doing?" she asked.

Jeremiah reassured her with his gentle face. "It's a common custom to shake hands when a deal is struck."

"Interesting." She extended hers to meet mine. Her hand was rather wet and cold, with a sticky feel and webbing between her fingers. The handshake was made, and we sat down. Just then, the waitress returned with a crew, and they served up the main course hidden under squared, blurred-glass containers surrounded by decorations.

"Now that we are done with the important matters, I figured we could enjoy a meal before your big task. Jeremiah will have all the details, and we'll have transportation waiting for you at first light the day after tomorrow. Until that time, I will allow you to stay in a guest house. Help yourself in any way to prepare for the journey. It's all on me."

We applauded her generosity. The servers took that as an opportunity to wheel the food closer, and the smell snatched control of my nose in an instant. And I wasn't the only one who was swept away by the aroma. I could feel the water building in my mouth.

There was much more than we expected: Grilled trout fresh from a river, butter and honey and Bammberry preserves, a rasher of tender meat strips layered with fat and soft-boiled eggs as large as my fist, a few wedges of cheese, and a pot of thick sauce.

The hot food warmed my belly and lifted my spirits, as it did for the others. Our dinner continued with conversations of the light-hearted variety all the way through dessert. It had been a long time since we felt this good and light of stress.

Chapter 8: The Seer
December 7, 2111

James Stone

Expressionism and art seemed to be a large part of the culture of the corelinn species. Here I was, moseying my way through the guest house, when I came across a collection of formatted music and a player. I sat on the couch, avoiding the watered parts of the floor like a plague, since that seemed to be a thing in practically every structure, albeit an annoying thing at that. Once settled, I popped some music into the player; a small device looking more like a harp with waterfalls instead of strings. Then the music played; no words, just classical-like string instruments in tempo with something that had a kick to it. Most fascinating of all, the waterfall on the player danced to the music. And just like that, I found myself a time-killer for the following hour.

One of the two suns began rising through a nearby window. It was a new day on the planet. However, ARW time just peaked past midnight. Since there were two suns, there was little time for night, and I heard from a local that a fair portion of this planet was desert as a result of the suns.

Shadow-Walker entered the room I was in and stopped by the front door. "James, I'm headed out."

"Where to?"

"Same shop as Brad. I'm going to see if I can modify Silent Dagger to use their crystalized water munitions."

"All our weapons are low on ammo, but if you can manage to modify more than just your rifle, we could really benefit. We'd have the best of both worlds; our superior tech matched with their means of harming the shjarrs."

"I'll see what I can do." Shadow opened the front door. He jumped back. "Shivf, Jeremiah! You startled me!"

Jeremiah entered. "My apologies, that wasn't my intention. I just came to speak with James."

Shadow shook his head and sighed. "You make me want to go to where you live, toast all your bread, and put it back in the bag." I chuckled as he slid past Jeremiah and out the door. Jeremiah watched him go, not sure about Shadow's joke.

"There really isn't any bread on this planet," Jeremiah said, with a deadpan expression.

"Shadow was messing with you," I assured.

"Where're your teammates?" Jeremiah cupped his hands together over his waist and stood straight, formal both in dress and stance.

"Shadow headed to the same smithhouse where Brad had been spending his time. Frost is exploring the city and Valiic... I'm afraid he's locked himself in his room for personal time. Poor teddy bear has been struggling with being out of contact with his cohinla."

Jeremiah gazed down, his expression filled with pity. *"--and Luvamoureus took his mate in his arms, and she took him in hers - for their soul melded together as one and forever they shall be together in this life and the next, forever journeying down one path - and he whispered to her: My cohinla. Solvia 2:14.* It's said that was the origin of the word cohinla. And I personally find that verse purer than any other. It always rejuvenates my faith in our galaxy to know we have such a compassionate species as the maelkii." Jeremiah had a tear in his eye. "I will pray for Valiic."

Waterworks? I thought, *I feel for Valiic, too, but tears are a bit emasculating.* "I know he will appreciate it," I said.

"Sorry, I've always been a tad emotional." He wiped the tear. "I came here for another purpose. Before tomorrow, I'm supposed to show you to Anighta."

"Just saying her name out loud doesn't really tell me much." I made the comment in good fun and showed with a smile I didn't intend on teasing him.

"She has information... *and* something we will need to earn this weapon."

"So she's important. That's all you needed to say." I stood up and followed him out the door.

*****

Chapter 8

To say I feel comfortable in thick crowds makes as much sense as a raindrop pleading to join the ocean. Jeremiah and I were working through such a crowd in the rich part of the city, and we were on the way to see someone. However, in moments like this, I wanted to find a quite tree in a quite spot to bask in serenity. I'm the raindrop that falls on the beach, sits on a pebble and adores the ocean from close by, savoring the salty aroma and motion of the waves. Not the one that lands in the ocean.

The crowd had a life of its own; the vibrant clothes glimmered in the morning light, and the people moved like enchanting shoals of fish. There was chatter between sellers and buyers, old friends catching up, new friends made. It was busy for sure, but the hustle and bustle brought a life to this city.

We cleared the herd of corelinns, and Jeremiah was cheerful. "Don't you just love this part of the city? Flowers everywhere, the markets bursting with food, the spring-grown grapes used for wines are so cheap and so good that you can almost get drunk just breathing the air. Everyone in this part of the city is happy and friendly and rich."

"I'm the kind of tree that grows best in its own sunlight, not light shared by a forest," I answered.

He tried to cheer me up with his smile. "Well, we are almost there."

As we continued to walk, the amount of corelinns around dropped exponentially, and I was happier for it. "You wouldn't hold it against me if I told you I was no longer a believer in God."

"I've never been one to force my beliefs on others. I believe if it is God's will for them to hear me, then they shall listen."

I nodded. "I'm glad to hear it. We don't need conflict among ourselves. In my experience, I find it doesn't mix well with battle."

He nodded. "I agree. Being that I'm the new one of the group, it doesn't surprise me you'd question where I stand."

I gave him a friendly pat. "You seem to have a good read on people."

"Are you the only one?"

"One of what?"

"Only one who doesn't believe in something higher?"

I rubbed my neck. "I've heard Frost and Valiic express faith, but I can't say the same for Shadow or Brad. If I'm laying the cards out on the table, it's not really something I talk with my unit about much."

"I appreciated your honesty. It will be important as we work together."

"On the subject of honesty, I still have more than a share of doubts that you should be tagging along. With the very destruction of this planet hanging on our success, the last thing my unit needs is to babysit you."

"I have no fears facing what we are to face."

"Oh, yeah? What fuels your confidence?"

"Because I stand on the promises God has made for me."

His unshaken poise forced a few good laughs out of my gut. "I'm going to need you to elaborate."

Jeremiah stopped and stood in front of me with a twinkle in his eye. "The Bible says in *2 Corinthians 5:21* that *God made him who had no sin to be sin for us, so that in him* - not because of what I've done, but because of what Jesus has done - I can become righteous for God. That I can be justified just as if I had never sinned in the first place. That I'm already good enough not because of the sacrifices that I make, but because of the sacrifice that Jesus made. And in this day and age, those such as you may question if I would be harmed or something will happen, but the Bible says in *Psalm 91:10-12, no harm will overtake you, no disaster will come near your tent.* For he has guardians all around me. *They will guard you in all your ways,* and *they will lift you up in their hands, so that you will not strike your foot against a stone--*"

I noticed a small crowd of corelinns stop to listen.

Jeremiah was still going. "--And look, if something goes bad I didn't expect or I feel it will be a problem, the Bible says no problem at all. *Romans 8:28, and we know that in all things God works for the good of those who love him, who have been called according to his purpose.* I don't have to worry about my financial life either, because *my God will meet all your needs* - not according to what happens in my economy, not according to happens in this galaxy - but *according to the riches of his glory in Christ,* I am financially protected; *Philippians 4:19.* And if I get sick, the Bible says *by his wounds we are healed; Isaiah 53:5.* I don't have to worry about the future, because the price has already been paid.

The stripes that Jesus bore on his back purchased my healing. And I can live with peace, *the peace of God, which transcends all understanding, will guard your hearts and your minds in Christ Jesus; Philippians 4:7.* And when the enemy comes in like a flood, they *will fear the name of the Lord, and from the rising of the sun, they will revere his glory. For he will come like a pent-up flood that the breath of the Lord drives along; Isaiah 59:19.* I don't have to be strong, because it is not what I do *by might nor by power, but by my Spirit says the Lord Almighty; Zechariah 4:6.* And I can stand on God's word because *2 Corinthians 1:20* tells me *no matter how many promises God has made, they are "Yes" in Christ. And so through him the "Amen" is spoken by us to the glory of God.* That is why I have no fear, because God is there for me."

At this moment, I was damn near overtaken by his overflowing confidence in his belief. And I knew then what drives people into faith in something bigger than themselves. Even if I believed it was all bogus, true believers are empowered by their faith in something larger watching their backs. That was something I had no right to take away.

Some in the crowd clapped and cheered. After they dispersed, I cleared my throat. "When I said elaborate, I didn't quite mean whatever the hell just happened."

He laughed and adjusted his glassed with bright cheeks. "I apologize. His word is in my heart like a fire, fueled by my soul. I'm weary if I try to hold it in, indeed, I cannot."

We were almost there, and after a short walk I pushed through the opening of a merchant's tent with a sign that read *"Seer,"* in the corelinn language. Anighta sat alone in her hut; fairly elderly and losing the shine in her skin tone. Rugs, lively with colors and patterns, covered the entire floor space. Besides her chair was a table, one of three more like it. On top were many exotic artifacts, relics, and décor. Each added a vibe of mystery to the inside this place.

I cleared my throat. "I came here--"

"I know why you are here," Anighta cut me off.

"Of course you do," I mumbled under my breath.

"I am gifted like you, James. I believe the word you use is... *ace.*"

"You're an ace?" Surprise came over me. "What's your ability?"

"The words of the universe can be seen by me. Often, I find that they are too confusing to make sense. Rare as it may be, I can sometimes pull information and riddles from the miasma of nothingness." She turned to me, and her eyes immediately stopped my feet and stole my attention. They were glowing, full of dots of light inside a vast ocean of blackness, like stars shining in space. "I see you believe me now."

"So then, soothsayer, I'm told you can offer us advice on this weapon we are supposed to scoop up."

She got up and walked into an adjacent room, out of view. Only a few seconds passed before she came back out with a hardcover book as thick as the Bible. She handed it to me; black with golden symbols and patterns filling the cover. "All the advice you seek is within this. The Book of Sin. And my words are truth."

Sin? I wondered. "A crusty, old book. What else you got?" I asked, with unbelieving eyebrows.

"Experience." She waited in silence for a moment before starting. "What you seek, James, is not an easy thing to obtain, let alone control. For generations, my species has been trying to obtain the weapons with absolute nil success. My team and I, we didn't even make it past the second test."

"Test?"

"Are you not aware of what these caves were created to do? They are trials to be completed in order to obtain its reward. Through the harshest labyrinth you must traverse." Her eyes went to the hut's ceiling, as if she were watching something past the fabric. She continued. "The creatures within the labyrinth are the blood of the cave, and they feed on certain emotions. I was alone, at the second challenge. Oyemar, the last of my team remaining alive, had gone missing. I thought Oyemar dead until I heard his tortured screams. I followed the echoes down, to the darkest ends of the caverns below. What I saw... what I witnessed is what we all fear - the wickedness of the damned on full display. Among a sea of crystalized cocoons, and surrounded by thousands more freshly spawned pools of slime, the damned held Oyemar's broken body in a vice of metal and pain. It was peeling the life from his body - his soul. How? I can't imagine, and I have tried. Tendrils of luminance tore away like flesh. With every strand, Oyemar's scream cut the dark and was met with a chittering chorus from the unborn. I can't say if they were feeding off his soul, or the pain, but my guess is both - somehow they ate both. And my words are truth."

Chills ran down my spine. What are the damned that she speaks of? Shjarrs? Second thoughts about this mission began to shove their way up to the top of my mind.

Anighta shook her head in a swift, rapid motion, closing her eyes for a moment. She turned back to me. "Please don't let what I said spook you. A monster of the forest will bring destruction to this planet... a monster your team can stop. A great risk I have taken by bringing you here."

I felt a bit of ire fill my blood. "Come again? You saying you caused our ship to malfunction?"

"Directly, no. I was the one who asked for it to be done."

I was lost for words due to the revelation, but that ire in my blood soon faded away when I remembered what Witna had said during our conversation in the restaurant. She was desperate and believed we are the only thing left to save her planet. So when the opportunity presented itself, she wouldn't've hesitated to bring us here. Despite having some spite over being forced here, I understood why. "Can't say I blame you. And a deal with me might as well be written in stone. I'll hold up my end. I'll save your planet," I promised.

Anighta nodded in graciousness, and I headed back out.

✳✳✳✳✳

Most of my team and I stood around the island countertop back at the guest house. Each of us, including my giddy self, were eager to take a peek inside this strange book Anighta gave me.

"What do you think's in the book?" Valiic asked.

To satisfy everyone's curiosity, including my own, I opened to the first page for everyone to see. What was shown was not at all what I expected. Clear as day, the words were in English. How could this alien novel from an alien planet, of whom the inhabitants speak and write in an alien dialect, be in English?

"The words are in my native Quallic Dialect," Valiic stated, with surprise.

"Really? I see Jav'colo," Shadow-Walker added. Jav'colo is a dor'o language Shadow-Walker grew up speaking.

Jeremiah gazed at the words in silence

"Plain as day, I see English," I said.

"Make that two," Frost backed me up. "Uzzos... I think this book somehow projects whatever native language we speak onto the pages."

"How?" Valiic questioned. "If this were so, how do each see different languages?"

Frost answered, "Sight is only a sense, one that can be exploited. I think the book is reading us, rather than the other way around."

"The corelinns don't have the brain power to produce such a complex antique," I added.

"Well, the prime keeper said the caves weren't created by them either. Maybe whoever created the caves created this book, too."

"Devisors?" Shadow-Walker asked. Jeremiah raised an eyebrow to that word, probably unsure of what we referred to.

"I guess we will see when we enter the caves. Devisors seem to have a particular architectural style that we can keep an eye out for," Frost finished.

I closed the book and handed it off to Jeremiah. As our guide, he was going to be responsible for it. It was not our place to trudge through all that material. We had to rest. So I headed off to my quarters to turn in for the big adventure that started tomorrow.

Chapter 9: A Quest for Sin
December 8, 2111

James Stone

Dawn had hit, and the sky glowed orange and yellow, with thin
streaks of green streaming from one side of the sky to the other. It was
gorgeous. My unit and I didn't, however, have much more than a few
seconds to soak in the view. We were on the move. Already on the
outskirts of the city, we came to a seaport. Down a vast network of stairs,
all of us followed Jeremiah towards the docks.

"This may be the mercenary in me talking, but are we really just
going to trust altar boy over there with our lives?" Shadow-Walker, next
to me, whispered.

On the other side of me, Valiic had overheard Shadow-Walker and
answered for me, "I, for one, sense that trust is a cherished virtue in
him."

"I don't trust someone without a dark side. And besides, didn't he
seem just extra eager to join our super elite boy band."

I added, "Considering our situation, I believe putting our faith in the
man of faith is our best route home." Shadow-Walker and Valiic
nodded their heads. "Anyway, Shadow. That's of little concern to me at
the moment. I wanna know if you were able to convert our weapons?"

"Funny story there. See, I was able to convert Silent Dagger and
Valiic's cannon... his especially took a while. By the time I got to yours,
my hands, my beautiful mechanic's hands, were smoking out. Flat tire or
something," he snickered with his nose.

I was a bit disappointed, but I knew the matter couldn't be helped.
Shadow-Walker did his best, and for me that was enough. "It's fine. I've
a feeling Frost and I won't be sent to the lion's den empty-handed."

Shadow agreed. "With so much on the line, they'll let us use all the
weapons we need."

My gaze switched to the wooden docks within the confines of a
miniature gulf; a massive boatyard as silent and motionless as the still
waves. "How long till we arrive?" I called to Jeremiah.

"Two weeks even. Our boat will be filled with supplies, and I've planned two rest stops on the way. After all, we'll need to restock."

"Why so long?" Shadow asked.

"The land of the Blood Forest is expansive, and we have to sail around it in order to avoid danger."

Jeremiah nodded me over to him and led me directly to a wooden booth at the gate entrance of the docks; the rest of my unit hung back. Walls of wooden stakes lined the area, keeping people from entering. He reached in the windowsill opening of the booth and pushed a button. There was a tumbling sound from within before a corelinn male appeared. "Two humans!" He paused. "Oh, you must be the ones Witna spoke of. Jeremiah, right? Jeremiah Sun of-or something like that?"

"Jeremiah's good." He nodded. "And we are."

"Well, best of luck, then." He pulled a level down, and the gate lifted up.

Jeremiah signaled for all of us to enter, and we followed him to a boat. It was the first one on the dock; large and styled artistically in a manner similar to many of architecture of the city. Design-wise, this boat looked like it could be a cousin to old-age, human-created deck boats mixed with yachts. One by one, we climbed a tiny ladder to enter the boat. I sat at the back left with Shadow-Walker. Frost was laying down on the back right. Jeremiah took the captain's chair. Valiic took a front seat, with Brad occupying the adjacent couch.

Jeremiah turned the engine over, and the boat hummed. He backed us out of the dock slot, and we began our journey to retrieve this ever so special weapon.

Minutes in, the wind was in my face, and the spray of water cooled me down. The journey heading towards inevitable conflict to save a planet had begun. I, however, wasn't about to let the direness of it all eat away at me. Instead, I opted to let the moment take over me. The ride was relaxing, so I let my feet extend to the foot stool in front of me; my back and ass were against the waterproof padding.

Shadow-Walker, eyes partly closed to the wind, reminisced, "I don't remember the last time I've been on a boat."

Chapter 9

"That's about as surprising as seeing green in spring. Ever since hovercraft options became more military-viable, boats have become a niche commodity," I added.

"Outside the military, boats only serve for leisure and sport," Frost agreed from the back right seat.

After about half an hour, Jeremiah pulled open a drawer and tossed back two binocular-looking devices to me and Frost. He pointed to a cliff face at the corner of the Blood Forest far in the distance, which looked like a dot sticking out of the ocean-river. "Look there."

I placed the device to my face and tried to adjust the length to fit both eyes, but they were too wide - clearly made for the different facial structure of the corelinns. Instead, I used just one eye and gazed in the direction he pointed. The view made the hairs on the tips of my toes stand. The cliff jutted sharply out of the ocean-river at steep inclines. Jagged rocks protruded where the water met the rock, but in contrast to the barren cliffs, atop lay what appeared to be fertile grasslands large enough to build a colony. Further past the grasslands were thick forests full of black and dark-gray trees - the Blood Forest. Along the grasslands were the ruins of a trailer park, with a research center at the middle of the colony. The stomach-tuning part was, it had the same technology and design characteristics of humans and qwayks. It must've been remains of Project Outreach.

"That's where I'm from," Jeremiah said.

"I wanna see." Shadow-Walker reached for the device, and I handed it to him.

"How did you survive where others weren't so lucky?" I asked.

"Faith."

"Walked headfirst into that one." I rolled my eyes.

"--*Truly I tell you, if you have faith as small as a mustard seed, you can say to this mountain, 'Move from here to there,' and it will move. Nothing will be impossible for you. Matthew 17:20.*" Jeremiah gave a subtle tip of his head.

"Once, a long time ago, I believed in the divine. But even then, if someone told me faith alone can move a damn mountain, I'd look up and down at them stupid. In my experience, faith only gets you so far.

I've found that only the bonds we have as brothers in arms is what has kept us alive." I gestured to my crew.

Jeremiah smiled. "Such a bond is a gift. *My command is this: Love each other as I have loved you. Greater love has no one than this: To lay down one's life for one's friends. John 15:12-13.*"

"I'm glad you, me, and the lord can agree on one thing."

"If you want a mountain moved, it's as easy as talking to the dor'o. Mountains are kind of our thing," Shadow-Walked weighed in. "And it is science that moves that mountain, not faith. Science is what disproves faith."

"Science doesn't replace God. No, science leads us closer to him," Jeremiah claimed. "To say science and faith are mutually exclusive from each other is an injustice to them both."

"But of course it is, Jeremiah," Shadow said, with sarcasm. "Especially when his name has goody-little angels like you to defend him." Jeremiah was kind enough to laugh with Shadow.

I got up. Valiic was sitting in the front, silent for too long. Today was an especially hard day on him, since it was the day of his cohinlation - the day Narrisa and Valiic became partners in life, and a day especially sacred to many maelkii houses. I couldn't find it in me to see him this way much longer. So, I made my way over to his seat and sat next to him. With the heavy wind, I knew we could keep our conversation away from prying ears.

"Valiic. We'll get off this planet, and you'll be able to talk with Narrisa again. On my life, I promise you." I placed my hand on his back to comfort my friend.

"I can see her, James. I can see her. When I close my eyes at night, I see her."

"In your dreams?"

He nodded with a heavy head. "I'm there in a dark room and the only light is coming from the window. I see her and those dytirc children. They wonder why their mother is so sad. They stare at Narrisa as she stares out the window in tears. She's waiting for me, James. I can see it clear as day."

I didn't know what to say. Her being alone, raising two dytirc children on a qwayk home world is no small feat. She traded one hostile territory for another. The key difference is, those living on Jaba-Qwayk won't be hostile towards her as much as they would towards those poor kids.

The other matter, of course, came down to how she would make it financially. Given that we are MIA, that would also mean our paychecks had stopped flowing. As soldiers of the ARW, we are paid on a per mission basis with a small base cut. As legionnaires, one of more elite ground units, our pay is rather handsome. Yet, none of that money will see Narrisa with us gone. Even if Valiic hadn't thought of this himself, I wasn't going to be the one to add more worries to him.

"Narrisa's strong-willed. No doubt lays in my mind that she'll be able to handle herself." I patted him on the back, hoping to ease his depression away with each pat.

"I pray every day to have half her strength and will. I can't live without her, and every day I'm away-- I know this is a test placed on my path as a warrior, but I'd be lying if I said it wasn't challenging."

"Guys like us will face obstacles every day. And those obstacles will mess with your compass. But I know you'll always remember true north." I gave him one more pat. He acknowledged my words with a subtle nod.

"So what is this weapon that we're supposed to get?" I caught Shadow asking Jeremiah.

"It's a sword called the Blade of Wrath. One of the Seven Weapons of Sin."

"Did you say seven deadly sins? As in what old Catholic churches preach against?" I asked.

"There's nine mentioned in the Book of Ancient Prophets," I heard Valiic mumble to himself. He seemed too occupied with his own sadness to want to contribute to the conversation, and I couldn't blame him for it.

"Big Daddy heard weapons," said Frost.

"Yes, weapons," Jeremiah reiterated. "Granted, it does seem to have similar symbolism to the capital sins. *Pride* - hubris and arrogance. *Gluttony* - Wasteful consumption, not just of food. *Envy* - desire, wanting what others have, critically, in a resentful manner, which tends to be more about depriving others of what they have. *Sloth* - less about laziness, as it is about apathy and unfulfilled potential. *Greed* - desire, specifically about the accumulation of material things, to hoard them and own them for the sake of ownership. *Lust* - desire, not of material things or of things others have, but of everything else. Lastly, *wrath* - vengeance, inability to forgive, often fueled by rage."

"So even the sins are the same. Sounds like these weapons were named after the seven deadly sins," I concluded.

"Or the sins were named after the weapons," Frost countered.

With aid from the water's breeze, I felt my hairs stand up as the ship fell to silence. There was something unnerving about that idea. Yet, our quest hinged on obtaining one - a quest for sin, so to speak.

Chapter 10: Prison of Darkness
December 8, 2111

Airra

When a warlord is in need of assistance, it is Airra's job as the head warlord to see that each and every warlord helped so that they can continue to do their part in the war. After all, she was above all the warlords and needed to make sure everything ran as smoothly as possible. Not a task she enjoyed, of course. Other people's problems were not her problems, so she couldn't care less about them. Yalfari Soodo, one such warlord, had called only a moment ago with an urgent matter. As an elderly lycargan with a battle injury to his knee, he had trouble walking. If it weren't for his ability, he might've already been put down. Nonetheless, she was on her way to meet him.

Airra marched down the familiar ostensibly endless halls of her home; a vast quantity of ancient harren-tree doors, hand-chiseled stone walls, shades-of-gray pictures that were almost high enough to touch the five meter high ceiling, and dim lights that flickered as candles would. She breathed in the sweet smell emitted by the wooden doors and carved walls. In these halls she walked since she was still just a little girl; halls that were located within a mansion residing on a combination of two planets called Thearend. It was home.

"Sister." Maliv Kuss, her dear stepbrother and fellow warlord, closed a door behind him and caught up to her.

"Walk with me." Airra motioned down the hall she was going.

They began to walk. "Father was impressed with the results you obtained from the omelic prisoner."

"It was pain that got the information, that's all. Pain runs the galaxy." She gave pause. "Enough about that, what does he want me to do with the information?"

"Nothing," Maliv informed.

Airra stopped at his words. *"Nothing?* Is he still upset about my failure to take that stupid key from James Stone?" she asked, with some sadness in her tone.

"Come on, sis. You know he never stays angry for long. He just told me to put a pin in that for the moment."

Airra let out a breath. She was relieved to hear her stepfather was not angry anymore. She never had much room in her twisted heart, but her stepfather managed to push his way in, as did her stepbrother. "Then it's time to go back to leading the legion." After the words were said, she realized she said them with distaste.

"You sound as if you don't want to. If... if you want, I can keep on leading them. I'm sure--"

"Now, now, dear stepbrother. I know you had your fun as acting head warlord while I was away, but I still don't think you are ready."

Maliv nodded, and his head sunk.

"But you could definitely use more responsibilities." Airra smiled.

He perked back up.

She continued. "With Steion dead, and now Dro'Zer, too, we will have to promote more dytircs and lycargans to Ultras to maintain a solid chain of command. With the inclusion of korkyran warchiefs, our presence on the ground should see a significant increase in success rates."

"Remind me how that works again. I'm not sure I understand how lycargans and dytircs are supposed to work with korkyras. Our ideologies are quite different."

"It's simple. Korkyran warchiefs will command ground parties in pairs. Each star cruiser will have at least one Ultra in command, and should any of them find themselves not on a star cruiser, they shall take the reins of a unit all to themselves. Ideologies aside, it's by far the best tactic. After all, I came up with it."

Maliv joined in her happiness. "I've always believed in you."

Airra stopped. They had almost arrived at Yalfari's quarters. She placed her bark-layered palm on top of her stepbrother's head. "I want you to take lead in the Ju-Sana System - take Yalfari, too. I expect he has found the location of the last key, meaning he is free to leave this place again. Take a large force of vicious, belligerent soldiers that are ready to bathe themselves in their enemies' blood. I trust you with this task."

His gleaming eyes stared up to hers. "And what will you do?" asked Maliv.

Chapter 10

Airra grinned, laughing, "I will do my part and snatch up the fourth and last key, hopefully stirring up mischief while doing so."

Maliv nodded, and Airra let him leave. After he'd gone a distance down the hall, Airra knocked twice on Yalfari's door.

It took a moment. Airra could hear the slow steps and thumps of his cane as he approached. The door opened with a creak.

Airra walked inside, past the old lycargan warlord. The reptilian scales below his eyes sagged. His claws and bumps had lost their sharp edge, and the natural shell around his body had a dull yellow tint to it. Yalfari was closing in on seventy, which to a lycargan was nearing the end of life.

Even with his cane, he struggled to make it over to his chair in the corner. "I'm glad you came, Airra. I have sensed a prison of darkness encircling Mara'Sane's mind. She is not well, and I fear we are going to lose her."

"How can you be sure?"

"I'm not. However, every day her mind becomes more and more shrouded to me. Something is wrong with her, and we must act now." There was clear panic in his elderly voice.

Despite her burning abhorrence for Mara'Sane, Airra knew she had no choice but to help. Mara'Sane had a vital role to play in the near future, meaning Airra needed her to live.

"Frak me," Airra cursed. "As much as I hate that ruddy bitch, what can we do to help?"

"I'm going to attempt to enter her mind with you. My hope is to find answers in there. And we must act now, or I fear it will be too late."

Airra nodded and took a seat on the ground next to the chair Yalfari sat in. She reached out her hand, and he grabbed hold. She closed her eyes and waited as Yalfari mediated.

Within a few seconds, Yalfari had pulled his and Airra's consciousness into Mara'Sane's inner mind.

It took a few seconds for Airra to regain her composure, and her senses quickly began to search for answers as to her location. She and Yalfari were near the entrance into an underground mine, with a broken down ramp leading up and out into the darkness of night. From the outside, Airra could hear the sounds of war; gunfire, explosions, shrieking, all the sounds Airra enjoys so very much. She didn't even realize she had a grin on her face from it, as it was so natural to her.

Airra headed over to the entrance of the mine and looked up the ramp leading out. There were beams of wood placed down the tunnel like a spine, used to sturdy the place. Outside, she saw only a black void. No sky at all, just streaks of a mist-like dark haze swirling around outside.

Airra looked back to Yalfari, who seemed too nervous to move. "My-oh-my, I would've thought her head would be emptier, but there seems to be a surprising amount of detail here. Quite imaginative." Airra laughed.

"It isn't that. Mara'Sane's brain has regressed back in time and locked her consciousness into this memory," Yalfari said, with a visible breath of air.

It must have felt cold for him. But being her, cold would feel just right.

"Dro'Zer mentioned a Final War his species went through. I'm sure I'm correct in saying that this must be from that time period," Airra informed.

"Maybe so, but that isn't why we are here. The day Dro'Zer died, I've felt something dark in Mara'Sane spread. He was her intellectual bar'won. They shared thoughts, they shared feelings. Meaning, she would've felt Dro'Zer's pain as he burnt to death. One cannot imagine what that would do to someone. And for it, Mara'Sane inner mind seems to be morphing into something else."

"Well, let's go see for ourselves." Airra grinned an overly curious grin. And they began to walk. For a second, Airra began to wonder if she made the right decision letting Dro'Zer stay behind on that doomed planet Idor. It was never her intention for him to die. In a way, it was partially her fault he suffered such a horrific death. Burning alive; she wondered what that would feel like.

The tunnels they walked looked like veins with its many winding routes, blackened by the abuse of explosives and tunneling. Many paths went on and on into the swelling clouds of darkness, without an end in sight - steel tracks abandoned to rust. Mine carts and crates rotted away in the damp tunnels, while old machines withered away.

Chapter 10

Torches lit the way down the widest of the tunnels. As Airra and Yalfari ventured further into the abandoned mine, the sounds of war in the near distance grew quieter, and the sound of crying came closer. That was the sound they followed until they came around a bend. Just before the corner, from the ground to the rock ceiling, loomed an archway. Airra ran her hand over the decaying wood, it had all the softness of driftwood, with none of the charm.

"Careful, Airra. I feel a lot of pain and despair in that room," Yalfari warned.

"Sounds like my kind of place." Airra felt her body tingle with excitement and intrigue, and she shivered.

Airra led the way. They entered through the archway and followed a narrow path that led up to two rocks. Airra went behind one, and Yalfari stood behind the other. She was ready to take a look at the scene.

The barely decomposing, fresh remains of a half-dozen korkyran adults decorated the room with their gore. There was a fire in the corner, with a korkyran arm over the blaze. Sitting on a broken down mine cart, in the darkest part of the room, was a small korkyran child; her hands were over her eyes as she wept. Airra hadn't seen Mara'Sane much, but the resemblance was undeniable. This child was definitely her, but obviously from the past. No other korkyra bears a black pelt like Mara'Sane.

Airra and Yalfari stayed put behind their rocks, studying the scene. To many, a sight such as these would send them away in fear. Airra was not one of those. She was accustomed to gore. She was practically born into it.

"I don't get it. There has to be more than just a sobbing child." Airra whispered.

Yalfari gestured further behind the sobbing child to a dark shadow extending against the rock of mine's walls. "Her shadow doesn't seem to be crying." Yalfari shivered. Airra studied it with sharp intrigue, not afraid.

Almost on cue, the shadow began to creep towards Mara'Sane. As it got closer, it formed into a mirror image of her, like a twin. Then it began to hum a slow and grim melody. Its head bobbed from side to side to the tune. When it reached her, the shadow put her hand on

Mara'Sane's crying shoulder. Airra sprouted a grin as her interest soared.

Then the scene changed! It was the same setting, only the time seemed to shift backward to a previous event. Those korkyran corpses were now alive, walking about, worrying over something with distorted mumbling amongst themselves. The korkyran adults bickered with each other, guns and weapons over their back, and some clutching their stomachs. Mara'Sane was still on the cart, no tear lines down her cheeks, just her playing and giggling.

Soon, one of the adults went over to her. Mara'Sane was in conversation, laughing in-between words.

"Who are you talking to?" the adult asked Mara'Sane. The room went to silence as the two began to talk.

"Dar'Ra, silly." She giggled.

"Dar'Ra?"

Mara'Sane pointed across from her and laughed. No visible person was there.

"Oh, right. Your imaginary friend, Dar'Ra," the adult muttered softly, looking to the floor. She put her hand over her stomach, holding back its groans and grumbles. The other adults were all staring at the two, with eyes sharp like stalking predators. "You are but a child. How are you not hungry, Mara'Sane?"

Her face was the definition of childlike ignorance and joy. "Dar'Ra helps me find food some nights, silly."

"Food? We are in a wasteland - a warzone. What food exists to find?"

She stopped playing and looked up to her clan mate. "How weird. I don't remember." She tilted her head in confusion.

The adult was furious, as was the group watching. "I was hoping it wouldn't come to this, Mara'Sane. I was betting on you. But it turns out you are just the weak link that everyone else says you are. They are right. There is only one source of food left." The adult's eyes were like rabid dogs as she came nearer to Mara'Sane. The group stepped closer and closer!

"Let me in," a faint voice whispered.

Chapter 10

Time distorted again, and the scene was back to how it started. Mara'Sane was back to crying on the cart, with the shadow-thing touching her shoulder.

Mara'Sane looked up to the shadow image of herself, eyes reddened and wet. Airra had a sudden idea what this imaginary friend might be. She remembered Dro'Zer once said Mara'Sane had dissociative identity disorder, which meant she essentially has more than one personality living in her body.

Was Dar'Ra one such personality? Airra wondered.

Mara'Sane stared at the shadow and sobbed. "They're all dead. I woke up, and everyone's dead. They were my clan."

The shadow twitched its neck. "They thought you were the weak link. They *thought.*"

"What do mean, Dar'Ra?"

Dar'Ra grinned but ignored the question. "I cannot wait to show you what I've learned."

"Learned? I-I don't understand what's happening," Mara'Sane sobbed.

"I was you, and you were me. In the beginning, we were the same."

"No. You're Dar'Ra, and I'm Mara'Sane. And we are friends. An-and you are all I have left." Mara'Sane sniffled.

Dar'Ra twitched. "Yes. We are all we have left. Just us. You and me, strength and weakness side by side. Now, no one can truly hurt us. And I'll always guide the way, and all you have to do is... *let me in.*"

"B-but what about my clan?"

"You don't remember?"

"I-I fell asleep. And-and now they-- If I didn't fall asle--"

Dar'Ra put her finger to Mara'Sane's mouth. "Ssshh...sssshhhh. Quiet down." Dar'Ra stepped around until she was in front of her. She took a knee and looked up at Mara'Sane. "They were hungry and psychotic. But they weren't the psychopath. I was."

"Huh? I-I... I don't know that word."

"But it's okay. It's okay to express yourself in any way you see fit." Dar'Ra's head moved from right to left over and over. "Art is art. It's perfectly okay to express yourself in any way you want. Whether it's humming, drawing, or... ripping ligaments away from bones."

Mara'Sane's eyes enlarged in shock.

"No, no. Sorry." Dar'Ra ground her teeth with each twitch of her neck and wrists. Each movement made by the shadow was quick and sinister, not like any creature Airra has seen. She loved it, intrigued by the sight and mannerisms of this thing.

"Dar'Ra, are you okay? You're scaring me."

"I've got a secret, Mara'Sane." Dar'Ra grinned.

"What secret?"

"There is a lot of darkness inside of us. But I learned how to control it, harness it. The darkness, I let it in." Dar'Ra shook and twitched violently.

"What darkness?"

"Oh, don't you worry about that. I let it in for the both of us. For us. I can be anything you need me to be."

"You're a sicko."

Dar'Ra clenched her fist, and her voice went sinister. "I'm *not* a sicko. You know that."

Mara'Sane was horrified.

Dar'Ra continued. "You and I know what it's like to be different. It's only been us, me and you, forever."

"But you're scaring me."

"The fun never has to end. We're always together."

"I-I don't think... I don't think we can be friends." Mara'Sane sobbed. "I'm afraid."

Dar'Ra hugged Mara'Sane. "People worship what they fear. Fear is power. *We* are power. We are the same. You never need to fear me. Only others will fear us, because we are fear." Dar'Ra voice distorted into darkness. "Let... me... *in.*"

Almost in an instant, both Mara'Sane and the darkness morphed. Mara'Sane was no longer a child; she was her current age. And the darkness stared back at her like a twisted, broken mirror. Though it resembled Mara'Sane almost completely, its eyes were black, with dark smoke foaming out of it. The same dark stuff leaked from her nose and ears.

"I'm really glad we're friends. And I hope our friendship never ever ends," Dar'Ra hummed. Mara'Sane didn't move. Dar'Ra continued.

"You said those words to me here in this mine, all those years ago. When you needed me, I was there. I *was* there. And you *needed* me. I killed them and saved you. You survived because of me." Mara'Sane looked up into the all-consuming eyes of the darkness, her own eyes were still reddened. She stared, and Dar'Ra twitched her neck. Dar'Ra added, "I knew we'd see each other again. I saw it. I *saw* this coming. Did you miss me?"

"They killed Dro'Zer," Mara'Sane mumbled in grief. "I want revenge. I want them all to suffer," she growled, and her body shook with anger and hate.

Dar'Ra smiled. *"Let me in."*

Mara'Sane grabbed her hand. "Happily." And their bodies joined together, filling the room with hate and pain. Airra loved the feeling of it. Airra looked down to see Yalfari trembling.

"We have to leave," his eyes begged her. "I'm ending this connection now." As he was about to pull them out, his eyes nearly jumped out of their sockets as he looked over Airra's shoulder.

Airra spun around to see those evil, black eyes of Mara'Sane. "You let him die!" She grabbed Airra by the neck and smashed her against the mine wall. "You let Dro'Zer die!"

Airra laughed hysterically, enjoying the moment. Even with all of the strength of a korkyra, Mara'Sane's grip was not enough to choke Airra through her bark skin. "You can't kill me. Just like I can't kill you. The fight would last an eternity."

Mara'Sane growled and let her go. "Who killed him?"

Airra smiled. "Yalfari told me his name is Brad Swift--"

"Leave me out of this," Yalfari cried from the background.

Airra continued. "He is some insignificant, ruddy human among the squad of the James Stone who wears a marked helmet. I'll send you everything I've got, because I know you'll do right by that information."

Mara'Sane's eyes never left Airra's. "First, I'll tear him apart, arms first, and stuff them down his throat. Then I'll find a way to kill you and use your bark-skinned body as a toothpick." Her carnivorous teeth were bared, and her voice dipped into darkness. "Now get out of my head!"

In that instant, Airra and Yalfari were snapped back to reality. Airra's eyes reopened to see the surroundings of Yalfari's quarters. She was back home.

"What just happened?" Airra shook her head out of the daze.

Yalfari said, "I've lost my link with her mind completely."

"Can you reconnect?"

"I can't. She is now one of a few that I can't link my mind to."

"Who cares anyway? She'll go do her thing and leave us alone to do ours. As far as I'm concerned, that couldn't have gone better."

"But Airra--" Yalfari began to protest.

"Enough with all of this. When you urgently asked for me, I expected that you had the final key's location. So do you have it?"

"I umm...the thing is... this last one has been tricky--"

"I did not come for bloody excuses. I mean, frak, all I need is a damn planet!"

He was speechless.

"You have till the end of this month. For your sake, figure this shivf out!" Airra stood up and left Yalfari to his chair, without saying any more words. She'd have to inform her stepbrother that Yalfari couldn't join him after all.

Even though she didn't have a location, she had an itch that needed to be scratched. While she waited for that old bag, she decided to spend time doing her favorite pastime. It was time to go kill things, to feel pain through their dying eyes. That was the drug she craved in this moment.

Chapter 11: Aces of the ARW III - Drayvan's Pride
January 16, 2112

Night-Shade

By complete accident, Night-Shade found herself floating in the white nothingness of someone else's dream. It wasn't her fault. Along with being able to walk outside her body, she could walk among other's dreams. But it was all new to her, and she had little control or understanding of how to use her dreamwalking power. Last time she dreamwalked, Night-Shade touched the forehead of someone sleeping while already out of her body. It only works when that person is sleeping, and even then, it fails sometimes. In fact, she had more success dreamwalking when done by accident. Just as some people sleepwalk, she finds herself accidentally dreamwalking into another person's dream without having any intention of doing so. She always was a klutz.

It had only been a few days since the aces of Project Aurum were sent on mission. The Broker came through with his promise. After Day-Bringer made a deal to exchange someone for information, The Broker gave Kalvin and Day-Bringer a series of coordinates to use in the hunt for this unforeseen, unknown threat to the ARW. Now on a mission, they traveled on a star cruiser, and this was the first night aboard.

A shallow female voice whispered into the wind.

Night-Shade turned her heard in the direction of the voice, but there was nothing. Every direction was white space in which she floated. She couldn't make out any words as the voice whispered once more. A rush of happiness flooded her body and mixed in with her intrigue. It wasn't her feelings that she felt, however. It came from whomever was actually the one dreaming. Sharing dreams with someone else came with this side effect, feeling what they felt.

Night-Shade always found wonder in the experience. It happened so little, but she loved being someone else from time to time. Walking in their shoes, seeing through their eyes, experiencing what they experience; all of it was thrilling. It's the feeling she has inside of her in the dreams she shares, the people who pay a visit in those dreams, the ventures she takes, the places she goes, the things she tastes; even if they're not real, she still feels every bit of it. Like quenching a thirst she never knew she had.

A dream, so magical, so unbelievable, so perfect.

"Drayvan," the same shallow female voice from before whispered into the wind.

On the words of the wind, she now knew whose dream she was in. It had to be Drayvan Pryde's dream. It could be no other.

"Drayvan Pryde. That's a good name, my cohinla." This time, the voice in the distance was male.

Then Night-Shade could see. But not much was there. Two silhouettes of black shapes held a baby maelkii in their arms together. The baby, it shared a similar skin tonality to Drayvan and was the only thing visible with any makeable details. Everything else, setting especially, was blurred and not in focus. Night-Shade could make out what seemed to be a nursery of some kind, but it was not clear. It was like trying to look through a smoke-filled room.

"She will be the pride of our house," the same male voice boomed.

But there was a silhouette, one farther away from the rest, that began to grow into shape. And even covered in black, Night-Shade was able to make out the cruel sting of jealousy; tight lips, sour gaze, crossed arms. Its eyes were focused on just one thing - Drayvan.

This was no fictional creation. No, Night-Shade was certain this dream was replaying real memories from Drayvan's past.

The dream shifted. The setting swirled like a tornado around her and started to sprout into somewhere new. When her vision had time to adjust to the rapid change, she noticed an open field of obsidian rock. Outside in the rather barren area, there was a maelkii, and it was beating down on another, younger maelkii. Repeatedly, the older male child hit the female with a rock until she was on her knees, looking into the ground. Bruised and blood-stained, Night-Shade could feel her own empathy radiate for the poor girl. It was overtaken as a sudden pulse of anger and pain surged in her body. But it was not her emotions. She could feel what Drayvan was feeling during the dream, and she understood the girl getting beat on was Drayvan. The very same rage grew and grew as Night-Shade watched a younger Drayvan get beat to the ground.

"How come Mom and Dad only dote over you? What makes you so damn special, you cocky brat?!" The male hit Drayvan again with the rock.

"Stop!" Drayvan yelled, and the rock hit her back once more. "I said stop hitting me!" Drayvan grabbed the arm of the male maelkii and squeezed. He let go of the rock and fell to his knee in pain. Drayvan did not relent, and Night-Shade watched as she snapped his arm!

The moment switched away just as it happened, leaving Night-Shade relieved she didn't have to see it all through. The swilling dark clouds of the dream opened away to Drayvan standing over ten hurt maelkii warriors. Each hunched, and in pain in the mud as rain poured over their shamed faces. Drayvan did not share that look, she had a glow of pride over her work. And Night-Shade felt that feeling through Drayvan. So much of it, and so strong was the fire fueled by Drayvan's pride. How can someone be so sure of themselves, so unrelenting in their belief in their abilities?

The crowd of maelkii gave Drayvan a warrior's shout of honor. Their cheers roared. Their stomping feet shook the ground, the surfaced ice pillars, and the structures built around and into them. The village was at the base of a volcano, with a small stream of molten rock pouring down a side. Among the setting, someone came forth; another maelkii, older and wearing decorated armor. "I'm proud of you, Drayvan. In our history, you will be the youngest ever to take charge of our house."

Drayvan bowed. "I accept, Father."

The members of the crowd cheered once more. But it was all interrupted as a starship came zooming above. Night-Shade recognized the Order of Aegis symbol over the hull.

Pieces of the scene then started to fall away into detail-less empty space until the setting was gone completely. Night-Shade was soon taken elsewhere. Another place put itself together like a magic puzzle. Inside a hut of some kind, Night-Shade watched as Kalvin Keefe entered. He was wearing a breathing mask due to the harsh air of Maelkiin and escorted by some maelkii warriors. Drayvan waited for him, with her father at her side.

Kalvin stopped in front of Drayvan. "My name is Kalvin Keefe, director of the Order of Aegis. Am I in the presence of the one called Drayvan Pryde?"

Drayvan stood tall. "Do not speak to me as if we're friends. And I ask that you do not waste my time either, for my time is valuable because it belongs to me."

Kalvin's eyebrow raised to her words. And he didn't hesitate to jump to the point. "I hear you are quite powerful. Join me and fight for the ARW, and you shall bring more honor to your house than any maelkii before you. That is my proposition to you."

Drayvan looked to her father for advice. He nodded. "You'll be a shimmering ray of hope to your allies... to those lucky enough to fight alongside you."

Those words of encouragement echoed over and over, becoming quieter each time. They were a trigger that sparked the dream to change once more. Everything began to fade away to nothing. No, not everything. Kalvin remained, and the image of him grew shadowy, even as the scene drowned out and Night-Shade was left with almost nothing again. Until it all formed back again, every detail formed around the image of Kalvin. And Night-Shade recognized the new setting as one of the training facilities of Project Ace; a wide open rectangular room with a viewing glass on one side and a few double doors throughout.

Drayvan stood by Kalvin. "The Bruising Brothers asked me for a challenge. I say you give it to them," Kalvin said and began to walk to a double door behind them. "I want to see for myself just how strong you are."

Drayvan didn't look away and waited until both Geariic and Alabon came through the doors at the other end. Drayvan walked forward, unarmed and without armor, until she was just a meter from the Bruising Brothers. Both the twin brothers marched in confidence, both with their signature weapons, and both baring their metallic skin courtesy of their ace ability.

There was a look of disgust in the eye of Geariic, and he spat at his side. "Kalvin didn't mention we'd be fighting another honor-high maelkii of some snobby house," he growled.

Chapter 11

Drayvan moved forward until she was eye-to-eye with Geariic. "Do not mistake me for a lesser house. You stand before Drayvan Pryde of the glorious Escanorinn House. Honor has never held a higher meaning than when uttered in the same sentence as the name of my house, for our honor is greater than any other because we embody it through our own prowess."

Geariic smirked. "I don't care what your pigshivf house believes in. You're all the same to me - hypocrites. What honor is there in deserting your own kin? Tell me, Drayvan! Tell me what honor came from leaving Alabon and myself on the streets to fend for ourselves?" Alabon nodded in agreement with his brother's words.

"Your hunger for my sympathy bores me, and your demeanor is that of a pouty child. A shame, really; you two are as unlucky as you are foolish, seeing as you've come before me, only to forfeit what's left of your pitiful reputation." Drayvan flexed her shoulders, and the tattoos on her back began to glow.

Alabon left loose a laugh. "Can you believe the mouth on this girl? Who is she to talk to us like that?"

Taken aback for a moment at Drayvan's unabashed words, Geariic questioned, "Wait a second. You're not a maelkii, are you? You're an ace, just like us."

"I *am* a maelkii - in blood and spirit. But--" Drayvan put one finger high in the air, "--I am also the one who stands at the pinnacle of all that live in this galaxy."

Geariic laughed at her. "Pretty bold of you to claim you're at the pinnacle of this galaxy. You are, without a doubt, the cockiest person I've ever met. Tell you what, let's put what you say to the test. I've got a game in mind."

Alabon clapped his hands. "Oh, boy! I love games!"

Geariic continued. "We each take turns hitting each other. Last one standing in this spot wins. What do you say? I'll even give you the first punch."

"I accept your terms." At that moment, Drayvan brought her fist straight down into the jaw of Geariic, with lightning speed. Night-Shade almost missed it, and she almost missed the ink of Drayvan's tattoos run back up her arm and back to its original location. Geariic was sent right out of his laughter and to his knees.

"Brother!" Alabon was shocked but did not leave his place.

"What's the matter? Can't find your shattered ego down there on the ground?" Drayvan taunted. Her eyes met Alabon, as if to gloat. And he stared back, unable to shake away the shock on his face.

One strike! That's all it took to send Geariic down to the ground! Night-Shade was beside herself in amazement.

"Don't pat yourself on the back just yet. My brother is far from done. I promise you it is not over," Alabon said.

Geariic growled, rubbing at his jaw. After collecting himself, he stood back up to face Drayvan. The sourness of his mood shifted, and he became spirited. "You're strong, I'll give you that. However, Alabon and I rank above all other aces in the ARW, so it'll take a lot more than that to beat me."

"I'm aware of that, of course. And I'm grateful, otherwise this game wouldn't be as exciting for me."

"You make it sound as if you intentionally held back," Alabon added. "You really are arrogant. But you'll soon be put in your place."

Geariic grabbed his warhammer from his back. "Let's assume for a moment that what you're saying is true. I'll still make you regret ever playing this game with us. Your mistake was not finishing me off with that first blow." Geariic lifted his warhammer over his head, and the back of the hammer's head gave way to an engine. Suddenly, fire erupted from the back of the warhammer, but Geariic held it at bay over his head. All that force was building up for one massive attack. "This next attack is quite impractical in an actual fight. Even for someone of my strength, this amount of energy is tough to hold at bay, making it too hard to land on a moving target. But you have to stand still and take my strongest attack, or you lose."

Drayvan stood still and did not flinch as dust and wind kicked up around them; all due to Geariic's warhammer. Alabon energized his two war-glaives with electricity, and both prepared to strike Drayvan from both sides.

They made the move! Sparks flew, the warhammer exploded, dust and smoke blasted all around the room - all making it impossible to see what had happened. Night-Shade waited as the dust cleared, and when she saw the scene, she did not believe her eyes.

"You're kidding, right? That was the absolute best the both of you could do?" Drayvan sighed. "And here I had my hopes up." She had both arms up, guarding against both strikes. Standing there with no visible damage at all in spite of the fact that both Geariic's and Alabon's weapons had made contact. Her tattoos had moved from their original position and covered her arms and seemed to act as some kind of protection for the areas that Drayvan was struck.

Geariic and Alabon's eyes were wide. "Impossible! Y-you stopped... you stopped both our attacks! How?" Geariic stumbled on his words.

"Brother. We need to flee this fight!" Alabon pleaded, dropping his war-glaives.

"Never! I will not lose to this arrogant fraker!" Geariic pulled back his warhammer and smashed the head into the ground. He pointed to Drayvan. "Come on! Let's keep this up till the end."

"If that's your wish. I believe it's my turn, right?" Drayvan cracked her knuckles and looked directly at Geariic. Her eyes were dark and intimidating. Night-Shade found herself trembling just being close to her presence. Drayvan then readied herself for another go and made it clear she intended to hit Geariic. Only this time, she didn't look like she was going to hold anything back.

Geariic let it all get to him, and he bolted out the door, bashing it open as he left. He was gone without a second thought. Drayvan then looked to Alabon, who was stuck staring at the dust kicked up from his fleeing brother. Drayvan sighed. "What a shame. I was prepared to show him a glimpse of my true strength. Though I can't really blame the guy for running away, since he was up against me."

"Brother." Alabon's voice was soft and trembling.

She continued. "Now, then. This game has gone and got me in a good mood. As a special favor, Alabon, I will allow you to back out now. Make your decision while I'm still feeling charitable."

Alabon left without saying a word, dragging his feet away in defeat and shame. Drayvan and Night-Shade watched him go. All the while, Night-Shade could feel her body getting hotter under the burring sun that was Drayvan's immense pride.

As the time went on, the setting began to slowly decay until she was left in that same white empty space as when it all started. Then something else began to bloom. Just like the scene, the pride she had in her was gone.

After some time, the distinct image of Alabon walking away in shame came into view. He kept walking, endlessly, in the white space, and Night-Shade was forced to float behind him. Never getting closer or further. Endlessly watching him drag his feet in shame. He was not alone. Night-Shade shared that same shame; rather, the feeling came over her like a dark cloud. That moment, she realized it was not her who felt it. It was Drayvan's emotions that she was experiencing.

There was a voice in the air. "You'll be a shimmering ray of hope to your allies." It was Drayvan's father's words.

As Drayvan watched Alabon, she was contrite and full of guilt. Drayvan had let her own pride get the best of her. Instead of being a beacon of hope for her ally, she was an instrument of intimidation and only forced him away. That was the origin of the shame and regret.

Chapter 12: Duty or her Sister
December 11, 2111

Catharine Darcrose

The wood of the holy cross, hung high at the back of the congregation room, was the color of a maraschino cherry. In front of Captain Catharine Darcrose, captain of the 707 Wolf-Pack, was beautiful, old grit and stained glass to decorate the congregation room. Pine-wood benches, padded with cherry-red cushions, lined the room in rows. A room that had an atmosphere to it and was unique in aesthetic compared to most other places on the Whispering Dragon. Some ARW ships had more prestige woven into their respective monasteries, some not so much. It didn't matter to Cathy. A church is a church to her, a place where she can worship in peace. She always felt connected to something higher than herself when in religious houses. The comfort of prayer had helped her through much of her hardships growing up. And though it may not seem like it to most, Cathy had a lot to pray over.

Today was strange. Gone for months on two separate back-to-back missions, Cathy expected to return and for everything to be the same. It wasn't. She didn't quite feel at home here. She had only been back for a few hours, and all she got was uncomfortable stares gazing her way while she marched for the ship's church. Almost like they didn't want to approach her or congratulate her on another successful mission.

In prayer, Cathy didn't notice a solider approaching to her. She lifted her head as the soldier placed his hand on the bench next to her and cleared his throat. "Sorry to disturb you, Captain Darcrose," he paused, "the commander would like a word with you."

"What does she want?"

"Wouldn't say. I do know that it is urgent." The soldier gestured to the chapel doors and began to lead the way.

"No need for that. Despite the long time away, I remember the way." Cathy referred to the unrelated missions her unit only returned from hours prior. In fact, she hadn't even taken off her veridium armor before entering the church; her signature Darcrose family armor, shaded with black and red roses.

"As you wish." The soldier nodded and went off in his own direction.

After a long walk and a few elevators, Cathy found herself inside the debriefing room. On one wall was a hard-glass window peering out to the stars, bright and glowing. In a corner of the room was a table with coffee on one end, an energy drink created by the qwayk called Pighmix on the other end, and cups in-between.

Cathy took a seat at the long table next to Commander Dancing-Sky, who sat at the head. "I've called you here for a debriefing of your last mission," said Dancing-Sky.

"Which one? First, we were sent to aid some valistare rebels. Then, before we had even wrapped up that mission and returned, you sent us on another mission regarding a mercenary."

"The latter."

"I wrote a report."

"I'd rather hear from you," Dancing-Sky responded.

Cathy studied the face of Dancing-Sky for a moment. A rather plain face for a Dor'o, little wrinkles, no discolorations. Unlike many in her species, her face really didn't have too much character to it. "Alright. As you know, we have been tracking down recent partners of the renowned mercenary, Erryn Wolph."

"Were you able to finally put a past to her name?"

"I did." Catharine pulled up bits of information over a hologram emitted from her cyberwatch. "Like the rumors suggested, she is a descendant of King Kaylob, the fabled king of the ancient Tolkran Kingdom. Her father, King Garrol, was murdered by Erryn, and she fled. A bounty was put on her head; one her uncle Bearon failed to complete. She's a survivor. That much is for sure. I've done my duty by this mission and have already began to upload the facts into the ARW's database."

"I'm glad you have, and it brings me right into your next mission."

"Can I expect more intel with my intel this time around?" Cathy asked, with a mix of dry humor.

Dancing-Sky shook her head. "I regret to say that it is even less this time around."

"A bit unfortunate, but I trust command."

"You're a dependable soldier, Cathy. And the lack of intel... well, it is a result of who you are tracking."

This made no sense. She was unaware that she was tracking anyone. "And who am I tracking?"

"A group - or rather a cult, really - called the Brotherhood of Relics. It's why you were sent to verify rumors about Erryn Wolph and the house she came from... all to build up to this."

"The Brotherhood of Relics? I've heard of mercenaries supposedly dressing as brotherhood knights to strike fear in their targets. But is that the extent of it? I've heard there is no such thing as the Brotherhood of Relics, that it is all a myth."

Dancing-Sky swiped over files from her cyberwatch to Cathy's. "A few weeks ago, you may've been correct. But we've come across eye witness testimony of their existence. Captain Wild-Heart has returned from a recent mission--"

Cathy smiled, interrupting on accident. "My sister's team! How is she?"

Dancing-Sky's expression shifted. "Oh, uh... I'm not sure I'm the best person to tell you--"

"No! She isn't... d-dead, is she?"

"No, no. She's MIA."

"MIA! How?"

"She was unable to make it back on Captain Wild-Heart's rescue ship. Instead, she escaped with Captain James Stone on the last ship out of Idor. Due to unidentified reasons, his ship seemed to have malfunctioned and wormholed to some location that we couldn't track."

"So she may be alive?"

"We believe so."

"Rescue operations?"

Dancing-Sky cringed. "Lying to the unit under my commander never was really my style, so let me give you it straight. All teams have been instructed to keep an eye out for any tips or clues as to Captain Stone's location - just like all MIA soldiers - but that is all. There're no actual search teams looking for them."

"Forgive me if I'm stepping out of line, but that--" Cathy stood up and pointed out the window to the stars, "--is my little sister out there.

I've already lost my dad and brother, I don't need to lose her, too! And does my mom even know yet?"

"She's a chief admiral, of course she knows. And she also knows that our military resources are needed elsewhere. Your best option is to just trust that Captain Stone will get her and his team home."

Cathy was unhappy, but she could see the logic behind what Dancing-Sky was saying. The ARW is losing the Wersillian War and needs all the manpower focused on fighting the threat. "James Stone better return my sister, or he'll regret it."

"I'm truly sorry, Captain Darcrose, but it is time to return to the mission briefing."

"Sure... proceed." Cathy tried her best to keep her head on straight. Duty has always come first.

"Captain Wild-Heart has confirmed that on their last mission at Idor, Captain Stone and Brad Swift witnessed a member of the brotherhood. She says that the brotherhood even aided them in escaping the planet by sending out rescue plans to my ship."

"Alright, they exist. But if the rumors are correct, they would be the single most difficult group to locate in the entire galaxy."

"Correct, but this is where Erryn Wolph comes in. According to the legends, her ancestor, King Kaylob was king over the ancestors that first started the Brotherhood of Relics."

"So you're thinking that the Wolph family may know where the Brotherhood of Relics are?"

"We are hoping?"

"We?"

Dancing-Sky shrugged. "This mission comes direct from the top. Chief Admiral Day-Bringer personally requested it after a meeting with the other chief admirals."

"What does she expect me to do if I find them?"

"Deliver this message." Day-Bringer gave her a data chip to upload her cyberwatch.

"So is that all?"

"It is."

Cathy had a wry laugh. "You weren't lying when you said there wasn't much intel."

Chapter 12

"I don't like to lie."

"Yeah, you've said. So when would you like my unit to start?"

"At midnight tonight, a transport will be waiting for your team. Day-Bringer arranged for you and your team's clearance into the Tolkran Kingdom. I'll send over the details, and I recommend that you start with the king there. See what he knows."

"It's true what they say about the wolf-pack units - we are always on a mission," Cathy said, more to herself than to Dancing-Sky.

"Good luck, and Godspeed." Dancing-Sky led Cathy to the door.

Cathy halted and pressed her palm to the frame of the doorway. "I've never asked anything of you before. Now, I intend to break that precedent. If I complete this mission successfully for you and the chief admirals, will you allow me a leave of absence to search for my sister?"

"If you do this, you will've earned it."

Cathy nodded her head with appreciation. And with that, her meeting was over.

Chapter 13: Space Guard
December 15, 2111

Catharine Darcrose

Alone, Cathy Darcrose sat in the cockpit of the dropship she was piloting. Traditionally, a captain of a ground-based unit such as hers doesn't fly starships; however, wolf-pack units are something of an aberration in the force. Given the high variation their missions often present, they are forced to be a jack-of-all-trades. For this reason, Cathy and a few others on her crew were trained on the basics of piloting dropships. That, naturally, was one small reason her unit's the most decorated of all the wolf-packs. Her individual skill and the loyalty of each soldier under her command has given her a sense of pride. Her crew consisted of Kenny Morison, first lieutenant and medic; Vayhara Lomia'dicia, second lieutenant and engineer; Edward McCollister, weapons specialist; Tommlar Wloque, navigations specialist; and Skolla, warwolf.

The view as Cathy approached the home world of the omelics was stunning. Omulice was given a great gift not seen anywhere else in the known galaxy. Their oversized planet is surrounded by motionless asteroids netted together in thousands of energy lines bursting with pulses of energy every few seconds. Essentially, Omulice was surround by a web of defensive energy. Located throughout this defensive network were stations, and starships must have clearance to pass through. And all the above may seem implausible to achieve, and it would've been had the technology not already been installed ever so generously by the Devisors. Or so it is believed. The omelics just learned how to work the defensive network of their planet for themselves and have never seen a threat brave enough to attack their home planet in all its history. Lucky them.

Looking up at a mirror, Cathy adjusted it towards herself. She put her thumb to her lower jaw and gave her skin a small tug downward, checking her skin coloration. Her hair was dyed coal-black to match her sister Beverly Darcrose. Cathy and her younger sister had more resemblances than just hair; expressive eyes bright with color, cheekbones that sat high on their faces, curved lips, and hourglass figures. But Cathy lacked her sister's smile that sent people gleaming with happiness. Cathy's smile was more strained, and she sometimes looked like she was forcing it. What she lacked in that appeal, she made up with a body that was more toned than her sister. Maybe even more so than her younger brother, Alexander. Then again, that enthusiastic geek was no crowing jewel of physique.

At the memory of her brother, she had to hold back a tear.

In solitude, Cathy pulled a bowl filled with freshly cut watermelons closer to her. It was her favorite snack food, and she started to munch on some as she stared into the vastness of deep space.

The lieutenant of the 707 Wolf-Pack, Kenny Morison, entered the pilot's den. "Hey, look. We're almost there." He pointed out the window.

"Good observation," Cathy said, with her brand of dry humor.

He tapped the bowl of cut watermelons. "See you still got a taste for strange snacks."

"It's the *best* snack. You can never eat too much of it, low calories, mostly water, and most importantly... watermelon is damn good."

Kenny gave her a few judging laughs through his nose. Even so, he was curious enough to pick up a piece and take a bite. "Not for me." He tossed the rest of his piece in a trash bin, and Cathy looked at the travesty with mournful eyes.

"Go! Get! I don't want a watermelon waster in my cockpit. Leave me in peace." Cathy shooed him off with half a laugh.

Kenny held up his hands and left her alone.

Taking a bite from another slice, Cathy piloted the starship into the space station where she was supposed to visit. She was no professional at this, but she had enough skill to get the job done.

The ship passed through a massive atmospheric door that covered the entire side of the hangar. Ships and other material could pass, but the air and pressure were held at bay.

The starship landed with a short skid, and Cathy cringed a bit at the landing. Even so, it was time to meet the Space Guard, the watchers of all that enter and leave Omulice.

"Everyone wait here. I'll go out alone," Cathy commanded her crew as she departed.

Outside the ship, there were more than a dozen omelics, most of whom were performing chores in the hangar and tidying up ships. Not to her surprise, she didn't see a single female. From the books she read about omelics, it was in their culture to ostracize their women. Such a shame, too, for lack for a better word.

There was a welcome party for her, three omelic men with one at the head.

"Welcome to Omulice, human. Do you have an authorization chip?" the one in the center asked.

Cathy pulled it from a pocket and handed it to the man. He inspected it and then scanned it with his cyberwatch. "So that's who you are... one Catharine Darcrose. I was told to expect you from the king of the Tolkran Kingdom himself." The man pushed a button on his helmet, and it retracted into his armor, revealing his face; sharp-featured and gaunt as a mountain crag, but there was a glimmer of affability in his blue-gray eyes. "Nice to meet you. I'm Wouren Lightbourne, Station Commander of this particular outpost. Come. Follow me while these two inspect the ship."

"Will it be long?" she asked him.

"I assure you it won't."

Wouren Lightbourne motioned Cathy towards the other end of the hangar, and they began walking. As they walked, she noticed she was getting some rather obnoxious, even objectifying signals and stares from some of the crew. Such brazen, crude gestures was nothing anyone should be used to.

With a quieter tone, Cathy said, "I can't tell, but it seems some of your crew have it out for me."

"Don't mind them. The Space Guard consists of men from various kingdoms, and some of them come from places where older ideals reign supreme. And... and not many of them have ever seen a human before."

"Older ideals?"

"Many kingdoms treat their women less than should be." Wouren nodded to one omelic cleaning a ship part as they passed. "He came from the Surben Kingdom... has three wives, all of whom probably wish they were born elsewhere."

"So the rumors are true. Omelic women are treated as objects."

"Sadly in many kingdoms, that is the truth."

"You're different. I can tell."

Wouren smiled. "As it happens, I'm from the place you're headed, the Tolkran Kingdom. I don't want to ruin the surprise, but my home kingdom has come a long way."

"I'm glad to hear that, or else this would be a long mission." Cathy's small joke fell flat. She cleared her throat. "How did you end up here anyway?"

"The Space Guard consists mostly of volunteers taking tours of duty. No one's life bound here; rather, it's seen as service to our planet."

"Is that *your* reason for being here?"

"Well, my house has always held a tradition that at least one person per generation take up duty and guard our planet. Although--"

"Although what?"

"Omulice is a big, beautiful world, and most of the omelics that inhabit the world live and die in the same kingdom they were born to without venturing out to explore all that the galaxy has to offer. I don't want to be most."

Catharine understood that sense of wonder and excitement. Once, she used to be the same way. Then duty took over.

They arrived at the edge of the other side of the hangar. Through the atmospheric field, she was able to see the legendary world of Omulice.

"It's beautiful," Cathy marveled.

"I've heard it called Earth's Big Brother. And really it is. The surface is thrice as big. The mountains are bigger, the oceans, the land, trees, and... and the creatures of course. There've been creatures on our world that would dwarf your dinosaurs." Wouren chuckled.

"Should I be worried? I've read that Omulice has some of the deadliest wildlife of any known planet."

"Absolutely, you should be. But it is other kingdoms that you should watch out for most of all. People are always more dangerous. Make sure you stay over the clouds and head straight for the Tolkran Kingdom."

"I will." Cathy nodded.

Wouren stuck out his hand. "It was a pleasure to meet you. I wish you safety on your journey."

Cathy shook his hand. "I thank you for your advice."

Wouren motioned her back to her starship, and they walked together in silence. After listening to what Wouren said, Cathy had a wrongful gut feeling, and her inner conscious urged her to stay away. This planet may be more dangerous than any other she had visited. However, that was no excuse to stop. The mission comes before all.

Is finding the Brotherhood of Relics going to be worth all the trouble? Cathy wondered to herself. But who was she to question authority?

Chapter 14: A Dangerous World
December 16, 2111

Catharine Darcrose

Their starship was on fire, and falling fast! Red lights flashed in sync with an ear throbbing alarm. Even after heeding the advice of Wouren Lightbourne, disaster struck. A hovercraft with impressive assault capabilities stopped their starship over the clouds and didn't bother to hail Cathy. They did what omelics are stereotyped for; they shot first, without caring to ask any questions.

"Everyone strap in! Now!" Cathy shouted over her dropship's intercom.

She had no time to check on her crew. But she knew she wouldn't need to. They could handle themselves. She had a duty to land the ship the best she could and not kill everyone aboard. And that duty was closing in fast.

As the ship dipped below the clouds, Cathy had a few precious moments to take in her surroundings; a vast swampland and swampy forest surrounding a few steep mountains. There was an edge to the forest coming in fast, but there looked to be a large village with walls thickened towards the forest end. Innocent lives could be lost if she aimed at the village. Lucky for her, there was a large moor deep in swampland. That was her chance.

Cathy pulled up on the steering control with all her strength, clinching her jaw and holding the control with a vise grip. The ship angled itself toward the moor.

Shaking as if in a windstorm, the starship scraped against the tops of some trees before touching ground, burying itself in the dirt with a massive crash. It came to rest quickly, which of course was no help to Cathy, as the lock-in straps barely were able to brace her from the impact.

Dazed, she held her hand to her head, feeling as though her brain collided with her skull. She took a few moments to shake off the pain and slight confusion.

There was no time to waste. Cathy forced herself from her seat and pulled a lever to open the door. She soon found her way to her squad, with slightly swaying steps. She was relieved she saw her allies already up. Kenny was still by the closed dropship hatch. But he didn't stand still for long. His attention, followed by his movements, went another direction.

Cathy's eyes followed to the seat of Vayhara Lomia'dicia, who sat docile in her seat; no movement, no motion of her chest. As Cathy's eyes adjusted, she saw a river of blood flowing from her shoulder, at the point where a piece of the ship had impaled itself in her, and trailed down over her lap. Her head hung over the lock-in straps, and her arms rested in the pool of blood.

Kenny stared as Cathy went to her neck to check for a pulse. Nothing. She used her cyberwatch to confirm that Vayhara was dead.

The reality set in, and Cathy felt a pain in her chest; a pain that didn't so much come because of her dead ally, rather she felt sick for not feeling more grief than she did. That was Cathy's reality. Many of the captains she knew had such close bonds with their unit, bonds like brothers and sisters. Cathy was not one of those captains. Her unit was loyal to her as she was to them, but she always held an emotional distance from the people under her.

Still, Vayhara was the first person to die in her unit in over two years. That was where Cathy felt she failed Vayhara the most.

Cathy turned to Kenny and shook her head. "She's gone."

"We should bury her," said Edward McCollister, who was now up.

"Impossible. The metal in her shoulder made sure of that. And whoever shot us down may come looking. We'd best go."

Her unit understood the situation. Times like these demanded them to wait and grieve later. Tommlar Wloque already had the hatch open. The rest of the crew marched outside, with Cathy being the last.

There was no denying the heat. Cathy could feel the cloth under her armor, clinging to her chest. Thick, moist air covered the moor like a damp woolen blanket, and the nearby swampland had grown unruly with the breeze.

"Fraken omelic bastards just had to make it hard on us," Cathy cursed.

Chapter 14

"No wonder outsiders rarely visit this shivfhole," Edward added.

Tommlar, on a knee with both eyes looking through a landscape scanner, pointed toward the trees leading to the mountain they'd seen earlier. "Scanner indicates structures that way. Roughly a kilometer from here."

Cathy looked at the map of Omulice on her cyberwatch. It indicated they were in the deep north of the Tolkran Kingdom. And the structures would lead them south and towards where they needed to be - a stronghold known as Direclaw. That was where the king would be.

"Time to move out," Cathy commanded. She took the lead. Her squad positioned themselves as they followed the wide open heath until they reached the tree line of the marshes.

They entered, pushing in past the brush. This was no glade. The fallen trees and branches all pushed together, creating a wet web of moss, branches, and leaves. Ancient willow, hardwood, and cypress trees dominated the area, which was larger than on Earth and with branches darker in color. Vines interlaced through the branches and then hung to the ground. The vegetation had an aura to it, like a mystic life force surrounding them like a fog. There was a path to follow that went around infected trunks of decay, others full of moss. Unconcerned, a speckled frog, all brown skin and beige dots, blinked lazily as a swarm of gnats buzzed by. A large frog at that, likely three times the size of one on Earth. Overhead, some creature hooted.

Soon, the path led to swamp water that was thin like a tiny river; mists off the river had wreathed it in wisps of gray. They followed the bank towards the direction they needed to go.

Kenny was at the head with Cathy. "Captain, you are glowering more than usual, I must say."

"I don't glower," she responded. Her thoughts about her dead second lieutenant were hard to ignore and undeniably the culprit of her semi-sour mood.

"Not that it's a bad thing. Nobody glowers quite like you. Well, none that I've met anyway."

"You sure are a talker," Cathy remarked.

Kenny chuckled. "I met this girl I think you'd like. She's quite like you. Dutiful and loyal, yet stiff. Fair and just, but wooden and uncharismatic. Damn, now that I think about it, she's practically your twin."

Cathy ignored him.

"You know what? Maybe we should all visit one of the brothels when we arrive. Get us a whore each with the exception of Skolla. Actually, frak it, let's get him one, too. We could all use something to help us grieve," Kenny joked.

"Vayhara's death isn't something to joke over. And we're not here to bed harlots. Do well to remember that we're on mission."

"There she is, serious as ever." Kenny pointed at Cathy. "Finally got you to stop glowering."

"You should switch positions with Tommlar. Skolla would be a better conversationalist than me."

"Your call, Captain. But we both know you'll miss me." Kenny dropped back and out of Cathy's view.

He was right in a way. And she couldn't much blame him for joking. It was in his character, and also his way of getting through the loss of Vayhara. Kenny, along with everyone else, was loyal to her, and she was to them. They had been together as a unit for years, sewn as one team by the harsh trials of combat. She has never wanted anyone else on her unit, and never will.

After a couple hours of hiking, the path eventually led into a town, which was clearly long abandoned. The architecture looked at least a century old by modern omelic standards; buildings rotted away, streets started to give way to vegetation, and wreckage lay all over the town.

"Man, it is bizarre how similar omelics and humans are... even down to their architecture. Gable roofs, solid brick siding, concrete foundation, shingles-- If you went back to the mid-1900s on Earth, these buildings would fit right in," Tommlar said.

"The saying that omelics and humans derive from the same tree seems to hold true," Edward added.

"Only the omelics never left their medieval era," Cathy said.

"Their technology sure did, though," said Kenny.

In those streets, her unit seemed to be the only beating hearts, the only things of warm blood and flesh. The structures around were once homes to many, yet now it was a shadow of its former past. The light of the sun was high over the streets, and buildings caste low shadows over the ruble and debris, unaware that the civilians had vanished. Silence covered the place like a fog, no boots to walk the streets, save the wolf-pack.

They kept marching onward. "It's quiet." Tommlar swayed his weapon from door to door.

"I hate the quiet," Cathy heard Kenny say from behind her.

Banners hung with sigils to be read only by the dust-laden wind. A market was all set up like it was awaiting the stall holders arrival any moment, only now it was covered in webs. Ahead was a clock tower, forever stuck at a time long ago.

They then stopped at a sudden crash of wood and metal coming from the clock tower. Skolla halted, head and tail up. All weapons were raised.

Cathy signed towards the door. "Skolla, Tommlar. Clear the door."

Tommlar nodded and stepped with slow steps towards the wooden door. He stacked his body against the side of the door, Skolla was behind him as he pulled down the knob with caution. Suddenly, he flung open the door! No! It was kicked open!

Two knights, armored in silver metal, rushed out. Tommlar fired his laser pistol, the first shot of which hit the armor of the omelic knight. He seemed to take notice of the hit but still ignited a sword made of finely focused and rapidly spinning energy from a plate of armor just over his wrist. Tommlar's second laser shot was absorbed by the sword just as it came down and through his neck!

"NO!" Kenny shouted, starting to fire his assault rifle. Cathy's adrenaline spiked, and she fired as well.

Skolla growled and sprung at the knight that killed Tommlar, bashing him to the ground. His paw stepped on the wrist omitting the sword before Skolla's barred teeth dug into the space between the knight's helmet and chest plate. Blood squirted over his face as his teeth tore into the knight's neck.

The kinetic damage from Cathy's and Kenny's assault rifle had a much greater impact against the knight's armor than laser weapons. It tore holes in the plates, and the second knight fell to the ground dead before even pulling a sword.

Two more omelics revealed themselves in the shadows inside the clock tower and started to shoot bolts coated in energy using their advanced looking crossbows. The wolf-pack returned fire, sending the two back into cover.

That moment was short-lived as the knights bolted for a back door, shouting in fear.

"Damn grunts!" Kenny spat at the ground.

As Cathy turned her head to face Kenny and Edward on her left side, the sight of moving stone caught her attention. That was all was able to see before fingers extended into long needles, one of which stabbed Edward right through the heart. His eyes went wide, and he dropped his weapon. Cathy dodged to the side to avoid more needles, as did Kenny.

She was now on full alert at the monster before her. What she saw stunned her. A beast of stone-like skin, mossed over, and moldy-brown in color. Thin eyes and a symbolled chest marked similar as to what you would see on a black widow, both glowed a hot red. No mouth or ears, but twin horns extending from both sides of the head, this monster was three times the height of Cathy, but not much wider. And its fingers were long and thin, sharp at the ends. Edward, who was still impaled by one, began to turn to stone before her eyes!

Almost in a trance, and not seeming to be paying attention to Cathy or Kenny, it pulled back its fingers and lashed them out again. Of course, that move caught Cathy off-guard, but it was a testament to her training that she was able to jump away.

She fired her weapon but might as well not been firing at all, as the bullets did nothing.

"Cathy!" Kenny's voice pulled her attention, and her eyes met his haunted face. His hand covered his check before he pulled it away to reveal a tiny slice in the skin. A single drop of blood leaked out a moment before the skin started to turn to stone. Another member of her unit died a death straight out of a horror film. His screams rang in Cathy's ears; every pitch and blood-filled gurgle. Soon, his fearful eyes were forever looking back at Cathy, after giving in completely to the transformation.

Chapter 14

Cathy was utterly horrorstruck. In mere minutes, her teammates had fallen before her eyes, and she was helpless. Never had she felt that out of control.

Skolla came running to her side, growling, but she held out her hand to stop him from attacking the beast. She then took off, with Skolla running in front of her. The monster gave chase, its long legs seeming to glide over the streets.

The wind picked up all of a sudden. The trees in front her swayed, and the debris was blown away. A hovercraft had just flown over the abandoned town, stopping above. Ten knights, wearing different banners than those before jumped from the open hatches on the side of the dropship - landing between her and the monster.

She stopped and looked back to see them in formation. Nine knights in black metal with white stripes, and one in all white and shiny armor. They ignited their swords; seven were silver, one was blue, one was yellow, and the one in all white ignited a sword to match his color.

They charged at the beast, and it sliced right through one knight's armor like a hot knife through butter. Another knight sliced the monster's leg. That was the opening the rest needed, and they slashed right into the monster, cutting it down with ease. Each energy empowered sword hacked through its skin with what looked to be little-to-no resistance.

The creature was dead, and Cathy held her weapon ready as the knight in all white came up to her. The blade sheathed itself back into the handle, and he placed the handle back into his arm piece, which retracted over it. He allowed his helmet to retreat from his face. Without knowing why, he looked familiar to Cathy. "My name is Mauga Lightbourne, head of House Lightbourne, Warden of Northpoint, and First Under-Reign." Those words took away all her fear and stress, and she now understood why he looked familiar. She was looking into the face of another Lightborune. In some way, Mauga was related to Wouren, who she met in the Space Guard.

"I'm Catharine Darcrose." She was motionless.

"We saw your ship crash and came to offer aid. Only, it looks like--" Mauga took half a step backward and looked to the tragedy that befell her soldiers. "I'm sorry for your loss. Grenjores - they're brutal and merciless."

"Grenjores, huh. That's what killed my men." Cathy's nose flared, and her face filled with hatred towards the beast.

"Some call them stone giants. And I really hate to be the one to say that those two in stone aren't dead."

"Aren't dead?! How's that possible?"

"When stone giants cut into skin and infect the blood, the victims will become stone giants themselves soon enough."

"So they might as well be dead." Cathy clinched her fist.

"Sorry to say," Mauga confirmed. His head dropped, feeling her pain.

Cathy stared at her closed fist. She knew what had to be done, but she was silent. All she saw was her shaking hand as she struggled to ask, "How do I stop them from turning?"

"Blade to the heart or removal of their head," Mauga said softly.

Cathy was not ready to do the deed, but it had to be done, and she preferred the former approach - a blade to the heart.

She marched forth, letting duty muscle her feet forward. It was duty alone that kept her moving until she reached Edward first. She looked into his stunned face. Skolla whimpered at his unmoving feet, pressing his nose to the stone.

"I need a sword." Cathy looked at Mauga. He nodded to one his men.

He came up to her and held out his right arm, palm facing the ground. The metal plate over his wrist retracted, and a hilt became visible. He pulled it off his arm and handed it to Cathy.

She looked over it; brown hilt with tan grip, basic circular pommel, and a cross guard. She ignited the blade, and first came blocks of thin metal extending out of the center of the hilt, one after the other until it was about a meter long; altogether the metal blocks were called a stearth, as she recalled from an omelic book. Then the energy, silver in color, roared over one end of the cross guard and around the extendable metal, or stearth, to the other cross guard. It formed into the shape of a longsword, only with intensely focused energy rotating so fast, it looked motionless.

Chapter 14

She placed her free hand over the stone cheek of Edward and thrust the blade into his heart. She felt every motion of it, as if the act was done to her and she was unable to hold back a tear as it came down her check. Edward crumbled into nothing.

Somehow, she held the will to make it to Kenny. She clenched her jaw and drove the blade into him. She wanted to scream but held it in. His haunted gaze was soon no more as he fell apart just like Edward.

Wouren warned her about the creatures, but she never expected this. Seeing it for real, she realized many of the creatures of Omulice were ancient predators of immense power and strength. When she was young, she read stories that some could grow as tall as mountains. It seems everything on this planet was extreme in size; trees as high as skyscrapers, flowers and brushes as thick as buildings, and bugs as big as birds. Knowing that now, she had a feeling mountain-sized monsters must be true, too.

She stood there in grief for her lost soldiers, and she already missed them. When she finally was able to come to her senses, she realized all the knights had moved over to the bodies of Tommlar and the two knights who initially attacked her and her unit. She was so focused on her duty to her stone-turned men, she didn't realize the knights had moved in the first place.

"Did you kill these two?" Mauga asked.

"We did. They attacked us, and we retaliated."

His eyes went back down to the knight he was inspecting. "Hmm, this is troubling. They are knights of our neighboring kingdom to the northwest. We were supposed to be at peace with them, but their uninvited presence in our kingdom may hinder that peace." He looked to Cathy. "I must travel to Northpoint, but I'll have our dropship take you to Direclaw."

"Before you go, please... can you please bury them? I hate to ask this of you, because you've done so much already."

"You can never sacrifice enough for those in trouble. I will do this for you." A bright smile was on Mauga's face.

"Thank you. Thank you so much."

Mauga nodded to her and instructed one of his men to take Cathy to the dropship.

Skolla scurried to her side as they departed. Despite the tragedy, she couldn't lose her head. She must remain focused on the task at hand. If she can't, the mission would be over before it began, and that simply cannot be allowed to happen. It was her duty, not only to her commander, but to her lost sister. For once she finishes the mission, she can focus on finding her.

Soon, they were on the dropship and off to Direclaw.

Chapter 15: Direclaw
December 16, 2111

Catharine Darcrose

Side hatches of the dropship still open, Cathy gazed out on the land in the Tolkran Kingdom as the wind caressed her face. Direclaw was visible in the distance, the capital and strongest fort in the Tolkran Kingdom. The walls were magnificent, tall, and guarded; blocked, darkened stone powered by a field of energy and towering above the lands like a fruit tree over a desert. The capital was on fortified land, terminated on the south by a ridge of mountains hundreds of kilometers high, which are altogether impassable, due to the volcanoes upon the tops. Two of the other sides were surrounded by open farmland and several large villages which looked to be bustling with activity and trade. The last side touched a sea as far as the eye could see. There was one seaport in the whole kingdom built around patches of jagged rocks. The sea looked so rough, there was no venturing outward without the use of massive ships.

The dropship landed in a shipyard near the castle. It was wild with life. Ships of all designs were coming and going, nearly all covered in sigils and markings designating they belonged to a house. Omelics left and right; citizens, common folk, knights, lords, traders, and a many more.

There was a security check from the shipyard to the castle they had to pass. They did with no trouble. Outside to shipyard, wagons and riders were still pouring through the castle gates, and the yard was a chaos of mud and horseflesh and shouting men.

It is common knowledge omelics and humans are similar in many things up to and including appearances. So much so, humans and omelics can sometimes successfully have an offspring together. Such a thing was still considered taboo to both cultures. There were, however, obvious differences, such as skin tone, less body hair, hair and eye colors, and those black markings that were natural on their skin. Though, looking over the crowd, Cathy's sharp eye could see ever so slight differences in body type. On average, omelic men carry broader shoulders, slightly wider feet and hands, and denser muscle definition. Women, on the other hand, are more likely to have wide hips and fit bodies. When taking into consideration the omelic culture, it makes sense. Darwin's theory and all.

Leading up to the castle lay a market square. Manses and bowers and granaries, smithhouses and starship depots and intergalactic pawnshops, brick warehouses and timbered taprooms and merchant's booths, taverns and cemeteries and brothels, all piled one on another. With a finer eye, Cathy could see the market was skewed. Everything close the castle was richer in design and clientele. However, as the market continued away from the castle, dropping down hilled roads, so too did the quality drop.

"Nice to see so much activity," Cathy said to the knight guiding her.

"It never gets old does it? Not long ago, these roads hardly felt the patter of feet."

As they went through the right edge of the market square leading to the keep, Cathy could hear the clamor of the fish market even at this distance. Between the buildings were broad roads lined with trees, wandering crookback streets, and alleys so narrow, two men could not walk shoulder to shoulder.

The knight led her and Skolla inside Wolph Castle. When they reached the gate to the throne room, one of the guards welcomed them. "Welcome to the Tolkran Kingdom," he said. "I have been informed the king would like to meet you."

She entered the Great Hall, a large, cavernous room. Its entrance was made up of two huge bronze and wood doors. The White Throne sat on the opposite side, atop a raised dais where two sets of wide steps of rough black stone led up to the throne. Decorative, lavish chairs were placed in a row to the right of the throne for use by members of the king's council. Above the throne, hung as high as can be, was the sigil of the king; a red-eyed direwolf, white fur, over a snowed field - the sigil of House Wolph. Vaulted ceilings with massive arches and columns towered over the patterned marble floor. A raised gallery connecting other areas of the castle lay to the right of the throne. Decorative stain-glassed windows depicting former kings and their accomplishments lined the left wall, lighting the room in a multitude of colorful light that danced across the room.

King Kaydon leaned back on his throne as he awaited her approach, leg resting on a padded leg stool. He was thin for an omelic male, not much muscle either, which was surprising given he was royal. However, much could be hidden due to the thick clothes and cloak he wore. There was just a small patch of black streaks below his nose and another between his eyebrows, making it seem as if he had a unibrow.

A nearby royal knight informed her, "You stand before King Kaydon, king of the Tolkran Kingdom and head of House Wolph."

"Your Grace." Cathy bowed. "I was told you wanted to meet with me."

King Kaydon half-grinned. "There is no need for such formality. You'll find me quite approachable."

Cathy tipped her head in appreciation.

"Besides, I wanted to see our honored guest firsthand. It isn't often outsiders visit our world, and even less so to our kingdom. Though I heard there were to be five of you total and a--" his eyes locked onto the warwolf, "--wolf. Ironic; a wolf in Wolph Castle." He smiled.

Cathy's expression grew mournful. "The rest--"

"--died before we arrived," her guide finished the sentence for Cathy.

"Oh, I'm quite remorseful to hear that. My well-wishes go out to their families and friends," the king said. "Is there anything I can do for you, Cathy?"

"Point me to where I can start my research. I wish to start immediately."

"As you wish." King Kaydon gestured to the knight. "Escort our guest to Saulomon's Temple."

He nodded and approached Cathy. "If you will, follow me."

"Lead the way," Cathy responded.

He marched onward.

Skolla and Cathy were led through a few halls before they arrived at the wooden double doors that led inside the temple. He pushed them open. "Find our Master of Scrolls, Kaizerious. He runs the daily operations here and can help you with your study, for he himself has already taken an interest in the topic you seek."

"How will I know what he looks like?"

"He is the only non-omelic in the room, and, ah... the tallest. Hard to miss, he is." The knight chuckled. He then left her.

She began walking through row after row of old books, scrolls, manuals. You name it, it was there. Saulomon's Temple housed all the knowledge, stories, and teachings of this kingdom's omelic ancestors. That was the claim anyway.

There was a section entitled *"Hyperswords,"* that caught her eye. She pulled out the first book she saw. *"Guide to Building a Hypersword."* On the cover was a picture similar to the swords she saw those knights wielding before arriving at Direclaw.

Hyperswords, she remembered reading that word long ago during a time when her mother forced her to read omelic history and culture. Hyperswords, the chosen weapons of knights, lords, and kings.

She started rummaging through a few books, reading the titles:

Hyperswords & the Science
All 9 Blade Shades in Detail
The Eight Combat Styles for True Swordsmen
A Many Framing Techniques to Build your Hypersword
Lost & Legendary: The 4 Mystical Blade Shades
Triangle of Ren: An Experimental Study

All of it looked so rich and interesting to read and research. To her disappointment, she hadn't the time to mess with it. She needed to focus on the mission at hand, the one that had claimed her team. She needed to find clues to the location of the Brotherhood of Relics. She put away the books and left that section.

As she continued searching for Kaizerious, she stumbled on a steel gated section of the temple. She looked around; only her warwolf was in sight. Quickly, she pulled a utility kit from one of her pouches and used a few tools to pick the lock. It took some time, and she struggled. A few broken pins before she had it unlocked.

Now inside, she began to look through some of the texts. She started with a row entitled *"Reign of King Kaylob"* and began pulling everything she could get her hands on. The writing was in ancient umomah, an outdated omelic language, and was too smeared and distorted for the cyberwatch to translate. Lucky for her, her mother had her trained in various omelic languages, including this one. Though tough to decipher, she was able to read the words.

She took a seat a nearby reading table with arms full of material to research, Skolla at her heel. She was surprised to see stuff was already laid over the table, some open, but most of it was closed. She started with a journal she pulled earlier, written by Arkenlord Izayhah Hartmon, and flipped to a random page.

Our kingdom continues its decline. King Kaylob hasn't been the same since that dreadful day, and now turns to drinks. He spends most days in a tavern, drinking his emotions away. If things continue down this way, I fear our great kingdom will fall to ruin, cursed by the leadership of a drunk fool.

The material was familiar to Cathy. She recalled hearing about the fall of the Tolkran Kingdom during Kaylob Wolph's reign during her studies of the omelic species. Even so, it wasn't going to help her.

The next book she pulled was entitled *"Time, Reality, Existence, & Death: 4 Constants of the Universe."* Theory work, nothing more, and not much useful.

She pulled a collection of tattered scrolls part of a collection. *"A Man Who Dreamt Hell,"* the collection of scrolls were titled, authored by Arkenlord Mozaru Vox. Each in a series of at least five total. Was this fiction similar to The Inferno? Too bad it would likely not be of help to her. Thus she had no time for it. Among the table, she noticed a particularly dulled and worn journey; black and full of cresses. A rectangular image of a hand-drawn enormous warehouse of scrolls and knowledge was stitched to the cover of the journey.

Cathy turned to the first page, and there were inked words in small print. She read in her head:

The fire consumed it. A sea of red, yellow, and orange. A smoke cloud that covered more height and distance than a volcanic eruption. I saved what I could. It wasn't much. For the great Mousseion burned to the ground that night. With it burned all the knowledge it held. All of it, except what lays in this journal.

Cathy did a quick flip through of the journal and was surprised to see the rest of the pages were full of burnt pieces of paper that were stitched to each page in the journey. When she turned back to the second page, she began to read what she could inside, but some of it was burnt and scorched:

I dreamt I was the enemy, walking in their skin. The enemy - the d   to my   . A   n born of the dead. In the dream, I walked on a lone path of glass and rock, beneath the blossoms. At th end of the path grew a flower in the shape of a gray pulsing heart. Unable to shake the trance, I reached out to pluck it, and it cut me with a thorn. I bled and the blood was   ack like ink. The flower said to me, "You are   dead thing made by a dead pow   in the shape of the dead... all you will ever do is plague the universe... you do not belong here; this is a sacred place - a place untainted and balanced."
I responded, "You're wrong. I'm born of   and not death. Y u're a creature devoid of a soul, and you seek to deceive me." But I looked down on myself and realized I was no longer a   . I was me again, an   . And my cut now bled white.
The flower repeated, "You are a dead thing made by a dead power in the shape of the dead... all you will ever do is plague the universe... you do not belong here; this is a   place - a place untainted and balanced."
I looked behind me, down the long slope where the blossoms tumbled in the war wind, and the great trees wept sap like blood or wine, and I felt doubt. When I awoke again by the sea, there was a thorn-cut on my left hand, and it has not healed since.

-- Lady Serafina L

Cathy flipped the page. There was more:

Chapter 15

My dreams have gotten worse. No, I can no longer call them dreams, they are nightmares. The looming threat of the enemy of the Prism of Life haunts every second of my dreams, every restless night. They are a flood, held at bay by a dam. But I can see the cracks forming, and I'm helpless to stop it. The Tri   lation will be upon us. For the last 'seven' of the seventy 'sevens' has yet to be spoken. They will come again. And I fear our galaxy will not be ready for them.

There was a time when I tried warning beings of tw   ht. I tried warning countless civilians. They called me a witch, zealot, radical, doomsday sp   ker. To them, I'm insane. So I gave up trying to convince the crowd of underdeveloped beings of   l ht. I'm from a different time, after all. A time of li   , d   ess, and more. A time of

Wars and miracles. And there is one miracle that still holds my heart. A man placed out of time; my love, my G   . I will wait for him.

-- Lady Serafina   ne

Caught up in the text, Cathy was startled as the gate slid open and heavy footsteps thumped from around the corner. "I see our guest has arrived. If you wanted to get back here, all you needed to do was ask." The man spoke just as he revealed himself. His voice was deep, and he spoke with a harsh and hesitant tone; each word came slow but had a ring to it, like it was stuck on a specific emotion that was trapped in each word.

She stood up and tilted her head in respect. "I got a bit curious and carried away. I'm Cathy Darcrose, in case you couldn't already tell."

The being before her was larger than any intelligent species she had seen before. If she were standing, her head would only come to his waist, and she was taller than an average human woman. She could stretch out her arms, and her wingspan would barely measure the width of this behemoth of a being. And his appearance was intimidating; jagged skin that almost had an uneven crystal-like texture to it, smoky black highlighted heavily with an ice blue. Parts of his body, especially around the limbs and eyes, carried characteristics of a maelkii, only larger.

"I take it you're Kaizerious." Cathy's eyes studied him, though she believed she knew the answer.

He nodded. "I am." He then sat opposite of her. She hadn't realized until he sat that the chair was much larger and sturdier than hers. He must have been back here before. Probably why some material was already spread on the table when she arrived.

Her eyes studied Kaizerious. Never had she seen anything like him. If he was to be trusted, she would have to get to know him a bit better. "You're big." Cathy shook her head. "I have never seen anyone like you before."

Kaizerious expended a wry laugh. "You're not the first to say that. As it happens, I'm the last of my kind."

"Really? I'm sorry to hear that. I hope I'm not stepping over the line by asking what happened."

There was moment of silence as he lingered on what she asked. He then cleared his throat. "A catastrophe happened - genocide. Not something I talk about. I still carry the scars, you see."

"Sorry. I didn't mean to push." She paused to take a breath. "Strange, though. Omelics never seemed the type to allow outsiders a seat at their king's council, Master of Scrolls." Her eyebrow rose.

"I think you'll find this kingdom isn't like many of the others," he responded. That wasn't the first time she heard that. Stands to reason he wouldn't be lying, then.

"So why, then? Why would a place like this interest you?"

Kaizerious eyes glared toward the stack of books. He spoke with soft words. "My interest is the same as you: To take care of those I care for." Cathy stared for a moment. Her mind was on her lost sister. Kaizerious continued. "I may be the last of my kind, but I still have those that I love."

"How did you know? How did you know I am here for family? That this isn't just a mission to me? It is possible hope."

"When you're as old as me, you start to sense patterns in people... see motives in their eyes."

"And how old are you?"

"I've lost count. Slow aging is a trait of my species."

"That's a gift not many species have."

Chapter 15

"I like to think I spend it well. It's allowed me time, lots of time, to really understand life in this galaxy clearly. And I'm thankful. That clarity is the reason I can take care of all of whom that are dear to me."

"Even if I had time, I'm not sure I'd benefit much from it. Life for me has been a series challenges. So I've not had the luxury of thinking about my life long term."

"What challenge do you face right now?"

"Finding the Brotherhood of Relics, delivering a message to them, and then finding my sister."

"And once she is found?" he pushed.

"That's just it. I don't know. I mean, how could I... this war... the Wersillian War-- I may not get to see the end of it, so why should I try to think past it?"

"You really believe you will not live through the war?"

"I mean, I hope I do... that's really all I can... all anyone can. Until the day the war ends, I follow orders and do my duty for those I care about."

"You carry yourself with strength. In my experience, people like you survive more often than not."

Doubtful, Cathy thought, if only he knew of her family's cursed past and burden. "Strong? Me? I look nothing of the sort compared to you."

He smirked. "You mistake me, Cathy. I am no fighter. I have not fought anyone in decades. And I never wish to in the future."

Cathy was surprised. "With your size and strength, I would've imagined you would've been a great warrior."

"Maybe in another life."

Cathy smiled. "You know, you are an interest to be around. And I don't really say that about a lot of people."

"I appreciate your compliment. And please, Cathy, allow me to assist you."

Cathy nodded and said, "I just got started looking into the reign of King Kaylob, and from what I understand, he was supposedly the king of the Tolkran Kingdom during the time when the Brotherhood of Relics started."

"You're right."

"Any advice?"

He looked to the book she held. "I recommend tossing that. It won't help you with your task." From the pile, he handed her a thin book that was old and held together by breaking seams. It was untitled, and the cover was a blank red.

Cathy thumbed to the first bookmarked page and saw a section circled. She read:

February 30, 2084

King Garrol, first of his name, rightful king of the Tolkran Kingdom, Sword of Spikes; has theorized that the Tolkran Kingdom is cursed. He believes it runs far back... as far back as the reign of King Kaylob. This information has been entrusted to me and me alone.

Cathy finished reading the circled text. She looked up from the pages. "Who's the author?"

"It never says," Kaizerious answered. "I found it hidden in this locked room and circled the useful information from it."

There were more bookmarked pages. Cathy turned to the next one and began reading from the circled text:

October 18, 2092

King Garrol commanded I follow him. I didn't know any details of where he wanted to go or what he intended to do. All that was found out later.

It was a meeting. Far below Wolph Castle, hidden deep in a dark alleyway of a deserted part of the stronghold. It was just the king and me, and I was on edge. No guards to accompany us.

We waited for a long time, longer than a king should ever have to wait for someone. King Garrol was determined. I saw this in his grit.

Eventually an athletic man showed. He didn't look omelic - his skin was tan in color, hair golden-brown, and some of his physical appearance did not fit, such as his arms and fingers and claws. Hidden behind a black spiral-patterned mask that focused and spiraled around the eyeholes, only his golden irises were visible. Clothed in a kilt that was lopsided, much of the rest of his body was wrapped with tape-fabric.

"You're Reality?" King Garrol asked.

"One of many names I've been called," the man confirmed.

"What took you so long?"

"Another deal. It took longer than anticipated." Reality's tone and accent were new to me. Ancient and of a time long ago.

"I've waited for this moment for ten years. Long have I been searching for the mythical creature know as Reality, the Wish-Granter, the Man-a-Mystery." King Garrol bowed to give respect. I joined so as not to look out of place.

"Now that you've found me, what is your wish?"

"I want the Tolkran Kingdom to return to its former glory. I want whatever curse on my kingdom lifted."

"That's two requests. I can grant you one."

"Then tell me, is my kingdom cursed as I believe it to be?"

"The simple answer is yes. The long answer, I'm afraid, is far more complicated."

"Then remove the curse. That's my wish."

"Do you know what it will cost you?"

"I've read the stories. I know."

Reality and King Garrol made a deal that day. Reality conjured up a golden, double ankh pendant for both to grip on either side. The deal was made, and Reality's glowing eyes brightened for a moment.

"The curse has been lifted. What befalls your kingdom will now entirely be up to your choices henceforth." Reality left us there.

There was one more bookmarked page that Cathy turned to and read from:

January 13, 2094

The events of December 18, 2092 still occupy my thoughts. I had no idea that Garrol was looking for this mystical creature for ten years. What exactly befell that night still keeps me up in my bed. Garrol never told me anything more on the subject, even when I asked. He is dead

now, and I'm the only one left who knows. One thing I am happy to see:
Our kingdom is on the rise again for the first time in my lifetime.

Cathy closed the book. "Curses, Reality. All seems like a bit too much."

"My thoughts were that the creature called Reality was a member of the Brotherhood of Relics."

"Really, now?"

"Just a hunch. No more than that, I admit." Kaizerious gave pause. "I have more clues that I left back in my chambers. I can bring them to you tomorrow if you're interested."

Cathy gave a nod to show she was. In the meantime, she and he spent much of their time looking over the pile of books on the table. She spent the rest of the day researching and putting together clues, with Kaizerious's aid.

Chapter 16: Lost Brothers
December 22, 2111

James Stone

Two weeks had passed, and in that time we met a few locals as we made stops to resupply our boat. In a word, they were kind. One may even say too much so which a trait not too often witnessed in the galaxy these days. In truth, maybe that is what has held the corelinns back from intergalactic travel. But really, would these beings even fit in the twisted-up, upside-down galaxy of ours? It takes a thick coat to make it from day to day through a war as massive as the Wersillian War. A coat that not everyone can bear to carry. From where I'm sitting, the corelinns may be better off waiting a few decades to join the list of intergalactic species.

We were close to our journey's end. Our boat drifted towards the last bend that would lead us into a cave. Cliffs on both sides, forests and brush so thick, light could barely pass through lined the tops of the mountains, all along with an unnerving silence as we neared our destination. Fog flowed over the top of the wakeless, blue water and sharp rocks forced Jeremiah to maneuver our watercraft carefully. One brush against these rocks could mean the end of our ride, and instead, we'd end up neck-high in water.

It took a bit, but we eventually made it through the cave. On the other side were some docks. Up and past the docks was a rather small colony with big walls and defenses, all made of dense stone logs.

Both suns were high in the sky, yet both moons orbiting this planet were visible in the sky as well. Humid air blew over the sky-blue ocean-river and the wake of our boat swished against the patterned, composite docks. Jeremiah eased the boat into the edge of the marina just as a dock worker came over to help; stomping with loud sandals. "Would you like help, si--" The worker's eyes caught notice of us. "More otherworldly visitors?" Another observation I have made of these people is, they are a lot more likely to accept alien life than humans ever were. Sure, they are surprised in the immediate moment after catching sight of my handsome, war-hardened face. Though after that, they accept it; rather nonchalantly at that. Quite an interesting species indeed.

"What is their purpose on our world?" the worker asked as he tied the boat to the dock.

Jeremiah stepped off the boat first. "They seek to go home. But first they are here to enter the vault."

His eyes grew wide for a second. "Dangerous."

"I'm surprised that Witna hasn't mentioned them," Jeremiah responded, gesturing for us to follow him.

"She probably has, but you know our leader. He doesn't tell us much news from the mainlands." The worker stepped aside to let us pass.

Behind myself, everyone in my crew followed. Valiic came to my side. "The longer we stay on this primitive planet, the more at risk we place our alliance. Engaging with underdeveloped worlds will began to anger species all across our galaxy."

"As long as these people choose to take a metaphorical key and lock away their knowledge of us, then we shouldn't have an issue. Plus, what other choices were on the plate fate handed us? You don't think others will see this?"

"Some species aren't as understanding as others. The last thing we need is more enemies to fight against."

"And you think I didn't give this a second thought? Thus far, the people here have yet to let a word slip about our presence to other species across the galaxy--"

"To our knowledge," Valiic interrupted.

"Let's just meet with the leader of this colony, get the weapon, kill the monster, leave, and the people here will probably just forget we were ever here."

"I hope you are right, for the sake of our alliance."

The stairs led us to a gate already opened for our arrival. The fencing around this colony consisted of carved stone logs spiked at the tops and posted into the ground. Hundreds of these spiked stone posts boxed the colony in, each placed right next to each other. Every corner held a sentry tower, with all four being the tallest structures around.

Inside, guards lined up on either side of us and welcomed our arrival. They formed a path through the tents, barracks, and other wooden structures to the center, where a larger town hall marked the center.

As we came closer to the stairs outside the town hall, a soldier said, "Momotashi Boo'Thuur will be out to see you shortly."

The leader, Momotashi, rushed outside to meet us just a second later, scampering down the stairs and nearly tripping over himself. "There you are. I cannot tell you how glad I am to see you." The words came rushing from his mouth.

"I'm James--" I began to introduce myself.

"I know your names, so let's skip the introduction. I've had my men prepare supplies for your journey into the vault." He motioned to three men, who stepped forward with backpacks stuffed tightly.

Valiic stepped forward and grabbed them by the straps.

"You're eager to shoves us into the vault. What's the rush? Seriously, we've had a long journey and haven't even had a chance to get our bearings."

"I'm afraid I don't have time to explain--"

"Hold your beer for a second. I've heard that platitude before, so instead, let's make some time."

"Look. I'm sure Witnamerrys mentioned an inevitable threat. Well, that threat was reported by my scouts to be two weeks away from reaching this fort. If you don't have the weapon by then everyone here *dies*. A week after that, it will reach Surradimoor."

Jeremiah whispered in my ear, "That's the formal name of the Treasured City."

Frost jumped in to answer the leader's plea. "Consider it done, uzzo."

I nodded. "We have our share to lose. Alright then, just show us the way."

Momotashi bowed. "Thank you. But before you head into the vault, you will need a seventh member for you team."

"Got a soldier in mind, I take it?"

"One of yours, actually."

"Mine?" I frowned, not sure what he meant by that. All my men were presently in my company.

"Yes. In our medical center." He tapped on the shoulder of the closest soldier to him. "Show them." He then went back inside the town hall.

The soldier marched onward.

"Fine." I started forward. "Valiic, with me. Everyone else - wait for our return, and take inventory of the supplies."

Valiic handed the bags over to Frost and Shadow-Walker, then we both followed the solider. After just a hop, skip, and leap in distance, we arrived to the medical center. The back end of the building was pushed against the fencing. The center, however, was nothing special by any means. It looked like everything else, maybe just a hint wider.

In the medical center, we were taken to a room on the right of the first hall. No doors were separating the rooms. I was eager to meet this mysterious person who, supposedly, was team ARW.

I was the second to turn into the room, behind the soldier leading us, and I just about fell over when I caught eye of the two men before me. Maelkii twin brothers; one on a medical table with a blanket over him, and the other on a chair at his side. They looked up, their metal skin reflecting the light of the room into my eyes.

"What in bloody Sam-Hell are you doing here, James?" Geariic jumped out from his seat.

"James?" Alabon asked, not believing his own words until he saw me.

It was the Bruising Brothers! Here, on an unknown planet within our vast galaxy, in the same camp, and looking quite alive. The odds were astronomical. "You ask me that?" I asked louder than I meant to. "Seriously, what the holy hell?"

Geariic came closer to me, warhammer strapped over his back. "Yes, James. You aren't supposed to be here."

"Not that we aren't happy to see you," Alabon added before groaning with some pain.

Valiic moved past me and placed his hand over Geariic's shoulder. "It's good to see brothers as valiant as you two."

Geariic seemed uncomfortable with Valiic's gesture before losing it to laughter - untempoed and deep. "You're just as I remember, Valiic."

Valiic moved over to Alabon and pulled back the sheet. "What's the injury?"

"Leg." Alabon pointed to the bandages wrapped over his leg.

"Rest now, warrior. Tell me what happened."

Chapter 16

"We tried to win the game," Alabon grunted as Valiic touched the bandage.

He removed his hand. "I apologize."

"Game?" I asked Geariic.

"He means the vault. We attempted to face its trials and claim the prize. Made it to the first champion before Alabon took a blow strong enough to pierce his skin. I barely managed to drag his ass out of that Sam-Hell."

Pierce him! What monsters lurked in our future? I shuttered at the thought.

"I can't believe you two were bested," Valiic said.

Geariic stomped on the ground, shaking the room, and turned. "Don't go spewing that garbage."

Valiic raised his hands. "I mean you no disrespect. All warriors have their shortcomings when facing the challenges placed in their path." Geariic stepped closer to Valiic. "Warriors, such as you two, are never defeated, only made stronger by such loses."

Geariic gave Valiic a disrespectful sneer, but he left it at that. Valiic seemed to ignore or miss Geariic's gesture all together. That sneer left a bad taste in my mouth, but I let it be. He was our ally, even if he was taking Valiic's words deeper than they were meant to be.

"You still haven't told me why you're here," I continued.

"You should just tell him, brother," said Alabon.

Geariic faced me again. "Kalvin sent us here."

"Kalvin did?" I was suspicious.

"Who else would?" Geariic asked me.

"It's just... just--"

Geariic tilted his head. "I don't like that look in your eye, James. What happened?"

"We all thought you two might've died," I responded after a moment of silence.

"Dead? Us?" Geariic and Alabon burst into gut-wrenching laughter. Alabon was cut short by the pain. "What gave you that impression?" Geariic questioned as he recovered from his laughter.

"When we were on the mission on Idor, your squad went and dropped off the fraken map. Gone... like a puff of smoke. And man, we could've used you two!" I shouted. "People died!" I stepped forward, a meter in front of him, pointing. "You two could've saved many lives!"

Geariic pushed down my hand. "Bring it down, James. Shivf, I would've liked to have bloodied my warhammer with some korkyran blood, too. But hell, we didn't have a fraken choice. Kalvin's orders."

"And Kalvin gets what he wants," Alabon added.

"And I swear to you, James, our unit was fine when we were picked up. Captain Waseem was supposed to inform everybody of the situation during the next captains' meeting."

"He never made it to that meeting," Valiic informed.

I let my blood lighten up. "You're right. Kalvin does get what he wants, and I'll make sure to take it up with him. Until then, we need to work together if we ever want to see this planet in the rearview mirror."

"How do you propose we do that, James?" Geariic crossed his arms.

"If we manage to claim this weapon from the vault and kill their planet-killer, the corelinns will let us use their communication tower. That's our ticket home."

"Shivf, you think we're going back in deathtrap? Not with my brother in the condition he is in."

"Not him. Just you."

"And leave my brother. Frak that," Geariic refused.

Alabon grunted. "Brother. Go with them. We still have our mission."

"Mission?" My eyebrow went up.

"Kalvin's mission," Geariic reiterated. He walked to his brother and looked down at Valiic. He gave up the chair to Geariic, who sat at his brother's side. He put his hand over his brother's head. "If Kalvin wants one of those weapons, he can come take them himself. There isn't a place in Sam-Hell that I'd ever leave you, Alabon."

"Brother... if you can't retrieve that weapon, we'll all die here."

Those words seemed to shake Geariic, and his head popped up. "Frak it. Why do you have to be right, Alabon?" He patted his brother on the chest. He looked to me. "Very well, James. Count me in."

"You and the big-ass warhammer will make an excellent asset to our squad." I was thrilled.

"Aces should stick together," said Alabon.

Chapter 16

Geariic looked down at his brother once more before standing up and leaving the room. He grunted, "Let's get on with this shivf." We and the corelinn soldier all followed Geariic and emptied the room.

Chapter 17: Vault of the Seven
December 22, 2111

James Stone

Our number was now at seven and we were but hours away from entering a place few corelinns have ever come back alive. Geariic, Valiic, and I were led by a soldier to the far side of the colony. Against the deepest edge of the back wall surrounding this place was an outpost reinforced with thick doors and defenses. It was coated in webbed nets, murky green in color, and had a three-riser staircase leading to the door.

"Your allies are inside," the soldier informed us.

"For what reason?" Valiic asked.

"Tunnels," Geariic stated.

"Tunnels?"

"Yes," the soldier said. "We dug deep tunnels leading to the Vault of the Seven... only a kilometer away from this colony."

"Made for going under the forest and avoiding the shjarrs above, I presume," Valiic said.

"Correct," the soldier confirmed.

As we approached, the outpost doors were opened by two guards. Up the three risers I went and was inside first. The room wasn't large by any definition, and it was filled with tables stacked with military crates, weapons, and ammunition. Everything was ready for our choosing, we need only grab it. At the back was the gateway portal to the tunnel, which dipped sharply downward.

My squad was gearing up. Frost noticed Geariic.

"Geariic, my uzzo! I thought I'd seen the last of you." Frost sped over to Geariic and pulled back his hand.

Geariic reciprocated, and together they high-fived into a shake. "I'm harder to kill than most." He laughed with his belly.

"Hah. Ain't that the damn truth? But what in the hell are you doing here of all places?"

"Kalvin sent us here."

"Before Waseem's unit went MIA," I added.

Chapter 17

Frost looked from Geariic, to me, and back to Geariic. "Really?" His voice dropped a bit of enthusiasm.

"Sure did," Geariic reaffirmed. "My brother's injured and resting here in camp. But I'm here to smash the shivf out of the enemies in the vault."

"Having someone like you around to take the enemy focus away from me just warms my insides," Shadow-Walker jested.

Jeremiah joined Frost and stood before Geariic. He studied him with friendly awe. "Who's this little twig?" Geariic asked Frost. "I can just about use him as a toothpick."

Jeremiah extended his hand. "We haven't been introduced. I'm Jeremiah, your guide through these trials."

Geariic looked him over. "And why do we need a shrimp like you to guide us?"

"Because not having one worked out damn well for you last time," I joked.

"You went in already?" asked Jeremiah.

Geariic retorted, "How do you think my brother got injured?"

Jeremiah backed away. "I'm sorry."

I went over to the front of the entrance of the cave. I looked down to see stairs leading downward, carved from the stone of the cave floor. It was lit by lights hung on the cave ceiling and strung together by cords for power. With so much on the line, the time to wait was over, and the time for getting our asses in motion was now. "Listen up." I grabbed everyone's attention with some command in my voice. "We've got our mission. Lives depend on our success. So let's cut it with the howdy-dowdies for now and start chewing some dirt. As legionnaires, our motto is: *To you, each is a weapon.* And it's time we made good on those words for these people. Everyone clear?"

My words received acknowledgments back from everyone, and I started down the stairs into the cave. Everyone grabbed their gear and our supplies and followed my lead.

"Aren't we just a big bunch of circus freaks now?" Shadow joked.

"Don't call me a freak." Geariic's voice deepened at the remark. Shadow-Walker didn't seem to care much, keeping his jesting smile and attitude.

Jeremiah was right on my trail. "We are on God's quest now," he added, with cheerful glee in his words.

"Calm down with that do-goody-good horseshivf, good pastor," I teased him.

He laughed. "Remember James, those on the side of the lord are on the winning side. And who wouldn't want to be on the winning side?"

Geariic snorted, "And what makes it the winning side?"

"Because the victory was already secured. Against all of the darkness and evil in the galaxy, God already defeated it. For the devil is a defeated foe. And for it we've already won."

"Can't say he isn't a positive man," Shadow-Walker added, with a laugh. In spite of his humor, Jeremiah's words did kill off a few of those pesky butterflies in my stomach.

With so many of the corelinns relying on us, I felt the pressure like a weighted backpack on my shoulders. Being relied on wasn't what was new to me. I felt that weight every mission to the point where I no longer noticed it there. Instead, it was the do or die of it all. The dark shadow of doom lingered in my mind. Fail, and a whole civilization crumbles away into sand and ash.

*****

Seven circular gates, gold and obsidian, were before us inside an expansive and domed cavern. This was it, the big moment, the beginning of the Vault. Written words and symbols unknown to me were carved above each gate. Not even my cyberwatch was able to recognize it. At the center of the domed cavern, with a ceiling high over our heads, was a pedestal-shaped device; gold and obsidian like the gates, with a round inclined control panel on top. Seven slots rounded a concentric circle that was centered around a central white orb glowing with white smoke.

Seven gates of the seven different trials centered around seven different weapons of sin. Seven, seven, seven; yet, the number didn't seem so lucky at the moment.

Jeremiah, now near the control panel, held the book in his hand and was our designated navigator. He turned to the first page. *"The Vault of the Seven. A wound in time, a landmark to the Precursors. Seven weapons of sin for seven worthy sins of darkness,"* he read.

"Precursors? Never heard of 'em," said Frost.

Jeremiah flipped the page. *"In the beginning, life stood two; light created what darkness destroyed until one gained the favor over the other--"*

"Holy shivf! I've heard that before!" I shouted.

"Same!" Frost nearly jumped back at the words.

My head was damn-near sent spinning as well. Those words came flooding back into my mind as I remembered my vision in the tunnels below Garatopia. It was clear as day, playing like a movie in my head.

"That's well and good, you two. But what does it mean?" asked Shadow-Walker. He sat against the cave wall as we waited.

"Who gives a shivf?" Geariic grunted. Near Shadow-Walker, he held the handle of his warhammer as the head of it rest against the stone floor.

"I'm wit Hammerhead ova here." Brad, crouched with his shotgun at rest, pointed his thumb back to Geariic. Geariic grumbled inaudibly at the comment.

"In the beginning, life stood two," Jeremiah started. "Some who believe in-- What is the name of that ancient extinct species?"

"Devisors," Valiic informed.

"Ah, yes. Some who believe in the Devisors, believe them as the oldest known species in the galaxy. In my travels through the inner parts of the Enchanted System, I've heard another species with this same claim - the Precursors. What if both claims were true?"

"In the beginning, life stood two," I muttered to myself.

"The architecture of those gates and that pedestal don't carry the same characteristics as what I've seen from Devisors," Valiic, a believer in the mythological species, agreed. "Looks like the book answered your question."

Jeremiah turned another page. *"The Seven Weapons of Sin: The Axe of Pride, Staff of Gluttony, Claws of Envy, Blood of Sloth, Spikeburst of Greed, Serpent of Lust, and the Blade of Wrath. Weapons enchanted and cursed with charms."*

"And of these seven weapons, which have been claimed?" Geariic's voiced boomed with more curiosity on this topic.

Jeremiah looked in the pages for an answer and seemed to find one. "Hard to be sure. But it seems to me that the Staff of Gluttony and Blood of Sloth have champions that wield them. Or so that book seems to make it out that way." He adjusted his glasses.

Luckily, the Blade of Wrath is still without a champion, I thought.

"Does the book tell us why the Blade of Wrath will kill the foretold monster?" asked Valiic.

"If you believe your weapon can murder all in existence, then so it shall - thus is the Blade of Wrath," Jeremiah read.

Geariic grinned. "Sounds like my kind of weapon."

Jeremiah continued to flip through the pages. "And I think I've found how we enter. *In the Vault of Seven, those seeking status of seven sins shall bequeath on the Pillar of Sin. Seven is the number."* Jeremiah, who was standing next to the pedestal in the center, placed his hand in one of the seven slots. "I believe each of us must do this to enter."

Geariic grumbled as he dragged his warhammer over. "I could've told you that."

Everyone encircled the device and started placing their hands on the slots. I was the last to do so and felt the ice-cold panel against my palm. It didn't feel completely metallic or solid; it had a moist, gel-like sensation against my skin. Then there was a tiny prick of pain on the center of my hand. After this, we all extracted our hands from the device. The ball in the center activated, and the clouds within gave way to images of our faces. It ended by displaying some unknown symbols that led to the furthest gate on the right opening up. It was the only one of the seven to open.

"When Alabon and I did this, all the doors except the furthest left opened," Geariic told us, seeming to be puzzled by it.

"Which did you choose?" asked Valiic.

"The middle."

Jeremiah looked through the pages. "God is on our side. The gate that opened is the trial for the Blade of Wrath."

"That's good enough for me. Time to introduce some monsters to Big Daddy." Frost was the first to enter the gate.

Chapter 17

Brad was damn near at his side. "Iceberg got da right idea. Waitin' iz ah bitch."

His actions of gallantry inspired us all to follow suit. We entered the trial to claim the Blade of Wrath, and the gate closed behind us. Our trial awaited.

Chapter 18: Two War-Blooded Families
December 23, 2111

Catharine Darcrose

Catharine Darcrose comes from a family engrained in war throughout human history. Up until the year 2069, history recorded that Charlotte Carter Lee had died at seven weeks old as a result of premature birth and sickly health. She even had a grave marked in what was once known as Shockoe Hill Cemetery in Richmond, Virginia. This was wrong. Fact was, the family doctor of Charlotte Georgiana Wickham and William Henry Fitzhugh Lee stole the child at birth and faked the Lees' newborn daughter's death. This, of course, meant Charlotte Carter Lee was the grandchild of General-in-Chief Robert Edward Lee, commander of the Confederate States army for the Confederate States of America in the American Civil War, and great-granddaughter of Henry "Light-Horse Harry" Lee, the Lieutenant Colonel in the Continental Army and Governor of Virginia. The doctor who stole her, whose name was lost in history, raised Charlotte Carter Lee, and she lived to a healthy age of seventy-one under the name of Anna Wallace Darcrose before she passed. She was never made aware of her heritage. Her legacy carried on, generation after generation. And the true linage of Anna Darcrose wasn't discovered until Cathy's grandfather, Sir Hearty Darcrose, made a name for himself in World War III. His first-born daughter and Cathy's mother, Elizabeth Darcrose, followed in his footsteps. Elizabeth Darcrose is the current chief admiral representing the humans in the ARW military - the highest rank achievable. Thus, war runs in blood of the Darcrose family. It always has.

Cathy had spent ten hours a day researching with Kaizerious for six straight days after her arrival. She was tired, her mind was tired. Cathy had turned into her quarters for the night, lying in her bed with Skolla, the warwolf, beside her. Warwolves are genetically altered wolves; twice as strong, twice as large, and smart enough to understand ARW soldiers on a basic level. In 2062, the Order of Aegis first began experimentation on genetic therapies and manipulation. Decades later, the process of breeding warwolves was perfected - a process that was slow and took years to complete. Once warwolves are bred, they are placed in training simulations with their designated wolf-pack unit.

Just as she was settling in for the night, there was a knock on the door. Cathy answered, albeit slowly.

"The king would like a word. Follow me," said a royal knight.

Hesitantly, Cathy followed and signaled for Skolla to stay. After leaving one tower, the knight led her into another tower, down some stairs, across a small sunken courtyard, and along a deserted corridor where empty suits of armor stood sentinel along the walls. They were relics of House Drayfus - black steel with snake scales cresting their helms now dusty and forgotten.

Cathy was led to a door in a high tower. Inside, there were a few bookshelves filled with books, some luxurious chairs surrounded by lavish decorations; statues and paintings among other things. The room was carpeted, bright in color, to match the walls and ceiling. There was an open double-door leading to a balcony, with a telescope angled to the stars.

The royal knight gestured for her to go inside, and then he left. From another door in the room, King Kaydon entered. He was rubbing his hands when he noticed Cathy. "My apologies. I just came from the privy." He grinned.

"You summoned me, your Grace?" Cathy put herself on one knee and bowed.

He gestured for her to rise. "Like I said earlier, no need for all of that." He tapped his finger to his chin in interest. "It does surprise me to see that you're so familiar with our customs."

"Simply due to training, really. Nothing more."

King Kaydon nodded toward the balcony, heading there himself. "Come."

Cathy followed. The king put his arms over the parapet walls of the balcony and stared at the stars. Cathy mirrored him, not too sure what to make of this situation. She had never been alone with someone of royal lineage before. It's hard to know exactly how to act.

After a minute of silence, Kaydon asked, "What's it like out there?"

"Empty. Vastly empty. But then, not so much, if you know where to go." Cathy answered.

"I've often wondered. No room for a king who would abandon his people to travel among the stars. You wouldn't often think it of a king, but it can often feel like you're trapped."

Cathy waited in silence.

King Kaydon turned to face her, leaving one arm on the wall. "Trapped for all eternity to live in the same place."

"You're the king here. I'm sure you can travel if you so choose."

"And you'd be right to a degree. Only, it would be rather irresponsible for me to do so. But there is a better option."

"What option?"

He smiled. "Unite our world under one king. If I were to accomplish such a goal, there would be a lot more time for leisure such as travel."

"Sounds like an impossible task in the World Unknowing Peace."

"Yes, it does. The kingdom directly west of us is run by a backstabbing usurper who once was part of the Tolkran Kingdom. To the east is even worse... might as well call that kingdom a kakistocracy. And those are just two of the Grand Thirteen Kingdoms. But those who dream little accomplish little. But I don't. I don't dream little. I want to unite our world."

Cathy felt for that particular sentimentality. She knew all too well of war running in the blood of a family. That very thing is commonality on this planet. Never-ending conflicts of kingdoms fighting for the upper hand surely meant that war ran in just about every creature here. "You'd be a very powerful man if you were able to unite Omulice."

"That's way too much responsibility and work for me," Kaydon said, with a guffaw. As he laughed, he found his way off the balcony and onto one of his couches. When he sat, he pressed a button on the table next to him.

A servant came through the door. "Wine, please," he said to the servant. "Want any?" he asked Cathy.

Cathy took a seat on another couch. "I don't drink. Never liked the taste."

"Fair enough."

The servant left and returned very shortly with a glass full of red wine. She then let herself out of the room.

Chapter 18

Kaydon took a sip. "In truth, Lord Mauga would be a better king than myself. He was the one who ruled in my stead until I came of age, which was not too long ago. We have him to thank for the turnaround of the kingdom."

This was only recent knowledge to her. Before her trip here, she understood the Tolkran Kingdom was nowhere near the giant it was centuries ago. But she had been under the impression the kingdom was still on the decline. Interested, Cathy asked, "He sounds quite impressive. How did he turn it around?"

"The story is a long one, but I'll give you the short version."

"We have time," Cathy insisted.

Kaydon half-smiled. "Once upon a time, the Tolkran Kingdom was one of the greatest and largest kingdoms in the world. At its height, during the reign of King Kaylob." He hesitated for a moment. "Then it wasn't. Our luck turned sour, and our kingdom declined all the way, even through my father's reign. My father, King Garrol - he died when I was too young to remember him - and was killed by my sister, Erryn Wolph, who incidentally also murdered my uncle Bearon Wolph."

"That's a lot of family bloodshed to bear. I'm sorry," Cathy offered her condolences.

"No need. If my father was left in charge, our kingdom might already have been gone. But his death lead to Lord Mauga, who was the Warden of Northpoint and First Under-Reign, becoming acting king. Lord Mauga has always been a gentle and forward-thinking man. It was him, after all, that vastly progressed women's rights in our kingdom. Now women can become just about anything they ambition and train towards. All that was because of Lord Mauga, and it wasn't easy on him. It took him many years to do what he did with just as many years of backlash and resentment."

Cathy was silent.

"He did something I don't think I would've ever thought of. Now today, due to Mauga's foresight, the Tolkran Kingdom is on the rise for the first time in centuries. Who knew women could make such a difference?"

"Everyone else in the galaxy," Cathy joked, with a dry tone.

The king laughed. "You're probably right. The logic does seem simple, doesn't it? If a kingdom constantly suppresses half of its population, like so many kingdoms do this day and age, it suppresses half its potential."

Cathy held back a response. After all, she didn't want to offend a king.

"Of course, we still have a ways to go," Kaydon admitted. "Anyway, tomorrow we are celebrating the anniversary of my coronation. I want to invite you as an honored guest. What say you?"

Cathy wasn't too keen on the idea of wasting a day that she could otherwise spend productively. She was still in search of answers to the Brotherhood of Relics. Yet it would be bad manners to refuse a king. "I'd be honored of course," she said.

"Glad to hear it. I'll have someone escort you back to your chambers." Kaydon pressed the button, and someone entered the room. "I enjoyed our talk."

Cathy stood up. "Before I go, I would be remiss if I didn't ask about what you knew about the Brotherhood of Relics."

Kaydon smiled. "When I was informed we would have guests wishing to study that folktale, I didn't believe it at first. But here you are."

"Sounds to me like you know nothing."

"Sorry to say, I only know them as a myth. In time, I believe you will come to that conclusion yourself."

"Thanks for your time." Cathy bowed before following the lead of the king's servant. If the king himself knew nothing, Cathy wondered if she truly was wasting her time here. Alas, it was her mission, and she planned to see it through.

Chapter 19: The First Trial Begins
Error 66b

James Stone

"The trials that are held in the Vault of the Seven are unique in our galaxy. Other realities exist simultaneously and brush up against our own within the confines of the vault, which acts as an anchor. The Vault of the Seven, guardian of the Seven Weapons of Sin, serves as a meeting point between the past, present, and future. It is where all timelines converge and where every moment of time exists in one instance - the ultimate defensive tool against those unworthy," Jeremiah read from the Book of Sin.

Valiic and Geariic were at the head of the group as we stood just past the entrance gate. "Other realities, time convergences. Such technology is unheard of by any existing culture I know and is undoubtedly not Devisor in origin. And yet these... Precursors that created such a place as this must've been just as enlightened," said Valiic as he shifted his forcidion shield forward.

"Devisors versus Precursors, a race of technology, that I imagine must've been quite an exciting time in history," I stabbed away at the tension with a joke.

Jeremiah carried a calamitous look at my words despite it being well-received by the rest.

Everyone had their weapons pulled out. Geariic held his bulky, glowing warhammer tight in his hands. Shadow-Walker clutched his beloved Silent Dagger at the ready. Brad was loose with his shotgun, not fearful of what lay ahead, geared up in power armor and strapped up like a walking arsenal. Frost was light of arms and carried just a pistol-like corelinn weapon. Shadow was unable to convert my weapons to use the crystalized ammunitions the inhabitants of this planet use, leaving me to use corelinn weapons. That was the opposite story for Valiic. Shadow was able to convert his plasma cannon into a cannon capable of firing bursts of crystallized blasts.

The setting was elegant and mystical, yet dark and foreboding. Surrounding us was a cerulean rocky cave illuminated by the light of alien vine growth that crawled up the walls, some of which were even spreading into the cracks and burrowing into the rock like thick, indigo tentacles. Yet, this cavern of wondrous mythology was home to more than just the run of the mill rock. Much of the walls were streaked with a glass-like solid that glowed a deep blue and fought with the rock for dominance over the space.

To our luck, the cave called to us. The sole path was lit with only one direction to go.

As we stood, our collective cyberwatches started to go off, beeping red in alert. I read the display in my head: *"ALERT: Substantial Time Relativity Change Detected. Error 66b: Unable to compute change, cannot display ARW time."*

The fact that everyone who had a cyberwatch experienced the same thing all at once told me this wasn't just a malfunction.

"I'm no science wiz, so, uh... the hell is time relativity," asked Shadow-Walker.

Frost pulled up a holographic display on his cyberwatch and began to fiddle with the settings. "It means time in this location is moving at a significantly different rate of time than we're used to."

"Faster or slower?" I asked. My bones ached in anticipation of an answer I would otherwise rather not hear.

"It can't seem to tell."

A realization dawned on me. "Which means we could finish this trial in an hour and an entire year may pass by on this planet. In the words any idiot can understand, our efforts here may not amount to shivf. Our ball is completely out of our control, and fate has our balls in a vise grip." I kicked a rock. "Frak!"

Geariic was just as agitated as I was. "This is some pigshivf!" He slammed his fist into the wall hard enough to blast out debris.

Jeremiah closed his hands together and began to pray silently to himself.

"No use in feeling sorry for ourselves, uzzos. Let's get our heads in the game and get this shivf done." He gave pause and looked over at us. "Now tell me, who among you wants the smoke?!" Frost pounded his chest, which seemed to get a response. "I said, who wants the smoke?!" His call to arms successfully hyped everyone up.

Chapter 19

The mood lightened at his words, and there was a resounding, "Oorah!"

"Valiic, take point and look scary. Geariic, on our ass. Jeremiah, you're in the middle. Everyone else, we'll fill the gaps," I commanded. "Everyone on alert. Others have taken shots at these trials before and no longer have their lives. Anighta even lost her whole team. This isn't going to be like walking through the breeze."

We formed a column formation, which was a common military formation to take, especially in narrow environments. Starting at the lead, we spaced each other off into groups in case of ambush. Valiic, being in front, controlled the group with arm or verbal signals. Each of us had a standard position we took but must be flexible for any given situation. As a group and independently, we worked to make traversing hostile territory as safe as possible.

"Who's this Anighta?" Valiic asked.

"The lady who gave us that book." I nodded to the book in Jeremiah's hand.

His eyes went low. "May her team rest in comfort and peace."

"That must've been hard on her," added Frost.

"Chill, guys. Those people you never knew died," Shadow-Walker gave laughter to his joke, brightening the grim mood. "But that's not going to be us."

Valiic continued to lead us down the stone pathway that wound like a snake. I was right behind. It started around a right bend, then a left, and back to a right. This occurred for just roughly ten minutes, all while taking us lower and deeper into the caves. Eventually, we reached a point where the cave ended into a small open, with rectangular boulders pinching the gap tighter. We crawled through the tunnel, which barely allowed Valiic and Geariic room to maneuver, until it gave way to a larger opening, which made our whole company stop for a moment to scout our next route. Before us lay a ravine, the emptiness of which was vast, and the walls were not as shiny and bright, but dulled and aged.

Valiic pointed with his weapon to a path next to him. "I suggest we try the pathway instead of scaling down the ravine."

"I'm all the way with Valiic. Let's try the easy way." Shadow-Walker turned to Geariic behind him, who stared back with a bit of mockery.

Geariic snickered. "Afraid of a challenge, Shadow?"

Shadow-Walker joined in and laughed with Geariic. "I'm a sniper for a reason. I prefer to stay far away from danger."

Frost joined in, with a grin. "Careful now, Shadow. If you stay too far away from the enemy, you'll have to mail them your bullets, you bum." Shadow-Walker got a kick from that.

Following Valiic, we walked through the archway of the path and found the cave scaled up in size exponentially; matter of fact, it hardly looked like a cave any more. I felt small, like a toy soldier in a room made for giants. Below were two oversized floating slabs of rock and glass leading onward, but below that, which tugged at me wrong way the most, was nothing but a vast ocean of emptiness that seemed to descend forever. An endless abyss of purplish fog, with no visible floor.

"Well shit, I ain't 'bout tah stand 'round wit my thumb up my azz." Brad leaped to the nearest rock. I followed right behind him, jumping a distance of a few meters. Each platform was about three or four meters.

"Nah, Brad, you got me twisted. Big Daddy came for the smoke, so you best believe I'm coming." Frost was next.

"Den don't fall behind, Iceberg," Brad poked back.

Shadow took the hint and did the same. Jeremiah, Valiic, and Geariic were hesitant. Valiic, at the edge of a flat surface, looked down at us. The floating rock was a few meters jump to get to and a few meters lower than the surface.

I looked over at Brad, Frost, and Shadow, all of which shared the floating rock with me. "Clear out, boys."

Brad caught on to what I was thinking fast. "Next one. Now." He led the three to the second floating platform.

"James, I don't know about this. You may've cleared room for me, but if I misjudge where to land--" Valiic started.

"No. I get it, Valiic. I'll stop you from falling."

"That's a lot of meat to stop," Shadow joked. I shot him a sour look.

"Frak it all!" Geariic took a running leap past Valiic and landed at the front edge of the floating platform.

His weight caused the whole thing to dip to his side suddenly! And I flailed my arm backward to stay afoot. Geariic landed hard and started to fall forward towards me. Then the platform recovered, which stopped both of us from falling.

Geariic added with wry amusement, "See? No reason to cower. Well, actually, not very warrior-like either. Aye, Valiic?" he teased.

Valiic ignored him and prepared to jump. Geariic, seeing this, stepped to the other end of the platform. Valiic hit, and with a more balanced weight, the platform handled it better. Meaning we did, too.

Jeremiah was last. He landed on the platform with relative ease, almost touching down as light as a feather.

"Someone's light on their toes," I said.

"After following two maelkii, I would assume that's how it would look." Jeremiah smiled with his eyes.

He has a point, I thought, leaving it at that.

I was the first to take the next leap to the others on the second platform. With the ace ability I was fated, such a task as this was as easy as tossing a rock into an ocean.

The second rock was a twin in appearance to the first rock. In spite of that, the orientation was different. The first was straight ahead, while this one was to the right of the first. And from the second, I could now see our next destination like a glowing sign. Multiple flat surfaces of rock, meters in area, made a jagged and rough staircase downward and led down into another cavern. The first step of which was also to the right of the second floating platform, completing almost a spiral of steps when everything was laid together in my noggin.

As we jumped lower and lower, I began to question the space around me. The rocks seemed to float or hang, but there was far too much space for this place to make any sort of sense. The last step led into a small cave, which bent sharply to the right. We waited, as Geariic and Valiic were the last two to join us. We took the same formation as before and traversed through the cave, only to find the right bend was the only turn. It gave way to a long, ten meter surface that overlooked an unending gorge which surrounded everything now.

A few of us marched to the edge of the overlook to see what stood before us. A sight that was something to gawk at. In simple terms, it was the largest floating platform of rock thus far. But that was just a point on the painter's brush, and he had only begun paint the picture.

What was before us was nothing short of a damn battleground. Columns crafted of a combination of glowing vines, glass, and rock towered at different heights, placed all around the arena to act as lighthouses of sorts, for every single one of those columns had several bulky stones imbedded inside that illuminated the battlefield like yellow stars. The brightest of all the lights was carved in the center of a massive gate that carried strikingly similar characteristics to the gate that first led us into the trial, only it was scaled up to fit a far larger behemoth.

Under the light of the columns, the battleground was designed with three main lanes, with the singular goal of hashing one enemy against another. A place of fighting to test one team's will to the will of another. A warrior such as Valiic should get a thrill out of it. Then again, he wouldn't be the sole one among us partial to a good battle here and there.

Most of the battleground was structured around the middle of the three lanes. The aforementioned enormous gate was at the far end of the middle lane. The same middle lane leading to the gate started with high-ground nearest to our side and ran down a set of stairs with a dozen steps. Those stairs gave way to a flat area with a circular ring glowing of foreign symbols and elevated from the floor. However, it would be foolhardy to take such a path if one wanted to reach the gate, and that was due to the hard fact that the gate was level more in line with the start of the middle lane. Meaning, the area under the stairs was a few meters lower than the perch of rock the gate rested.

The other two lanes were more simplistic in design; the right started low and gave way to various flat boulders that led up to a hidden area covered by a roof of rock and glass, while the left lane started with a wide platform nearest to us then gave way to an even larger area below it. Half a dozen pillars of floating rock surrounded the battleground at higher positions and gave sightlines to the right and left lanes. Hopefully, that wouldn't leave us preverbal fish in a barrel.

I held my closed fist over my head. "I can't imagine that I'm the only one who believes our first trial will be held here." I gestured to the floating battleground.

"Agreed," said Valiic. His eyes were studying the layout of the arena. "It's an area made for battle."

Chapter 19

"So what's the plan?" Shadow asked.

"Jeremiah. See what you can find out in the book," I commanded.

Jeremiah, still furthest away from the edge, began to dig through the book for clues. Interested, Frost hovered over his shoulder.

"So we wait." Shadow-Walker sighed. He found himself a boulder and took a seat on it. "So if we complete this entire sin-test-thing or whatever, does that make us heroes on this planet or something?"

"They should've never needed us in the first place, if you ask me," Geariic scoffed. "How weak does a species have to be to have outsiders like us fight their battles for them?"

"They tried." Jeremiah stopped reading to reply.

"What do you mean *tried?*"

"They did. Many volunteers attempted to enter these trials, and very few made it back alive."

"Maybe they deserve their fate, then," Geariic snarled. The head of his warhammer was against the ground, and Geariic passed the handle of his hammer from left to right hand repeatedly, moving it like a lever.

Not wanting to get dragged into this debate, Jeremiah left it alone and went back to reading.

"And your brother, Alabon? Does he deserve the same fate?" Valiic countered. He stood beside Shadow, who was still sitting and waiting for his question to be answered.

"Leave him out of it!" Geariic snapped back.

"He was wounded during a trial, was he not? I mean not to anger you, Geariic. All I aim to do is for you to see the position of these innocent citizens."

"Nobody's innocent," Frost added.

"Maybe not, but they're in need, and we're in a position to help them. It is the honorable thing to do," Valiic insisted.

"Honor." Geariic spat down the abyss. "A true warrior seeks power. Not honor."

Valiic slammed his shield on the ground. "Steion said that same thing to me once!" Rare that I see Valiic so worked up. "You sound more like a dytirc than a maelkii to me."

Geariic stopped playing with the handle of his hammer and instead picked it up a bit before slamming it back down. "Blame your own species! It's the maelkii's fault. I wasn't raised in a glorious house like you or your darling cohinla Narrisa--"

"Watch it!" Valiic snapped. I stood up, ready to stop a fight.

Geariic ignored him. "I was cast out. I was left on the street to fend for myself. I was called a freak. A monster. I had nothing from the moment my skin turned metallic. I fought my way to the top, and not with your pigshivf morals. My brother and I both did, and we did it alone."

Neither made a move, nor did they back away. I stepped in the middle of them. Brad, who had his legs over the edge of the overlook, stood up as well and joined me. "You've both said your piece. Now it's time to put it away. We will have plenty of time to hash this out after our mission. Right now, we need to stay allies."

"Fools give full vent to their rage, but the wise bring calm in the end. Proverbs 29:11," Jeremiah added.

Geariic spat in the abyss again and turned away from Valiic so he could no longer see him.

"Gotta say... not quite the answer I was looking for," Shadow jested, looking to Valiic, hoping to catch a laugh. Valiic, while not giving in to laugher, loosened up at the joke.

Valiic looked down at Shadow. "Heroes are born of ashes and tragedy and rise up to face extraordinary odds. I never claimed to be nor did I want to be a hero. I only ever wanted to be one thing - a noble warrior."

There was silence for a while until Jeremiah jogged over to us, Frost right behind. "I think I've got this figured out. I have a direct quote. *For the Blade of Wrath is not merciful on the soul and cannot be sought by those who are weak of will or strength. Before those can be tested worthy of wrath, those must prove worthy in the eyes of darkness."* Jeremiah looked up to us. "I believe we are to face foes as the first test."

"I take it we need to defeat the foes and the gate will open," Shadow theorized.

"Sounds just like a game. And I'm the cheat code, baby," Frost cheered.

"Hold it." Jeremiah pushed his finger against the nose bridge of his glasses. *"A champion will arise to guard his gate. Those do not enter less the champion gives way."* Jeremiah took a breath. "I believe this part of the trial will be more complicated than just defeating a champion. There's much more written, but I'm having a bit of trouble unjumbling everything."

"So we'll figure it out as we go," Geariic growled. "But if we stand here for one more minute nerding over a stupid book, I swear I'm just going toss someone on the battlefield."

"We're on the clock," I informed. "Can't afford to wait forever."

"So it's game time?" Frost brightened.

"It is."

"Whoo hoo, baby. Big Daddy's coming! Time to clown on fools." He pounded his fist to his palm.

I jumped down off the rock surface first and landed at the base of the battlefield. I looked back up and shouted, "Shadow. Stay up there in case we need sniper cover. Once you are down here, there's no getting back up."

"Cool with me," I heard him respond.

Just in front of me, at the base of the middle lane, was an oval-shaped machine made of onyx and gold shards of glass and metal, with many metallic spikes extending from the machine like branches on a tree. An aura of alien symbols and words swirled around it like a haze.

Everyone except Shadow-Walker followed me down one way or another. We stood at the top base of the middle lane - a large platform that sat opposite the massive gate. Two large columns cut the centers of the three lanes and acted as large pieces of cover. Of the three lanes, the left was the most exposed, which could bone any one of us if we left our asses wide open. For the badasses of the group who enjoyed close quarter combat, the right lane was just the thing. Consisting of many small boulders and tighter corridors that led into a rock and glass ceilinged room. However, the middle lane seemed to be the focus of everything. Down in the area with the alien ring, below the gate's platform, it was covered on all three sides by small roomed corridors primed for funneling in whatever foes were to come our way. Needless to say, our hands were going to get dirty.

I commanded, "Scout right, Valiic and Frost. Geariic, take middle. Brad, with me up the right. Jeremiah--"

"I'll stay here," he finished for me.

I nodded, and we all went our specific ways. I maneuvered down the few boulders on the right, with Brad behind me. That led me to a small rectangular open space not many square meters in size that connected back to the middle lane with a small corridor. Turning left, I was able to see Geariic march down the stairs of the middle lane. The very same corridor led to the leftmost lane, where I saw this Valiic and Frost march deeper into the open area on the left side.

I headed up the short batch of risers, which took my ass into a much larger room flanked all around with pillars and rocks that would be key for cover. At the center was another mysterious machine of Precursor creation, a twin of the one at the base of the middle lane. Lining the left wall of the room were a few cutouts between the walls that overlooked the middle lane and one that connected to the surface that led to the gate. At the back of the room was a cave that dipped slightly up and towards the left. I took a peek inside and saw Frost and Valiic marching down.

"Seems the left and right lanes connect at the back," Valiic observed.

"Almost like a horseshoe," I added. "Geariic?" I called over my cyberwatch.

"The middle is a fishbowl, with many angles looking down at it. You don't want to fight in here," said Geariic.

"I think I just heard a challenge." Frost smiled, with his finger in the air. I gave a disapproving nod.

"Shadow. How's it look from up top?"

"Lonely." He half-laughed

"Speaking of... where the hell are the foes?" Frost balled his fist repeatedly with irritation.

"You know, guys, maybe if we push really hard on that big gate, it'll open," Shadow-Walker joked.

"Instead, you could do something useful, like be on the lookout for approaching enemies," I joked back, with a voice that was light hearted.

Valiic and Frost joined us on the right side, out of the cave, and caught sight of the mysterious machine. "We had one of those on the left," said Valiic.

Chapter 19

"That makes three," I concluded. "I think it's time we count heads and regroup at the base," I commanded over my cyberwatch.

We all made it back to the base of the middle lane quickly. I arrived to see Jeremiah touching the machine. "I believe the book references these as confluxes." He looked back into the book. *"Confluxes - pillars of information. Shjarrs seek to sacrifice themselves to a conflux, attempting to create another place of time and reality. In this act, they chance their life for an existence where those have lost or do not exist and pull that existence into fruition."*

"Those... I'm thinking *those* is us," I pondered.

"You're right," he confirmed.

Jeremiah's hand never left the conflux. All of a sudden, the ground started to rumble, the haze around the machine started to glow light as if it ran electricity, and an alien circle began to build up around the machine similar to the ring in the middle.

"Looks like things are 'bout to get spicy," Frost roared, with anticipation.

The book flipped pages all on its own. Jeremiah looked inside. *"In come the legions of priests and fanatics to spread their disease and light. Confluxes, keys to bring forth the champion, must be defended if those wish favor in the eyes of darkness,"* he read.

There was a startling screech that resonated off the walls and turned our heads.

"Incoming!" Shadow said over the comms.

Walls gave way down the back of the middle lane, sliding into the ground like doors, and shjarrs poured out. They were heading up the stairs for us.

These bread of shjarrs carried with them many similarities to what we witnessed when we first arrived on this planet. Dripping of black goo, these slender and long-limbed shjarrs shrieked and trotted up the stairs. None of them carried what you would call a face, and instead there was a jumbled mess of vein-like stems around where a face would normally be. Shadow-gray with violet accents, the creatures, looking metallic and robotic in nature, were not quite the size of the ones from the forest. The ones that came for us now were not as large as maelkii; no, they were roughly the size of humans. They gained speed with their burly legs. Both arms were extended out, ready to claw us to pieces with seven bladed fingers.

As far as time went, we were coming up on empty. We fired bullets, dropping those shjarr priests faster than I could count. Each one that died exploded into parts with small sparks like busting confetti. We had but a single goal - protect the conflux.

"I don't mean to break up the group, but some shjarrs are heading to the right and left machine-thingies," Shadow called.

Shivf! We have three to protect!

I joined Geariic's side. "Take the middle, and buy us a moment."

Geariic grinned like a child and blasted off, pounding through shjarrs like a train. He stopped by the stairs and started to swing his warhammer, launching herds of shjarrs away.

"Listen up!" I shouted over the battle. "Valiic, cover the left conflux. Frost, you got the right. Jeremiah, stay with me by the center one." I looked to Brad, his visor stared back at me. "Do what you do best, route and aid where needed." Everyone gave me acknowledgement and were off.

Valiic started down the left platform and jumped to the open space. His side seemed the lightest on foes. Frost already had built up ice armor over his body and slid down some boulders to get to the right.

"Heads up! The pain train is coming through!" he cheered. Brad followed Frost, picking off shjarrs heads with well-aimed shotgun blasts.

"You all good, Jeremiah?" I asked. He was half-behind the conflux, with one hand over it. He looked up from the book and nodded.

I raised my endothermic rifle and got to work. Geariic did most of the heavy lifting in my lane, while I picked off stragglers. Though we had a rough start, we began to clear the shjarrs faster than they could enter the battle. Could they really be as powerful as Witna claimed? After all, not a single shjarr was getting within licking distance of the confluxes. Was this all? Or are we just too strong?

"James! Bigger shjarrs incoming!" I heard Valiic shout.

"Must be the fanatics," Jeremiah said from behind me.

Christ almighty!

I rushed over to the left platform and saw Valiic shielding the conflux. His shield was planted to the ground, and he was blasting away crowds of shjarrs. Multiple levels of staircases led up to openings at the back. Shjarr fanatics, the same monsters we saw in the forest, came charging out. I focused my weapon on them, taking one, then two out. They took many more shots to drop than the priests did.

One charged into Valiic's shield dead on, and Valiic slid backwards but held his ground. Shadow hit it in the head with an accurate sniper shot.

Two more fanatics charged at Geariic. He took one swing and smashed one, launching it with an explosion that blasted from the head of his warhammer. The other hit his other side and fell upon impact. Geariic snickered. "Haha. Pathetic." He stomped the fanatic into the ground, crushing it apart, its goo getting all over his leg. Geariic took another swing into a crowd of shjarrs. Then another and another. His next swing missed completely, then another hit nothing but air. "GAHH! What in Sam-Hell is going on?!" Geariic's swings became wild and frenzied.

I jumped down from my perch, covering myself, and was over to Geariic in seconds. His swing came at me! I ducked under and slid to his side. I grabbed his arm, trying to calm him.

"Who's that?" Geariic jerked his arm, and I had to let go so I didn't go flying.

"Geariic! Geariic! Calm down. It's James," I shouted.

"James?"

"Yes."

"I can't see!" He looked towards me, and I saw his eyes. Over his metallic skin were black, smoky veins stretching over his neck to both eyes, which were covered with a green sludge.

"Hang in there, Geariic." I tapped him on the chest.

Brad peeked from one of the right lane perches and fired an explosive blast from the underbarrel of his shotgun, and it blasted away dozens of shjarrs with an explosion of crystalized water. He switched to his light machine gun and covered us.

"Jeremiah?" I shouted at him.

He was still behind the conflux. "What?"

"Geariic can't see!"

Jeremiah rushed over to us, taking me a bit by surprise. I didn't expect him to jump so fast into danger. He saw Geariic's eyes.

"He touched the goo!" Jeremiah eyes went wide.

"And?" I urged him on.

"The goo causes blindness within seconds of touching it... and eventually kills."

"Kills!" Geariic jerked from shock.

I shoved Jeremiah on the shoulder. "You knew that, and you didn't mention it?!"

He was frozen, unsure of what to say.

"Can it be fixed?" I asked.

"With medical attention. Nothing here."

"There's gotta be--" My eyes caught sight of the book. "Book! Check the book."

He turned through the pages. "Oh, here-here! *And so the essence of the fanatics leaves those cursed. Those cursed must seek perfection in the dark eye.*"

"Dark eye?"

"Stonewall!" I heard Brad call.

My eyes darted to his location; he was on an overlook between the middle and right lanes, and I saw him nod towards the middle.

"Dat shit lookz like ah eye from up here," Brad said.

"The ring! It's the ring in the middle!" I started to lead Geariic through the crowds. "I got you, Geariic. Follow me."

He did as instructed.

"Hear that, everyone?" Shadow called. "Avoid the goo dropped by dying fanatics. If you goons can't manage that, the circle in the middle will unblind you."

Brad cleared the way, with some help from Shadow-Walker. I led Geariic inside the circle. There was a faint breeze, and the circle lit up blue. Like magic, the goo vaporized right off Geariic. None was left.

"James. I don't know if I've been so happy to see your ugly face in my life." Geariic jabbed me with a friendly punch in the shoulder.

I didn't let his insult phase me, especially knowing it wasn't true. "Alright, you big bastard," I laughed, "don't get all emotional on me."

"Snipers!" Shadow shouted.

"GET DOWN!" Geariic shoved me to my ass. I saw glass shards as thick as daggers plunge into Geariic, hitting him in the chest where my head would've been. Those glass shards fell to the ground, with blood on the tips. Blood! They made Geariic bleed! "If you die, this mission gets a whole lot harder. Can't have that. Got my brother to think of." Geariic wiped at the wound.

"You're injured."

"It isn't deep. Worry 'bout yourself." Geariic ran up the stairs and pounded away some shjarrs.

Jeremiah shouted from the back, "As written in the book, those snipers are called shjarr zealots."

Does it matter? I thought.

I stood up, gathered some strength in my legs, and leaped up to a ledge that connected to the right lane. I shot a few shjarrs and caught sight of Frost sliding on a frozen floor, encased in ice armor, and slicing down a shjarr with a sword made of ice.

"Whoo hoo! Robot or not, you're *getting* this ass whopping," Frost taunted. Another shjarr, hiding from his view, bashed him to the ground. "Damn baby, you gonna do me like that?"

"You good, Frost?" I called.

Frost was up quick. "Hang on, uzzo. Big daddy has a date with this turd with teeth. Promise it'll be a short date." He tossed his ice sword into its chest, and it exploded into shards.

I realized worrying about him was a misplaced feeling. He was well-equipped to handle his own shivf. Weapon high and ready to go, I made my way back to the middle conflux to protect it. On the way, with aid from Shadow-Walker, I shot down some of the shjarr zealots perched on the floating platforms past the arena.

Shjarrs were coming in hot, just as before, and coming out of the walls. Only now they were swarming in faster than we could dispose of them.

These shjarrs were stronger than the ones from earlier, and upon looking with a longer eye, I noticed their armor seemed a bit thicker. In actuality, the shjarrs numbered roughly the same, but they just took longer to kill, making it seem like there were more.

I kept firing until I heard a click. As I grabbed for another clip from a pouch, I felt nothing but lint.

"I'm out of juice!" I shouted.

"Here." Jeremiah unstrapped the backpack and shoveled his hand through it. He found more clips and tossed them to me. I shoved the extras in my pouches and reloaded safely behind some cover.

Just before taking more shots, I tossed in an endothermic grenade. It exploded in an array of blue-tinted crystals and took down half a dozen shjarrs. I turned to a group and fired at a shjarr priest. It was killed in seconds as the bullets melted its body. The shjarr then exploded in sparks and brilliance.

"James!" Jeremiah yelled.

I turned to see a behemoth of a shjarr centimeters in front of me! Big, bulky like a bear, I barely managed to duck under its bladed arms. It then dematerialized in a second.

"Behind you!" Jeremiah shouted.

I turned once again to see it in front of me. It had teleported! Just then, a few bullets caught it in the face, and it stumbled backwards, nearly falling. I put a few rounds in it myself until it exploded, dead.

"And the great apostles shall be called in the eve of the confluxes complete connection," Jeremiah read from the book.

"So we're almost done babysitting these things?" I asked.

He nodded. "I believe so."

I smiled and kept firing. Geariic, now a professional at dodging the leftover goo of fanatics, was in a tussle with an apostle. He gained the upper hand and tossed it to the floor and finished it off with his warhammer. Then I saw him spit on the thing with disrespect.

The shjarrs fell faster than I could see them, but still the numbers were piling up, and we were in danger of being overrun at some point. More fanatics started coming out and charging. I pulled out two pistols and started to dual wield. Brad blasted another group of enemies with his underbarrel launcher.

I heard a sudden stir of noise behind me, and I rotated to face the disturbance. I caught the end of a tussle between Jeremiah and a shjarr he had just tossed over the ledge.

"Good shivf." I saluted him, but he wasn't looking just yet.

Chapter 19

Bang!

I found myself lying on my back, with my head aching. I looked around and saw Jeremiah also pulling himself up. But that wasn't what caught the bulk of my attention. I was on the edge of a small crater. I noticed some blood leaking from a few cuts on my shoulders and arms.

Jeremiah rubbed his head. "You alright, James?"

"I'll be fine. Just gotta rub some dirt on my cuts and walk it off." I responded over the ringing in my ears.

"One of those apostles warped right behind you just as it exploded," Jeremiah informed.

Just then, Shadow-Walker landed by us, rolling awkwardly and finishing on his back. His scout rifle was aimed above him, and he shot once, swiped his rifle over a bit, and shot again. I saw two shjarrs' broken bodies land on the sides of him.

Shadow-Walker sighed. I reached my hand to help him up. "They started coming from behind me. Had to break position."

"Nothing to do about it now." I pointed to the high surface over the left lane. "Take position there, and support Valiic." He nodded and marched over there. "Let's thin these numbers!" I commanded everyone.

Thus far, none had managed to make a significant dent in the confluxes we were protecting. I dropped to my knee, feeling some fatigue from the battle. My lips felt dry, my stomach empty. We had been defending this area from what seemed like hours but in actuality may've been thirty minutes. There was still gunfire from the left and right sides; however, the middle lane was beginning to look dry, mostly due to Geariic's efforts. How he could still swing that big-ass warhammer with the power he did was beyond me.

"Above us!" Jeremiah warned.

I turned my gun and fired at the shjarrs leaping down at us. They must be leftovers from when Shadow-Walker was up there. A few landed by Jeremiah, but I couldn't let up on the ones above. I heard a struggle. Shivf, I can't let him fend for himself.

I brought my aim down and saw a few of the shjarrs falling off the edge, and a few more on the ground in pieces. Jeremiah was unharmed.

Not one to witness what took place, I could only spin the wheel as to what happened.

Focus, I thought.

Just then, the last dozen landed on the battlefield. I dodged two, losing my rifle in the process. I pulled out pistols and was able to blow holes in a few. My senses caught fire, and I was just in the nick of time to avoid a fatal slice from a shjarr priest that came from behind. However, it still managed to slice up my tank top and part of my upper chest before I blew its metal face in with a good shot.

"AHH! Mother of... FRAK!" the voice of Shadow wailed.

I finished off the foes in front of me and saw a shjarr right behind Shadow, who had fallen to his side. Thick blood dripped down the shjarr's claws. It went for another swipe at the downed Shadow-Walker!

I nearly shivfed my guts right out. How could I let this happen? Not again. I can't lose another one. *I can't.*

Mother's mercy answered. Or rather, Brad did by her grace. He was there in time. He intercepted the shjarr's attack with his gun. He then kicked the shjarr on the knee, twisting it off its footing. With his shotgun back in place, he blasted it in the head.

That's when my legs started moving. On their own, they took me to Shadow's side.

Frost came in through the comms. "What was that screech?"

"Don't worry about it. Hold your location," I answered.

Multiple open, gushing wounds started at the blade of his right shoulder and stretched down his back. Blood mud-red and darker than human blood had already spilled its way to the surface Shadow-Walker lay on.

Now on my knees, I looked down at him. He was shaking.

"Frak, James. This... grrah... really hurts," Shadow said through grinding teeth.

"Don't talk, Shadow." I pulled out medical bandages given to us by the corelinns.

Jeremiah joined me. And without needing to be asked, Brad was at the front edge, defending the area.

"James, you better give a hell of a speech at my funeral, or I'm not going," Shadow joked, his voice almost at a whisper.

Chapter 19

His joke dragged a light laugh from me, but it was in spite of the situation. His ordeal was crushing my heart to watch. Each moment he drew closer to death, I could feel myself giving in to sorrow.

"Hold the bandages." Jeremiah grabbed my arm. "Let me try something first."

I nodded.

"But I need you to cover us. I can see more enemies coming."

He was right. In they poured through the doors at the back of the left lane. They came as if knowing our unit was in a weakened, fragile state.

"Brad. Protect the middle. I'll help Valiic," I commanded.

He took off without acknowledging my words.

I had to do my part in all this. I got to my feet, leaving the bandages by Shadow-Walker. Guns ready, leaping down to the same level as Valiic, I started punching holes into whatever unfortunate enemy I saw. A fanatic charged right at me, but I sidestepped and tripped the creature. With it on its back, I dowsed it with more rounds than was probably needed, but hell, did it feel invigorating. I was pissed off and showed no mercy to these fraken machines.

Eventually, I made it to Valiic's side, and we both held the area.

"Tell me he's going to make it." Valiic's eyes begged for a specific answer, an answer I knew I wouldn't be able give him.

"It's bad." That was the only way I could think of to respond.

He fell silent, and I thought I could see a tear falling down his check. In the middle of a battle, it was hard to be sure. But we did what we had to. We kept fighting. I faced the enemies head on and gave no ground. Even though I was fierce in my will to fight, I couldn't blame Valiic for occasionally sneaking peeks back at Shadow. Maybe I should've, too. Then again, is that a truth I wanted to face right now? Honestly, I'd rather face a million shjarrs by myself than see whether or not Shadow was still alive.

That was the last wave of enemies. The time came when we finally finished the last of them. All without another major incident. No more came from the doors. Matter of fact, the doors had closed themselves.

All of the shjarrs were destroyed, and only one thing lingered on my mind. Valiic was already looking backward. Tears were in his eyes - tears of joy. "James. Look," his voice creaked.

I finally forced myself to look backward. And to my delight, Shadow was sitting with his legs over the edge of the surface, overlooking us. His shoulder and back were completely wrapped in white bandages. I smiled, holding back tears. Nothing else could've lifted my spirits like this moment did. Valiic tugged on me. We both made our way back.

As we were approaching, Jeremiah helped Shadow-Walker up and back to the middle. We arrived seconds after them. Shadow was resting with his back against one of the columns, with Jeremiah next to him. Brad was on recon, walking around with his gun up and searching for leftover foes. Frost just came in from the right side and took in Shadow's injuries for himself. Geariic leaned against a boulder next to the conflux, eating food from our supplies.

Shadow smiled. "Valiic, you're looking a bit red in the face. Those tears for me?"

"Tears of joy. Training a new recruit to take your place is no fun."

Shadow laughed. "I'm quite irreplaceable. Really one of a kind."

I found myself at Shadow's side, lightly pulling up a bandage to have a peek.

He swatted. "Come on, dude, be a man. It's only a near-death wound, nothing to see," he joked.

I ignored him and snuck a peek of the wound for myself. The light wasn't there to aid, but what I did see was nothing short of a miracle. I saw no stitching; however, the wound looked to be seared shut. From what it was previously to now looking damn near healed, and I was in awe.

"That was bloody fine work, Jeremiah." My eyes were still glued to the wound.

"God's will is strong. It is Him you should thank."

"Please," Geariic sneered. "There is no such thing. What happened was all your own skill. Recognize your own abilities instead of thanking an imaginary being for them."

"Let the man believe what he wants," Frost countered.

I was not one to believe in fairy tales. Surprised to say, I was with Geariic in that. Only question was how he managed to save Shadow-Walker. I let the bandage fall back into place. I stood up, looking at

Jeremiah. "How? Don't get me wrong here, I'm thankful as all humanly possible. But really, I must know."

Jeremiah shifted himself. "You flatter me. All I did was use a powerful healing agent and pray."

"Healing agent?" Frost asked.

"The corelinns may not thrive in areas of combat, but their technology for healing is rather advanced."

"I'll be damned," I smiled. I was never more thankful that we were in the good graces of such an unbelievable species.

Brad came up to me, just now wrapping up his recon. His visor glued to me, his arm pulled out something from one of his pouches, and he reached out. Gravity pulled a cross necklace down, and it spun in his hand by its chain. It was mine.

I quickly gazed down to my upper chest and realized that necklace my mother gave me was gone. Likely cut off when that shjarr sliced my tank top.

"Here." Brad handed me the neckless. "Next time, don't lose somethin' so preciouz tah yah."

I nodded, and he left.

I let myself fall down and rest on my back. We may not be done, but I needed a moment. Valiic and Frost started to pass around some quick snacks and drinks for everyone. I was tapped on the shoulder and handed some water, which I took my share of gulps from. It was our moment to rejuvenate and resupply our munitions from the backpacks.

Chapter 20: The Gatekeeper
Error 66b

James Stone

The first trial was not over. That much was as clear as freshly spit-shined glass. Though our aching, bruised, and weary bodies had some much needed time to recover. Geariic and Brad had split off earlier to scout around, neither being much on sitting around.

"We can't just sit here forever," Frost said after a few minutes.

"The gate's still sealed, and there are no enemies in sight." Shadow shrugged. An action he regretted by the wince of pain that came over his face. He rubbed his shoulder.

Jeremiah had been looking through the Book of Sin for some time. He read, *"The champion waits... waits for eyes of darkness. For the eyes will judge those, mark those, and sing to those. They will decide if you are real."*

Shadow chimed in. "Is it just me, or is this stuff starting to sound like we are going to get boned eventually? I really don't like the sound of the darkness and eyes and other weird shivf this book is talking about. Hell, the thing is called the Book of Sin. That shivf doesn't sound like a good thing."

Frost nodded in agreement.

"I hate to interrupt, but I must ask: How long has that been there?" I heard Valiic ask.

I sat up and looked at him and then in the direction he pointed. We all saw a bright fluctuating cube floating just at the top of the stairs, down the middle lane. Lime green in color, it illuminated the area around it and carried a subtle hum. Frost was already up to it.

"Frost, hang on there," I reached out my hand.

Frost stared for a second, squinting, then finally reached out his hand. As he touched it, the cube let out a single note chime. Frost grabbed his throat and fell to the ground! His hands fought over themselves, going from his throat to his head, and he gasped for air. He was choking and clawing at his head.

"Frost!" I shouted.

Everyone was up and coming to his aid.

Jeremiah and I tried to calm him down, while the others watched. But we might as well have been on another planet, because he was oblivious to us, clutching his head as if he couldn't hear us. We then saw his eyes. They were the same as when Geariic went blind. The cube must have cursed him!

Brad dashed over with his shotgun and shattered the cube with one shot. That was when we heard a chime go off, and then another, until five total rang.

Valiic picked up Frost and put him over his shoulder. He flailed around and screamed. Even still, he wasn't able to get out of Valiic's clutch. Hastily, Valiic took Frost to the lower level in the middle and placed him in the circle.

Frost recovered, coughing. "That... that hit me hard. I felt like...like something was screeching in my head. But, it was so hypnotizing."

"Why did it affect him much worse than Geariic?" I asked Jeremiah.

"Maybe it has different effects on different species."

Shadow tapped on my shoulder. "I hate to interrupt... actually, I don't, but uh--" He pointed at another cube. It was just past the edge of the left lane.

"There's more?" I asked.

Suddenly, the Book of Sin flipped open to a page. *"Oracles blink awake, the weapons of The Gatekeeper... speakers of time and reality, they construct existences where those are no longer real. For then The Gatekeeper can erase those from existence. Beware, for he is near."* Jeremiah stopped reading and gave me a haunted expression.

I knew immediately what had to be done. "Everyone spread out like wildfire! Destroy those green oracles before we're all six feet in the ground!"

It was do or die. Destroy the oracles before they kill us. That feeling had my nerves running races, and my reflexes benefited. I raised my rifle and fired at the one Shadow pointed at. My eyes and rifle then tore away from one location to another in search.

"I got one under the roof of the right lane," Valiic called.

"One'z down n' da back cave," Brad spoke.

That's four, I thought, *one to go.*

I cleared the way back up to the right lane's boulders and turned to return to the middle base by the conflux. Jeremiah and Shadow-Walker were already up there. I gazed over the arena and turned up to the area Shadow used to snipe from. Where the frak was the last oracle?

"Come to Big Daddy!" I saw Frost use some ice to climb to the base of the gate. From the top, he fired a few rounds from his pistol. "Kaboom! Got that boy!" he cheered.

There was a resounding horn-like sound that echoed off the walls, a deafening mechanical cry.

The book was active again. *"He comes. The Gatekeeper comes,"* Jeremiah muffled the words.

"On your toes, everyone," I commanded over the cyberwatch.

From the bottom of the middle lane, the surface gave way, and a monster rose up on a platform. He smashed through the ice recently created by Frost, and I was able to get a long look at the monster.

A few heads taller, The Gatekeeper looked to be the steroid-addicted, bigger brother to those shjarr apostles from earlier. With meatier armor, darker in tint, this beast started to loosen up its joints. It carried an arm congealed with dozens of glass shards spread sharp like a porcupine.

Just then The Gatekeeper closed his fist and extended his neck forward to let out another reverberating, booming cry; a sound loud as a Gjallarhorn.

Shjarrs seemed to pour in by the dozens! And a series of chimes started. Brad, like a cat, jumped on a near stone pillar and leaped even higher to a thin perch with a bird's eye view. He pulled out a trigger and clicked the button.

A series of explosions in the back cleared almost all the shjarrs out in seconds. Is that what he was doing earlier while we sat on our lazy asses for a break?

"Kaboom, baby!" Frost cheered and saluted Brad.

I pounded my chest and smiled. "Hell, yeah." The opening gave my ass the opportunity to rejoin Jeremiah at the middle lane.

Brad aimed his LMG and began firing it with incredible handling of the weapon directly at The Gatekeeper. No effect. In fact, it seemed like the bullets were being stopped before they even hit him due to a hexagonal shield that only appeared when it took damage.

"Everyone! The oracles are back!" Valiic informed.

With all the crazy shivf going on, I hadn't even caught eye of the oracle glowing in the middle lane. Quickly, I destroyed it with gunfire.

My teammate's voices rang in, and it was evident we managed to take out the five oracles in time.

I started, "Here's the game plan--"

"I love a good game plan," Frost jumped in.

"--We hold this arena down by zones, making sure to stay in line of sight of the oracles and take them out as soon as they chime back in. Cover your areas from enemies, and focus fire on The Gatekeeper when you see an opening. His shield has to break at some point."

"No, it won't," said Jeremiah from behind.

I didn't turn. I was close enough to hear him over my weapon. "What do you mean?"

"*The Gatekeeper bares a barrier unequaled, a barrier that exists in multiple realities. Destroy it in one, and The Gatekeeper replaces it anew. Forged in basks of darkness the Shield of Sin creates an isolated event to disrupt the barrier's manipulation of reality,*" Jeremiah finished reading. "And I think that's it in the circle."

Just as he said, lying down in the circle that uncurses you was a shield shrouded with black luminosity and color. It vibrated with power and dark energy that pulsed through the frame.

Only problem, and a dense problem at that: It was smack-dead in the middle, right at The Gatekeeper's feet. Figures.

I pointed my endothermic rifle at the metal monster and fired a whole clip. It didn't even get to him. The white holographic shield absorbed it.

The monster's eyes grew in anger. It raised its glassed arm, and the shards fired out - fired at me! I dipped out of the way and took cover, and the shards exploded into pieces as they collided into walls and boulders. The glass that was fired regrew back on its arm.

I gazed around my cover and saw Frost sneaking his way behind the beast. From behind it, he materialized as much ice as he could over its upper arms, shoulders, and torso. The kid had a pair, but the act only angered The Gatekeeper. It dematerialized itself and reappeared behind Frost, all the ice gone. He braced as the beast backhanded him in the chest, shattering layers of ice armor and knocking him towards me. Frost landed over the stairs, skidded, and collided into the wall in front of me. He couched, pulling himself up to a knee at a snail's pace.

Shadow-Walker and I unleashed our weapons on The Gatekeeper. In that very second, The Gatekeeper translocated right in front of me! On instinct alone, I activated my stasis shield just as it brought its sharp arm spinning around at my side. His power was that of a battling ram, which was sure as shivf more than I had anticipated, and I was knocked back towards the middle stairs. I landed on my feet and stopped myself. Mother's mercy let my shield take the full blow; however, the result was a nutt-pincher. One hit, and it flickered before the device sparked. Now complete trash, my stasis shield was fried and of no more use to me.

The Gatekeeper teleported in front of me again! Frost was behind it and tried to freeze it, but that hardly seemed to slow it down. Just then, Geariic came charging. With momentum on his side, he swung his warhammer straight into The Gatekeeper's body. The force, along with the explosion, knocked it backward a few meters. Even then, it still stood.

Geariic wasn't done. He closed the distance for another hit. The Gatekeeper used its arm to block the swing. Its free arm, the bladed arm, sliced at Geariic. It barely reached him, but the tip of the blade cut through his armor, exposing his stomach, back, and torso completely.

He let go of his warhammer and threw his shoulder into The Gatekeeper, attempting to bring it down. It was forced back, closing near the edge of the battlefield, but it held on from falling. Frost came around and started freezing the ground behind the machine, allowing Geariic to force it back further. It was nearing the edge.

The next moment was mine. With covering fire provided by Brad and Shadow-Walker, I dashed forward. I jumped over Geariic's back and slammed myself into The Gatekeeper. That last bit of force was enough to knock it off the edge.

"Oh, yeah! That's what you call a team freven effort!" Frost pounded Geariic on the back multiple times in celebration.

"Now all we gotta do is clear out the--"

I was cut off by Jeremiah. "Behind you!"

My instincts lit on fire, and I sidestepped a lightning fast slash by The Gatekeeper. It was back!

I forgot this thing teleports!

It spun itself, and the same arm came at me again. Only I didn't fully dodge this time. It sliced and drew blood from my chest, cutting through my tank top and skin like air.

I didn't hesitate and slid between its legs. My gut took me running back up the stairs to the top of the platform in the middle. A round shot right over my head. I dove into cover as Shadow-Walker sent back shots with his scout rifle, slowing the approaching shjarrs. His gun was resting against his wounded shoulder, and I made out spots of blood through the bandages.

"You'll reopen your wound if you push yourself too hard," I said.

"Because dying in this cave is a much better option," Shadow shot back, with a sarcastic jest.

"He'll be fine," Jeremiah reassured.

"Oh, and feel free to help at any time, Pastor," I half-joked.

"I'm best suited to you by providing informational aid." Jeremiah smiled, his eyes glowed with positivity.

Right as he finished speaking, more shards of glass smashed to pieces off the cover and walls. The Gatekeeper had made its way into the middle again. Geariic and Frost worked as a team to make its life hell. Geariic went for the legs and returned upward. He slammed the beast back down with a suplex, all while Frost continued to slow it down with ice.

The giant machine started to screech from frustration. For a second, its core glowed a hot array of colors before unleashing a devastating barrage of glass. It cut through the ice, forcing the two to step back. Some of the shards managed to cut small slices through Geariic's skin, while Frost managed to avoid most of the destruction.

The chimes sang again, and it had us all on edge. The oracles had reappeared all around the battleground, each one glowing brighter than before. We were not ready for this. Most of us had returned to the middle to help with The Gatekeeper. There was no way we can make it to all the oracles before they erased us from existence.

I reached for my rifle and pointed it at the nearest oracle in the middle, but The Gatekeeper's body was in the way. Shivf!

I was aghast as four simultaneous explosions ruptured around the battleground, shaking the rock beneath our feet. The oracle in the middle was then swiftly taken down by Brad, who just appeared by the gate.

"That'z all of dem," Brad said over the comms. "But don't expect 'notha one, cuz I'm outta explosivez."

That's what the explosions were for, my heart cheered with joy.

That moment was cut short as half a dozen apostles warped into the battle from seemingly nowhere. I unloaded my rounds at one right in front of me.

Click.

I was empty and out of time. The apostle downward-slashed at me, and I blocked with my rifle. It worked, but that stupid move cost me my weapon.

"Gun now!" I shouted the words to anyone who would hear.

I turned back and caught one of our spare weapons, tossed by Jeremiah, and aimed. Weapon up, I finished off the apostle attacking me and then aimed at different targets, unleashing my speed with rapid trigger presses.

Shadow-Walker kept pace, and I was unaware of how many shots we fired, because it would have been impossible to count. We didn't halt firing until the area was cleared of the sudden reinforcements.

The Gatekeeper, the sole foe, absorbed the bullets of all who fired at it. It lurked behind its towering shield like a snake ready to strike. Its eye gave away its intention to release a major attack like before.

But my eyes lingered elsewhere. Down the middle lane, Jeremiah grabbed the Shield of Sin, and he stuck it on his arm.

"When in Sam-Hell did he get there?" I heard Geariic's voice. And I was thinking the same.

The Gatekeeper let out a vengeful mechanical roar and disappeared in an instant. It was on one of the platforms hovering on the outside of the arena, charging itself for a massive attack. To make the shivf smell worse, more shjarr units were swarming in on us.

Geariic and Frost looked up to me for a plan.

Chapter 20

"I'll hold on to the shield so everyone can focus on the threat before us," said Jeremiah. He slipped into one of the small pathways near him.

"Brad, Valiic. Stay at the back of the battlefield. Keep enemies away from us if possible, but most importantly, make yourselves available to clear the oracles if they come back."

"Copy," I heard Valiic respond. I hadn't thought much of it until now, but it was especially soothing to hear from him since I hadn't seen him in an uncomfortably long amount of time.

My eyes jumped to Geariic and Frost, then to Shadow-Walker behind me. "Our task is killing us a gatekeeper."

We turned our attention back to The Gatekeeper, who was seconds from firing. Right as the storm of glass was freed, we jumped out of the way. Frost jumped to the top level on the right side, and Geariic to the left. Shadow and I stayed in our positions, where cover was the most generous.

We returned fire. The Gatekeeper fired off two more bursts of glass in quick succession, which Frost blocked one with a wall of ice. We evaded the second one. Shadow-Walker sniped a few rounds at The Gatekeeper's head, but its shield protected it. It teleported back to the middle and blasted at us again. Frost flared up his hand and created a small half-dome to protect himself. Geariic tucked himself out of the way for a moment.

While it was distracted, Jeremiah rolled out from his cover and stopped on one knee, with the shield pointed at The Gatekeeper. It spun towards him with a low metal grumble and readied another attack, but Jeremiah was quick and knew what he was doing.

The shield energized, and the black electricity flowed around it at incredible speed. The shield formed a swirling ball of goo. When it was nearly the size of the shield, the bolt of energy was unleashed. The shot made impact with the shield, and the shield shattered apart. Shadow-Walker and I were quick on our trigger fingers, and we unloaded our guns into The Gatekeeper. A grenade, courtesy of Brad's underbarrel attachment, exploded with direct impact on the machine. It tumbled back. Frost had frozen some icicles over The Gatekeeper and shot them down with his weapon. He then tossed a spear of ice right into it. The blade pierced its stomach.

It translocated away, attempting to hide. I heard Valiic's cannon start firing.

"Over here!" Valiic informed.

Shadow-Walker and I moved to position on the left lane. Valiic was at the back, using his shield to protect himself from a few enemy shjarrs and The Gatekeeper. We fired, and that's when I noticed its shield was once again intact.

Jeremiah ran up the stairs with the relic. "I'm going to hit him again. Be prepared."

The Gatekeeper was not able to go in peace. He aimed all he had at Jeremiah, who had started to create another energized ball. The glass came, but Jeremiah was nimble and able to keep concentration while dodging the glass.

Even then, he wasn't going to be able to dodge everything. That's when a few shards hit him on the shoulder and side. Then Geariic came to the rescue. His body blocked the rest, some of which even pierced his metallic skin.

Jeremiah was ready. He jumped past Geariic and fired the shield's bolt in the same manner as last time. The bolt splashed across The Gatekeeper's shield and shattered it to pieces. At the same time, everyone with a sightline on The Gatekeeper fired their guns, which tore into it as it let out an angry cry.

The chimes then came ringing in the caves.

Shivf! The oracles are back!

"The stupid things are getting faster!" Shadow yelled, with annoyance on his tongue.

"Everyone shoot down The Gatekeeper now!" I shouted.

"But the oracles--" Jeremiah started.

"It's a long odds chance, I know. Just do it."

I unloaded clip after clip into the machine. Shadow and Valiic fired as fast as they could pull the trigger. Frost let loose a few spears of ice, firing his pistol in between. Brad had out his LMG for maximum damage. Geariic, not having a ranged weapon, focused his efforts on the shjarrs.

"We are running dry on time!" I was sweating from fear and anxiety. The Gatekeeper needed to die and now.

Chapter 20

My heart pounded to a high tempo just as my instincts alerted me of something behind me. I didn't have time to turn but saw a jet of light fly by me. Like a sharp arrow, the beam of light pierced into The Gatekeeper. And it seemed to feel the power of the attack, falling to a knee. The arrow then exploded into tiny particles that then exploded once more. The force shattered the metal casing of The Gatekeeper as its glowing eye went black. It went silent and crashed to the ground, sparking and exploded itself apart into heaps of metal.

The oracles then disappeared as fast as they came, and the remaining shjarrs deactivated. I looked over my arms and down myself, almost not believing we just survived. I spun around.

"That light?" I was lost for words, not knowing what more to ask.

"I don't know. It flew right by me, just as it did you," Jeremiah admitted.

"I can give two fat shivfs where it came from. It bloody saved our lives!" Shadow-Walker cheered.

Geariic and Frost had formed up around the broken body of The Gatekeeper that we had just beaten. Frost fiddled around with the parts until Geariic interrupted by kicking it, sending a few pieces flying away. Frost looked up at Geariic with an irritated expression, and Geariic grinned with teasing teeth.

I reloaded my weapons and checked on my reserves. I was light after all the fighting.

"Jeremiah, how's the reserves look?" I pointed to the backpack.

He shuffled through. "At least half our stocks are used up."

Brad and Valiic had the other two backpacks. I wondered how much ammo was left in those.

Right before we began to relax, we heard a rumbling and looked to the gate that was blocking our progress. The gate spun back and disappeared. Trial one was now complete on the death of The Gatekeeper. A new path was open to us, and with it a new trial surely awaited. Seeing as how we kicked this trial right up the ass with zero graves dug, I had a better feeling about the second one.

Chapter 21: Coronation Anniversary
December 24, 2111

Catharine Darcrose

Cathy Darcrose rode on horseback towards a tourney held in honor of the anniversary of the king's coronation, escorted by Lord Mauga Lightbourne and a dozen of his men. Bannermen carried curtains of golden silk so thin, she could see right through them.

The entirety of King Road was decorated in honor of the king. Direclaw citizens stood at the edges of the road, cheering and waving banners in honor of their king. Cathy had heard talk that a hundred pavilions had been raised beside rivers and down main roads beyond the stronghold walls. Word was spread afar in an effort to attract attention to the event. She heard thousands of common folk were to watch the tournament.

After nearing the main gate leading into Direclaw, they turned off King Road and eventually found their way inside an oval shaped colosseum built close to the walls surrounding Direclaw. Cathy was led to her seat near the front row and down-path of the king's perched loge, where he sat on an extravagant throne. Royal knights accompanied King Kaydon. In the colosseum was a rectangular stage built up a meter above the ground with concrete.

The crowd soon filled the seats.

On the stage, a man came forward, and he waited as a crew placed a small booth in the center of the stage. Cathy watched as knights and warriors rode forth to enlist themselves in the tournament. Some were amateurs looking to make names of themselves, others were veterans named in a dozen songs and folktales, and Cathy knew just about none of them. Every entrant inscribed their names onto parchments for the man in the booth to shuffle into a deep bucket.

The splendor of it all was new to Cathy; the shining armor, the great chargers caparisoned in silver and gold, the shouts of the crowd, the hovering starships, and the banners snapping in the wind. Most of all, the knights were something to see. To her, all these fighters were just unnamed, unsung freeriders or men with no great deeds to their name, none that she knew anyway. Of all the contestants that entered, she only knew Mauga Lightbourne. But that didn't take away from the magnitude and atmosphere surrounding the event.

Someone caught Cathy's eye, and she saw an omelic man in armor take a seat next to her. Being that her seat was aloof from other seats, the man took the only seat next to her. He wore dressed armor the color of milk, his cloaks as white as fresh fallen snow.

"Who are you?" she asked.

He removed his helmet and placed it on his lap. "My name is Ser Jeeryn Ghallows. I'm commander of the Royal Guard."

"What are you doing next to me?"

"Just what the king asked of me. He didn't want you to be lonely."

"He's too kind for his own good."

"Agreed," Jeeryn nodded.

After all the contestants cleared, the man who had taken all the names took center stage. Around him, a few servants cleared things out. He spoke into a microphone that projected his words around the stadium. "Over one hundred contestants have entered today, but only one takes home the grand prize. We have finished with the random drawings and are ready to announce our first two contestants for the first duel. Let's hear it for the Warden of Northpoint, Lord Mauga Lightbourne! And his opponent, a young knight of Dove's Ridge who's looking to make a name of himself, Ser Gregor Mallister. Let the contestants take to the stage."

Uproarious cheers came from the crowd.

Mauga took the right. He wore the white cloak, and beneath it he was shining whitegold from head to foot, with a helmet carved smooth like a lake at the dawn. His shoulder plates and helmet were both marked with his house's sigil, a golden sun with a halo ring around it in the night sky. Gregor took the left. His armor was bronze and rigid. Each bowed in respect of one another.

"As with all duels today, first one to either lose his lifepack or fall out of the stage loses. Let's begin!" The announcer stepped off the stage, and the two contestants moved towards each other.

"What's a Lifepack?" Cathy asked Jeeryn.

"It's that little device stuck to both contestant's chest and back. If one is cut, they lose."

Mauga and Gregor ignited their hyperswords. The crowd was astonished at Mauga's blade, which was the same white-bladed, short-framed sword Cathy saw before. Gregor's was deep blue in color and a standard broad-framed hypersword.

"Aren't they worried about cutting each other?" Cathy asked.

"All hyperswords can have their intensity adjusted by the user. Right now, the blades won't cut through the armor."

Not what Cathy expected of omelics or what she read about common tournaments held by kings on Omulice.

A servant came forth. "Would the lady and ser care for any beverages?"

"Wine for me," Jeeryn said.

"Water," Cathy said.

The servant left them, soon retuning with their drinks.

Meanwhile, Mauga and Gregor had started to spar. Gregor's footwork was fluid and light and carried smooth rotation with his blade. Just what you'd expect from a young knight. Even so, his movements and attacks weren't working for the moment, as Mauga's guard was unshaken.

Jeeryn let loose some laughter.

"I missed the joke," said Cathy.

"Ser Gregor doesn't stand a chance."

"He's bigger than Lord Mauga. Surely, that works to his advantage."

"Take a look at Mauga's form."

Cathy's eyes watched Mauga. He used the entire ring as his playing field, deflecting away Gregor's attacks. Every advance Gregor made on Mauga was countered by swift and defensive agility. His body was lower to the ground, and his blade was always in front of him.

"Enlighten me. I'm no expert on swordsmanship."

"Take a look at his grip. See how he uses a reverse grip... some call it an icepick grip. Practitioners of Style V, also known as Jarrlinbar, use such a grip, and Lord Mauga is quite adept at this style of fighting. Notice his bent knees, how he keeps his center of mass lower to the ground, and how he is always behind his blade?"

Chapter 21

"I do."

"Those are all keys for Jarrlinbar duelists such as Lord Mauga. It is a great defensive technique, and I'm afraid Gregor's meager use of Style I, called Barriz, won't be enough. Needless to say, this is no match."

Almost on his words, Mauga parried a misplaced attack. Gregor's footing wavered, and Mauga sideways-swung with a downward attack. Gregor blocked, but Mauga's momentum let him jump into another swiping slash. That attack forced Gregor back, and he wildly brought an attack over his head and down at Mauga. Mauga dodged to the side and spun over Gregor's hunched body, back to back. From the other side, he dropped and spun his leg to trip Gregor, which left him wide open. Mauga capitalized and was able to cut straight through the lifepack on Gregor's chest.

"And that's the duel!" shouted the announcer.

The crowd applauded and cheered. Both contestants bowed and left the arena. The next duel was prepared. Before Cathy got to see it, a servant came to her.

"Lord Lightbourne would like to speak with you."

Cathy looked to Jeeryn, and he nodded. So, she followed the servant.

Cathy was motioned into a room inside the inner layers of the coliseum. She entered. Hypershields displayed on the wall, hung high next to armor. Along the room were plentiful tables with scraps of spare metal and tools. A liter of wine sat adjacent to a cup made of a polished horn.

In the pale light of a center, single bulb hanging from the ceiling, the lord sat on a stool, looking to the ground as if in a trance. He held some rough-hewn features and scars that had come from a fair amount of battle. Cathy looked at his face, noticing a birthmark just over his chin resembling a sun. She wondered if it was mere happenstance that his sigil and birthmark looked so similar.

Another individual was in the room - a thinly male omelic. He loosened the shoulder plates before taking them completely off Mauga's armor set. Next, he began to work on the piece around the lord's torso.

Mauga pointed backward. "This is my squire, Heuw. Found him begging for coins when he was only five."

Cathy bowed to the lord. "My lord. You summoned me."

"Forgive me for intruding on your festivities, but I hadn't had a proper chance to greet you."

"Pleasure's all mine. King Kaydon had a few good things to say on your behalf."

"He gives me more credit than I'm worthy of." Mauga turned his head to face Cathy.

"He says you helped save the kingdom."

"I purely led by values taught to me by my father. What resulted should be credited to him."

"It takes more than just values to reshape a kingdom."

"Perhaps you're correct."

"Take this colosseum, for example. When I was little, I read stories about tournaments like this. From every story I've read, there's always blood, and even death. But this tournament is different. And I take it you had something to do with that."

He scratched his chin. "Life has value. No sense in wasting it with games such as these."

"That's why you created lifepacks, correct? Other kingdoms fight in a more tradition sense, allowing their knights to potentially die, while your kingdom's knights live with the experience gained from dueling."

"You're quite the tactician," Mauga complimented. "And while all of what you mentioned has its strategic value, it was always about the lives for me. If I had my will sought through, all kingdoms would be living in peace, not war."

"You don't sound like a man that enjoys fighting."

"A knight should never shed blood in hatred of the enemies in front of him. Instead, a knight should fight for what he loves behind him." Mauga paused and looked down to his side. "That's something my father taught me."

"He was a wise man."

Mauga brushed off the compliment. "What is it you fight for?"

"Freedom."

Mauga beamed.

Heuw, his squire, finished removing the armor from around his torso. He followed with the under layer of cloth, leaving Mauga bare-chested. Cathy noticed that vein-like abrasions seemed to originate at Mauga's back, some tunneling over his sides.

Cathy pointed to it. Mauga looked down and back at Cathy. "See for yourself," he said.

Cathy began to walk around Mauga, circling him until she could see a shelled creature dug right into the center of his back, right at his spine, with what seemed like tiny tentacles penetrating his skin and creating those vein-like abrasions. The creature had three heads, two of which seemed to have their jaws clamped firmly against two different gems - one like a diamond, the other yellow in color. She remembered reading about these creatures once before but had since forgotten.

"They are called scarlencouls. Before one is knighted, the individual must've gone through the bonding process with one of these creatures," Mauga informed.

"Does it hurt?" Her interest was piqued.

"Our bond is symbiotic. It feeds off the energy created by my body. In turn, I can wield a non-neutral hypersword. Without scarlencouls, omelics would only be able to operate silver-based hyperswords."

"And what about humans?"

"No other species can bond with scarlencouls. And scarlencouls are the only creatures that can manipulate geminite, otherwise known as the minerals that power our hyper-weaponry." Mauga looked to his squire. "Bring me that chart over there off the wall."

The squire handed Mauga the chart, who handed it to Cathy. The chart showed images of nine different colored blades and listed them as follows:

Silver-Base: Neutral, requires no scarlencouls.
Sapphire-Base: Commitment & Loyalty
Citrine-Base: Duty, Honor, & Justice.
Amber-Base: Exhilaration & Enthusiasm.
Ruby-Base: Fury & Strength.
Amethyst-Base: Gallantry & Courage.
Emerald-Base: Patience & Composure.
Bronzine-Base: Valor & Empowerment.
Bloominite-Base: Peace & Love.

Cathy handed Mauga the chart back. "I'm not sure what to make of all this."

Mauga let loose some laughter. He reached and grabbed a marker and began to write on the chart. "Maybe this would help a bit." He handed her the chart again. It read:

~~Silver-Base~~ *(Gray): Neutral, requires no* scarlencouls.
~~Sapphire-Base~~ *(Blue): Commitment & Loyalty.*
~~Citrine-Base~~ *(Yellow): Duty, Honor, & Justice.*
~~Amber-Base~~ *(Orange): Exhilaration & Enthusiasm.*
~~Ruby-Base~~ *(Red): Fury & Strength.*
~~Amethyst-Base~~ *(Violet): Gallantry & Courage.*
~~Emerald-Base~~ *(Green): Patience & Composure.*
~~Bronzine-Base~~ *(Brown): Valor & Empowerment.*
~~Bloominite-Base~~ *(Pink): Peace & Love.*

Mauga continued. "Hyperswords are more than just swords of intensely focused, rapidly spinning energy. Every sword has character. Every tint has its own emotional mark." Mauga's eyes sparkled with joy as he spoke. "A blue-bladed hypersword is created by using sapphire-based geminite in the sword. And the user of such will have urges partial towards commitment and loyalty. And through training, one can learn to control these heightened urges properly and proportionally."

Cathy was left wondering about Mauga's white-bladed hypersword. "I don't see the chart mention any hyperswords like yours."

Mauga stepped off the stool, moving with excitement in his steps. He grabbed his hypersword and handed the handle to Cathy. "This treasure has been passed down my family for generations. The diamond-based geminite that powers it is legendary and extremely rare to find."

"So some tints aren't common?"

"That chart you looked at also lists the tints in descending order from most common to the least common being the bottommost tint."

"It's all so fascinating. But this raises a question. I noticed pink-bladed hyperswords inspire peace and love. If that's the case, would the world not be better if more used this blade?"

Chapter 21

Mauga went hysterical. "It all sounds great in an ideal world. But in all my time alive, I've never seen an omelic male choose to use pink geminite. They associate it with weakness and femininity."

Sounds like this world still has a ways to go, Cathy thought.

"Besides, it's all relative. What if one believes peace is brought by regicide or has love of violence? Every emotion is malleable to the man who feels it - another thing my father once said."

There was no denying that Mauga had a solid point there. "You're right," Cathy agreed. She handed Mauga back his hypersword. "I enjoyed the show you gave. And you were great."

Mauga was humbled. "I appreciate your praise. My father spent a lot of time training me himself when I was but a young man. I've him to thank."

"Ser Jeeryn was sure you were going to win based on your swordsmanship style. It was all too technical for me to follow fully."

Mauga gestured to the counter. "Heuw, grab my copy of *The Eight Combat Styles for True Swordsmen.*" Heuw retrieved a book that looked familiar to Cathy and handed it to her. Mauga explained, "This is a great starter book to read if you are interested in hypersword combat. At the beginning, it gives a summary of the eight main styles that you could look for as the tourney continues. There are more specialized techniques used in hypersword combat, but the eight in this book are the most versatile and well-recognized. I hope this will make your experience today that much better."

Cathy bowed in graciousness. "You're too kind."

He nodded. "Please. I've taken up too much of your time. I'll have my squire show you back to your seat." He gestured to his squire.

"Just one more question, before I leave. Ever heard of the Brotherhood of Relics?"

Mauga studied Cathy for a moment. "Only what everyone else has heard."

Like she figured. He wasn't going to be able to help her. In fact, it seemed like it was going to be all on her.

Cathy rejoined Ser Jeeryn in time to see another duel start. The stands were beginning to stir. Fat sausages sizzled on spirts over grill fires, spicing the air with the scents of garlic and pepper. A servant with a goose under his arm strode past the seats below Cathy. The crowd was even more engaged than before.

Just as that duel started, Cathy opened the book given to her by Mauga and turned to the summary. It listed the eight main techniques, also called styles, of hypersword combat with a brief description that would help her recognize it. The rest of the book was dedicated to explaining in more depth each of the eight styles by listing training methods, motions to use, mindsets to study, and much more. Cathy read the summary in her head:

Technique I - Barriz: A technique for amateurs learning the craft. Barriz covers the basics of attacks, parries, body target zones, and practice drills. Utilizes fluid legwork and sweeping motions. This well-rounded technique focuses on disarming opponents instead of landing fatal strikes.

Technique II - Delfvii: An effective defensive technique. Best used if wielder does not wish to be hit, or if wielder is facing many opponents with ranged weaponry. With a hypersword blade and enough skill in anticipating attacks, Delfvii is an excellent defensive tool, but in combat against another hypersword wielder, it merely delays the inevitable. Utilizes tight moves, subtle dodges and short sweeps designed to provide maximum defensive coverage, leaving the duelist less exposed to ranged weapons. Stresses quick reflexes and fast transitioning of position. Mindset is to always be moving opposite of attacker so as not to be hit.

Technique III - Toloum: Technique that carries a heavy focus on protecting one's hypersword to avoid being disarmed. Anticipation of a hypersword being swung at wielder is a focus, and as so requires very fluid movements of both the hypersword and the body. Timing, accuracy, and skill, rather than strength, are relied upon to defeat one's opponent. This is a duelist techniques suited for one on one combat which specializes in using opponents attacks against them. Unlike many techniques, it is based on holding one spot. This technique is best achieved by either positioning one hand near the top of the hilt and another at the bottom or with an angled grip, which is recommended.

Technique IV - Parmudo: Utilizes distanced attacks with long, thin swords and agile dodging. A technique that focuses around avoiding close combat with other hypersword duelists. Utilizes quick jabs and swift strikes. Mindset is if an opponent cannot reach duelist, then they stand no threat.

Technique V - Jarrlinbar: Defensive technique that is focused on utilizing a reversed handle grip for highly mobile defense. Better for protecting others than most other defensive techniques. Achieved by putting hilt close to wielder's center mass. Knees and body should be bent to lower center of mass, and blade is often kept in front of person. Utilizes atheism, agility, and awareness.

Technique VI - Aargo: Though this technique is highly aggressive, it is focused, and its best use is in combat against other duelists. Utilizes power and strength into strikes to overpower enemies. Powerful, wide attacks are to give wielder complete domination of opponents. Often incorporates hand and leg attacks. Larger framed swords are recommended.

Technique VII - Svyn: Utilizes speed and haste to move past enemies' defense. Best used with advanced knightly technology to move quickly. This technique is best suited for one on one combat. Can exhaust wielder much sooner than other techniques but is very difficult to defend against.

Technique VIII - Dezzlow: Form involving the use of more than one blade at once. Often combined with other techniques for fullest results.

On occasion, Cathy looked away from the summary to catch highlights of the duels. She found once she finished reading that summary, the tournament became more enjoyable to watch. Knowing how the swordsmen fought helped her appreciate their time training even more. The duels went on all day and into dusk. A dozen times, Cathy heard the crowd cry out in unison as fighters clashed blades with each other. Lifepacks exploded into splinters while the commoners screamed for their favorites.

The time came when it was down to the final two, both names Cathy had already forgotten. Then the sun went behind a cloud and disappeared. The fighting began and ended rather rapidly. A man in blue armor with a violet hypersword bashed the other knight dressed in red armor and a yellow hypersword out of the arena.

His head hit the ground with an audible crack that made the crowd gasp. But it was just the red antler on his helm. One of the tines had snapped off beneath him. When he climbed to his feet, the commoners cheered wildly for his well-being and, of course, for the winner of the tournament. He handed the broken tine to his conqueror with a gracious bow. The champion snorted and tossed the broken antler into the crowd, where the commoners began to punch and claw over the keepsake until some guards walked out among them and restored the peace.

The servants kept the cups filled all night as an entertainment show commemorated the day. It was a show with actors playing characters of a well-known folktale in these lands. Singers eventually came to the stage, filling the dusk with music as the show continued through the night. At one point, a juggler kept a cascade of burning clubs spinning through the air.

Later came the course meals of the event. Sweetbreads and banana-strawberry pie and baked apricots fragrant with cinnamon and lemon cakes frosted in sugar. The banana-strawberry pie was Cathy's quick favorite. That is to say, it didn't quite reach the level of watermelons for her, however. The end of the show concluded the event and the night. The commute out of the colosseum was slow and tiresome. But eventually Cathy made it back to her chambers after almost an hour of riding. She tossed her exhausted body on the mattress and dozed off in preparation for the next day.

Chapter 22: Walls of Perdition
Error 66b

Jeremiah

The gate closed behind them, locking them in the walls of the second trial. Looming danger on the horizon with no clear way out, Jeremiah wondered if this was what Daniel felt when he was locked away in a den of lions. Prayer saved Daniel then, and it will be Jeremiah's saving grace now.

In a brand new cave system darker than before, the black stones carried veins of blue, like glowing rivers in the night of the black walls. Moments earlier, James had called for a brief rest after the onslaught they had faced. And just as God did on the seventh day of creation, Jeremiah too rested. At least for the brief moment.

Many in the group were in conversations as they enjoyed some snacks and drinks. Though Jeremiah's mind was not attuned to the conversations. It was on the marvel of this place, and his eyes were reading the cave's curvature like a canvas.

The surface rock below his feet was smooth and flat, similar to the arena. The ceiling was also stone, but more jagged like the walls. Between the rocks making up the wall, Jeremiah took a look through the gaps. They were nowhere large enough to squeeze through, but they graciously offered a sight into a vast void of emptiness. Though it was just a trick of the eye. He could only see emptiness due to the dust and electric clouds most certainly put there to obstruct his vision of what lies beyond. To him, the sight was a reminder of all he didn't know, all he wished to know; vast and mystifying.

Never did he ever expect to be in the Vault of the Seven. He had heard stories told of this Precursor monument when he was young of years, but words only went so far. Truly a place lost in time yet full of stories he only wished he knew. If his kin could see him now, what would they say? Of that, he couldn't be sure.

Jeremiah, using the light from the glowing stones woven throughout the walls of the cavern, had the Book of Sin ready to read. He gazed at the scramble of words, phrases, and puzzles. With every page, the book seemed to get harder and harder to decipher. He thanked God the words were portrayed in his advanced native dialect. He had found many of the concepts written about wouldn't be very translatable in many of the basic languages of this galaxy. ·

After some time, he found what he was looking for. *"And to those whom still remain shall be tested not of prowess but of ingenuity within the Walls of Perdition,"* he read the put-together phrase in English after translating it in his head from his native language.

"So... hell. We're in hell," Shadow-Walker said, with a hint of sarcasm.

"Not literally, I would guess," Valiic reassured Shadow-Walker, with a pat on his uninjured shoulder.

Letting his eyes meander some, Jeremiah caught sight of James pushing a few boulders that were not small to reveal a pathway. Each boulder had to weigh close to a ton. In many ways, James reminded Jeremiah of Samson of the bible, both blessed with prodigious strength no ordinary human could achieve. Samson's downfall was women, and Jeremiah wondered if James would fall victim to a downfall of his own.

James grabbed Geariic's attention with a wave. "Time get this gear in rotation. You first, big guy." Inside the small pathway, James pointed down an opening between three flat rocks leading down almost like a chimney.

Geariic grunted, but he unattached his warhammer from his back and leaped down. James followed. Then Frost, Brad, and Shadow-Walker, in that order.

As Jeremiah approached the ledge, he noticed the jump was only a couple meters down. He crouched his body, then placed his legs over the ledge and pushed off. Landing with ease, he was presented with a tight corridor in front of him. It was the only way to go and pathed with many flat rocks descending down like a staircase. He let his faith be the strength to guide his feet onward.

Newly healed after the break, Jeremiah was ready. He was the second to last in the line, with Valiic Bessile covering him from behind. Here and there, gaps had formed between the group of men, with none too big to lose sight of each other. Valiic and Jeremiah were not as separated from each other as Jeremiah was from Shadow-Walker, who was ahead of Jeremiah.

Within a minute of moving, he noticed Geariic disappeared down another drop in the form of a chimney. Members of the unit began to follow his lead until it was Jeremiah's turn. When he looked down, he noticed the drop was at least three times deeper.

James and Geariic had their arms up. "Jump. We've got your ass," James said, gesturing him down with his fingers.

Jeremiah leaped into the catching arms, and they released him and made room for Valiic. He thudded against the ground shortly after.

His eyes mooched around in a room more open than the previous. When he noticed himself, he realized his gaze was fixated on a glowing, ponding pool of steaming water building up on the left corner. A rock, shaped almost like a volcano, extended out the middle of the pond, and spring water poured out from it. A breath of life in this otherwise dark tunnel.

Before he had a chance to comment on it, Geariic was already leading the group down another opening. Again, it was the only one, leaving Jeremiah a bit underwhelmed with this particular trial. It promised that which would call on one's ingenuity to complete. In spite of that, every space they'd entered had only one path leading out.

Maybe it isn't meant to be a maze, Jeremiah then thought. *Perhaps a different challenge lurks.*

He realized then he didn't see the big picture; just the tunnel he walked. Therefore, who was he to question his path? There's no reason to strike the stone twice, as Moses did when he questioned his path.

Within a tight corridor that led downward, Jeremiah continued onward. The spacing of the path often varied in this particular corridor. At one point, he found himself stepping over a blockage. At another, he was dipping below a lowered ceiling. The long corridor wasn't as much trouble for him as it was for Valiic, who was behind him. Jeremiah, being the gentleman he was, didn't let his pace get the better of him so Valiic wouldn't fall too far behind, as he had with Shadow-Walker.

"Psst," Valiic whispered from behind to get Jeremiah's attention.

"Speak your mind, o' wise soul." Jeremiah let his pace slow even more so Valiic was closer.

"Maybe this isn't the right time for this, but I have something I'd like to discuss with you. Something that has been on my mind."

"Do you wish to speak to me as a pastor, or as a comrade?" Jeremiah ducked under a hanging piece of rock.

"Well, I wouldn't say either. It has more to do with you, and not me."

Jeremiah was taken a bit off-guard by his statement. He was used to being sought after to aid in others' inner questions of themselves or help with other matters pertaining to them. "Did I do something to hurt or offend you?"

"No... it's--" He was silent for a moment. "During our battle, I could see you helping Shadow-Walker, and I mean not to make spite of that. What you did for him and us - it will never be forgotten."

Jeremiah hesitated before asking, "You saw me helping him?"

"In the heat of battle, I'm not sure exactly what I saw. But if my eyes are to be trusted, what I saw was... bizarre." Valiic's voice softened, almost unsure of himself.

The path veered right and down some steep boulders laid out as steps. Jeremiah made a small leap to the first step and then to the next. "I don't follow."

He heard Valiic following him down the steps, the metal of his armor and shield creating noise as he descended. "It looked like light, glowing over his back... and from your hands. The light wasn't bright, but subtle," Valiic whispered. "I keep thinking about what I saw, and the only thing that makes sense to me... is an ace. Are you an ace?"

Jeremiah pondered for a few seconds on the words spoken. "Have you told anyone what you saw?"

Valiic, of course, was apprehensive. "Is this something you mean to hide?"

"No, it isn't that, and I'm no ace, I assure you," Jeremiah was quick to respond. "What you saw was no trick. I mentioned a healing agent to everyone when questioned before, but it was a half-truth. It does heal, but that isn't all. The host who uses the substance gives up part of his or her lifespan to trade for miraculous healing of another. They call it Life's Barter here, and it is astronomically rare."

Chapter 22

"You gave away some of your own life for his?" Valiic's voice was shaken by this revelation.

"That's why I didn't want anyone to know. Promise me you'll keep this secret."

Jeremiah could hear a sniffle. "I will," Valiic promised.

They were almost at the bottom, having descended tens of meters in all.

"I appreciate it." Jeremiah graciously turned back to Valiic and gave a quick nod of respect. Gazing up, he noticed him reciprocate with his own sign of respect.

Jeremiah reached the last step, which lead into another corridor similar to the last, only much shorter in length. At the end of the corridor, Shadow-Walker was waiting. Jeremiah stared at him for a moment, without moving.

"Oh yeah, Pastor... I'll just wait here another eternity while you stand there." Shadow-Walker rolled his eyes at his own sarcastic words.

"My apologies." Jeremiah moved forward.

As he neared, Shadow-Walker asked, "Seriously, though, what took you so long?" Jeremiah eyes went back to Valiic, then to Shadow-Walker. He seemed to understand. "Valiic! So you're the culprit." Shadow-Walker laughed.

Valiic forced his way between a tight set of boulders. He stopped and looked up. "Culprit of what, I ask?"

"Being slow as a motherfraker. No seriously, you both are slower than a one-legged grandpa on tranquilizers with no cane."

"The wise man takes his time in hostile territory," Valiic said with confidence. But Jeremiah had a sense he was really just trying to hide a bit of embarrassment.

"Be vigilant, then, how you walk lands unknown - not as unwise but as wise, making the most of every step, for there is evil and ill-intent on a warrior's journey. Klooberic 488:10," Jeremiah said to Shadow-Walker, coming to the defense of Valiic. In truth, he shared some responsibility. If not for the conversation, they might've held a faster pace.

Jeremiah reached Shadow-Walker and looked down the hole Shadow-Walker stood in front of. It was massive, deep - a hole to perdition, figuratively speaking. As deep as it went, it was generous, too, having provided a few rock ledges from top to bottom tens of meters apart. Geariic was already so far down, he looked to be an insect, while James, Frost, and Brad where higher up. Brad continued to scale down, while Frost was working on creating small bridges from one bumped out rock to another. James was looking upward, ready to assist in case of someone falling.

Shadow-Walker gestured to a rope tied with multiple knots to a thick rock. It dropped to the first boulder down the hole. "Any time now," said Shadow-Walker.

"I'm not comfortable with this," Jeremiah said. Nonetheless, he sat down over the edge and leaned forward to reach the rope. Gripping the rope tightly, he pushed off the ledge and scaled down to the first surface.

There was a tiny bridge of ice from the first to the second highest perch he used.

Valiic was much less fluid with his descent. He leaped to the first boulder. The impact caused a split to form, and Valiic tumbled back, losing his footing.

"Someone help Valiic!" Shadow-Walker called, catching the attention of the others.

Valiic flailed his arms around, trying to catch his balance, but the angle of the rock he landed on increased more as he neared the edge. He had no choice. Valiic turned and gave a wobbly leap to a different rock.

"No! Not that one!" James shouted.

His words came far too late. Valiic flew and crashed into a small rock lower in the hole; one protruding apart from the rest. His weight forced the rock from its place, and he had no chance. He started to fall with the rock to an early grave!

Jeremiah had a moment where he thought he should intervene. He then saw James preparing to jump. As Valiic fell in level of where James was, he jumped from his spot and caught Valiic's extended arm. James, with a sharp bolt in his free hand, stabbed into the first wall he hit. The bolt impaled in, and after dragging down the wall some, both of them came to a halt.

"Christ! You're one heavy brother, Valiic." James strained as he struggled to hold them both up.

Chapter 22

You're not supposed to take the lord's name in vain, Jeremiah thought but didn't say aloud.

"As are all maelkii." Valiic's eyes were down, looking at the abyss, as he responded.

Below them, Frost had started to form a slide of ice to another boulder. "Hang in there a bit longer, uzzos," said Frost.

When he finished, James let go, and they were both treated with a gentle slide to the next boulder. James took a moment to stretch and massage his arms before everyone involved started down again.

Jeremiah and Shadow-Walker now had some catching up to do.

The rest of the way down went off without a hitch, but the journey down seemed endless. Jeremiah had no sense of time anymore, much less how long they spent descending.

He hit the lowest surface with a jolt but was still on his feet. When he reached the bottom, everyone was waiting, breaking for the moment, snacking and taking in water. The last one to land was Shadow-Walker.

"Jeremiah, Shadow. You guys need to rest your feet, or can you two soldier on?"

Jeremiah gave a smile as he adjusted his glasses. "I'm ready as long as he is." His look moved to Shadow-Walker.

"Just 'cause I got injured, doesn't mean I'll be the one to hold everyone up." He gave way to some laughter.

"Then it's decided." Geariic, already on his feet, strode right into the next tunnel.

Frost followed. "I like a soldier who's always on the go."

James sighed. "Those two were born to be on a team." He was next, with Brad behind.

Shadow-Walker tapped on Jeremiah's shoulder as he passed. "Don't take so long this time, boys." His eyes met Jeremiah's, then Valiic's.

Jeremiah went in after them, and it didn't take long for him to start falling a bit behind in the narrow tunnels. Mostly he was trying not to leave Valiic too far behind.

Some time had passed, but Jeremiah could not tell how much any longer. He didn't give up his pace and stayed close to Valiic. His journey was treated with light of almost torch-like patches of rock, smoking stars that bid him follow. After a few moments, the light seemed to disappear, but he kept on straight. And soon he found himself at the top of steep, narrow stairs that led down, another torch-stone glimmering far below him. He followed the call, down and down. Halfway down, he stumbled over a protruding rock and rebounded against the wall, and his hand found raw, smooth stone supported by Precursor columns, whereas before the tunnel had been dressed stone.

A bit after Shadow-Walker and James's voices had faded away, Jeremiah asked Valiic, "Do your thoughts still dwell on your cohinla?" As a pastor, he had grown used to these kind of troubles over the years.

"Are you asking as a comrade or man of the robe?" asked Valiic. His question was a play on what Jeremiah said earlier, and he gave a quick laugh at the humor.

"Both... neither. It doesn't matter. I'm here for you." He paused. "So do they?"

"She's in my thoughts always." Valiic's words came from a pit of sadness.

"She must be someone quite special to win your heart."

"More than words can describe. I have faith we will be reunited again."

Jeremiah smiled. He could feel in his heart Valiic had a bond true in the eyes of God. *"For we live by faith, not by sight. 2 Corinthians 5:7."*

"Forgive me, I've never read the Bible. I don't deny Christianity's similarities with Knoblelism, but I've always been faithful to the Book of Ancient Prophets."

"That's fair. Perhaps the verse of *Obitan 83:12. To have faith is to have confidence in our hopes and dreams, to be sure for what we cannot see."*

Valiic had himself a bit of laughter. "It is a rare seen talent to produce quotes not from one, but two separate holy books."

"When I was young, the lord put his holy words in my mouth. It was his greatest gift to me."

"I imagine a truly holy man such as yourself gained many followers on this planet."

"Not as many as I wish." In truth, Jeremiah was a bit ashamed of himself in this mission. He had always been partial towards the idea that everything has a purpose behind it. So when he remained the last survivor of a mapping and scientific mission on this planet, he believed it was for a purpose. He believed he could continue what he did on Earth by teaching spiritualty on this planet. Yet, he had fallen short of his own expectations.

"Really?" Valiic voiced with shock.

"The corelinn species have always held faith in their Holy Triangle: Oteyk, Guardian of the Oceans; Saeona, Guardian of the Skies; and Moonikwaa, Guardian of the Surface. I've had my troubles gaining follows since my message preaches otherwise. Nonetheless, I admire their devotion. Even so, God gifted me with the spiritual gifts of evangelism and apostleship. At moments I feel defeated, but I must keep trying. *Because of the Lord's great love we are not consumed, for his compassions never fail. They are new every morning; great is your faithfulness. Lamentations 3:22-23.* Every day is new, and I must make the most of it." That was a verse Jeremiah was partial towards.

Truth be told, he had more hope in these people than he did when he first got started. Back then, he preached to sinners who thought themselves in the right; today, he preached a different viewpoint to already faithful creatures.

"Even if it's not what I believe, I'm glad the corelinns have faith in something. It is my belief that a culture without a faith that upholds a standard of morals and good-hearty ends up building a culture of sin and evil. If they have no reason to live selflessly, they turn to selfishness instead. Too many species, in my eyes, have lost such an important part of being an individual with a living soul."

Jeremiah had a sense of warmth from what Valiic had to say. "I'm glad to have met you, Valiic. You truly are a good man."

"And you have a soul full of light," Valiic returned the compliment.

"Manner of speaking?"

"No. I mean every word. The corelinn are made better by your presence, whether they know it or not. One day, I believe you will accomplish your goal."

"I have faith." Jeremiah smiled and whispered softly so only he could hear, *"But when you ask, you must believe and not doubt, because the one who doubts is like a wave of the sea, blown and tossed by the wind. James 1:6."*

They must have been walking for at least another kilometer or two. Finally, the stairs reached the bottom, and there was no place to go but forward. And forward led to all consuming darkness. He found the wall and followed, blind and lost, letting faith be his guide in the darkness. Soon, he was knee-deep in sweet-smelling water and shivered at its icy touch. It was total darkness when finally Jeremiah and Valiic emerged into a massive, cavernous opening and into some light. The squad was there, waiting.

The air was clearer down here, but the surroundings were still dark and blue. Jeremiah stood in the arctic pool of water and looked around. He and everyone else were in a cavern, and all was quiet. Although much of the ground and walls seemed to be made of natural rock, some structures still seemed to be created by the Precursors; like lost treasures in a field. In some areas, the opening divided into tunnels, while other paths followed tiny rivers. Different paths led in different directions, but no clear answer indicated which one was the right one to take. It was the first time the path ahead was unclear. And Jeremiah prayed they would make the right choice.

"Now that we're all here, we have some decisions to make," said James.

Jeremiah already took the cue and was looking in the Book of Sin for answers. Ironic to be looking to sin for answers, but the lord works in mysterious ways.

The team sat down on the bank and laid their weapons on the ground as they waited.

Jeremiah found something of use to translate. *"Into the lair of the sandren those travel. Be wary, for if they see something they don't think should exist they remove it from existence."*

"Sandren?" asked Shadow-Walker.

"Imagine a religious extremist who works under a convert-or-kill philosophy - a person who lives only to convert others to their beliefs, else that extremist kills them in a ritualistic manor. Best translation I could give."

"In dummy words, you don't want to be face-to-face with a sandren, correct?"

Jeremiah nodded. "Precisely."

Chapter 22

"Yah boyz ready?" The group turned to see Brad reappearing from the shadows.

Jeremiah wasn't aware he had ventured away. Brad waved them on and started down a path beside a stream and towards the leftmost area of the labyrinth. The stream ventured right, but they stayed left and traveled towards the cover of a thick boulder.

The squad gathered behind cover. "Check it out." Shadow-Walker pointed at a shjarr sandren floating back and forth in a pattern in an open area. The machine glowed a teal light from its circular core, with six tentacles made of light and of similar appearance to the tentacles of a jellyfish. They waved in the air on high alert.

Has it discovered us? Jeremiah thought.

He snuck a better look, and it seemed to be facing them. But it had no eyes, so he was unsure.

Jeremiah scanned the area. He saw another shjarr sandren circling a massive boulder on the left, and another one even further with its own rock to circle. To the right of them were two sloped rock pillars many meters in length, and less so in width. Those two rocks split the open space into two main areas.

"We need to put air under our steps. Can't afford them seeing or hearing us even once," James whispered.

"Once is enough to wipe us from existence. And that don't work for Big Daddy," whispered Frost. Jeremiah was unaccustomed to him using a quiet voice.

Shadow-Walker was giving Valiic a funny frown. "We all know sneaky isn't this guy's specialty." He pointed. Valiic shrugged, knowing his words were the truth.

"Doesn't matter right now. Step one is to find an exit, and we need a brave volunteer to do so," James said.

"Just send the tiger." Frost's eyes motioned to Brad Swift.

Tiger? Jeremiah wondered, *what does he mean by that?*

Brad didn't even respond. He just started moving towards the center pillars, cautious of the sandrens. Not much of a talker, but quite one to take action. In spite of the darker mystic around that man, Jeremiah thought of him almost as a guardian sent by the lord, possessing talent and skill unrivaled by many. He was and continues to be a gift.

In fact, Jeremiah felt blessed to be within the company of such capable men. At moments, even he felt like a pup amidst a pack of wolves.

"That settles that. But what in Sam-Hell do we do?" Geariic grumbled.

"Wait," Shadow-Walker answered for James.

"I fraken hate sitting still." Geariic shifted in his spot, trying to make himself more comfortable. With his warhammer over his lap, he fiddled with the handle.

"Patience is a valuable virtue--" Valiic started.

"Oh, here he goes again," Geariic interrupted. His eyes spat fire. "That's a fine-looking high horse you got there, Valiic. I bet you're proud. But I came from a place where high horses only made you a bigger target, and an easy kill." Geariic's tone and voice were starting to become loud. Too loud given they were near the enemy.

James put his finger up to Geariic. "Enough of that! This isn't the time," James commanded, with a powerful whisper.

After a short time sitting in silence, Brad reappeared behind their cover. "Follow me." Brad motioned with his weapon and started toward the first of the large pillars, keeping his center of mass low to the ground.

The team followed Brad forward on a path straight from where they were sitting. Geariic and Valiic lagged a bit behind, and Valiic placed his arms around his armor and shield, trying to keep the metal from clacking against each other.

Brad leaped onto the bottom of one of the center pillars dividing the cavern and went upward with silent steps. The slope was forgiving enough to trudge up without needing the use of hands.

"I get it," Jeremiah glowed. "Most people would try to maneuver their way through the maze of rocks to find the exit. Ultimately, their chances of stumbling upon a sandren exponentially increase. The wise man avoids the challenge designed for failure and makes his own way, just like the story of Dahmathada the Wise, in the Book of Ancient Prophets. That's why going up this pillar over the maze is the best strategy."

"So the trick is having the sense of mind to see the big picture instead of letting tunnel-vision trick you," said James.

Brad was at the peak of the pillar. "Any assassin worth ah shit would avoid da target till da moment of da kill, controllin' every moment 'n-between." Jeremiah could hear a bit of excitement in the voice of Brad.

"I sometimes forget you were a hitman, Brad," Shadow-Walker added.

Brad, using a boost from his power armor, jumped from the peak of this pillar and landed on the second pillar. That one didn't have much of a low point and was fairly flat down its span.

James made the leap, while Frost prepared a bridge for the rest of the unit. He crossed, as did Geariic and Shadow-Walker. Jeremiah's turn came, and he steadied his arms out for balance. Over the ledge of ice, he could see a shjarr sandren patrolling the gap between pillars. The sight was like vinegar to the teeth and smoke to the eyes, and it tempted him to quicken his pace. Valiic was last and took the most time, inching forward so as to make as little noise as possible.

Brad was already at the end of the second pillar, waiting as the squad joined him moments later. He squatted down at the ledge and pointed down the right edge to three rocks patterned in a semi-circle - two were only large enough for one person to hide behind, while the middle one was roughly three times the size. Those rocks seemed to provide cover for a small dome-like indention into the pillar of which the group waited on top. "Exit iz cut into dis rock," said Brad.

Jeremiah noticed Brad reach for his pouch, and he pulled out a trigger device. "Rigged ah flash bomb to ah fuse." He pressed the trigger, and a flash of light went off in the near vicinity. The sandren that was coming up to the rocks by the exit pulled itself away and towards the flash of light. Brad jumped down and landed on the surface a few meters down.

"Haul ass," James whispered.

He jumped with Geariic and Valiic. Frost was a second behind and created a slide of ice down as he fell. Jeremiah, followed by Shadow-Walker, aimed for the slide, and both were down in seconds. Frost started to build some cover with ice to prevent the sandren from finding them.

Having recovered from the landing, Jeremiah's eyes looked back at the pillar. It was carved out and shaped like a dome, and just as Brad foretold, an exit led downward into a cave system, going deep below the pillar.

Frost finished, and everyone made haste down the path to the exit, away from the danger above. When they figured they were safe, they all slowed back to a march.

The path ahead had many low hanging ceilings, and each time Jeremiah had to crawl through. After spiraling a few times to the left, the group came out of the short cave. Jeremiah crawled past the last of the low ceilings, with Valiic behind, and met up with their teammates in a wide room.

A pillar designed by the Precursors was blocking the path onward. James was staring at it with Geariic and Shadow-Walker nearby, while the rest of the crew was off to the side, sitting against a batch of rocks with some snacks and drinks.

"Made it just in time," Shadow saw Jeremiah and said to him.

"For what?"

"James was just saying how he was going to move this damn thing."

James was now at the pillar and pushing with all his might before shifting to try to lift it instead. It was no good. Geariic then joined in on the other side to help. It was no good, and because of the position of the pillar, only two people could try and lift it at one time.

James and Geariic relented to catch a breath. James said, "For the record, this really sucks." He looked to Jeremiah, who took it as a cue to come over and help. Now beside them, Jeremiah was already flipping through pages of the book.

"Maybe you just need try harder." Shadow-Walker laughed at James and Geariic's expense.

James smiled. "We'd have better luck picking up a turd by its clean end than moving that son of a bitch."

"Let's see you do it," Geariic added, with a taunt.

"Sure. I'll tag right in." On his sarcastic words, Shadow-Walker held out his good hand.

The pillar suddenly started lifting to reveal a short pathway. Jeremiah looked away from the book to see Valiic holding his hand on a flat piece of rock now glowing at his touch.

Chapter 22

Valiic was glowing at his discovery. "I found the answer." Only, as he removed his hand, the pillar began to fall until Valiic stuck his hand over the rock once more.

James grunted. "Well, that's just dandy."

"One of us will have to stay behind," Geariic realized.

Jeremiah put the book away, since it clearly had no answers on this particular situation. "This trial is about ingenuity. So there must be a way to trick it."

Frost jumped in. "I'll do one better, uzzo. I already thought of something that will is guaranteed to cheat it."

"You always had a head on you." Geariic gave his friend half a smile.

"I bet those Precursors never knew about forcidion when they designed this little thing, since it only ever originated on Maelkiin. If we just stick Valiic's shield under the pillar, it should hold it up."

James was already doing just that. He grabbed the shield from Valiic and struggled as he carried it under the pillar. Valiic let go, and lo and behold, the power of the mind trumped sheer strength. A success in anyone's mind.

"Good thinking." Shadow-Walker nodded to Frost.

Everyone was able to get by, and Valiic pulled his shield out as they left the obstacle behind and soon entered a completely new area. Vast was the ravine before them where no one could see a bottom, much like the area of the battle arena from this first trial. Above them was a mirror of the bottom - no visible ceiling.

The rock around them could probably be scaled down, but it was clear they were supposed to make it to the other side of the ravine. Just like the side they were on, there too laid a cliff face that spanned right further than eyes could see. But as the cliff face continued left, it had an indentation into an opening to a cave. The cliff face was angled that way too, making it so the further right it went, the closer it was to them. On the same cliff was smooth dressed stone, with several footholds on the vertical surface. The distance away was probably a few hundred meters between them and the other side.

"Jeremiah? Any helpful tips from the book?" James stood closest to the ravine.

"Yeah. How the Sam-Hell are we going to get over there?" Geariic mouthed.

Jeremiah was just beginning to open the book as James neared the edge of the drop-off. A block of stone appeared from nowhere in a mere second. Suspended in the air, it was unmoving and only a jump away.

"Scratch that. I think we have our answer." James jumped to the platform. Others followed, as did Jeremiah.

Just then, another platform appeared, lower and at a greater distance from the first. Another came, and the team hurried to make it onto it. Valiic, unfortunately, was lagging behind. Geariic was not doing much better himself. They had just gotten to the second platform as the fourth and then the fifth appeared.

"Frak this!" Geariic cursed between breaths.

Jeremiah turned at this. Then he realized something haunting was happening. "What happened to the first platform?" He threw the question out to the group.

James, in the lead, ground to a halt at the words. Everyone followed and witnessed the second platform begin to disintegrate just as Valiic jumped to the third.

"Run, boys! Run! Don't look back!" James gestured for everyone to move on ahead. As Frost was about to pass James, he grabbed Frost's shoulder. "Start with the fifth platform, and build up some ice to land on. Do this every *two* platforms."

Jeremiah was now on the fifth, aiming for the sixth. Every platform was further away and farther down than the last. All the same, that meant the same strength was required for each jump, but the landings were getting harder.

Frost had finished with the fifth platform and landed on the sixth, using some ice to help the fall. Shadow-Walker was now on Frost's back, hanging on for dear life. Jeremiah landed on the sixth platform behind Frost. They were more than halfway across at this point. Every platform seemed to lead them closer to that cave opening.

The seventh was there, and the eighth was just appearing.

They sure are fast, Jeremiah thought.

He gazed back to see James give Valiic a massive boost with his hands. Valiic had gotten a running start, and James launched him up with cupped hands.

Now last, James was off the third platform a second before it completely dematerialized. He crossed the fourth with ease and jumped for the fifth.

James's boost allowed Valiic to skip the fourth and land directly on the fifth. He almost didn't make it quite there, but with an assist from the ice that increased the size of the platform, Valiic landed safety. Geariic was ahead, and he just made the jump to Jeremiah's platform.

That's when Jeremiah realized he'd better be on the move. He made it onto the seventh platform, then the eighth, still landing with relative ease. Brad had already made it to the other cliff face and was waiting on an angled platform that dipped into an unlit cave.

Ten platforms total. Frost and Shadow-Walker were just making their way to the tenth platform just as Jeremiah jumped to the ninth.

Jeremiah looked back to see James giving Valiic another boost. This time, James made the jump half a second before the disintegrating platform disappeared completely.

The timing's getting too close. Jeremiah stood still on the thought.

Valiic landed on the seventh platform just as Geariic zipped by Jeremiah. James was there in no time, and they prepared another round.

Valiic gave it a full run, then lift off!

The platform was gone, and James, having just started to push off, barely had enough momentum to reach the eighth platform. He caught the edge, pulled himself up, and ran for the ninth as Valiic landed.

Jeremiah looked back. Frost and Shadow-Walker were in the middle of jumping to the cliff face. Geariic wasn't far behind. They weren't paying attention to the situation like Jeremiah was.

Quickly, Jeremiah ran to the tenth platform and landed. Valiic was preparing another leap when the platform started to disappear under their feet.

They aren't going to make it! Jeremiah's mind raced.

It was gone. The platform was gone!

"Holy shiivvvvffffff!" James started to yell.

Valiic's running momentum took him into James, and they both were falling towards Jeremiah, with nothing below them.

Without thinking, Jeremiah extended his hand. James saw this and grabbed Valiic's hand as they were still in freefall. Jeremiah was at the furthest point of the front edge of the platform, and as they passed, Jeremiah caught James and used the momentum to swing them to the cliff face.

Heavy! They were much heavier than anticipated. Jeremiah was forced to let some of his energy flow through his body to complete the swing.

As they arched in the other direction, Jeremiah and James let go. Both James and Valiic landed safely.

Jeremiah had no moment more. His platform faded to nothing, and he fell. Not a moment later, he lost sight of the last landing zone.

His mind went into a spin, a million things at once. He couldn't let himself fall into oblivion. He had to see this mission through. People would die if he didn't. He had already used much of the power stored within him to heal Shadow-Walker, and even more just now. But he had some left. He let it flow and gave himself a quick upward burst.

It was just enough for him to shoot just over the platform. He landed harshly, rolling into the cave, losing all sense of direction, and crashing into Valiic.

Jeremiah shook his head to clear the daze and stood up rather slowly. He turned to see a few of the unit wheezing for air, hunched over; Valiic was in the worst shape.

James, not breathless like the rest, maneuvered around Geariic to get to Jeremiah.

"How did you do it?" James was too close to Jeremiah for comfort.

Jeremiah put his hand to his forehead, still a bit dazed and drained. "Do what?"

"Don't horseshivf me. You held both Valiic's and my weight. How?"

"Are you not thankful I saved your life?"

James let the tension in his face and shoulders relax some. "Don't take me the wrong way. I'm off-the-walls grateful that you did. But it would've taken magic pixie dust and a rabbit's foot of luck to get us out of that situation. What you did wasn't... human."

"God gave me the strength I--"

James's kindly mien shifted into a frown. "Tch. Pulling that hocus-pocus shivf isn't gonna work for this."

Jeremiah shrugged, not knowing how to answer. "Adrenaline, then?" He formed the statement into a question.

Just then, Jeremiah and James noticed Frost coming to them, having just scooped up something from the ground on the way. He extended his hand towards Jeremiah, with the object firmly in his grasp. "Uzzo, I think you dropped--" his hand opened, and all three were aghast at the object in his hand, "--this," Frost finished.

Jeremiah didn't believe his eyes, prodded his pocket, and soon realized nothing was there. It must had fallen out as he landed earlier, now in witness to all three.

James snatched the object from Frost's hand and held it right in Jeremiah's face. "Where did you get this?!" By now, the eyes of the rest of the unit were glued to the scene.

Jeremiah stared at the object that had once been in his pocket. An object he knew all too well, and by the tone of James's voice, so did he. What lay before his eyes was a Quondam Key, one of four - triangular, with two additional lines protruding from the triangle and converging down into the center of the triangle to form an inner circle. Tangible symbols created a pattern from key words and instructions.

Jeremiah was searching for words to say.

Frost cheered. "James, you know what this means, right? We have the last of the four keys. The Wersillian Legion may have two, but now we do too!"

The Wersillian Legion? Jeremiah had no idea what that meant. But that was nowhere near the most concerning thing spoken. Frost mentioned that the four keys were now removed from their original hiding spots. Jeremiah never imagined this would happen in his lifetime. Just how much had he missed in the galaxy outside this planet?

James pulled out a second Quondam Key, to the shock of Jeremiah. And it was the centerpiece, no less, the one that held the other three in place.

Geariic came closer, lingering over the three of them with heightened curiosity.

"It means we need to get them both back as soon as God's grace allows us," James spoke to Frost.

Did he say both? Was James really intending on taking his? Jeremiah couldn't allow that. He needed to guard it.

James turned his attention back to Jeremiah. His eyes were spheres bottling intensity. "I asked you a direct question, Priest."

Jeremiah ignored the stare. Rather, his attention was pulled away by something truly profound. The two keys touching in the hands of James were reacting to him. Those symbols glowed a very subtle red, and James was none the wiser. This was something Jeremiah never thought was actually real. Once he heard a tale about a being who would cause such a reaction within the keys, but it was just that to him, a tale.

Frost saw and immediately pulled James's eyes to them.

"Take it," Jeremiah blurted out. He had no idea just what the reaction meant, or why it was happening. The sole thing he knew about this phenomena was that those keys belonged with this man. "You must take them with you."

James was back to Jeremiah. "I planned on it. Do you plan on answering my question?"

Jeremiah was so aghast by all that just happened, he forgot to answer the question altogether. "That relic came from this planet, and I found it. Nothing more." Jeremiah intentionally decided to downplay his knowledge of the keys. Not doing so would only bring more mistrust, along with a string of interrogative question.

"Found it?" Frost was apprehensive by tone.

"Exactly."

"And the events earlier," This time, Geariic was the one who asked, his arms crossed.

"I don't have the answer you're looking for." Jeremiah walked backward to the edge until he felt his foot partially over. "All I want is to complete this mission. If you feel that is best accomplished without me, I'll fall willingly to my death."

James lost his built up ire and breathed it away. He took a few steps and pulled Jeremiah away. "Come now, no need to be so dramatic."

"Just when I thought this trip wouldn't get any stranger." Shadow-Walker was up with his weapon, giving in to a light laugh.

Chapter 22

The group rounded everything up and pushed forward on the path. Geariic gave Jeremiah a long look, and as he neared him, Geariic grinned. "Seems you aren't as weak as I thought you were."

Jeremiah wasn't quite sure what he wanted to say, so he stuck with a simple, "Thanks."

The path that led onward was short. And a door sat at the very end of the path. Once everyone got close, the door slowly opened. Everyone took a gander around at each other, knowing how close they had come to not getting there.

Light poured into the dark hallway from the new room. Jeremiah saw a few shield their eyes as they walked through the door. But Jeremiah was accustomed to light. They were inside and ready for what awaited.

Chapter 23: Blood Attacks Blood
December 30, 2111 - December 31, 2111

Catharine Darcrose

Cathy had just finished taking a shower in the privy located in her quarters. Still drenched from head to toe, she stepped out of the shower past the stained glass door and found herself in front of a mirror hung over her wash station. Almost another week of research had gone. She even missed Christmas, but duty came first.

She seized a towel from the hangar next to her and dried herself. Earlier, on the wash station, she had placed a bag of makeup she had brought on the trip. From it she pulled out a preparation bottle and sluiced the cold liquid over her body to help the makeup last longer and be more durable. A concoction made just for her. Next, she followed up with the makeup, spending most of her time touching up her skin around her body. Her back was the hardest as always, but she had a device that helped. The process of it all was nothing but a drag, but she was used to it. She wondered if other women felt the same over the matter, but then again, it wasn't the same for them. No matter, she knew she had no taste for these beauty products and was doing it mostly to maintain appearances at this point.

When she was finished and fully clothed, she reentered her chambers. She was almost ready to sleep. Tomorrow would begin another day of researching. After all, she felt as if she was getting closer each day.

The lights to her room cut off, interrupting the moment. Almost immediately, backup lights switched on, red and dim.

Power outage? she wondered.

A window was in her room, and she looked out and saw the darkness of night, which was made even darker by the lack of lights in the stronghold. Everything but emergency lights were off. Rain was falling hard, driven by wind and drumming against the wall and window. Rivers of black water were running down the glass.

She turned away from the window and saw movement on her floor. Shadows! She remembered the skylight glass above her room.

Chapter 23

Crash!

The glass above Cathy had shattered! She jumped back, barely dodging the broken glass as she caught a glimpse of two intruders. She felt vulnerable since she didn't have on her armor. They were dressed up in exaggerated outfits; one dressed as a blue clown, the other as a red one. And both were clearly omelics. Intelligent individuals would guess they were mercenaries.

They both noticed Cathy in an instant.

Skolla appeared at the door leading to the privy after hearing the noise. His teeth were bared, and his tail and ears were laid back with aggression. Cathy held up her hand to hold off Skolla.

"The briefing said this room would be empty," the red clown said.

"You weren't paying attention. It *said* this was a guest room," said the blue clown.

"That was supposed to be empty!" retorted the first. "Frak it, let's just kill the helpless bitch and be on with it."

"Helpless?" Cathy grabbed a nearby lamp by the handle and pulled it out of the floor it was attached to. "Let's see who's helpless."

Cathy was laser focused on the two foes that came at her. She had no weapons. But she had a lamp, and it was enough for her. One pulled a silver-bladed hypersword on Cathy.

A shifting sound behind her had her sudden attention, and she turned to see another mercenary had come through the window, shattering the glass. His blade was already lit and ready to attack.

Then Skolla slammed into him, grabbing him by the neck, and both went out the window!

"Skolla!" Cathy ran to the window and saw nothing but the darkness. She was high up and knew in her head there was no surviving that fall.

"A shame about your mutt," she heard the red clown say from behind her.

When she turned back, he was already attacking. She dodged the slash, grabbed the clown's wrist, and rammed her hand against his elbow.

Snap!

"AWW! FRAK!" he cursed and dropped the blade.

Quickly, Cathy swung the lamp at the red clown, knocking the shivf out of him. He flew to the floor. She dodged her second attacker's dagger and tossed the lamp at his face. The distraction allowed her to seize the fallen hypersword. It was silver, so Cathy was able to ignite it, and she sliced deep into the blue clown's rib before he could recover. Still alive, he gazed back and was aghast.

"You--" He dropped to the floor. The blade slid out of his body, followed by a river of scarlet blood.

The other was barely getting to his feet when Cathy decapitated him with a flick of her wrist.

The power going off, along with mercenaries coming through her ceiling at almost the same time, can't be a coincidence, Cathy thought, *some plan was in play here.*

It was in her best interest to defend this castle, despite having no obligation to do so. If this place falls, her mission did, too, and that wasn't something she was going to let happen.

"For a human, you are good fighter. You were able to take two cutthroats down that fast. That was... *fun* to watch," a voice called from the skylight above.

She looked up in time to see another mercenary jumping into her room.

He was an omelic as well, covered in cleaned bones in a variety of sizes. Tiny bones shaped like thumbs and teeth were chained around his neck, his armor was made of carved bone, and he even wore a mask made of the skull of a giant animal.

"And I suppose--" Cathy gestured to and around the bone man, "--all of that is what? Scary?"

He snickered. "One for every victim. Patchface and Slackjaw here--" he pointed to the dead, "--had a body count, too."

"A lot of good that did them," Cathy snapped back.

"Mine's multiple times larger." He smirked. "They call me Scourge."

"It only takes one person to snuff out that count," Cathy jeered.

He held an ill look in his wanting eyes. "I like your face. Maybe I'll sell it when I'm done." Scourge came at Cathy with a red-bladed hyperdagger. She blocked with the sword in a shower of sparks. The bone man pulled out a second dagger and came for her throat. In one swift motion, she whirlwinded her sword to swipe it away.

He came at her again with fury. She ducked, and he went past her. She spun and kicked him into the door leading out of her chambers. It buckled from the impact. Cathy slashed at Scourge. He redirected her blade with his daggers into the door, and the sword cut through the latch like butter. The domino effect of that action led to the door spinning open and causing Scourge to fall into the hall.

He was quick to his feet to match blades with Cathy once more. In the heat of the fight, Cathy barely made out another sound. It was another fight happening close to her right.

She turned to see Mauga Lightbourne protecting the entrance to a room from another assaulter. He looked to be a knight emblazoned with the banner of a different kingdom on his slender armor. He bore an orange-bladed hypersword. At Mauga's feet lay two dead allied knights. And Mauga was on wobbly legs, with blood dripping from his shoulder and down his left leg.

Mercenaries and foreign knights? Cathy asked herself.

The foreign knight came at Mauga with absurd speed and agility. One second the knight was at Mauga's left, then his right, then dropping from the air above him; all with the use of some kind of acceleration boots to amplify his attacking speed. Mauga struggled to defend against the insane barrage of attacks.

"Don't take your attention away from me!" Scourge shouted as he took a stab at her gut with his free dagger. She barely escaped with just a graze to her side.

Scourge and Cathy were now two meters apart. Scourge then halted, seeming to be listening to a voice in his left ear.

"Fine! I'm on my way, Erryn," he said.

Erryn! Cathy's eyes flared at the familiar name.

Nonetheless, this was her moment to strike, and she took it by swinging the silver blade at Scourge. He noticed and tossed both his daggers at Cathy. She had to slide to dodge under them.

He just threw his weapons, Cathy thought, *he'll be open to an attack.*

As Cathy recovered to her feet after the slide, her face almost collided with a night-black blade erupting with darkness and swirling with power. She stopped on a dime and barely managed to spin backwards into a fighting stance. Immediately, she used her silver hypersword to block the black-bladed hypersword Scourge had pulled.

The blades collided, and her blade snapped right in half! Dumbfounded and frozen by the sudden splitting of her blade, she didn't notice a hasty follow-up attack by Scourge.

When she did see it, she knew she wouldn't be able to dodge in time. She had failed.

The air was then forced from her lungs as another body tackled her to the floor and away from Scourge and his attack. The body slid off her, and she sat up, looking to her side to see Mauga wailing in pain. His hands covered his right leg, or what was left of it. Below the knee, it was severed completely off! Blood was draining like a hose. And she didn't have to look far to see the rest of it beside Scourge.

"You fraken idiot!" she cursed. Mauga was in too much pain to hear her. Sweating from the fight, with what little she had on, her clothes had started to cling to her skin.

"You've got quite the soldier's body," Scourge complimented. He was walking toward them. "Maybe, instead, I'll just cut off your limbs so you can't struggle as I take you."

"You fit the stereotype of omelic men quite heavily. You assume you have the right to take what you want just because your blood is up."

He let loose wild laughter. "Nothing like a good rape after a fight."

Behind Scourge, the knight that Mauga was fighting off earlier was heading towards them, too. And Cathy had nothing left to defend herself or Mauga. Even so, she stood up ready to fight, fist out and bared.

Scourge and the other knight stopped.

Cathy felt a hand on her shoulder. "Leave them to me. You've done enough today," a voice whispered from behind. She hadn't even heard his footsteps.

She turned to see another omelic in allied armor; chiseled and elegant, with a gold tint to highlight its black color. He held a brown-bladed hypersword. The stearth was curved, giving the hypersword blade a curve as well; saber-framed. Black with gold accents, the grip was stylish. What truly was the marvel piece of the sword was the design of the cross guard; one end formed into a knuckle guard that protected his hand. And the flowing energy made its way over the knuckle and cross guard.

"Who are you?" she asked.

"Qrow Jraxston." He stepped in front of her and was now in-between her and the enemies. "Help Mauga, please. He has done a lot for our kingdom and doesn't deserve to die today."

Cathy did as asked and bent down to help. She placed Mauga against the wall. He slouched, now recovering some from the initial pain of the lost limb. She took off her top and covered Mauga's cut. She used her belt to strap it tight. She now had nothing above her waist but a bra. His eyes caught the sight of Ser Qrow.

"It's him," he whispered to Cathy.

"Don't speak," she instructed.

"He'll save us. He--" Mauga coughed. "He's the best duelist I've ever seen."

Now interested, Cathy looked up to see Qrow still idle, waiting.

Scourge pointed his sword at Qrow. "I know you, Ser Qrow. Tell me, what is a shadow knight like you doing here?"

"I came upon intelligence about an attack scheduled to take place on Wolph Castle today. So I came to stop it," he answered.

"Only you?"

"I'm all that's needed."

"Arrogant fraker," Scourge cursed him. "But you'll make a fine addition to the collection on my armor."

"And you-- I recognized that voice. Ryben Bukkaro - the Scourge of the South. Said to kill his victims, eat from their corpses, and mold their bones into armor. Said to have killed three members of his own family, two when he was a young kid, and raped two more. Said to have cut the tongues out of his newborn sons because he couldn't stand to hear them cry. Said to have made a young girl fall in love with him - gave her gifts and made her feel like a queen - and when she got pregnant, he cut her tongue and chained her to the bow of his pirate ship, all just to prove a point."

"Lies! I never did half of what you said. I shall cut your tongue out for your slander." Scourge was livid, with his hypersword still pointed at Qrow.

"Cutting a man's tongue out doesn't prove he is liar, only that you don't like what he has to say."

Scourge and the other enemy knight were gearing up to attack. Scourge pounded his chest. "You! You fraker! I'll be damned if you think you can say that to me! Come, Ser Yarth." The hall was wide enough for Scourge to run towards Qrow's right, and the other knight to Qrow's left.

Scourge met him first. Qrow swiftly blocked a high and low attack before momentum carried Scourge past Qrow. Yarth was next, and Qrow blocked his attack just as fast. Both held blades together, leaving Scourge with an opening to strike Qrow's back. Qrow spun his blade around and ducked under Scourge attack. He gathered on the other side, in range of Yarth, who swung at Qrow's leg. He stepped over the strike and flipped over him completely and was now behind Yarth. He brought his sword around his body and came back down with the blade vertically. Qrow bent his back and spun the blade to block the attack over his back. He spun out again, causing Yarth to almost lose his blade.

Yarth recovered and powered up his boots and boosted to the ceiling, then to the wall. He attacked, but it was parried by Qrow. The next came from behind and then above and then to the side; all happening in quick succession of one another. Qrow's defense was ironclad. After another two swift attacks and blocks, Qrow snuck in a kick and knocked Yarth to the ground.

Qrow smiled and said, "You're an impressive user of Syvn in the art of hypersword combat. A style that utilizes speed and haste to break past an opponent's defense. But every user of this style is well-aware of its severe drawback - it exhausts the user quickly. All I needed to do was outlast your barrage of attacks and wait for an opening."

Yarth growled in response. He bolted up and attacked Qrow recklessly and paid for his mistake. Qrow dodged and bashed him with his knuckle guard, cutting Yarth's cheek and sending him to the ground once more.

Scourge was quick to capitalize. Jumping earlier, he came down with his blade angled straight down. Qrow dodged and the blade impaled the floor. He pulled it up and sliced at Qrow's feet. He blocked low, with his blade touching the floor. Yarth had gotten back to his feet and sliced at Qrow's exposed arm. Qrow let go of his handle for a mere instant to avoid the swing and grabbed it again with his other hand. Yarth's blade was now in-between Qrow and his blade, his momentum carrying his blade closer to the floor. Qrow angled his blade, which was still locked with Scourge, upward and kicked the handle of Yarth's hypersword towards Scourge. His blade had nowhere to go but into Scourge's now exposed stomach. His orange blade tore partly into Scourge, who fell to his knees.

Qrow pulled his blade free of Scourge and sliced Yarth from waist to shoulder. He couldn't pull his sword in time to defend himself.

With both enemies defeated, Qrow turned to Cathy. "Head down the left. I'll go right."

"And what about Lord Mauga?"

"I'll call an arkenlord and let him know this area is clear. The arkenlord will help him. But we have to find and protect the king. He wasn't in his quarters or his study. I checked."

"Very well. I'll do my duty." Cathy rose. She would've loved nothing more to grab one of those swords. However, none were silver bladed. Since she had no bond with a scarlencoul, she would be unable to use them. She had no choice to go left down the hall without any weapons.

She kept a quick pace, ignoring much of the details of her surroundings. She knew going left would eventually lead her out of the guest section of the castle, and she made haste until she was clear of it. After bursting into one of the main corridors, she had a few different ways to go. Directly left led to Saulomon's Temple and entrance to the throne room. King Kaylob wouldn't be in the temple, of that she was sure. But the throne room?

She listened and heard no sounds of fighting. Much of what happened in the area of the castle had already happened. There were bodies in the corridor, but no sounds of battle. So she chose to go a way she hadn't been yet, directly right.

Soon the sounds of battle found her, and she spotted a large doorway at the end of the hall. It was the council's chambers. A clash was going on in and outside of the room. The royal knights were fighting off mercenaries, along with enemy knights.

Behind her, she heard the roars of men. When she turned, she recognized them to be allied knights. She moved aside and let them take the lead. Following behind, she waited as they charged toward the enemies and took up blades. That distraction allowed her to slip into the council's chambers.

Inside was richly furnished. Expansive carpets covered the floor instead of rushes, and in one corner a hundred fabulous beasts cavorted in bright paints on a carved screen for décor. The walls were hung with tapestries from around the planet, and a pair of metallic sphinxes flanked the door with eyes of polished garnet smoldering in black marble faces.

At the head of the large table centering the room, King Kaydon was standing up, anxiously hoping for his guards to pull through and clear an exit for his escape. Kaizerious was rather calm given the circumstances, sitting in a chair a meter away from the king.

"How did you get in?" King Kaydon asked.

"I'm trained to get into places that I'm not supposed to," Cathy answered, with dry humor.

"You have no part in this. You shouldn't've come."

"No guest should watch as their host dies." Cathy picked up a hypersword from a dead knight and ignited the silver blade.

"You've got it backwards. The host is responsible for his guests, not the other way around. I cannot ask you to risk your life for me."

A sudden bang stopped her before she could speak. She turned to see the fighting had been stopped by an explosion. The last royal knight alive then fell from a shot to the head. As his body hit the floor, one last mercenary was revealed.

She was an omelic wearing a worn-down, brown western hat with two gold laced strings tied around it; a tattered scarf rested below her breathing mask but above her body armor. The mercenary's right arm was robotic, and a golden-ink and animated skelven tattoo decorated her left arm. She pointed one of her two ballistic revolvers at the king.

The mercenary was Erryn Wolph.

Cathy only had a hypersword, with no armor. From experience, she knew it would not stop a bullet. Nonetheless, she stood in front of the king, blocking him from Erryn. Kaizerious edged further up his chair, troubled by the situation.

"Move, bitch," Erryn panted from the exhaustion of fighting. "My only gripe here is with my family. Get in the way, and I'll shoot right through you."

"I'm not moving," Cathy promised.

"Have it your way, dear." Those words ended with a gunshot! Cathy blinked at the sound and expected to feel the pain of dying. Her eyes opened, and she felt nothing. In front of her was an arm thicker than her torso. She followed the arm back to Kaizerious, and her face filled with shock. But at the same time, she felt a prick in her heart at the thought that Kaizerious took a bullet for her.

Erryn fell to the ground after firing the bullet, panting still. She let the gun go. "Frak it all. That was my last bullet," she said. She didn't move, letting whatever happened next happen.

Guards stormed in and seized her.

"Take my sister to the dungeons," King Kaydon commanded.

It took nearly the whole night to stop the invasion. Most of the remaining mercenaries fled upon hearing Erryn Wolph had been captured, leaving the enemy knights outnumbered. Many of them were shown little mercy.

*****

It was the following morning, and at last Cathy sat face-to-face with Erryn Wolph. In a circular room of just a single table and chair, it was recently decorated with fresh blood. Erryn was beaten and battered; her ribs were tenderized like meat, and she had cuts and scrapes all over her body. Tortured. And yet Erryn smirked. "You're quite a beautiful specimen."

Cathy held back from blushing. "I thought you fancied men?"

"No dear, I fancy pleasure. When I'm offered love, I'm not choosy. Why indulge myself in only half of the galaxy's pleasures?" Erryn coughed, spewing some blood in the process. "You here to get your revenge?"

"Revenge?"

"I did try to shoot you."

"Yet, I'm unharmed. No, I'm here because I'm hoping you might be able to lead me on the correct path."

"What are you even talking about?" Erryn asked.

"I want information on the Brotherhood of Relics."

Erryn snorted at the mention of their name. "Then talk to Kaydon. He is the bloody king."

"He claims to not know anything about the brotherhood."

"That's because they aren't real, honey." There was mockery in her tone. "They're just a damn myth. So--"

Cathy stopped her. "I wonder how someone of royal blood like you ends up a mercenary on the run... on her own... alone in this grand galaxy."

"What the frak is it to you?" Erryn cursed.

"Most people have no clue you descended from a king."

"They know I killed my father... that's enough."

"But why?"

"You know how omelics treat their women. They--"

"Don't bullshivf me." Cathy slammed her hands on the table filled with torturous tools.

"What? Do you want my whole life story?!" Erryn screamed.

"No. I just want information on any clues that the Brotherhood of Relic's ancestors may have left here."

Erryn sighed. "I already told you--"

"Stop!" Cathy pushed aside the table and came closer to Erryn. "Let's stop wasting precious time with lies and deception. You remember our mutual acquaintance, James Stone?"

Erryn cheered up, shifting upright in her chair, chains clanking in her movement. She smiled. "Of course. How could I forget such a fine ass?"

Cathy rolled her eyes. "According to Captain Wild-Heart, James had a run in with the Brotherhood of Relics on a recent mission, and they were responsible for saving countless ARW and civilian lives. I want to thank them personally."

Chapter 23

"I thought you said not to waste time with lies?" Erryn retorted. "You wouldn't waste time *thanking* them. You want to meet them to form some kind of alliance, no?"

Cathy shifted upright. "That's ARW business."

"Save your time. The Brotherhood of Relics allies with nobody but themselves." Erryn's gaze turned to the floor.

"They'll want to hear what I have to say."

"And if I help you, what's in it for me?" Erryn asked.

Cathy pulled out a key. Erryn gazed in complete shock and awe. She began, "Is that--?"

"Yes. The key to your shackles."

"How?" Erryn's eyes did not leave the key.

"Snatched it from the guard. And it's yours... *if* you help me."

Through the bruising and pain, Erryn smiled with cheer. "Deal."

"Glad to hear it," Cathy nodded.

Erryn grinned. "Have you ever heard of the *Tale of the Lost Village?*"

"What does that have to do with the brotherhood?" Cathy questioned.

"Legend says the brotherhood's location lies hidden... riddled into the story."

"Hmm. You have my undivided attention. Where can I find this story?"

"In Saulomon's Temple, the children's section."

"Children? It's a damn children's story?!" Cathy was a bit miffed by that reveal. Not what she expected.

"Trust me. But look specifically for the call number: LVP 909.P57996. From there, read the book all the way until the end," Erryn informed.

"Anything else?"

Erryn looked to the door for a brief moment. "Just a word of advice. Your friend.... watch out for that one."

"Who?" Cathy had an idea of who.

"The big guy of course!" Erryn yelled.

Cathy gazed at Erryn for a few seconds, still not quite sure what to make of the warning. "And what is that supposed to mean?"

"When I said that *I'll shoot right through you,* I meant what I said. That bullet was forged from pure forcidion and packed full of as much airjin fuel that I could squeeze in. And... and that bullet - made of the most indestructible metal in all existence - bounced off that man like rubber! A bullet like that would pierce straight through a line of maelkii!"

Those words chilled Cathy. What could this mean if what Erryn said was true? "Why are you telling me this?"

"To scare you, dumbo! I mean, what the hell is he? Th-that he could take firepower like that without even flinching."

"I don't know! And you know what? I really don't care. Here!" Cathy tossed Erryn the key, and it landed on her lap. "Take the key, and leave this place." Cathy headed for the door. She looked back at Erryn, who had already somehow managed to shift the key to one of her chained hands. Cathy banged on the door. The guard opened it and let her out.

Chapter 24: Wolph Family Tree
December 31, 2111

Catharine Darcrose

As Cathy was on her way back to her chambers, she found Kaizerious in the Grand Hall, staring at the family tree of the royal family going up like vines dozens of meters high. But his eyes were locked onto just one picture - Erryn Wolph. He held a piece of paper in his hand.

"How did your interrogation go?" Kaizerious asked, his eyes unmoving, as Cathy arrived by his side.

"She gave me a lead to go on," she replied. Kaizerious nodded, almost not even acknowledging her. He was in a zone, deep in thought, distant even. Cathy hadn't seen him like this before. "Kaizerious?"

"There used to be a saying that the dermmotifs of a child would be the shadow of the parent that sat opposite," he spoke.

"Dermmotifs?"

"That is what the omelics call the patterned-black markings on their faces and skin."

"I enjoy fun facts as much of the next, but I'm not sure I follow your point."

"A bit before you showed up here, I came across an interesting study while browsing Saulomon's Temple - one done a long while ago. Depicted in the study, I read that omelic children can actually be traced back to their parents by their faces alone. All omelics have two major pigment genes that determine the tint of their skin and how the pattern of their dermmotifs will show. When a bunch of those black cells bunch together, the dermmotifs are visible to common eyes. However, some black cells would still remain separated, remote from the rest and mixed in with their normal skin cells. Those aren't things the common eye would see, but with the right kind of microscope, they can be seen. That riddle I mention earlier... it means that a child's dermmotifs would take after those hidden patches in the parent of the opposite sex. So a son would take after his mother, and a daughter after her father. Though, it's worth noting that this wasn't an infallible method."

Cathy's eyebrows furrowed. "I still don't see where this is going."

He pointed to the parents of the king, and Cathy looked. "When I saw Erryn, something about her stood out to me," Kaizerious said.

Cathy gazed at the pictures. Nothing stood out to her. All she saw were unique faces with unique dermmotifs. Erryn's was the simplest - two black lines starting just above both her eyes and going straight down and past them until it stopped halfway down her checks. The king's father and mother's masks were all around their face. And the king had just a small patch below his nose and another between his eyebrows, making it seem as if he had a unibrow.

"I don't see the differences," Cathy remarked.

"To the naked eye of a human, I would imagine so. To me, I can see those hidden black cells. The king's father, in particular, has some around his cheek bones. The king's mother has some around her ears and down her neck. Erryn - she just has a tiny patch above her lip and one in the shape of a teardrop above her right eyebrow." He handed Cathy the paper he was holding. It was dry with a thick texture and torn away from something. "That was taken from a mortician's journal nearly twenty years ago."

Cathy read the top of the page where Kaizerious pointed. *"Logbook December 2, 2093: Deceased body of the Queen Cateron Wolph identified. Beginning preparations for her royal sendoff."*

Kaizerious continued. "That logbook says she died on the second of December. However, King Kaydon's mother's official date of death released by the doctor at that time for Cateron Wolph was December 27 - three days after the day that the current king was born."

"That doesn't make any sense. His mother couldn't have died bef--" She stopped midsentence.

Kaizerious finally turned to Cathy with an expression of revulsion and alarm. She thought about what he said. The king's dermmotifs were patterned below the nose and between his eyebrows. Queen Cateron had nonvisible markings nowhere near the king's visible ones. But Erryn did!

Cathy's chest grew heavy, the hairs on her arm stood tall. She shivered at the thought - the vile thought. "No! It-it can't-- Erryn?!"

Kaizerious nodded. "Erryn."

Chapter 24

Cathy sighed. The palm of her hand ran up her face and through her hair. She couldn't believe it. Erryn was not just King Kaydon's sister, but his mother, too. "Frak. I gotta... I have to talk to her before she leaves."

Kaizerious tilted his head. "Are you sure you want to involve yourself in this... unclean family business?"

"I can't in good conscience let her leave this castle without saying what I have to say."

"Leave the castle? She's chained up, isn't she?" Kaizerious asked. By the tone in his voice, Cathy gathered he knew the answer.

"I gave her the key."

"Very well. If she hasn't escaped yet, I know where she is likely to go."

"Take me there."

Kaizerious led her through the lower parts of the castle past rooms and chambers long abandoned. Dust and old decorum were all over these damp and dark parts of the castle. Into secret rooms and hallways they ventured until Kaizerious led them to a tunnel opening. It was a surreptitious way out of the castle.

✱✱✱✱✱

Kaizerious and Cathy waited in the tunnel. The only light source was a flickering torchlight hanging just to the left of the ladder they had lit earlier. There was movement, and lo and behold, Erryn slid down.

She nearly jumped back at the sight of Cathy and Kaizerious. "Frak! I thought I saw the last of you," she told Cathy. Her eyes were wary of Kaizerious, however.

"Took you long enough," Cathy fired back.

"Had to wait for a guard to open the door to check on me," Erryn sighed. "What do you want now anyway? I mean, I already helped you with your quest and shivf... sooo--?" Erryn shrugged.

In the long while it took for Erryn to arrive, Cathy had been running scenarios as to what she should say when Erryn finally showed. Now that she was here, Cathy wasn't sure if what she had come up with was the right way to tackle this particular situation. "I just wanted to know how old you were when your brother was born."

Erryn shot her a sideways eye. "Fourteen. W-why?"

"That's umm... young to have a kid."

You could've heard a pin drop. Erryn was frozen in place for a tense couple seconds. She balled up her fists, cheeks turning pale. "Excuse me?!" she barked, holding back much of the anger.

Cathy took in a breath. "See uh... we know the truth. We know King Kaydon is your son. We--"

"You don't know a damn thing! You... you don't-- You couldn't even begin to understand--"

"I do, actually. I do understand. You killed your father. I now know why and damn-sure may have even done the same in your shoes. I mean, to have your very own father take advantage of you."

"Take advantage? Let's get this in the air, shall we? He raped me! Mother was too sick to carry a child, so he--" Her voice caught in her throat. Tears dripped from Erryn's eyes. Cathy couldn't hold back either. "He turned me into his object... his baby factory. He wanted an heir so so-very bad." Erryn used her arm to wipe away her tears. "I was held prisoner during--" She stopped as her voice caught.

"It happened to my mom, too," said Cathy. This was why Erryn's situation was all too close to home for Cathy. "She kept the child, though - my older sister. And... despite that she wasn't his, my dad, rest his soul, loved my sister just as much as his own children. And her other siblings never even knew." A tear hit the floor before Cathy started to wipe it away. By now, Cathy could feel Kaizerious's stare on her back.

Erryn was a mess. Cathy was just as bad. For a few seconds, no words were spoken.

"Was your mother raped by her father?" Erryn asked.

"She wasn't."

"Then it isn't the same."

"Maybe. I just know that my sister grew up to be who she was because of her parents. And her parents were so proud. Even if it wasn't by the choice of my mom to have a child then, my sister was gifted a life to live. That was something her parents never even considered taking away."

"Look, that's cute and all, but I didn't... I didn't have a choice. Mine was made for me. And if it had been my choice, the king wouldn't even have been born. They locked me up to keep the precious heir alive inside me."

"So what? You try to kill him to correct that?" Cathy was sympathetic, but she felt it was wrong what Erryn was trying to do.

"It's none of your business!" Erryn shouted.

"Oh, please," Cathy sighed. "We are so past that! Why try to kill your own son?"

"He never should've been born!"

"But he was. And that won't change. Why can't you let him have his life? For all you know, he could change the world."

"It isn't about that," Erryn wept.

"Then what is it about?"

"It's... it's about hate - my hatred of him."

"Did he do something to you?" asked Cathy.

"No. He doesn't even know th-that I'm his--" Her voiced pulled away.

"So why hate your child?"

"I hate him... I hate him because I never wanted him."

Cathy extended her palm, trying to sympathize with Erryn. She had to make her see, she just had to. "My mom didn't want a child at the time it happened. She went on to love her anyway."

"I hate him... because when I see him, I see his father, my father. I *see* that monster."

"King Kaydon isn't like your father. He has done nothing but good for this kingdom. He helped bring it back from the fringes of destruction."

Erryn was in tears. "I know, I-I do. I... I hate him. Because if I didn't hate him... I'd love him. And love... love is weakness. I will *never* be weak again. Never." She wiped the tears away and flexed her jaw. She used anger to fight away her pain.

"Weakness would be letting your past define what you do now. Every time you go after your son, you prove yourself weak. So don't let weakness be what kills your son."

Erryn began walking past them. Cathy didn't try to stop her or block her path, nor did Kaizerious. As she made it to Cathy, she gave her a long stare, then gave her a nod. She then trudged by them, without saying another word, until she faded away into the dark of the tunnel. That was that. They waited alone in silence, staring in the direction Erryn disappeared.

"You don't have an older sister, do you?" Kaizerious finally asked Cathy.

"I *am* the older sister."

Chapter 25: Tale of the Lost Village
December 31, 2111

Catharine Darcrose

Cathy explored the children's section of Saulomon's Temple and came across an entire row of *"Tale of the Lost Village."* She eyed each one. Every number matched the call number Erryn gave up until the last two digits. LVP 909.P57991; 92, 93, 94, 95. It stopped. She reached the end of the brown shelf. She gazed over to the next shelf: LVP 909.P57997, and a completely different book at that.

What? Where is it?

Her eyes returned to the original shelf and spotted something - something in the back. She shifted over the last book and reached back. Her fingers tipped against another book half stuck behind a hole in the wall that met a column between that shelf and the adjacent one. She grabbed it and yanked it loose. LVP 909.P57996! She had it!

She took it back to her favorite seat in the restricted section. Kaizerious was waiting there already. She opened the first page:

A long time ago, in a time of wonders and mystery, a king ruled with riches as deep as dreams. This king, a king named Kaylob, ruled over many villages and over land further than eyes could see. He had everything a king could want - riches, power, fame. Other kings envied him for his power and prayed for a day that they could take what was his. But King Kaylob did not fear them, for he was the most powerful king in all of the north. No, the king had but one fear - a prophecy. One day, at the height of the king's power and influence, on the day of his thirtieth birthday, a foremoth--

Cathy stopped reading and gazed to Kaizerious. "What is that?"
"Think of it as a fairy or pixie that can predict the future."
"Hmm." She continued to read.

--a foremoth came to the king in his dreams and foretold upon him a prophecy.

She whispered into the king's ear, "On the day of your next birthday, a boy born to a family of farmers, a firstborn child shaped by the land of the king, will bring your kingdom to its knees."

The king awoke, screaming that night and, out of fear, devised a plan. On the birth of the next morning, King Kaylob marched his army village to village and slaughtered every firstborn child of every family of farmers within his land. He believed the words of the foremoth to be a warning that the child was in his kingdom. Little did the king know, by acting to prevent his kingdom's fall from power, the king would only cause it.

Word spread as the king made his way to the outer villages and resistance formed. In battle and arms, the resistance fell that night. Time was bought, and the firstborn son of a pair of farmers fled at the dusk of the battle's end. His parents, among the resistance, died. The boy fled no longer a farmer's son; he fled an orphan.

By the next full moon, King Kaylob had killed every firstborn child of every family of farmers in all of his villages. Or so he thought. He did not know of the orphan. The child, now filled with fear of the king and pain over the loss of his parents, ran into hiding, believing the king would one day hunt for him.

Deep into an unending forest the boy traveled, deeper than anybody before. As years went by, the boy became a man who was forged by instinct and nature. The man, his name was Arathor. On the day of an eclipse, during a hunt that led Arathor further into the forest than ever before, he came upon a tree - an ancient tree unlike any in the forest. Its roots ran deep, its trunk as thick as a lake, and its branches extending over a nearby mountain. Arathor found an opening and slipped down between the roots. Tunnels, forged by roots, took him under the forest and to a room filled with treasure and magic.

"Magic? You expect me to believe in magic?" she asked. Her unbelieving eyes pleaded at Kaizerious. As the story continued, she grew more skeptical.

"This story is children's folktale coming from a time before science," he replied.

She continued:

Chapter 25

--In this room, there was but one thing that caught the eye of Arathor, for he did not seek treasure or riches, for he lived off nature. The one thing that captured his interest was a tomb in the back. Inside was a wizard held in a space without time and full of white light. Arathor placed his hand on the glass and shot back as steam and water came exploding out of the sides! He watched as the wizard, wet and weak, stumbled from the case and fell to his knees. Arathor reached out his hand to aid the wizard to his feet and was surprised to see the wizard rise as an ordinary omelic, a spitting image of himself. When the wizard stood at eye level, he asked Arathor how he had found him. Arathor, trembling, started from the beginning and told the wizard everything from the king to his parents to his journeys in the forest. The wizard, unfazed by the story, spawned a jacket out of nothing and gave it to Arathor.

The wizard thanked Arathor for saving him and spoke. "Take my gift. Take this jacket and wear it into the kingdom. For you have saved me, so shall I save your people."

"How?" he asked.

"Face your fears. Face the king."

"But who are you?"

"Murrlawn." Then the wizard vanished before Arathor's eyes.

Scared but trusting, Arathor eventually did as the wizard asked and made the long journey back into the kingdom. Jacket on, he approached the gate guard and told him his heritage. The guard escorted him before the king, spear aimed at his back. After the king was informed, he gazed upon the man and asked him why he had come. Arathor responded that he came to take the freedom of his village. The king and his men laughed and howled in jest before giving the order to kill Arathor. A guard plunged the spear at Arathor's back! It did not pierce. For the guard cried in pain as the spear shattered back into his face. The king, now dumbfounded, yelled out for all his guards to attack. Each swing of a sword or fire of an arrow would deflect back at the attackers.

Once the advances stopped, Arathor took the moment to speak. "You have shown no mercy and seek only power. Should you attempt to harm another innocent life in your kingdom, I shall show your kingdom no mercy and show you the true meaning of power."

Frightened, the king nodded, and Arathor left. Only a day later, the king rode with his army to the home village of Arathor, only to discover it abandoned. Upon searching the place up and down and all around, all that remained was a hardcover book with the words "tell my story" on the front. Enraged, the king rode to his castle and thundered up to his quarters. He tossed the book in the fire and cursed into the wind from his balcony. That night the king woke to a light in the corner of his room. As he rubbed away the sleep, the light moved toward him. It was Arathor! And he held the book that the king had thrown in the fire. Stunned, the king froze.

Arathor spoke. "You disappoint me, King. I saw you this morning with your army, seeking to enact your fury, and when you couldn't, you tossed my gift in the fire. Sadly for you, it cannot be destroyed. And should you try to lose it, it will always find a way back to you. Because of what you did today, I take away your kingdom, your power, and leave you only with this dull castle. Do not force my hand again."

Arathor handed King Kaylob the book and left him to his defeat. In trying to avoid the prophecy, the king caused it and lost everything. He lived out his remaining years in isolation. His legacy passed on the book from generation to generation, and the story spread across the lands. But his kingdom never regained its former power.

The end.

Cathy finished the story with nothing but a blank page left to turn. "Is this book mentioned in the story real?"

"You just read it," Kaizerious answered, pointing.

Cathy didn't expect that answer. "This?"

"It is just a folktale."

"It can't be. Erryn wouldn't have ju--" Cathy bit her tongue.

Frustrated, she turned to the last page - the blank one. A note! It was taped inside the back cover. *"At the king's fire, call my name,"* the note read. Another riddle! Freven great!

"Any idea what that means?" Cathy asked Kaizerious. Throughout her time searching for the brotherhood, he had been there to help every step of the way. She had come to respect his intelligence and this instance was no different.

Chapter 25

"King's fire?" His eyes drifted toward the ceiling. "In the story, King Kaylob threw the book in the fire of his fireplace. I'd start there."

"You really are a genius."

*****

Kaizerious asked around and found out that the current king's chambers were not in the same place as the king's chambers during King Kaylob's reign. Those old chambers where in an ancient, sealed off part of the castle. Kaizerious had to get permission from King Kaydon to venture into such a place.

At a sealed off door, a knight pulled away the nailed boards to allow it to open. He let them venture in by themselves.

It was an old study abandoned to dust and spiders. A decaying desk sat near one end of the room, while a carved bench decorated the other. Books doused in layers of grime and filth lined the shelved walls. At the back was a circular staircase leading upward.

They followed the creaky steps up and up the tower. They then reached the top landing, which led to a wooden door. Kaizerious pulled it open by the latch, and its creak echoed down the stairs. It was a bedroom that hadn't seen use in decades. A mattress had partially fallen to the floor due to a broken peg. Any furniture that had remained in this room was a shell of its former glory. Across from the mattress was a fireplace with a stone mantel, caste, and chimney.

Cathy stood in front of it and wondered for a moment how they would light it without firewood. That's when she saw Kaizerious snap apart pieces from the furniture and tossed them into the fireplace. She doused the wood with some airjin fuel from a bullet and lit a match. It was enough to ignite a fire.

They stood beside the lit fire, and Cathy shrugged and whispered, "Erryn?" as though asking a question. Nothing. "Erryn Wolph." Again, nothing. "What now?"

Kaizerious pondered the thought. "The note was attached to the book. What is the name of the book?"

"*Tale of the Lost Village.*"

The fire shimmered and roared. The red flames blinked blue before all was normal again. On top of the flames sat a book looking much older than those picture books in the children's section. Cathy reached into the flame and grabbed it. Remarkably, there was no heat, no burn.

"That does it. I believe in magic," Cathy joked dryly.

She turned it open and read. Every word was the same as what she already read before. Wait, no! The last page, it started differently:

That night the king woke to a light in the corner of his room. As he rubbed away the sleep, the light moved toward him. It was Arathor! And he held the book that the king had thrown in the fire. Stunned, the king froze.

Arathor spoke. "You disappoint me, King. I saw you this morning with your army, seeking to enact your fury, and when you couldn't, you tossed my gift in the fire. Sadly for you, it cannot be destroyed. And should you try to lose it, it will always find a way back to you. Because of what you did today, I take away your kingdom, your power, and leave you only with this dull castle. Do not force my hand again."

Arathor handed King Kaylob the book. But before going, he whispered on last thing, one last riddle. "In blood you sought to bathe my village, but our blood shall always conquer. Those of this blood need only seek home to find home."

Arathor left him to his defeat. In trying to avoid the prophecy, the king caused it and lost everything. He lived out his remaining years in isolation. His legacy passed on the book from generation to generation, and the story spread across the lands. But his kingdom never regained its former power.

The end.

"That doesn't make sense!" Cathy was running low on patience. *"In blood you sought to bathe my village, but our blood shall always conquer. Those of this blood need only seek home to find home.* I'd say that the first part is clear. It simply refers back to the story when King Kaylob tried to attack Arathor's village. It's the second part that must lead to something."

Chapter 25

"I think he says that anyone of his lineage - *those of this blood* - are supposed to go home." Kaizerious scratched at his chin, with his eyes up in thought.

"Home? You mean that village that King Kaylob tried to attack?"

Kaizerious gave it a moment. "I think that would be a good place to check." He hesitated, then put up a finger. "Hang on. I'll be back shortly." She waited for a few moments, thinking over the story and if there were any more details that would be helpful. She barely noticed when Kaizerious returned, despite his size and rather loud steps. "I found this on the shelves downstairs." He showed an old map from King Kaylob's reign and unrolled it over the dusty castle floor. "Please pull up the current map of the Tolkran Kingdom."

Cathy used her cyberwatch and enlarged the image before projecting it next to the old map. There were many differences, the biggest being scale. The old Tolkran Kingdom was far larger than what it was today. Cathy didn't know where to begin. There was so much.

Kaizerious raised his finger and pointed to a spot on the map. "I found it."

"Found it? Already?" Cathy looked at the village he pointed at and compared it to her map. In its place was a small town called Grimlock. It was on the very northern edge of the current Tolkran Kingdom.

"What makes you so sure?"

"Before you arrived, I remember reading somewhere about Lord Smyth Grimlock receiving land for himself and all his future generations in perpetuity for his valor in battle by decree of King Rickter. That land contained the abandoned ruins of a village that King Kaylob marked as cursed."

Cathy agreed. While it wasn't perfect, this was the best lead they had. It was well worth a shot. Only thing, they would have quite a long travel ahead of them. Being that it was past midday, they would likely get there close to midnight in ARW time.

✳✳✳✳✳

Kaizerious and Cathy were at the edge of Grimlock, having been dropped off close not too long ago. King Kaydon was nice enough to lend them transport via a dropship. There were gates and a fence of tall planked wood. Above it all was a tower with a knight on guard.

The gates opened outward at his command, and a man in armor came forward to meet Kaizerious and Cathy. The old man had no helmet; his hair was as pale as his armor, yet he seemed strong and graceful for all that. From his shoulders hung a pure white cloak.

"King Kaydon sent word of your arrival," He stopped before them, eyeing them up and down. "I'm Lord Smyth Grimlock II. Please follow me inside."

They went through the gates. Grimlock was a complex spanning several acres and protected by two massive walls. There was a village at the end, older than anything else in the complex, called the Grim Ruins. It was separated from the main town by a gate.

As they headed to the back of the town, Lord Smyth spoke. "Grimlock was built near an ancient forest which spread over a natural hot springs. The water is piped through walls and chambers to heat them, making Grimlock more comfortable than other complexes nearby."

"You'd think there'd be better technology out here," said Cathy.

"The far north is a land mostly of lowbloods. But we take care of our own in these parts."

Inside the walls, the complex was composed of dozens of courtyards and small open spaces. Weapons training and practice took place in those yards. Located next to a broken tower was an inner yard that was an older open space in the castle where archery practice took place. At the center of the town stood the inner castle, containing a great keep and a great hall. They passed fewer than a hundred omelics, and maybe a dozen of them were armed knights.

Many of the towers and halls had diamond-shaped window panes, constructed of materials including stucco, brick, and stone.

They reached an open gate at the back of Grimlock that led into the Grim Ruins. A dirt road wove its way through the ruins. Lord Smyth stopped. "Here we are. I'll leave you be." He left them.

Made of materials gathered from a nearby river, many of these abandoned homes and farms were degraded and spalling away. The limestone and river stones weren't made to last this many centuries. A very few of the structures used a wooden lap siding cut from the forest near the town.

The ruins were open to a forest - the same one Smyth mentioned. It was a dark, primal place of old forest left mostly untouched for thousands of years, even as this gloomy town rose near it. Covering as far as her eyes could see, it smelled of moist earth and decay. No softwood trees grew there. Instead, that place grew stubborn sentinel trees armored in gray-green needles, mighty oaks, ironwoods as old as Omulice. Thick black trunks crowded close together while twisted branches wove a dense canopy overhead and misshapen roots wrestled beneath the soil. It was a place of deep silence and brooding shadows.

There was an omelic here and there, but there wasn't much action as they walked the street through the ruins. The omelics they did see were coming back from a hunt with freshly killed prey.

Towards the end of the ruins was a chapel that fit the architecture of the rest. To what religion it was built for was unknown to Cathy. She vaguely remembered that places of worship on Omulice had a formal name, only Cathy couldn't recall. Even though it was the largest structure remaining in the village, it was the best maintained.

As they got to the entrance door, an omelic man came out and passed by them with an interested stare. Then they went inside.

The entrance door led right into the sanctuary room with wooden benches, each hand-carved to match the walls and ceiling. All of them had been maintained, polished, and stained. Lining the room were candles hung on walls and near benches. Cathy was amazed at the height of the ceiling - at least fifteen meters and supported by thick limestone columns.

"Welcome," said the omelic at the other end. He stood just past the deacon doors near the ambo, or preaching stage. Old and in traditional omelic religious attire, he stepped down to meet his new guests. "What brings you to my sanctum?"

"We believe this village was the home village of Arathor."

The omelic tilted his head with a funny expression. "The Grim Ruins were abandoned long ago."

"You're still here," Kaizerious prodded.

"I maintain this beautiful piece of omelic history and even hold sermons here once every fortnight."

"If you haven't heard of Arathor, maybe you've heard of the Brotherhood of Relics," Cathy queried.

"Only the legend."

"In any case, we would be honored if you'd kindly allow us to take a look around." Kaizerious was polite with his tone.

"Absolutely. This is a public monument." The omelic man stepped aside and allowed them room to press onward.

The sanctuary connected to a back storage door to the left corner and hallway to the right. Kaizerious led Cathy towards the hallway. He opened the wooden door by its cast iron latch and ducked under the frame. Four stair risers were to the left. Two doors were at the top on the right, and a table with candles was at the end of the hall for decoration.

Cathy noticed the omelic man was following them. So long as he didn't disturb them, she didn't mind.

The first door led into a utility area of sorts. Carved limestone for walls, drainage pipes were running along some of it. That short hall led down stone stairs into a room with a massive wood burning furnace the size of that entire wall. Left of it was a metal cabinet with mechanical equipment for maintenance. The technology was at least a century behind what she saw at Direclaw, but it was definitely not original to this sanctum.

"Quite the setup," Cathy observed. She got no response.

Over to the right, another short staircase led into a hollowed-out room. It was carved below the ground, and you could still see the bedrock being used for walls. This room could very well have been original to the sanctum.

They entered and realized in an instant they were in a catacomb. Each wall housed square, sealed panels of carved stone to protect the bodies buried within.

Cathy looked at the names, many of which were hard to read, being as old as they were. She scanned to the right as Kaizerious went left. In her head, she read:

Chapter 25

Lord Jaune Parkenton
Lord Jaune Parkenton II
Ser Jaydom Parkenton
Ser Fron Spiden
Ser Phuelix Dosk
Ser Phenrick Dosk
Ser Arathor Home
Ser Maxtron Gaytes

Wait. Cathy stopped in her tracks. *Those of this blood only seek home to find home. Arathor Home.* The second home is a person, not a place.

"Over here!" Cathy waved Kaizerious over to her. *"Seek home to find home. Arathor Home.* Get it?"

Kaizerious turned to the man. "Are you fine with me removing this panel?"

"This is a public monument. You are free to explore." He smiled. Cathy thought it was strange that he was being so accommodating.

Kaizerious pulled the panel loose. She expected to see a body within the tomb, but none was present. Webs and dust were all that was there. As she got a better look, she could see it led far into the dark.

"I think I can crawl in there." Cathy didn't give Kaizerious a chance to protest as she heaved herself into the tight space.

"Cathy." Kaizerious touched her leg. "I won't be able to follow you."

"I'll scout ahead. See if you can find another way." Using her arms and legs, she military-crawled her way deeper. Her cyberwatch offered dim light, but it only allowed her to see a meter ahead at most.

After just a minute, she reached an edge and pulled herself through into another room. She could hardly see, but on the wall was a torch. She ignited a match and placed it to the torch, lighting it up as well. The hidden room was small and square. There was just one way, and it was down some stairs. Cathy was surprised at just how much heat had built up underground.

Cathy looked back through the tunnel, and she could hardly see Kaizerious on the other side. "It continues onward. I can't tell how far or deep."

"Keep going. I'll try and find another way," he assured her.

Cathy knew he was far too big to fit into the tunnel to reach this side. She had no choice but to hope there was another entrance he could use to get inside.

Cathy continued down some stairs that were the longest set so far. It was damp, and cobwebs were all over the place. Eventually, the stairs opened to a wooden balcony. It creaked and crunched under her steps. Some boards had holes inside. She may very well have been the first person to come down here in centuries.

The balcony overlooked a circular cavern that went straight down too far to see. Roots of trees were vining downward with the cavern. The only way down was to take the wooden steps following the circular wall. She didn't feel good about it whatsoever. There was a hint of light peeking into the cavern, which may mean Kaizerious could find a way inside after all. He did know it was here, so he had that advantage.

After taking in a few breaths, Cathy started down the aching, creaking stairs. She used as light of steps as she could and took her time avoiding all the holes. It was made of centuries-old wood and centuries-old rope that barely looked to be holding her weight. Each step was a hazard.

Ten heart-pounding minutes later, she reached the end of the staircase and entered a bridge leading to a cave tunnel. It was short and led to a stone door. She pulled a lever and was inside.

Torches lit on queue when the door opened, and a box-shaped room was revealed. Inside were two things - a rectangular device with stairs leading up to it, and a pedestal with writing on the top. Cathy made her way down to it and read the writing engraved into the metallic pedestal. *"Here lies the entrance of the only pair of starportals created by the holy divisors. Those of blood may step through."*

There was a button above the writing Cathy pushed, which set off the device in the back. From each of the four corners, a field of energy trickled out until it covered the entire area of the rectangular open space of the device. The energy looked of plasma and bubbled.

She got on her comm. "Kaizerious. I found a portal, and I think it leads to the brotherhood."

There was a pause. "Go on without me. I'm afraid I cannot follow you."

Chapter 25

"Are you sure?"

"Absolutely. Find them, and then your sister." He cut out.

Cathy felt a sadness because she had to go on without him, but she had a duty. That came above all.

Near her leg, she felt something strange and looked down. She caught a glimpse of something zoom away from her and into the device.

Was that a spider? she thought.

With as many webs as there were in this place, the possibility was there. Nonetheless, it seemed to make it through just fine. Cathy was now filled with the same confidence and marched through the starportal. Her body felt like ice adrift on a slow river, and she soon lost all her senses, but not all the way.

Chapter 26: Final Quondam Key
December 31, 2111

Airra

Blood covered Airra like clothes. Crazed eyes, vines extending off her fingers into daggers, Airra and her clones ran face first into a unit of ARW soldiers. She dug her hands into the warm guts of the first soldier she reached, slashing him apart like a savage beast. Her clones followed her actions, and she could feel the soldiers all dying before her might, almost at once. The pain they felt was a drug she used to get high.

From sandstone tower to tower, she attacked whatever ARW soldier stood in her way. And they never stood in the way for long.

On the great mining planet of Laloth, at the edge of the Parth System, Airra led a great battle to claim dominance over this planet. The species of laburtles, ARW supporters, would soon submit to the Wersillian Legion. Cowardice was a common trait among inhabitants in the Parth System. Not the laburtles; they were brave enough to ally with the ARW. But they were right on the edge, almost in the Ju-Sana System. A place this far away from ARW territory was proving very hard for the ARW to aid. That didn't mean this was an easy victory. No, Airra would have to fight for it. Their ground-to-space weaponry was giving the legion's starships trouble, and their military might was not something to take lightly. But that was one reason she wanted them for her legion.

From the balcony of a sand tower, Airra saw another one of the ARW's machines blasting away her allies, sending bodies flying in the streets. It was some dor'o design, bipedal, walker-like vehicle. But that only made the fun that much greater.

Airra leaped from the balcony as the machine neared her tower and caught herself on the top. She started jabbing vines into the machine, creating holes and sparks. After enough damage, the machine started to fall to the ground, and she leaped away leaving it to explode in the sand.

She caught the eye of a korkyran warchief coming in her direction. Keeping low and maneuvering through a storm of weapons fire and explosions, he made it to Airra. This desert biome surely must've been

Chapter 26

hard for the korkyran species. Probably why there were so few engaged in the attack on this planet.

"We managed to capture an ARW captain alive," he informed her.

"Take me there at once," she jeered.

The korkyran warchief led her half a kilometer to a large sand tower. They entered what looked to be a reception area of sorts. Lined in front of a desk on their knees were six ARW soldiers, one likely being the captain. Three dor'o, a qwayk, and two humans. A few of her allied soldiers surrounded them, with weapons pointed.

Airra stood in front of the soldiers. Some were beaten and battered already, and one had an open, active wound on his arm. She caught wide eyes and looks of horror from each of them. This would surely give her some enjoyment.

"Who's the captain?" she asked.

One of the soldiers, one right in the middle, looked up at her question. He faced her eyes with a brave mask, hiding the fear he surely felt before her. "I'm Captain Francisco Reyes, of the 00942 Commandos."

Airra grinned at him for a few seconds of silence.

He gulped. "If I may... might I suggest using us as bargaining chips? The ARW has war prisoners that may be of interest to you. You could trade us for them. Or... maybe a peaceful end to this battle could come of it."

Airra knew the moment he opened his mouth, he was trying to convince her to spare their lives. It was obvious. While the Wersillian Legion did take prisoners sometimes, Airra was not in that sort of mood.

Airra moved to the human just to the left of Captain Reyes and speared him in the heart with her bare hand. Her eyes were locked with Reyes's the entire time.

"Christ, woman! What are you doing?!" he shouted out of shock and fear. "You could've used him for your own advantage. Have you no logic?"

"Logic's overrated." Airra had a taste for moments like these. Often, she found herself giving in to her emotions rather than choosing the logical choice. Screw bargaining chips when killing these helpless bags of flesh felt so satisfying to her. "Killing is just so much more fun. Feeling him die just now brought me more pleasure than you could possibly imagine." She sighed a breath of ecstasy.

"You're insane!" Reyes protested.

She pulled her hand out of the human and stood in front of Reyes. "Do you want to know why I wear this jacket?" Airra gave a quick pull on it to show. She, of course, was proud of this piece of cloth - a short-sleeved, long white jacket that covered the rest of her attire and closed in the front by a thin, orange rope. Her jacket was decorated with gold, flame-like motifs on the edges, with the dytirc word for "indomitable" written vertically down its back. All choices she made when she had it custom designed for her and it was made to last, though she had spares if this one were damaged.

He was silent, unsure of what to say or why she had asked in the first place.

Airra took a knee next to Reyes and put her hand over his shoulder, staring into his fearful face. She started her story using hesitant, breathy words. "My... dear dad... he had an obsession over power. Life and everything in it was... something to control. I was no different - a tool to him. One that he shaped into a weapon. One night, he came below our home with a look in his eye I will never forget; they were unflinching and relentless, and I could *feel* them burning a hole in me. He took off my chains... and he handed me a knife. He looked at me with a smile on his face, his eyes still on me, and told me: *I brought your mother here. Take this knife upstairs and show me you are mine... show me by opening her neck over the blade.* The moment came when my eyes and hers was locked, my own mom. I had all the power, but never had I felt so powerless in my life. That was the moment I told myself nobody would ever hold dominance over me again."

"Is that why you're doing this? To fill some sick need to feel powerful?"

"That's one perspective. Then again, my motivation was never completely about having fun. The Wersillian Legion has a greater purpose, and I must do my part."

"What purpose? What could justify killing and conquering so many?" Reyes begged for an answer.

"Peace, of course."

He stared in shock, clueless as to what she meant. Airra didn't give him time to think. She slaughtered him, then the rest of the soldiers before her, taking great satisfaction in her actions.

The korkyran warchief was disturbed. "Was that necessary? It was already over for them. We had them as prisoners."

"It's never over until every last one is defeated," she countered.

"They were on their knees. How much more defeated could they get?"

Airra grinned with joy. "They were still breathing, weren't they? Now they aren't. Sounds pretty defeated to me."

The korkyra was uncomfortable with her response and tone. But he gave no more mention of the matter. He left her to rejoin the fighting.

Her intercom started to beep. She looked to see that Yalfari was contacting her. "I better hear good news, for your sake. Tell me you have the location of the final Quondam Key," Airra barked.

"I know the location is near the Inner Core in the Enchanted System. The planet doesn't appear to be on our official maps."

"Is that why it has taken so long to find the key?"

"No. Whoever holds it is not what they appear to be. The individual is almost as hard to get a read on as your stepfather is and proves to be highly resistant to my ability."

"Do you know exactly where this unknown planet is located?"

"No. But, if you take me with you, I have every confidence I will be able to show it to you."

"Fine. No time to waste." Airra signaled to a nearby dytirc Ultra to come to her and she waited as he rushed over. "Call off the attack. We have something more important to do."

"Yes, honorable warlord." He bowed in submission before he went off another way.

Airra let out a sigh of disappointment. As much as she wanted to see this battle through, it would have to wait. Even though she was winning, the Quondam Keys took precedent - stepfather's orders. The laburtles get off lucky today.

Chapter 27: Aces of the ARW IV - Epistle of Jude
February 28, 2112

Night-Shade

Less than half of the Milky Way Galaxy has been charted by the ARW. Without proper slip space lanes pre-coordinated, using slip space is suicide. With no slip space available, flying a ship through uncharted space is slow, so slow that mapping all of it is virtually nil to impossible. Exploring space in this manor is a lone ant scampering though a planet-wide forest. That ant will never in a million lifetimes see every centimeter of that forest.

The hunt for this unforeseen, unknown threat to the ARW continued. All was made possible thanks to the deal made between The Broker and Day-Bringer. Even now, they were still following the coordinates he gave. Their journey started almost a month and a half ago.

Such a journey required a suitable ship, an exploration class of starship. Drifting Cloud, the ship was called. Order of Aegis made, this starship was a proverbial millionaire's yacht in space.

Night-Shade was sitting co-chair to the pilot of this operation, an Aegis employee named Tarstbin Afuljack; qwayk male, of course. He was silent, as was she. Each waited for the Drifting Cloud to drop out of slip space to what should be the last coordinate given to them.

The wormhole was elegant, a glimmering sphere showing distorted images of the part of space that lay ahead. What wonders the magic of space travel brought. Living most of her life on Dorrath, Night-Shade almost never left the planet until Kalvin brought her into Project Ace. Even in those travels, she never got to see what it really looked like, what slip space looked like. Looking through the hard-glass, the single barrier between her and the vacuum of space, and seeing so much and so little at the same time gave her twists of joy and sadness. She was excited for her future. Yet life was simple once, and she wondered if she would ever have that happiness again. In this, she was unsure.

As they veered to the end of the wormhole, it looked like they were closing in on the end of a wide tunnel. Soon they would be even further away from home, deep in a massive territory of unknown adventures and threats.

Ayeko snuck into the cockpit and asked, "We there yet?" A question that just about threw Night-Shade off the chair with her heart pounding. Recovering and looking back at the amused Ayeko, she gathered he meant to surprise her.

She gave him a strong nudge, using her foot to his shin. "Where do you go getting off scaring me like that?"

He rubbed his shin. "You're right. I deserved that. Really, I just came to see if we were almost there. But you were so quiet, so intensely focused on the outside, I saw an opportunity and took it." He laughed.

The pilot, who was unfazed and seemed to be rather annoyed, stated in a monotone, "We're here."

Night-Shade's attention swirled back to space to see a wall of rocks; no, rather it was an entire field of them. So many asteroids, with sizes varying from a walnut to a starship. Each like bumpy chunks of old broken-up concrete and full of ore, yet far darker shades of color - onyx-black, worn-gold, and dull-gray.

Ayeko shifted in-between Night-Shade and Tarstbin and pointed to the bottom-left of the viewing glass. "Wow! Look at that!"

It took a few seconds for Night-Shade to see just what he was pointing at, but when she did, her shoulders twitched. Partially hidden behind an asteroid was a damaged escape pod large enough to fit a hominoid being. Parts of glass were cracked, and the metal frame was bent in several places. At the bottom, a red light blinked at a steady pace.

Tarstbin adjusted some knobs on the dashboard. "Looks like it is sending out a distress signal. How should we proceed?"

"I don't know. I ain't cool enough to be mission leader. Maybe you should ask her," Ayeko referred to Drayvan.

Tarstbin pushed the ship-wide intercom. "Drayvan. There is something you should see." He looked back to Ayeko. "Best head out to give her room."

"Tch." Ayeko let himself out, showing a touch of annoyance.

Moments later, Drayvan entered the cockpit, arms crossed, eyes emotionless. For the first official mission under Project Aurum, Drayvan was put in charge. As to why, Night-Shade didn't know. After all, Night-Shade was still completely new to all of this.

Drayvan noticed the pod as soon as Tarstbin pointed to it.

He started to explain the situation. "It's currently sending a distress signal. I recomm--"

"Jam the signal, bring it in. That's an order." She left just as fast as she entered and gave no time for a response.

Tarstbin was baffled. "Okaaayyy." He pushed a few buttons and pulled a lever.

"I should join the others." Night-Shade pushed herself out of the seat and followed Drayvan through the starship to the cargo bay, with Ayeko at her side.

"I have a feeling this is why we are here," Ayeko said just as the two of them entered the wide storage room. "This is probably why The Broker sent us to this location."

They all gathered at the center of the room to wait as the tractor beam pulled the escape pod up and through a shielded hole in the cargo bay. The starship's engineer, Trevor Tarnish, was present with a holopad out. Tank was nowhere to be found.

The process finished, and Night-Shade had no intention of making the first move. Instead, it was Ayeko who went towards it after receiving a nod from Drayvan.

"Not much to look at, is it?" Ayeko jested.

"Is it a recon pod?" Trevor asked. "Technology looks almost like it could be ours."

"Sure as hell isn't dytirc or lycargan. But I'm going to take a closer look. So, with a bit of luck, we can figure this out." Ayeko scanned it with his cyberwatch, a process a few seconds long. He then he peered inside a panel under the glass barrier of the pod. He pulled away the panel and revealed a monitor beneath. The rest watched him work in silence.

Night-Shade got a bit antsy and couldn't bear to stand any longer. As best she could to make as little sound as possible, she scooted a small wooden box closer to her. When she sat, her eyes looked back to Ayeko, and she noticed from the corner of her eye she caught Drayvan's interest. She didn't dare look up and couldn't explain to herself why she was so uncomfortable near this person. Being introverted, she had always had some discomfort with certain types of people. Never to this extent. Was it intimidation? She couldn't tell.

After searching through a bag of tools, Ayeko finally pulled out a male-to-male connection wire; the ends were shaped differently. He stuck one end into the monitor and another into his cyberwatch.

"This pod is from an Immortal starship," Ayeko said early on.

Immortal? How can a ship be immortal? Night-Shade thought to herself, then asked, "What do you mean immortal?"

"You know... the gang... the intergalactic gang," Ayeko answered.

Night-Shade still wore a face full of confusion.

"The gang - they're called The Immortals," Ayeko added with haste to his first response.

She mouthed a big "oh" to hide her embarrassment.

"Anyway. I'm getting a read on a person in there. Based on the diagram, it's a male smokmorjorok. Guess it makes sense to find one of them with The Immortals. Ain't no species more notorious for drug operations than smokmorjoroks. However, there's an issue."

"Kindly explain." Drayvan gave him a nod. Her tone was surprisingly friendly towards Ayeko; almost encouraging her ally.

"Whoever he is, I'm barely registering a pulse. Pulling him out of the pod's stasis state would certainly kill him. So, I need to know what you want to do, Drayvan."

"I want information."

"I thought as much. Only chance we have to get that is for me to use my abilities and operate on him immediately." Ayeko rubbed his eyes and shook his head twice. "Shivf's gonna suck. I'm not so familiar with smokmorjorok anatomy."

"How can I help?" Trevor asked.

"Get some of the crew in here with a stretcher and standard operation kit."

Trevor walked away, talking over his cyberwatch.

Two crew members prepared a table and stretcher.

Before opening the pod, Ayeko created a bubble around the area. After some time for preparation, he initiated the opening process of the pod. It decompressed in seconds, and the glass cracked as the hatch opened.

There was blood, lots of it; green and thick like oil. The man inside was nearly frozen in time due to Ayeko's ability. This gave him full control, and he pulled the man out with help from a crew member. They set him on the table.

Ayeko started by cleaning the various wounds with a disinfecting agent. There were so many wounds. With time slowed to almost zero, Ayeko was able to take some time and study all the injuries.

He gazed up to Drayvan. "He has internal injuries by the dozens, and some still have objects in them. Even if I really take my time, we don't have the equipment to save him - specifically, we lack transfusionable blood for a smokmorjorok. The moment I drop my bubble, he maybe - and I stress *maybe* - has seconds before bleeding out."

"Can you delay his death for a minute?" Drayvan asked.

"If I remove some of the objects and stitch together the wounds, it should buy him some time."

"Give it a shot," Drayvan nodded.

Ayeko went to work. He pulled out tons of metal from the escape pod from the wounds, then stitched them shut. It took a while, and when he was done, he did a once over of his handy work.

"That's the best I can do. Time to cross those fingers...or pray...or wish on those charms...or whatever your fancy." Ayeko looked to Drayvan. "Ready?"

She gave him a nod.

Ayeko took a breath and closed his fist.

That sudden moment, the injured man shot up and roared in pain. Time was once again at normal speed for him. "ARGH!" he shouted before giving in to puking up his own blood all over his lap and the floor.

His eyes were bloodshot and wild with panic. "Y-you don't know!"

"We can't know what you don't tell us," Ayeko retorted.

"I'm the unending darkness and terror. You'll feel the wrath of my malevolence, and you'll reel as I pick your bones from your body and peel your skin back over your face, it said. The monster! It... it came for

us." He reached out and grabbed Ayeko's shirt and pulled him closer, eyes locked.

Drayvan took a step forward and stopped when Ayeko put up his hand. "Don't worry," he assured.

The man let go and gave in to more blood-filled coughs.

"Where was this monster?" Ayeko asked.

"Close." He coughed. "The ship."

"What's your name? What ship are you from?"

His coughs went wild, and he fell off the stretcher. Ayeko came over to him as he gagged on his blood. That very moment, he passed away in Ayeko's grasp. His finger to his neck, Ayeko looked up and shook his head. "There's nothing I can do. Even after surgery, his internal organs took too much damage. No blood infusions, no replacements for him, his chances weren't good."

"His death is not without meaning. He gave me the information I wanted." Drayvan uncrossed her arms.

"So we find the ship?" Ayeko asked.

"Of course we do." Drayvan left the cargo bay.

Ayeko found himself by Night-Shade. "I take it she's going to talk with the pilot and try to find the ship."

Night-Shade asked, "What should we do?"

"Load up the recon ship."

Ayeko grabbed a crate, and Night-Shade did the same. They brought the supplies to the recon starship located at the back of the cargo bay. Together they loaded crate after crate of the needed supplies. In that time, they received notice that the starship the smokmorjorok mentioned was spotted.

Night-Shade helped Ayeko carry in the last crate to the recon ship. They took it up the ramp and placed it against the wall of the small cargo hold. Trevor was just outside, making some last-minute scans with his holopad. Drayvan brought Tank along, and both went inside.

"Coming, Trevor?" Ayeko joked.

"Me? I heard the word 'monster' thrown around, so this recon mission is all you guys." He laughed and tapped on the hull of the starship. "She's ready to lift off."

Ayeko nodded. "You're a champ. I'll inform Drayvan."

Ayeko headed to the front, which wasn't far from the rear on the recon ship. Soon, Night-Shade watched from the corner of the cargo hold as the ramp closed and she felt the ship lift off.

Not long after, she found her way to a seat in the midsection of the recon starship. For safety, she strapped herself in with the lock-in straps. She put in an earbud and started her playlist back up.

Drayvan and Ayeko were visible at the front, and Tank was back with Night-Shade.

Ayeko was next to Drayvan and had his cyberwatch connected to the ship's main scanners. "The Immortal's cruiser is dead in space. Scans picked up signs of low electric activity on the ship, and I see no communications going out of it. Ship is definitely cold."

"Can we board?" Drayvan continued to steer the recon ship around the stranded star cruiser.

He pointed as they rounded to the back of the dead star cruiser. "Seems the hatch is wide open."

Drayvan steered them inside, and Night-Shade felt her chest pounding a bit harder. Her leg jittered from side to side. This was her first mission in the field, and she didn't know if she was ready for it. She had three other aces with her, so she supposed she should feel like the safest person in the ARW. But she didn't.

Eventually, she felt the ship shake as it touched down. They had landed.

The hatch opened, with Drayvan and Tank leading the four out. Night-Shade swiped her scout rifle around the damp docking port of the star cruiser.

"Lights," Drayvan commanded.

Night-Shade hit the switch that lit up a beam of light attached to the long barrel of her weapon. All four had lights up; Ayeko's and hers came from weapons, while Tank's and Drayvan's came from their attire.

Night-Shade's focus went to the ceiling, which was plated metal with leaking pipes hung all over it. She stepped forward with her unit and shivered as her eyes caught sight of her breath. She wasn't dressed for this.

Chapter 27

Ayeko noticed as well. "Life support systems could be down. But my cyberwatch shows sufficient oxygen levels... I'd say enough to last us hours, and that's if the systems are down."

"Keep it monitored," Drayvan commanded.

The surrounding area was empty save a few unused ships and maintenance gear.

"Follow my lead." Drayvan motioned forward.

She led the four through the ship's port towards the exit at the back. Nothing crazy caught Night-Shade's eye. The hallway leading out was illuminated with red. She assumed it must've just been a light somewhere she could not see.

As they neared the hallway, Night-Shade jerked back as a shadow zipped over the light. Drayvan halted the unit, and everyone was on alert. Night-Shade took a knee with her scout rifle raised, because all four of them were in the open. Nothing to use for cover. She gulped, her finger trembling on the trigger.

"Night-Shade. Up scope, what do you see?" Drayvan's eyes never left the hallway. She hadn't even pulled out her sword. That only made Night-Shade even more nervous.

As asked, she took a peek through her scope but could see nothing. It was so dim, and the hallway was too narrow with a bend, which didn't give much to look at. "Looks all clear," she responded, with little confidence.

"Tell that to whatever passed the light earlier," Ayeko added.

"I can scout with my ability," she offered.

Drayvan spoke. "Save it. No time." Drayvan stood tall. "This is the great Drayvan Pryde, of the ARW. Reveal yourself to me at once." She waited just a second. "I never ask for anything twice."

Drayvan gave it another few seconds, then two separate shadows jetted by the light once more, and Night-Shade's heartbeat jumped with each.

Giving them no more time, two hairy, ten-legged creatures scurried down the hall and took mighty leaps at the four aces. Night-Shade shot at the one closest but missed. All she could see were the fangs dripping with blue liquid, foaming from its mouth. And the eyes, the great many of them, were cold and black, with nothing but a reflection of the room. She shot again and missed, her arm shaking.

Tank had his totem pulled off his back and used it to bat away one of the creatures. The second was aiming for Drayvan. She hardly moved until it was an arm length away. Its fangs craved for her neck, but she never let it close. As the creature came, Drayvan snatched it by the neck and slammed it to the ground in a motion too fast for Night-Shade to catch.

For a maelkii, she is ludicrously faster than she should be. Night-Shade's eyes popped in awe.

"Waste of my time." Drayvan's eyes were dark. "You aren't worthy of the air you breathe." Drayvan crushed its neck and pulled back her hand, which was covered in its blood.

The one swatted away earlier was scurrying back, and Tank met it with a quick burst of speed. Spinning his totem around at dizzying speeds, he plowed it into the wall before hitting it two more times to finish the job.

The whole time, Ayeko stood by, comfortable in letting the other two handle the task. Moreover, he looked to have expected this.

"Ugh. What are they?" Night-Shade gagged in disgust.

"Spiasaurs. They are giant spider-esque creatures that are found on a few planets in the Enchanted System. I've heard that there are some who like to capture them and use them to fight each other and bet on said fights. Could be why they are on this star cruiser."

"So why aren't they locked up?"

"Beats me. Seems they escaped recently."

"No shivf," Night-Shade let out a breath. Her face paled at his response.

"Expect more of them," Drayvan warned before leading them to the hallway.

"Rabbit hunting. Oh, joy," Ayeko chuckled.

Night-Shade waved over her nose. "Damn, do they smell." She took a breath and tried to slow her breathing. She didn't want her rough start to get the better of her. Even though this was essentially her first time ever in the field, she told herself she needed to conduct herself like a veteran. Even still, training simulations paled in comparison to the real thing. Having her life in danger put so much more on her than she expected.

The narrow hall quickly bent to the right and opened up to give them some more room. Par for the course thus far, the hallway was dark save for the red light they were about to pass. About midway down the hall was the sparking of an active electric line that had split out of a hole in metal panel of the wall.

Their boots clanked over the cagy metal under them as they marched forth. Night-Shade's ears grew hot as her light was catching streaks of blood over the walls. There wasn't much, so she couldn't really see it in the dark room without the aid of their lights. Each time she saw blood, she felt her heart pound like a drum. But as they continued on, there seemed to be more.

"Oh, man. Looks like things around here are getting interesting," said Ayeko.

"You didn't notice the blood in the hangar?" Night-Shade asked.

"Shivf, no. Where?"

"Laced over the ships."

"Thanks for bringing us in the loop now."

Drayvan inserted herself into the conversation with a strong tone. "Rest easy under my presence. Nothing shall do you harm so long as I am here." Drayvan's words were reassuring to her allies.

Even with those words of encouragement, Night-Shade didn't feel it. There was something different about the way Drayvan spoke. Almost like she wasn't speaking to reassure, but rather to make a statement.

"All this blood, with no bodies. Seems off to me. Anyone else?" Ayeko held a hint of sarcasm.

"At least I have your lame jokes to help me feel better," Night-Shade responded, with as much sincerity in her tone as possible.

Ayeko laughed at himself.

They arrived at the end of the hallway and pushed a button beside the door. Inside, streaks of blood covered the floor, even more than in the hallway. Electric armor clad conduit lines were strung up high against the ceiling. The room had two elevators, one with the doors already open to a deep drop off, and a few military grade crates were busted open, with weaponry spilling out the sides.

The second elevator doors buzzed open. The scene and scent overtook Night-Shade and sent her head spinning. Another one of those creatures was gnawing away at the flesh of a dead human. Its eyes locked onto the unit and bolted at them. Night-Shade fired twice, with one hitting it in the head. Its now limp body slid across the floor in its own spilling blood before stopping at Drayvan's feet.

"Well, looks like the Immortals had quite a day," Ayeko joked.

Night-Shade's stomach had had enough, and she leaned over to empty her guts onto the floor. No training had prepared her for such horrific sights.

Ayeko put his hand over her shoulder. "Hey, no worries. It takes time to ease into all this."

Drayvan was over by the human body, her cyberwatch scanning the corpse. "Been dead a while."

"The spiasaurs didn't kill him?" Ayeko asked.

Drayvan pulled a piece of bone, shaped like a horn, from his abdomen and held it up. "This did." She tossed it to Ayeko.

"It's just like those photos Day-Bringer showed us. Whatever has been killing our soldiers seems to have struck this cruiser as well," Ayeko took one look and said. The visual image of those pictures Day-Bringer showed all four of the aces before the mission found its way to the front of Night-Shade's eyes. Her blood was already running cold before this news was brought to light. She never felt so scared.

"Think it's still here?" Night-Shade's skin was ice.

"As Drayvan said, he was dead for a while, so I doubt whatever killed him is still on the ship. But why go from attacking ARW cruisers to attacking an Immortal cruiser? It makes no sense."

"The objective, then, is clear. Information retrieval. Tank, find the bridge, and gather all information available from the computer systems." She looked back at Ayeko and Night-Shade. "You two, find the engine room. Navigation systems could be stored there. Report what you find. I'll recon through the ship and assess what I see."

Drayvan and Tank left through the door at the other end and split off in two different directions.

"Well, this mission is just off to a grand start." Ayeko laughed.

Chapter 27

Ignoring his quip, Night-Shade rubbed her elbow. "Why do you think she wanted us together?"

"How do you mean?"

"She and Tank are off on their own, but we aren't. Do you think she sees us as the weak links?"

"No. No, no. Come on. Drayvan is just efficient in how she does things. She knows your abilities aren't effective amidst combat, so she paired you with me for your protection."

"So she sees me as weak." Night-Shade's eyes hit the floor.

"I'll level with you. Drayvan isn't the type of person who considers our feelings when deciding things. Not her fault; she was brought up that way."

"If you say so," she mumbled meekly. Night-Shade, even after hearing what he said, still felt down on herself.

"No, really. Codependence is commonplace in many maelkii houses. A trait hardly shared in Drayvan's house, however. She isn't accustomed to thinking about others, because she never had to in her house. Each member is capable, and their belief in themselves is uncanny. So, to somebody like her, like Drayvan, we are simply tools to achieve her goal. And I tell you, I don't think there is ever a shred of doubt in her mind that she can't achieve what she sets out to achieve. I envy that tenacity."

Night-Shade remembered that feeling well from when she accidently walked Drayvan's dream. She looked up to Ayeko. "Must be nice."

"What?"

"To have so much confidence."

Ayeko laughed. "Yeah... that's one word for it. Let me just say that arrogance may not strictly be a trait of the Escanorinn House, but she definitely does it better than anybody I've ever met."

Night-Shade had a small laugh with him.

Ayeko pressed the button for the elevators, but nothing happened. "Well, shivf. We might have to climb down."

"Down?"

"Yep. Their engine room is likely on the lower levels."

Ayeko pulled out a water bottle and took a sip before starting down the rope of the elevator.

Night-Shade followed him. It wasn't too deep, to her relief, and they landed on top of the elevator, which looked to be stuck at a floor. The pulley systems were jammed as well.

The floor above was blocked off. But beside them was an access to a utility tunnel. Ayeko pried the grated cover off and tossed it aside. The metal-to-metal noise resonated in the elevator shaft.

"Quiet, dummy," Night-Shade expressed, with a nervous glare.

"Right, my bad."

Ayeko entered the shaft, which was large enough to crawl through. Night-Shade followed, which was easier for her to traverse than Ayeko. As a dor'o, she was naturally smaller, and dor'o had evolved through their history in mountain caves and tunnels. They were made for this. As a qwayk, Ayeko struggled a bit.

Inside the tunnel were pipes running along the side, along with some metal conduit lines. Above them were grated metal ceiling tiles that could be pushed up to allow access to various electronics. This utility tunnel was left unscathed, unlike much of the cruiser, leaving Night-Shade to wonder why some of the people who were on this ship didn't hide in one of these tunnels to escape whatever danger was here.

The tunnel curved down into a square room with more pipes running into a bus hub. In conjunction, the metal conduit ran to a subpanel that connected to a terminal. At the direct center was a closed hatch.

Ayeko plugged into the terminal and started to fiddle around with it. "It's as I thought," Ayeko mumbled, mostly to himself. He removed the connection from the terminal and pulled away a panel beside the hatch. "Shine your light in here," said Ayeko.

With her light over his head, Ayeko worked inside the panel. Shifting through the wires, he was able to splice open the hatch. Out blasted a fog. Night-Shade covered her nose.

"It reeks." She gagged.

Bars of metal were leading all the way down the hole, acting as a ladder.

"Bilges... they're often very similar in every star cruiser. Should connect to the engine room at some point," informed Ayeko.

Chapter 27

Ayeko was the first to start down the bars. He took a brightstone flashlight from his pouch and put it in his mouth. Night-Shade put her scout rifle back on her back and followed into the dark.

At the bottom, the floor was flooded with about a third of a meter of water. By no means was that normal. Ayeko jumped and splashed as he landed. He removed the flashlight from his mouth. "It's wet down here."

Night-Shade giggled to herself as she landed beside him.

"Come. Only one way to go." Ayeko led, flashlight forward.

The tunnels were wide, flooded, and had columns to support the beams every few meters. Sounds of dripping water in the distance echoed through the tunnel. A few lights were embedded in the walls, but almost every single one was burnt out from being under water.

Night-Shade kept marching on despite the water being over her knees.

Movement in the vent system in the ceiling alerted them. Night-Shade had her weapon ready.

"Hear that?" she asked.

The movement continued. "Sounds like lots of legs, probably the same creatures. If we move slow and stay quiet, we may avoid them altogether," whispered Ayeko.

Night-Shade nodded and slowed her pace to match Ayeko's.

Her eyes were focused on the vents above, and she didn't even notice the scrap metal in her path. Her foot caught on it, and she tripped, splashing down completely in the water. Her rifle went off, an accidental trigger pull.

She felt hands pull her to her feet. Wiping away the water from her eyes, she saw Ayeko's worried stare behind her. She looked and saw dozens of the creatures pour out the vents behind them, splashing in the water, headed for them.

Ayeko put up a bubble around some, but the rest evaded it altogether. "Not good!" he yelled. "Run!"

Both of them ran towards the end of the tunnel. "There's a junction up ahead!" Ayeko shouted.

Behind them, the beasts were catching up.

Ayeko bolted through the doorway, and Night-Shade dived inside. Quickly, she was up and firing her scout rifle. Ayeko put up a bubble in front of the small doorway, forcing the beasts to enter it if they wanted to reach them. And it worked at buying time. Ayeko had both hands up, concentrating to keep up the bubble.

Night-Shade emptied the clip. "Reloading!" she shouted and slid in another. There were dozens, and she noticed some weren't being slowed. Her eyes caught Ayeko struggling, and his nose started to bleed.

"There're too many!" he shouted.

He let the bubble go, then pulled out a frag grenade and tossed it back. It flashed, then *BOOM!*

The spiasaurs were eradicated, and both the aces were knocked backwards from the shockwave.

She got up and rubbed her shoulder. Blood appeared due to a piece of shrapnel that had punctured her skin. Damaged plates of metal from the ceiling and reinforced bars had piled in front of the entry. They had no way of returning down the path they came. That was the least of their problems. The grenade damaged the tunnel, and more water started to build. At least the monsters were on the other side.

"Blast it!" Ayeko barked.

The rush of water forced them back, and Night-Shade lost her footing. Stumbling, her eyes met the fangs of a spiasaur! Instinct took her out of its direct path, but one of its thorns scathed her arm.

Ayeko put a bubble around them and slowed the creature to a near halt. Inside, he pulled Night-Shade a distance away from it and took a dagger to its neck.

"Come on! We can't stay down here."

The water continued to build and was already past Night-Shade's waist. They turned the first bend they saw in the junction.

"There's the door!" Ayeko ran to it.

It was elevated a bit higher than the floor, so the waves were lapping at the base of the metal-plated exit.

Ayeko pulled down the lever on the side. Nothing. "Stupid piece of shivf!" he swore.

Banging and creaking sounds were coming from the pile of debris guarding the entry. Both their eyes met, and both knew it was the rest of those monsters seeking for a way to get to them. Who knows how long it would be until they found it?

Ayeko took that instant to pull the cover away from the lever and look inside at the electrics.

"Light." He waved her over.

Night-Shade shined her light inside, and he spliced together two wires and rigged it into his cyberwatch. Taking a moment to look at the readings, he started to reach into the back of the panel.

The sound of a metal beam scraping across the plates made her wince, sounding like nails on a chalkboard. From the shadows cast by the light, she could see a leg breach through the rubble.

"Hurry! They're getting through."

"Got it!" he shouted, and the door slid open.

Both booked it inside as fast as the chest-high water allowed. The door closed behind them, with an airtight seal separating them from the oncoming waves. They faced more metal bars bored into concrete. It led up like a ladder.

Ayeko started up, with Night-Shade right below him. After just a few bars up, Ayeko stopped. He bent up his head and listened. "Hear that?" he whispered.

Night-Shade's ears were tuned to the water trickling below, so she hadn't. Then she heard it. There it was, softly echoing down to them. A voice.

"The pilots, the runners. All dead," the voice wailed in sorrow. There was a pause for sniffles. "I could see it digging, sliding around beneath their skin! Ohhh-ughh--" cried the unknown voice.

Ayeko motioned his finger and started up. She shared his thought that whoever it was must be close to the top of the climb. They both started up again, quieter than before, with ears tuned to the voice.

"And-and-n' then... their bodies came apart. Ohhhh, God, their guts spilled over the floor. The blood... so m-much blood," he moaned. "Make it stop." The sound of flesh pounding on metal made Night-Shade shudder. It was followed by more groans of pain.

Ayeko peered over the edge. He pulled himself over and helped Night-Shade up to the grated walkway over various pipes and tubing with diameters as small as a coin up to those large enough for her to walk inside.

She grabbed the railing as they walked over the clinging metal and turned a corner. There he was, the human man behind the echoing voice, balled up against the rail, crying over his knees.

"I did it a favor," he sobbed. "Yeah, that's it! I helped it!"

Night-Shade and Ayeko looked at each other and continued to listen. It seemed as if this broken-down human didn't even realize they were there.

"Maybe... maybe I should help myself. And-and make it stop." He sat up slightly, revealing a revolver in his hand! Eyes dark as night, he put it to his temple!

"Wait! Wait, wait, wait!" Ayeko shouted.

Night-Shade turned away as the sound of a gunshot rang in her ears. The ring! It kept going, and her heart nearly burst in her chest.

Ayeko put his arm around Night-Shade's far shoulder, and his other hand over her gaze. "Don't look." His arms were trembling.

Nonetheless, he guided her away. He guided them both away. "That's some serious mental trauma. To-to be forced to do that." Ayeko's words were shaking with his arms.

"Ayeko--"

"Don't worry. The engine room is just ahead."

"But Ayeko--"

"Just... try not to think about what happened. We have an objective to complete. Let's do that first, then we'll have plenty of time after."

Ayeko removed his hand from her eyes. Night-Shade nodded in agreement.

Before them was the engine room. A convergence of four separate walkways intersected at a circular platform, with terminals at the center. Below, the vast space was filled to the brim with machines unfamiliar to Night-Shade - all of them twisting, turning, spinning. It was all jarring to look at. And look at them she did, for she dared not look backward, not after what happened.

She followed Ayeko to the central computer system and watched as he worked his magic. Plugging in his cyberwatch, it allowed him to gain some access to a terminal. Engraved over it was the ship's name. Translated, it read, "Epistle of Jude."

"Seems Drayvan was right. The navigational data is stored down here." His eyebrows arched.

"What is it?" Night-Shade asked.

"Seems the data was accessed recently - only a few days ago. It was very specific in what it was searching for." He paused. "Keyword: Damon Swift."

"I don't know that name."

Ayeko's expression looked troubled. "It's, ah, a rather infamous name, especially among higher-up Aegis employees. But usually that man is referred to as Brad, not Damon. I heard once that he was involved in a gang. The Immortals are just that, so the whole two-and-two thing adds up."

"Why him?"

He let out a wry laugh. "Beats me. But that name did pull up a very specific location. Based on the star system chart, I don't believe it is on the ARW mapped systems. Lucky for us, I can copy a couple slip space lanes that would take us from here to there."

"What's there?"

"Doesn't say outright. But in my experience, I have a feeling that's where we are going next."

Once finished, he looked down one of the walkways and back at her. His eyes told her it was time to leave. Night-Shade was very happy to oblige him.

Chapter 28: The Selection
Error 66b

James Stone

Into another room of another trial we marched. The room was rather symmetrical; built around a single floating slab of rock. Flanking the left and right of that rock there were two copper-esque circular gates crafted by a different hand than the gates we were accustomed to seeing. Just in front of both gates were chokepoints with columns and boulders around for cover and two platforms perched next to each of them. Each chokepoint had another machine in the middle, which was wasn't quite a twin to those confluxes we had to defend before fighting The Gatekeeper; rather, it was of the same tree and carried with it many similarities. The confluxes were oval-shaped, much in the same way as the ones before; however, these two were colored differently; made of blue and gray shards of glass and metal, with many metallic spikes extending from the machine, just like branches on a tree.

Each of the two chokepoints connected to two flat areas that led to stairs, completing a nice symmetrical design that was easy on the eyes. Up the stairs was a gate even larger than the first two. The design held the same copper tint, but glass crystals grew around its edges, and they lit up the entire room. That was the end. Nothing was past that monument.

As we pushed further into the room, one problem jumped out into the stoplight like a stripper on a slow night. And that problem was shjarrs. They were kneeling just in front of that massive gate at the end of the room. All were the basic architype, the priests, and there were only a few. As problems go, just like with a stripper, not a problem you hate to have.

I looked to Jeremiah, and he nodded, opening the book. Soon, he began to read, *"Those have wondered before the light of The Archpriest's selection. The Archpriest - a machine commander that can manipulate the Vault of the Seven and dictate every move the shjarrs make like a main processor. For it deems those few worthy a chance to stand before it to achieve the Blade of Wrath. Those who can last within its domain long enough to escape will face the final judgment of wrath."*

Chapter 28

I chuckled. "Damn riddles. Not even going to pretend that makes sense. Let's do what we do best and figure the shivf out as we go."

"What's our first move, then?" Valiic asked.

"The way I see it--" I gestured to one of the two chokepoints, then the other, "--we have a shivfstorm behind door one and a storm of shivf behind door two. Either case, we face shivf, so might as well split up into two groups. Maybe then we can shovel through it."

"Shivf, you said it, James." Shadow-Walker laughed.

Geariic readied his warhammer. "Let's hope those aren't the only ones." His eyes locked on the few bowed shjarrs.

"I, for one, am of the complete opposite mind, Geariic. The less, the better." Shadow-Walker sighed.

"Fewer," Jeremiah corrected.

"What?"

Jeremiah smiled. "The *fewer*, the better." Shadow responded with a long glare.

Frost gave Shadow-Walker a tap. "Where's your sense of adventure, uzzo?"

"It left the moment my shoulder was nearly severed," Shadow-Walker mumbled, with a light laugh.

"Right, that's on me." Frost's eyes were apologetic.

We had only taken a few more steps forward before the shjarrs awoke and more poured in from openings behind the gate at the end.

They fired a barrage at us, but they were too late. We split up and dodged. I moved left with Valiic, Brad, and Shadow-Walker, while the others went right. I reached the gate and leaped up to the perch next to it for an open look. At the edge, I reached down and helped Shadow-Walker up with me. Valiic planted his shield at the choke below, and Brad took up arms near him. We all returned fire on those machines.

We destroyed the frontline in no time and tossed a few grenades to disperse the others. Shadow-Walker did an excellent job taking out the fodder, while the rest of us focused on a shjarr apostle that came beaming towards us. The apostle started to teleport, making it harder to hit, but we were hardened veterans by now. At this point in time, each class of shjarr had a pattern we were getting accustomed to noticing. First it appeared in front of Frost, who speared it with ice right in its head.

Feeling the burn from our relentless damage, the apostle thought it better to teleport to my side. When it did, it was met by weapon fire from Valiic, Brad, and Shadow-Walker. This apostle was rather intuitive when it noticed one of us wasn't there - me. It looked up as fast as its parts allowed and saw death coming down as I spiked it with both my fists. It crashed against the ground and shattered.

The smoke from the attack cleared, and I took a look at the empty battlefield.

"If only it was always this easy," said Shadow-Walker.

"I wouldn't rest on it just yet," I added.

That sudden moment, we heard was a deafening shriek. I didn't have time to cover my ears before it ended.

Just then, the portal all the way in the back began to hum and glow around the edges. From the center, a black mass started to swirl and grow until it filled the whole area of the portal. Dark, like an abyss, radiating with smoke and dense like oil.

A leg stepped out of it, followed by its entire body. Blades for wings, shiny metallic armor covering its entire body, it was heads taller than Valiic. In one hand it held a pike longer than its height. It had a metallic eye that glowed green just below a crown-like mold on his head. Something looming in my gut told me this was The Archpriest.

The portal behind it closed.

Its green eye intensified into a flash of light. When I regained sight, it was gone. In the wake of its vanishing act, more shjarrs poured out from the back. All were the same basic fodder, and not too much in the weight of numbers either. There was no stress in keeping pace.

"What in the Sam-Hell, guys?! Where are you? Shivf, where am I?" The voice belonging to Geariic came through our cyberwatches.

I peeked over to the other side and saw it was just Frost and Jeremiah over there.

"Uzzo, you just fraken disappeared!" Frost shouted back before any of us could make heads or tails of anything.

I started, "What do you mean he--"

"Goddamn it! That thing just appeared here with me!" Geariic cut me off. "Sam-Fraken-Hell, it's coming for me!"

"Hang on as long as you can. We'll figure something out."

Chapter 28

"If you don't get me out of here, James, I'll personally kick your ass sideways!"

"Love you, too," I quipped, with sarcasm.

"James, take a look," I heard Valiic call from below.

I jumped down to the chokepoint to see him gesturing to our portal. It was glowing, and so was the conflux. I could think of only one man for the job. "Jeremiah?" I shouted. I didn't realize he was already at our side, head buried in the book. I glanced up to Shadow-Walker, who seemed to catch my drift. He positioned himself to help with Frost's side.

"It's all scrambled, but I think I got it figured out. As you know, each side has a gate which, as it turns out, is actually a portal. It seems that The Archpriest pulls one of us at a time into a different location based on a selection process of sorts. To pass his test, the goal is to stay in his *domain* until we can open a portal to bring them back to our location."

"So how do we do that?" I asked.

He pointed to the conflux in front of the portal. "It seems this device that looks like a conflux is actually a keyport. We need to be near it and guard it. After a period of time, the portal will open."

I let out a breath. "I didn't realize we entered the trial of puzzles. I mean, shivf, why does everything gotta be so damn complicated?"

"At least you don't have to decipher it all." Jeremiah adjusted his glasses and holstered the book.

Both of us made haste and took positions close to the keyport. Jeremiah and I were behind cover as he explained the situation through my cyberwatch and I laid out cover fire.

"So this *domain*-thing that you spoke of... did it happen to mention anything about a black circle?" There was an explosion from his warhammer as Geariic talked.

"I believe so," Jeremiah responded.

"Damn it all! I already left that thing before you figured it all out!"

"To tell you the truth, I don't know if that is a bad or good thing in your case." Jeremiah's ill attempt at reassurance didn't go over well with Geariic, and he cursed.

Just then, our portal ignited in the same fashion as the big one in the back did a bit ago. It took about five minutes total for the two of us to

activate it. Moments later, Geariic rushed through, and it deactivated.
He was breathing like a second-hand bicycle pump under the hand of a
crack junkie. "That stupid thing gave me a hell of a match. Not sure any
of you would've lasted that long."

"Now that we figured out what to do on this end, we won't have to." I
gave him a friendly pat on the back.

"What James was actually saying is, thanks for being our guinea pig."
Shadow-Walker laughed from above.

Geariic grunted. "You're laughing now, but wait till you're forced to
face that thing."

A familiar shriek interrupted us. We realized there wasn't time for
mouths in motion. Geariic and Jeremiah left to their side. I leaped back
up to the perch and saw The Archpriest had graced us with its presence
once again.

Just like before, his green eye flashed, and I was blinded. When my
vision was restored, I realized I was not in the same place as before.
Plucked from one location and tossed into another.

Everything had completely changed. The once gray and white
battlefield was now open to the sun. The floor was covered with sand
lost in time, and the sky was yellow-brown. Everything around me
seemed decayed and deteriorated by age. It was like a desert. I did a
quick once over of myself and found all my gear and clothes intact and
still present.

It must be my turn. With that thought, I prepared myself under a
sense of urgency.

I looked down and realized I was at one side of a black circle at least
ten meters in diameter. It was a spinning mist of darkness floating just
above the floor itself. The Archpriest appeared at the other end.

No time to waste, I got on the comm. "Don't know if you boys
noticed, but I'm locked up with a bigass Archpriest and its bigass pike,
and that son of a bitch is glaring at me, waiting for me to drop the damn
soap."

"Have no fear, my friend. Geariic and Brad went to open the portal."
The reassuring words of Valiic gave me a shield of serenity.

Five minutes, I've got to last just five minutes. Shouldn't be issue for
me.

Chapter 28

The Archpriest burst forward! It was fast, and even I had barely a scrap of time to dodge. Now left of it, I planted a foot like a tree and landed a powerful kick. The thing staggered and slid back in the sand, neck vibrating with anger. It slammed its pike down at me. I took a step forward and caught the handle. My arms were shaking, and it took all I had to keep it at bay.

Then an idea hit me. In a swift move, I sidestepped and let go. The pike crashed into the sand, leaving The Archpriest open to attack. I made like a wrecking ball and slammed myself into it, powering it backwards, driving it to the edge of the circle.

If I were to throw it out of the circle, could I end the match earlier? That was my intention, and my thirsty curiosity wanted to find out.

The Archpriest countered with a swipe of its pike, which knocked me off my balance. I was centimeters from going over the edge. Cold, metallic fingers grabbed my arm and began to drag me closer to losing the battle.

With my free hand, I drove a knife into the dirt to halt it from taking me over the circle. Then I kicked it away, which gave me a moment to kick to my feet. It was short-lived, and The Archpriest burst towards me with a powerful flap of its wings. This time, I put some power under my feet and leaped over it. Flying past me, it turned and slid to a halt. Neither of us had left the circle. Taking a moment to stare me down, it then shoved a foot forward and used the powerful stance to toss its pike at me, which I dodge by a hair. My eyes followed the weapon as it sailed by me.

I heard the portal engage from the other side of this location and, upon turning back to The Archpriest, noticed it was gone. I was still within the bounds of the circle, which soon disintegrated. I did it! I passed the selection test.

"James. You're good to go," Valiic said over the comm.

I wasted no time dashing into the portal. As my body entered, I felt an almost goo-like substance on the outside of my skin. Before I knew it, I was back with the others. And that sensation was gone almost like the touch of a ghost.

I was greeted by Jeremiah. "How did you do?"

"I stayed in the circle." A smile jumped on my face.

He shared my smile and gave me a friendly pat on the back. Soon I was back to my original side, and the process began again. Next on the selection list was Frost.

It took only a moment for us to figure out he had vanished. Given some time, we had grown accustomed to the parameters of this trial and were expectedly getting better at this.

"Imma 'bout to end this priest's entire career!" Frost shouted over the comm. It was clear he was hyping himself up. But that's how he was. Frost was a bit over-the-top for his recklessness and gung-ho brashness. However, he had his positives. In and out of battle, he had an inexhaustible amount of energy that seemed to leak like a hose and energize people around him, including myself. And with his childlike humor, he was able to lift the spirits of those around him all the same.

"That's the way to tell it," Shadow-Walker responded.

In the meantime, Jeremiah and I helped open the portal. It was on their side. The shjarrs kept flowing, but it was clear they were not meant to be the focus of this part of the trial. From my position, I was able to drop them in-between a yawn, which perfectly sums up the action on this end. On occasion, a stronger shjarr or two such as a fanatic or apostle would join the party. Even when they did, we had our focus fire down pat. They didn't stand a turtle's chance in an endless desert.

The portal opened, and Frost was back. He saw me. "Shivf, I think it might've got me out, uzzo." There was genuine nervousness in his tone.

"What do you mean?" I asked.

"Big Daddy was really putting up a good fight, like always. I was giving it to that machine good, and I lost track of my footing. Not sure, but I may have stepped out of the circle."

"I'm sure you're good, brother." I grabbed him by the hand and pulled him in for a moment. "Now get back out there." I gave him a friendly pat as he went.

He smiled. "Big Daddy ain't done yet, I promise you."

I returned to my post, and the fighting continued. Next one to be plucked from our company was Jeremiah. When he disappeared, a sharp jolt came over me, and I realized I was more worried for him than I was for the others when their turn came. As of late, he showed himself to be more capable than I initially gave him credit for, but to fight off

Chapter 28

The Archpriest might be stacking the plate to much against his poor, nimble body.

This time, the portal was on our side. I jumped down and instructed Valiic and Brad to help me. Par for the course, the shjarrs of this trial were not much of a threat.

Sooner than expected, the portal opened. That couldn't've been only five minutes. Then it hit me. We used three able-bodies this time. Turns out if you get more guys near the keyport, it opens the portal at a slightly quicker speed.

Jeremiah was out. "I stayed in, James. I did it." He was excited.

"You did it?" I was aghast. "How?"

"Simple. I dodged."

"You *dodged?*"

"I dodged." He laughed.

"At this point, I'm no longer surprised by anything you pull out of your ass. Crazy priest... maybe I should give you a gun."

"I'll be honest, I don't mesh well with weapons."

I tilted my head at that obvious remark. Jeremiah took the time to scurry back to his side, while I repositioned myself.

I started to wonder to myself why this trial was such a cakewalk for everyone other than the one who had to face The Archpriest. I understood the main focus of the test was placed on that situation, not on the outside; still, this was as easy as pissing in a lazy river. Then the thought dawned on me and I realized how fortunate our group was. All other groups I'd heard about struggled with these trials and lost many in their group. Given that this was the third test, one would almost expect to have lost members of the unit - any normal unit, that is. And you would need a minimum of two healthy souls left, else the person facing The Archpriest would never be able to come back. And the fewer people you have, the longer they'd have to fight The Archpriest. This would all be happening while the people outside the portals were struggling to fend off the shjarrs trying to prevent the portals from ever being opened.

At that moment, I realized just how high our luck gauge was to have so many strong members in the unit. Having all of us here was truly why this last test was easier than expected.

The screech came, followed by The Archpriest, and the next one pulled away was Brad. We had the portal opened in no time, and he was out. I felt I knew the answer, but I needed to ask.

"How did you do?"

He walked past me. "Don't ask stupid questionz." A hint of humor was in his tone.

I returned to my post, and we continued to eliminate the shjarrs. A minute came and went, but The Archpriest hadn't made another appearance. That's when I noticed the shjarrs where no longer coming. It was no time at all before the battlefield was clear. Only then, The Archpriest reappeared, which was a longer wait than anytime previous. Something changed upon his reappearance. The shroud of unease that once filled the dense air was lifted away. The aggression The Archpriest once radiated was no longer there, and it didn't have its pike anymore. It gazed back with calmness in its eye. At the back, the big portal opened in the same manner as it did in the beginning. The Archpriest retreated through it, but the portal never closed.

I held up my hand to halt my group from leaving their positions and gave Jeremiah a nod. He took to the book.

Meanwhile, we waited with guns still at the ready. The third trial couldn't be over just yet. Neither Valiic nor Shadow-Walker had a chance to face off with The Archpriest. Not that I'd want Shadow in there. In fact, I'd rather he sat that one out.

"I don't get it. Valiic and I are still here," said Shadow-Walker.

"Isn't it obvious?" A hint of anger was in Valiic's voice. "You and I weren't even considered worthy enough to be selected." I felt that in his words. No wonder he was angry. A warrior like him being told he wasn't good enough, worthy enough, must sting worse than hugging a nest of wasps.

Jeremiah cleared his throat. *"For it deems those few worthy-- those few.* It goes on to say *in his selection not all will be chosen."*

"So that's it, then?" I asked.

I saw him give me a nod and noticed Geariic and Brad had already made their way by the portal. I gave the go-ahead to move up, and we all joined them just in front of the still-active, massive portal in the back.

Chapter 28

Valiic was the last to join, and I saw him carry himself with heavy strides.

"Figures that you weren't worthy," Geariic teased, with a mocking grin all over his face. He wanted Valiic to feel it. "What kind of warrior are you, anyway? Can't even--"

"Shut your mouth!" I shouted, cutting him off. Valiic's pride was too wounded to defend himself, and I had no tolerance for what Geariic was saying. I was unable to help myself. "I seem to recall that you failed."

"That's because little Jeremiah over here didn't tell me the rules in time!" Geariic defended himself, then his mocking smile returned. "I just wanted that so-called honorable warrior to know how much shame he brought to his beloved species of tradition-loving pricks."

Before I could come back at him again, I saw Brad come from behind him and kick down at the back of his knee joint. Geariic fell to a knee. That next second, Brad was at his side and fired his shotgun parallel to Geariic, with the butt lined up to his face. The blast sent the butt of the shotgun into the side of his jaw, and he jumped up in surprise.

He was just about to shout, but Brad beat him to it. "Da fuck'z wrong wit yah? He'z yer goddamned ally."

Geariic was facing down at Brad, who didn't budge an inch. Geariic's hand was hovering dangerously close to his warhammer before he finally gave way. He stepped back and mumbled inaudibly to himself.

Frost went over to him and whispered something to Geariic. He put his arm over his back and seemed to calm him down. At least I hoped it was working, because I was unable to hear.

Shadow-Walker started bringing everyone water and snacks, and we sat for a minute in silence to let things cool down.

Jeremiah read from the book. "I know what we have to do. We all enter the portal - doesn't matter in what order - and we can even enter simultaneously. It seems we will be split up based on our results thus far for the fourth and final trial."

"How will we know what to do?" I asked him.

"It's a mystery. The book doesn't say a thing about the fourth trial at all."

"Anyone care to place money on who passes, if any?" Shadow-Walker finished his snack.

There wasn't an answer, and Shadow-Walker's happy face ballooned into utter disappointment. I felt for him, but I think even he wasn't able to lighten the mood.

All of a sudden, I saw Geariic get up and enter the portal without saying a word.

Frost turned to us. "Geariic said he wasn't going to keep his brother waiting any longer." I saw Frost head to Valiic until he was face-to-face with him. "Geariic means well. Trust me, he does. I've known him a long time, and he feels hurt and betrayed by the maelkii. That's why he's been lashing out at you, Valiic."

Valiic stood up from his spot. "I know," he said in a soft tone.

"Come. We can't fall too far behind," I commanded the crew.

With that, the rest us entered the portal simultaneously. As my body entered, I felt that near goo-like substance on the outside of my skin again. It might've even been thicker. Before I knew it, my world was black, and I felt only the sensation on my skin. It was soothing, calm like a sea of nothingness.

Chapter 29: Wrath's Judgement
Error 66b

James Stone

After an unknown amount of time, my eyes opened to a building in rubble, burnt to a crisp. That sensation on my skin was gone completely. Smoke was still simmering from the charred beams and joists. It rose to an atmospheric void of nothingness, devoid of anything of mass, and pitch black. I had no idea where I was anymore. No idea where that portal had taken me. All that stood before me was a driveway leading to a burnt house.

I found my way to the center of the burned down house after navigating through some rubble. The walls had long since crumbled, and in their place stood thick beams of wood, blackened and charred from where flames had licked at them. The ruins were still smoking, and I could see the faintest glow of embers, indicating the fire must've been somewhat recent. Black dust hung in the air and invaded my lungs as I stood in the former living room of this house. Nothing had escaped the fire. Glass littered the floor where the windows had broken, and the metal base of the grand chandelier lay blackened and twisted on the ground.

I bent down and touched the chars of what had been and watched my skin turn charcoal gray. Being this close to the wood, I got a good whiff, and the smoke and ash filled my mouth, nostrils, and lungs. I quickly stood up and coughed it away.

Hold on. As my eyes were now away from the floor, I noticed someone was now in the living room with me; a man hiding under a ski mask and wearing thick black clothes.

I went toward him. When only a meter away, I asked the unfamiliar person, "Where are we?"

His voice had a hint of mockery. "Wrath's Judgment."

A strange sensation came over me, starting with my right hand. Something was now in my grip, as if materializing from nothing. My fingers wrapped around a smooth handle, and I eased the object into view. It was a blade, longer and thicker than a knife, but shorter than a sword. A sharp eye with a thin amber iris like a viper stared back at me from the center of the hilt. Mostly black in color, the top of the hilt and hand guard pulsed with blood-red veins that grew up part of the black symbolled blade and down the handle.

My entire arm was shaking. Something was alive within this cursed steel, as if the ancient blade had been forged from flesh, blood, and bone. There was a taste in my mouth, like iron, and my inner rage was on the rise.

My vision was so intensely focused on the blade, I missed what happened around me. The house was back intact. And the man in the ski mask was hard at work in the center of the living room. He set down a propane tank among many more, then turned them on.

My eyebrow rose. *What was he doing?*

He walked past me into the kitchen and turned on the gas-lit flame of the stovetop. That's when the realization hit me. He was going to blow up the whole house!

I heard some creaking on the second floor above me, which startled the arsonist. Soon followed the clatter of steps as someone started down the staircase at one side of the living room. It stopped. No more footsteps.

"Is anyone there?" The woman's voice pumped ice in my blood.

"That voice," I said out loud. I recognized it clear from my past. It belonged to my mother. But that was impossible. I didn't recognize the house. She couldn't be here. She was already dead.

I then remembered she and my grandparents moved while I was still being held by the Order of Aegis. And I never got a chance to see the new house.

All my rationale ran out the door, and my eyes bolted to the stairs. There she was, natural red hair to match mine. Wearing pajamas, her green eyes staring back at me with fear.

No! Not again! I can't have this happen again!

I ran over to the stove to stop the flame. Only the man was now in my way. All the while, my ire was a raging fire. I let it all out, every bit of my wrath. Consumed by my own hate, I blacked out.

I came to without any regard as to how long I was out. Still shaking, I noticed blood all over my arm and hand. The blade was dripping in it.

Chapter 29

More was on the carpet. So much was slathered over it, I could feel my stomach turn. I followed the trail with my eyes and instantly regretted it.

Tears overwhelmed my eyes. I fell to the floor on my knees, losing the blade. All the rage in my body was overtaken by grief and pain. The image before me will forever be burnt into my mind. I will never forget the sight of the cold corpses of my grandparents and mother, along with the arsonist, piled over each other. Blood still leaked from the many stab wounds, and there were *so* many! My gaze fell to the blade, and I knew. I knew that moment what the cause was. It was me.

I lost the will to stay up and fell face first into the blood. *I'm a monster! How could I?*

Everything started to fade into nothingness. The room, the blood, the blade, the bodies, and even my emotions started to fade to nothing. Soon I was just lying there, floating in a void.

I stood up and met face-to-face with the arsonist from before. It had begun to dawn on me that none of this was real. It didn't feel like a dream, but I knew it wasn't reality. In the moment it hurt, but I forced myself to understand what I saw was never my mother; rather, it was an illusion of some kind - a trick, a shadow on the wall.

"It's you again," I said.

The arsonist spoke. "Wrath judges you unworthy. Subjected to your own rage, you were consumed by it. You destroyed everything in sight. There was no control over your passion. True wrath consumes everything silently, like a deep sea."

I had no time to argue. Before I knew what was happening, I was sent away. No longer could I see anything. Had I really failed the last trial?

Chapter 30: Aces of the ARW V - Battle of Darkness
March 6, 2112

Night-Shade

More than a week later, Night-Shade had more butterflies in her stomach than ever before. The last time she was in the field, she was traumatized after that human committed suicide in front of her. That gunshot still rang in her head. And whatever beast it was that drove him to that point was very likely on this unnamed planet.

Ayeko saw her shaking and came up to comfort her. "You're going to be okay. When the time comes, Drayvan, Tank, and I will be the ones to face it. Not you. You sit this one out."

Night-Shade felt much better from the words. She wasn't going to protest. Not anymore.

The hatch of the recon ship opened to the new world. All four aces were there waiting. It was a world engulfed in a sandstorm with grains of sand flying at many kilometers an hour. Out there, it would be nearly impossible to see past your own hand. Night-Shade was glad not to have to go out there.

Drayvan stared out the opening, and after a moment to think, she said, "I see one option. Night-Shade, your time is now. Use your ability to find the Immortal hideout."

Being called into action by Drayvan sent tremors down her spine. She looked to Drayvan and protested. "Please--"

"Be brave. You're on this mission because you deserve to be. And be thankful, for with me as your leader, you can accomplish anything. Remember that."

Night-Shade nodded. She didn't want to, but Drayvan needed her, and she finally had a chance to prove her value to Drayvan. With her ability, the grains of sand would pass through her, and she would be able to scout without shielding her eyes. It would still be a challenge finding the hideout, but it was more efficient than those three wandering aimlessly through this sandstorm. And Drayvan was all about efficiency.

Night-Shade sat down on the floor and relaxed her mind.

Chapter 30

"You got this," she heard the encouraging words from Ayeko. "Nothing will happen to you with us protecting your body."

She was out of her body and into the sandstorm. She could maybe see a meter, even without having to protect her vision. She was maybe ten meters from the recon ship when she began to wonder how she planned to do this. Was she really supposed to wander around until she found something? Even she would lose all sense of direction in no time.

She put her hands to her eyes, trying to think of a solution. Astral projection is all about spirit and mind, right? Maybe if she focused hard enough, she would be able to sense the things around her. She then remembered that feeling she felt at Station 51 when searching for Tank. If she could somehow look for what she wanted in that same manner, it would guide her.

Night-Shade focused on a single thought, searching for the presence of anything within the range of her ace ability. Anything at all. She called to it, honed her mind on that singular idea that something was out there. Then she felt it - a feeling of utter despair and darkness in the distance. It was malicious, pure hate and fear bottled in a singular spot.

Night-Shade hesitated before telling herself that she could do it. After all, the others were counting on her success. So, she forced her feet forward and marched through the sandstorm.

By her estimate, she was about five hundred meters away from the landing spot before she pushed past some kind of field. Inside was open sand, with hills throughout the nearby patch of land. This piece of the planet was shielded from the sandstorm by a dome made from the same technology used in atmospheric doors, only much larger by comparison.

The sky above had traces of clouds, or smoke, or fog. It was hard to tell, since it looked like nothing Night-Shade had seen before. Nonetheless, the weightless mass of black particles floated high in the sky. At least it looked black to her; being out of her body made everything appear in shades of gray.

Must be something with the planetary weather, she told herself.

Night-Shade marched to the top of a hill, and from the top she spotted a single structure not far from her; made from wood as sturdy as steel. Just past it she could just see the left lip of rocks protruding from the sand, and it looked to have an entrance into it. She would have to get closer to know for sure.

Night-Shade crept to the edge of the structure. Even knowing she couldn't be seen in this form, she still took precautions for the stability of her nervous mind. She was getting close to reaching her limit on how far she could venture away from her body, which she could still feel in the distance.

She peeked past the structure, and there was no doubt in her mind the rocks led downward into the sand. It was a cave entrance for sure. She remembered Ayeko mentioned this Immortals location was likely a mortan sepulcher, which was a place dedicated to their members who had fallen. The cave supposedly houses hundreds of tombs and other memorials for dead Immortal gang members, whilst the structure kept records on all their achievements while in the gang. Together the two made up the mortan sepulcher.

Interested, Night-Shade found herself wandering closer to the cave and past the structure. She stopped immediately when she saw the bodies lined up on the other side of the structure! Every one of them had been skewered like a rabid animal; no skin left, just blood, muscle, and guts impaled through and through with bones and left for the scavengers. Night-Shade felt the urge to vomit, but she was unable to in this form.

Such a horrid image brought back that feeling she had from earlier - the one of pure darkness. It was close, and her eyes looked past the massacre. It was there! The monster was there! Just staring at the entrance of the cave and as motionless as a scarecrow.

Her eyes couldn't turn away. Even though she was unable to be hurt, she dared not move closer to that monster. Her veins pumped frozen blood through her body, then she let herself fade back to safety.

"I found the threat! I found the monster!" She shouted the sentences as fast as she could upon waking up.

Drayvan was as calm as ever and spoke politely to her. "Would you be so kind as to point me in the right direction?"

Night-Shade did as asked and pointed in the direction she had traveled. Her voice was shaky. "It's a bit further than five hundred meters straight that way. You'll see a building, and it's just past that."

Chapter 30

"You did well. Now stay put," Drayvan told Night-Shade. With her chin, she motioned the other two aces to follow her. Then they left her.

After a minute or so, Night-Shade had a sudden urge. She didn't want to be alone, and that reality was setting in for her. So she left the recon ship. She trudged through the sandstorm, shielding her eyes, until she reached the dune hills near the perimeter of the dome. Despite being closer to the monster, she felt safer knowing she could see her allies. Just seeing anything at all was assuring.

After plowing up the sand, she reached the top of the five-meter-tall sand dune. Her allies had just passed the structure and were headed towards that cave. But she wanted a closer look.

She closed her eyes and let herself pull away from her body. Everything that once had color was now shades of gray. With haste, she ran through everything until she was there with her team. Only not there at the same time.

"--and whatever those cloudy-things are in the sky, it is disrupting communications equipment," Night-Shade caught Ayeko as he finished telling Tank and Drayvan.

Drayvan stopped them once she saw the threat. "Flank around its sides. Wait for the opening that I create." Drayvan's words were directed to Tank and Ayeko.

Without seeing if they would answer or acknowledge her words, Drayvan stomped towards the creature in the distance. Night-Shade followed, feeling empowered by Drayvan's lack of fear. Tank and Ayeko waited a few seconds, then started to circle around.

The ink embedded in Drayvan's skin began to move, then pulled out of her back, tiny droplets ejecting themselves from her skin. Despite the unsavory and seemingly painful sight, it had no visible effect on Drayvan. Now outside her body, the ink spun together into two separate circles of swirling matter, each looking like black holes a meter in radius, both following Drayvan, seemingly under her control. Drayvan took a spherical device from her waist and pressed a button on the top. It activated, and the core glowed a bright orange, and Drayvan tossed it into the ink. It disappeared inside, engulfed like a stone thrown into a lake.

What was this unnatural power of hers? Night-Shade wondered.

As they neared, Night-Shade was able to make out features of the threat. And what revealed itself was not what she expected. This beast was not a beast, but a korkyran warrior. It was the first one she had ever seen in person.

Night-Shade remembered hearing that Brad Swift had killed a korkyran warlord named Dro'Zer. Was this the reason this korkyra was looking for Brad? To get revenge?

Night-Shade didn't expect the korkyras to have such a prominent muscle structure. Its physically intimidating physique was incredible, as every muscle fiber looked to be bulging against its back. Four horns protruded from its bull-esque head, and its pelts and manes were coal-black. Being unable to see color in this state, she could still tell this creature's fur color truly was black because of how dark it looked to her. As they got closer, Night-Shade noticed an odd steam or fog radiating off its skin, similar to those clouds in the sky.

It must've heard Drayvan approach, because it turned to meet her. The eyes stopped Night-Shade in her tracks; they were black, with that same dark, smoky material foaming out of them, and intense enough to make just about any sane person shivf themselves. That mad grin was a similar fear-inducing catalyst. None of that stopped Drayvan, nor did she slow in pace.

In no time at all, Drayvan stood face-to-face with the threat, nose-to-nose, only centimeters away and looking down with an arrogant smirk. Drayvan was just a hair taller, but both looked equally intimidating.

Its face carried just a hint of surprise. "What's this? You don't fear me?" it asked in a crazed voice.

"Of course not. Why would I fear someone who is obviously weaker than myself? No, all I feel is pity towards you," Drayvan taunted.

It purred, "So full of pride."

"That's who I am - Drayvan Pryde. Do well to remember my name before I bury you into the ground."

"You stand before Mara'Sane, warlord of the legion. I will enjoy tearing your intestines away and using them as a scarf." Mara'Sane let loose an overwrought, monstrous string of laughs.

"My only request for you is to make this fight memorable. Don't disappoint me as many others have."

Drayvan grabbed for her sword. That action ushered a response from Mara'Sane, who closed her hand into a fist. There was a crunching and swooshing sound as her arm distorted and two bones punctured through her skin, tearing it open and letting loose blood. The bones were sharp and grew past her fist. She lunged it at Drayvan's face. Those dark circles of ink intercepted the blow at lightning speeds. But the bones were not engulfed like the device from earlier.

Night-Shade closed her arms over her chest. What she witnessed Mara'Sane do made her feel cold.

Drayvan held a look of disgust. "I asked myself over and over, why so many bones? Seems you're the answer I sought."

Mara'Sane's neck twitched with disturbing snapping movements. "You saw my art, then. Did you appreciate its complexity?"

"The only art worth my time is that in battle."

A monstrous grin rivaling a hell spawn spread from ear to ear. "Then you shall be my next work of art. Tell me, does your blood taste sweet or salty? I would love to run my tongue in it."

"The sight of my blood will never be seen by such an unworthy foe as yourself." Drayvan had yet to pull her sword, a mistake Mara'Sane took advantage of. With her other hand, she did the same thing with her bones and came in for an uppercut-slash. Drayvan let go of the handle of her sword and swiped away the attack with ease. Her free hand balled to a fist and cracked into Mara'Sane's jaw. The force sent Mara'Sane to a knee, laughing.

Blood poured from her mouth, and she smiled with blood-soaked teeth; a crooked smile since her jaw was half-hanging from her mouth. She took a hand and snapped the jaw back into place, then laughed. "Yes! Oh please, *please* make it hurt more." Mara'Sane shuddered with delight.

Sick freak. Night-Shade looked on in horror.

"What you witnessed is just a taste of my prowess," Drayvan taunted.

"Pain and punishment are an art. I seek it! I want it! Give it to me!" Mara'Sane lunged up, bones protruding from her fingers.

Drayvan had her sword pulled now and blocked with the blade. Mara'Sane's eyes narrowed. As she looked at Drayvan with those all-consuming eyes, her skin began peeled away from her body. Bones broke through in all directions. Drayvan stepped backward.

Night-Shade was horrified. Every time Mara'Sane manipulated the bones in her body, it gave off horrific sounds of breaking and snapping.

Just as Mara'Sane took a step towards Drayvan, a golden sphere formed around them both, and she was stopped in her motion.

Drayvan and Night-Shade turned to see Ayeko had stepped in. "I was wondering when you would enter this fight," Drayvan said to him. Tank was beside Ayeko.

His face was filled with a hint of disgust at Mara'Sane. However, he responded, "I was just enjoying watching you fight."

"I figured as much. I am quite the sight to behold."

"I can see that." He grinned. "But as much fun as it is to watch this masochist and you go at it, we've been away from home for, like, forever. I just want to end it and leave."

"Fine, then." Drayvan took the sword and cut clean through Mara'Sane, from right shoulder to left hip. Night-Shade turned just as the blade left her body. She didn't want to see all the guts pour out of her leftover torso. "Just a nobody," said Drayvan, displeased with the outcome of the battle.

"You seem upset by that," Ayeko pressed.

"I yearn for the day that I can feel the thrill of a fight once more. Such a feeling is lost on someone as strong as me."

Night-Shade watched Ayeko drop the bubble and start walking away with Drayvan and Tank. The job was done. Night-Shade, not interesting in sticking around any longer, was ready to return to her body. But just as she was about to jump back, she saw Drayvan stop.

"What is it?" Ayeko asked.

Drayvan didn't answer. Instead, she turned back to Night-Shade, and her expression shifted in a way Night-Shade had never seen from her. Drayvan looked straight at Night-Shade with a look of disbelief and intrigue. Tank was appalled, and Ayeko's mouth dropped open. Night-Shade knew this was not her doing. It had to be what lay behind her, and she could not stop her body from turning.

The body of Mara'Sane, laying in a blood pool of its own making, carried a thick steam over where it was cut. As if on fire, black clouds radiated out of the body and hissed in the wind. Almost that instant, the stuff latched onto each other. The fluid, or whatever it was, grabbed onto itself, from one piece of the torso to the other. It pulled itself together, and the body pieces with it, and Mara'Sane was sewn back together by it.

"Did... did she just pull herself back together?!" Ayeko shouted from behind Night-Shade.

Mara'Sane moved! She was still alive! But how?!

"I was sure you killed her," said Ayeko.

As Mara'Sane stood, her head creaked from side to side, and she stretched her back.

Night-Shade didn't know what to think. Her head hurt just trying to.

Drayvan stepped through Night-Shade and marched up to Mara'Sane, chest high. A light grin was on her face. "You are full of surprises. I apologize for calling you a nobody," Drayvan commended.

"Praise gets you nowhere with me. I'm still going to bore a hole in your throat and suck the air from your lungs. Don't think you'll get off easy, because nothing you do will end the darkness within me. For I am fear incarnated."

"I'm thankful for that gift of yours. Otherwise, this fight wouldn't've been anything worth remembering." Drayvan had a thrill in her voice.

Ayeko came in hot, daggers drawn. He created another bubble around both Drayvan and Mara'Sane, slowing only Mara'Sane. "Looks like we'll have to just keep cutting until you die," he shouted.

From under the ground, tons of bones erupted outward, straight at Ayeko. He was quick enough to jump to the side but lost control of his bubble, and it popped. Mara'Sane was released.

"What an annoying fly you are. I shall treat you accordingly and squash you beyond recognition," she growled.

"Blast it! She already figured out I can't slow time below ground," Ayeko muttered to himself, within earshot of Night-Shade.

Drayvan unleashed a thunderous strike against Mara'Sane that launched her backwards a few meters. Tank had leapt in the air and was coming down near Mara'Sane. Bones sliced out of her arm and beamed for Tank. He had to maneuver that totem of his to block them, but he was still knocked away.

With a burst of speed, Drayvan was in front of Mara'Sane once more and sliced three times so fast, the motion was a blur. Blood exploded out of Mara'Sane, and multiple limbs were sliced away. Night-Shade was sure she was dead. No one could survive that much blood loss.

Mara'Sane gave herself to laugher, laughing through the blood soaking in her throat. "Yes! The pain! I've never felt so alive!" Her body was sewn back together once more. Small bones burst out of Mara'Sane's fingers like bullets, forcing Drayvan to block with her spheres of ink. They bounced off and lost much of their momentum.

She fired the bones from her fingertips. Night-Shade was stunned.

Drayvan followed up with a stronger swing of her sword. Mara'Sane laughed, and tons of bones shelled over her side like armor, which blocked the sword.

Tank was back and slammed his totem down onto Mara'Sane while she was still on the ground. Nothing. She blocked him, too, with the bones, and some actually managed to puncture his skin.

There was a sharp, sudden look of pain in his expression before Tank jumped back. The bones that had punctured inside of him had grown some. Tank placed his hand on his side, covering his wound.

"It feels good, doesn't it?" Mara'Sane taunted Tank. "Please come back over here. I want to cut you more and drown you in your own blood."

Ayeko had another bubble over them. But it was no good. More bones launched from the ground and forced him away.

Bones piled over Mara'Sane's free hand and created a long pike. She launched it at Drayvan, who blocked it with another sphere of ink. She continued to put pressure against Mara'Sane to keep her on the ground. It only made Mara'Sane fill with rage.

An entire field of bones started to jump up from the ground like spikes. Drayvan blocked a few before leaping out of range. It was a boneyard now. Tank crashed the totem to the ground and cleared the area around him of the bones. Ayeko used a bubble around himself to slow them and dodge them. All three were now a good distance away from Mara'Sane.

"Time to fill you with holes and turn you into a shower." Two objects started sliding under Mara'Sane's rib cage before popping out of her skin. They had handles and triggers. Mara'Sane pulled them out of her and pointed them at the aces. Each looked like shotguns made of bone and cartilage and drenched in Mara'Sane's blood.

She pulled the first trigger, then the other one, and repeated as dozens of tiny bone projectiles exploded from the barrels. So many, at such a massive spread. Ayeko was forced into a bubble. Tank leaped at her, which only drew her attention to him. He took some damage, but most of the tiny bone bullets seemed to bounce off his skin. Night-Shade noticed it was vibrating furiously and acted as natural armor against Mara'Sane's insane attacks.

Tank landed by Mara'Sane and bashed her with the totem. A bone spike jumped from the ground and blocked. Mara'Sane fired. Drayvan burst forward to help, and both attacked from either side. Mara'Sane was somehow holding them both off but taking some hits. Tank and Drayvan coordinated attacks managed to sneak past Mara'Sane's many attacking bones.

Her rage engulfed her, and a cloud of smoke released from Mara'Sane. She started spinning like a tornado, and her body seemed to partially turn to a gaseous state. That very instant, she fired off hundreds of bones at the same time. Tank took some major hits and was forced to run and used Mara'Sane's own boneyard for cover. Drayvan slapped the two ink spheres into one larger sphere that covered her entire front side from the storm.

Drayvan put her sword on her back and burst forward faster than even before! She landed a seismic punch on Mara'Sane and knocked her out of her tornado attack. She was sent cascading a dozen meters off the ground. She got up, a hole in her side. Drayvan covered that distance in a flash and landed a second blow. Mara'Sane didn't fly as far.

When she got up a second time, Night-Shade noticed a layer of bone membrane in her second hole. "Even though I grew a bone membrane under my skin, that powerhouse still punched through it. How can that be? It's as if she is getting stronger as the fight goes on," Mara'Sane growled to herself and Night-Shade overheard. Mara'Sane then put a hand over her face and laughed hysterically into it.

Drayvan marched up to Mara'Sane. "This fight is over. Your ability, while impressive, is inconsequential compared to mine. Submit."

Mara'Sane let her laughing die, then spoke. "The last person who talked to me that way no longer has a tongue."

"I offer this chance solely for your benefit. I don't care whether you live or not. But if you wish to continue to fight, it will end with your demise."

Mara'Sane laughed as if she had heard a joke. "Never. When I find someone as fun as you, I tend to focus on them... quite intently."

In blinding speed, Drayvan had removed her sword and sliced too many times for Night-Shade to count. The attack left a cloud of dust, and Night-Shade was sure that had to do the trick. That many cuts would've sliced Mara'Sane to tiny pieces.

The dust faded, and something was off. None of the attacks connected as they should have. She then noticed Mara'Sane's cells, every one of them, seemed to have changed into a gaseous state before becoming solid again.

"So you control more than just the bones in your body. Quite intriguing," Drayvan praised her foe.

Her ace ability seems ridiculously strong! Night-Shade awed.

A bone a meter thick suddenly erupted from the ground at Drayvan's feet. It startled her for a moment before she used the ink to block. But the speed and power behind it was immense, and it carried Drayvan far away and out of sight.

A bubble formed over Mara'Sane, to her surprise. This time, Tank was there to protect Ayeko from the attacking bones. Ayeko made his way closer to Mara'Sane, with a large grenade in his hand. He was able to maintain the bubble with Tank's help, and when he was close to Mara'Sane's near motionless body, he tossed the grenade at her. "Eat that, you demented freak show."

The grenade stuck to her head and exploded. Her entire torso and head were completely gone. Ayeko let time resume at a normal speed but maintained the bubble. What was left of Mara'Sane fell to the ground with a thud, and blood poured out like a spilled vase.

She had to be dead. She just had to. Nobody could survive without their head and body. All three aces watched, making sure this time.

A hissing sound originated from the body, shattering all their hopes and dreams. Steam omitted from the wound. This time, her body repaired itself from what was left of it, and she regrew her torso and head. Her cells multiplied and multiplied until Mara'Sane was whole once again.

She stood up and faced Ayeko and Tank with a fat grin. "I'll skin you alive for that."

"Wha-- H-how can you remember? Not only did you come back from a fraken exploded head, your neural impulses came back intact! How can you defy the very laws of nature?"

"You don't get it by now?" Mara'Sane created a blade made of her bones and shoved it into her heart. She pulled it out and shoved it into her brain next, and finally one of her eyes. Each time she pulled it out, all her wounds healed in a few seconds. "Every cell in my body is mine to control, multiply, and change. And it's the darkness within me that binds it all together. You can hit me with all you have, but I will *never* die."

She took just one step towards them. Ayeko and Tank took a step back. Fear covered their eyes and face. "Stop! Don't come closer, you monster." Ayeko's voice quivered.

She took another step. "Tell me, have either of you ever experienced so much pain that you wished you'd die?"

They took a step back. "I said stop," he begged.

"Those men guarding that structure. They felt that pain that I gifted them. They begged me, just as you are. They pleaded. After I had my fun, I used a razor wire of my own bones and veins and strangled them until their heads came clean off."

Mara'Sane took another step, but neither of them was moving. Paralyzed with fear, even the bubble popped. Everything that came out of Mara'Sane's mouth was dark and vile beyond all that is natural. How can someone have so much darkness in them? It was disheartening and draining to the soul to go against. Her very sight carried an encumbering presence that filled her victims with so much fear, they lost the will to fight. Night-Shade was never happier of her ability, but her mind was heavy on Tank and Ayeko. Was no one there to save them?

She had been so distracted, she didn't notice Drayvan had returned. Confidently, she marched past Tank and Ayeko and put herself in-between them and Mara'Sane.

"Drayvan. We... we can't win. Mara'Sane is immortal! And if we can't kill her, we have no hope of beating her. Please... we have to leave," Ayeko begged her, with a heavy tone.

Drayvan stuck up her hand. "Unkillable and unbeatable are entirely separate things."

"But--"

"Stop and use your head. Mara'Sane can still be contained, but as we have no method of doing so, I opt for another option. She is flesh and blood and can be knocked unconscious."

Mara'Sane halted. "You're still alive? Better enjoy it while you still can." She stuck out both arms, and the cells around her arms dispersed and showered the ground. All that organic material formed into two beasts. Made out of exoskeletal bones and black, foggy skin, they had claws for hands. All they had for their eyes were two singular glowing dots.

"So you can just create life, too... just like that? Because of course you can... why not? After all, how much stronger can she get?" Ayeko's thoughts were all over the place. He was fearful and letting it out with his words.

"You talk a lot to ease your fear." Mara'Sane laughed at him. She turned to her creatures. "Go hold them down so I may slit their throats."

The beasts bounded towards them on all fours, tongues lolling at their prey. Drayvan knocked one clear out of view, and Tank engaged with the other.

Ayeko followed Drayvan's lead and attempted to put a bubble over Mara'Sane. She dodged, and he tried again. Mara'Sane unleashed a wall of bones separating the two of them, then a dozen bones popped up and surrounded Ayeko. He bubbled himself just before the bones started firing projectiles inside. Ayeko struggled to slow them all down enough to dodge them. His nose was dripping blood!

Drayvan hurried and attacked Mara'Sane. She pounded Mara'Sane against the bone wall, breaking through it. Mara'Sane pulled her spine out of her body and used it as an extendable sword against Drayvan.

Night-Shade quivered at the gruesome sight.

Drayvan blocked with her own sword and cut the spine in half before following up against Mara'Sane. She was able to block with more bones.

"You think my attacks will stop just because you hit me? Think again," Mara'Sane taunted. Drayvan's expression shifted, and she shot her eyes to Ayeko.

He took a hit from another of those tiny bone bullets.

No. Night-Shade had tears in her eyes.

The bones stopped firing. However, Ayeko let go of the bubble because he couldn't hold it anymore. Bleeding from his nose, arm, and side, he was hunched over and wheezing.

"See what your brash and pride has cost you," Mara'Sane mocked Drayvan. "Now watch your ally die!"

The bones surrounding him shifted and speared straight towards him!

That sudden moment, a flash pushed him out of the way. Was it Drayvan? No, she was unable to make it in time. The dust cleared. Tank, having had finished off that beast earlier, made it to Ayeko's aid.

Night-Shade was in tears. It wasn't for Ayeko. It was for Tank. All those bones, all dozen of them, had impaled him. His breath was faint, eyes dull and open, blood draining down the bones. He had taken the attack meant for Ayeko and was barely alive. At that moment, Ayeko put a bubble over him to slow down his blood loss, buying him time. But Ayeko could barely hang on to it. Already his nose was beginning to bleed more.

"Night-Shade. If you are there watching, I'm counting on you to aid our comrades," said Drayvan. That instant, she launched herself at Mara'Sane. She countered with a wave of bones Drayvan had to switch to block. It pushed her away and gave Mara'Sane an opening. She didn't use it to engage Drayvan. Instead, her nightmarish gaze found Ayeko and Tank.

Mara'Sane was on the move to finish them off!

On instinct, Night-Shade fell back to her body and shot awake. Her scout rifle was over her lap. She scoped in, and without even thinking about it, she took a shot. It hit Mara'Sane in the head. Her enraged gaze then beamed in Night-Shade's direction! What an intense thirst for blood; a feeling of sharpened darkness had focused on her. Night-Shade has never felt anything so chilling, as if her own life was being choked off. Her body shook, and she dropped the weapon. That feeling of darkness had intensified and focused on her. It overwhelmed her senses. So much fear engulfed her, like a prison, and she now knew what those killed by Mara'Sane's hand must've felt.

The distraction Night-Shade bought was enough for Drayvan to come back with a strike more powerful than any previous. Mara'Sane was sent flying out of sight. Night-Shade understood that moment Drayvan was going to keep Mara'Sane far from Tank and Ayeko so she couldn't kill them. Drayvan then leaped in the direction Mara'Sane flew, disappearing out of sight herself.

Night-Shade was still shaking out of her skin, but she had to help Ayeko and Tank. They could die if she didn't. That thought carried her there. Her body moved as fast as she could manage until she passed the structure and found herself in the boneyard.

Soon, Night-Shade was by Ayeko's side. His eyes didn't see her. They were locked on Tank. With all his will power, Ayeko tried to hold on to that bubble.

She entered the bubble with Tank. "What do I do?" She begged Ayeko for an answer.

"Cut... th-the... bones," he squeezed out the words. Night-Shade began to fire her scout rifle at each of the bones. One down, then another and another. Each took at least five shots, and she had to reload often. The last one broke, and Tank was free, but his body was still near motionless due to Ayeko's efforts.

She looked back to Ayeko. "Now what?"

His eyes were starting to close, and he was blinking in and out. Night-Shade rushed to his side. "Ayeko! Hang in there! You need to stay awake." It was no good. Ayeko had exhausted his ability. That very moment, his eyes closed again and didn't open. The bubble dropped, and so did Tank.

Night-Shade ran over to him and tried to drag him back to the recon ship herself. He was too heavy for her. Then his breathing stopped. Night-Shade pulled and pulled, an effort that amounted to nothing. She was useless. Why was she so useless?

Minutes went by, and Night-Shade fell backward trying to pull Tank. She landed by Ayeko and looked for a pulse.

Please be alive, she begged.

Chapter 30

Her plea was answered when she felt Ayeko's heart still pumping. He was unconscious, but alive. Knowing that, she went back to Tank. She started pressing against his chest and breathing into his mouth. Again. And Again. She kept at it and eventually dropped to her side. She couldn't handle it anymore. She was defeated to her very core. She had failed Tank.

Alone and in grief, Night-Shade stared into the sky for almost an hour. Her body didn't move. She didn't have the heart to. The last few minutes of that battle replayed over and over in her head. The sight of Tank being impaled by Mara'Sane haunted her thoughts. The fact that Ayeko went unconscious trying to keep Tank from dying, only to have her fail him in the end, ate at her soul. She didn't know what to do. What to think.

Hearing footsteps approach, she snapped out of her daze. She sat up, half-expecting it to be Mara'Sane. Her fear dropped away when she saw it was Drayvan.

Drayvan stopped in front of Tank and stared down for a few seconds. Her eyes turned to Night-Shade, which immediately caused her to look to the ground in shame. She couldn't face those eyes that counted on her, knowing she failed.

"In the end, Mara'Sane fled from me. Of course, with me in pursuit, I'd imagine anyone would cower from the sight. My only regret is that I wasn't able to avenge Tank's courageous sacrifice." Drayvan knelt beside Tank and closed his unmoving eyes. She heaved him up. "Rest knowing you died a warrior's death." Her voice was soft as she whispered to into Tank's ear. Drayvan was now over Night-Shade. "Would you be so kind as to bring Ayeko?"

Night-Shade nodded. "He's... he is alive," she mumbled the words.

Drayvan walked past her. "I know."

Night-Shade forced her tired body up and willed Ayeko into her arms. She followed Drayvan back to the recon ship. The journey felt much longer, and neither of them talked. When they reached the recon ship, Drayvan gently laid Tank's lifeless body on the ground. She then took over for Night-Shade and brought Ayeko to the tiny medical bay on the recon ship. Night-Shade informed their pilot it was time to leave.

Their mission to stop the threat was a failure. But that wasn't even what was so disheartening about it. Tank had died for nothing. That weighed heavily on Night-Shade. And with no way to find Mara'Sane again, they had no choice but to return to Station 51 with the bad news. Not that they should go after that thing ever again. Not ever!

Chapter 31: Awakening of Fire
January 12, 2112

Sunfire

Sunfire's eyes opened. Taking time to adjust, she could feel the goo around her body. She started to move in slow bursts. Dim rays of light crept their way inside the cocoon she was in, barely making it past the thick green shell.

She was ready - ready to emerge from the cocoon her body had created years ago. Her energy was recharged fully, and she felt renewed; completely reborn. Having the great power she had came at a hefty price. Once her energy depleted fully, her body created a cocoon around her to absorb solar and heat energy at a heightened rate. That was the price she paid for her glorious ace ability - a power rivaling solar stars.

With a clawing motion from both her hands, she tore through the shell of her cocoon and fell to the floor, covered in slime and goop. Naked, she felt the brisk air.

It took only a second before two individuals were at her side to help her to her feet. They cloaked her in a towel so she could cleanse herself from the layer of organic matter covering her skin.

She used the towel and targeted her eyes first, clearing the way for her to see the light of the room. It was just her and two bishops of the Brotherhood of Relics.

The room was familiar because it was hers. Built for the sole purpose of shortening the time she would have to spend in her cocoon. It was domed around the back of the room. Mirrors and artificial solar lights were strategically placed to direct all sunlight at the back of the room, where her cocoon formed. She remembered all those years ago when she sat in this same spot, when her energy was low and waited for her cocoon to form.

After many years of inactivity, how much has changed? Sunfire wondered.

Long before she first went into her cocoon, she was given a promise; rather, a prophecy. A seer by the name of Anighta told Sunfire she would be the light to cast away the shadow of war. But what war was she supposed to stop?

The bishops led her through the tall double doors and into the next room. She motioned for the bishops to step aside. Once they did, she motioned to a sensor, which sent torrents of water splashing down from above. After just a few seconds, she turned it off and let the water drain down the center.

Both walls were reflective like mirrors, and she could see herself. She was fairly tall, physically fit, and a well-toned woman with muscles lined throughout her arms, legs, and abs. Purple skin, yellow eyes, and shaggy white hair cut up to back of her neck, but with noticeably long bangs. Above her right eye was a small scar, and her black dermmotifs were set just below both her eyes and shaped like war paint.

Sunfire breathed in a full breath. Her pupils dilated and filled with fire - her fire. Her skin grew hot, and the water evaporated in no time at all. One of the bishops came forth and handed her a specially designed fabric armor. It was similar in looks to the fabric armor sets traditionally worn by knights of the Brotherhood of Relics, only hers was made of a drastically different material. It wasn't designed to protect against any kind of weaponry. Its sole and main redeemable property was its unmatched resistance to high temperatures. Extremely rare and expensive was this material. However, price was never an issue for the Brotherhood of Relics.

Sunfire motioned her finger towards one of the bishops. "Tell me who the current four other knights are."

He responded, "Starlight, Brawn, Castle, and Ghost."

Her mood turned dry. "You mean to tell me we have two falsebloods at the roundtable?!" She, of course, referred to Castle and Ghost.

"Falsebloods? I beg your pardon, ma'am." His eyes darted in confusion to the other bishop.

He came up to Sunfire. "We haven't used that word in almost a decade."

Sunfire grew more furious by the second. "Gather all knights present to the roundtable. I'll be waiting there." Sunfire marched off towards the door.

"But ma'am--" he started.

"That wasn't a request." She pushed open the door and followed the hallway to the roundtable.

Sanctuary, the home of the Brotherhood of Relics, was created by the Devisors long ago. For centuries, the brotherhood had maintained it. Every addition or change made was done under inspiration of this technological marvel of a palace. Emerald green and sharp silver, this hallway pulsed with power and majesty.

Sunfire entered the council chambers, accented by a roundtable in the middle, with chairs surrounding it. All furniture was engraved with the sigil of the Brotherhood of Relics and carved out of an ancient tree from Omulice that was important to their past.

A bishop in the room was cleaning and maintaining the table. He wore the mark of Sunfire and was once one of her bishops, temporarily lent to Brawn while she slept.

Sunfire addressed him by name. "Catch me up on the affairs of our galaxy. Start with the most important, and build towards the least important until the other knights arrive. Go."

He did as she asked, and she waited in silence, taking in every bit of information. She was shocked at all she had missed, appalled even by some of the news, but she kept a noncommittal expression throughout.

The door opened, and the bishop took that as his cue to leave. Sunfire stood at the end of the table, arms crossed, as three knights entered.

Castle entered first, smirking with charm in his emerald eyes and lots of fidgety micro-mannerisms. He carried himself the same as Sunfire remembered, although his gear changed. Castle, dressed in a knight's cloth, brandished a belt-like black cloth around his left arm and an overabundance of throwing knives along his waist, over his shoulder, and more hidden throughout his person. Sunfire didn't recall him using so many knives before. And the tattoos he bore were new. One thing was the same as before, his hairstyle; spiky and dyed black with a purple tint.

Ghost was not far behind. Unlike Castle, his gear was similar to before; bandanna and mask to cover his head and mouth. His knight's attire bore extra metal plating on his shins, arms, shoulders, chest, and waist. He gave her a quick glance with his unique set of eyes; one was yellow, and the other was purple - both irises looked of shattered glass.

Last in was a face very familiar to Sunfire; it was Starlight. She had known her for her entire knighthood and considered her a close companion. Her attire was traditional, save a few white-shaded tertiary cosmetic additions she made. Starlight didn't have her signature starlight bow or fabricator with her at this moment.

Sunfire's eyes went to Ghost and Castle, sharing contempt for them both.

Castle grinned as he took his seat. "The firehead herself walks among us once again. I should've brought flowers in celebration of this tremendous day." Sunfire thought she detected a hint of sarcasm in his words.

She ignored him. "Tell me where Brawn is."

Ghost took his seat. "He's leading his bishops against enemy troops."

"Sanctuary is under attack?" Her voice grew in volume.

"Of course not," Castle remarked, with sarcasm. "Ghost, a man who doesn't mince words, decided to say we're under attack when - get this - we aren't."

Ghost jumped in. "Our outer shields will hold for many months against their star cruisers and freighters. The only thing they can do for the moment is attack us on the ground. To which, they are finding our deception and ensnarement warfare tactics hard to overcome."

"That doesn't tell me how they found us."

"Recently, we took it upon ourselves to gather information from one of their locations--"

Sunfire shot Ghost a raised eyebrow. *"Gather information?"*

Castle jumped in. "We broke in. Apparently, they figured that out and made the first strike. We underestimated them. But those crazy bastards have no idea what they've just done."

"I'll have to deal with that later, then. First, I called for this roundtable meeting for one thing: I want you two, Castle and Ghost, to renounce your titles as knights so we can hold a trial for your successors immediately." She would rather them renounce their titles willingly, else it would be near impossible to remove them from the table, since removing a knight simply isn't a matter that can be voted on.

Chapter 31

Castle shot out of his chair, and it fell back. "What did you just say?!"

Ghost, calm, with his elbows on the table and fingers folded, said, "You can't believe we would ever do such a foolhardy thing."

"If you had any respect for the Brotherhood of Relics, you would do just that. It is a cruel joke that you falsebloods, born without brotherhood ancestral blood, would ever be knights. So, stop this insult to our ways this instant."

Ghost didn't move. "With respect--"

Castle could not contain himself anymore, interrupting Ghost and letting the words fly. "Oh, boo-fraken-hoo. Dear old Grandma Sunfire misses the days of old where everyone had to have the ancestral blood to be accepted into the brotherhood." He was standing, with expressive hands arching a rainbow over his head. "Here's the headline: We didn't just swindle our way into knighthood. We crawled and fought for every step *and* against elitist bitches like you--"

"Watch your mouth!" Sunfire roared.

"Or what?!" Castle marched over to Sunfire, spitting his words in her face. Starlight and Ghost were on edge. "You gonna burn me to ash? Break our most sacred rule? Do it! Prove yourself a hypocrite!"

"Step back! Now!" Sunfire uncrossed her arms.

Castle let out a sarcastic laugh. "Me step back? Really? As if I'm the problem here."

Sunfire glared. "You've been a problem since joining the brotherhood."

"What the hell are you trying to accomplish? We both know neither Ghost nor myself would ever renounce our titles. So, if your goal was to piss me off... guess what? Mission fraken accomplished, you jagg-off. You can take solace in the fact that one time, for like... fifteen seconds, you irritated me. By the stars, I hope you're proud of yourself."

Ghost came over and pulled Castle half a meter away. "Don't let her get to you," he tried to soothe Castle.

Sunfire didn't back down. "Both of you, look around. Sanctuary, our secret home, isn't so secret anymore. And as one of my kind bishops informed me moments ago, we have our entire galaxy at war."

Castle growled, "Who gives a shivf? Our brotherhood has only ever cared about protecting and studying all that the holy Devisors constructed. And once we deal with the enemies on our doorstep, we will relocate Sanctuary. Easy-peasy."

"Agreed. The wars of others don't pertain to us," Ghost added.

Sunfire slammed her hand to the table. "Wrong! Starlight, advise these two with some of your wisdom."

Starlight sat in the furthest corner, almost looking to make herself seem smaller and out of sight. She looked like she didn't want to be involved with this conflict; however, Sunfire called on her for that very reason. "Devisor's technology... equates to disaster in virgin hands," Starlight said in a mumbling whisper.

"What?" Castle's eyes were squinting, his head shaking in confusion.

Sunfire reiterated, "What she's saying is, there's a reason we take the technology for ourselves. It's dangerous for species ill-equipped to handle such powerful technology to possess it. Thus, the Brotherhood of Relics has always had the secondary goal of protecting the galaxy from itself. And this war - the Wersillian War - is threatening to destroy our galaxy if we do not step in."

Castle retorted, "That isn't your decision. You may not act the part, but you are a knight, same as us. We're your equals, despite how big that head of yours balloons up."

"So we put it to vote - we put involving ourselves into the Wersillian War to a vote - as all matters before the brotherhood should be." Sunfire tilted her head to Castle.

Castle sat down. "That's the first thing you've said that I agree with."

Ghost and Starlight both nodded in approval.

Sunfire started to the door. "But first, I'll go relieve Brawn of the burden of dealing with our intruders."

Castle joked, "Having just awoken, and you're already itching to get your hands dirty."

Just then, the door opened, with a bishop present. "Sorry to bother everyone, but the Devisor starportal in storage has just been activated."

Ghost reported, "That hasn't been used in at least a hundred years."

Castle stood up. "I'll meet our guest. After all, each of you has the conversational skills of a plant. Best leave this to the social expert of the group."

Chapter 31

Ghost and Starlight nodded. As Castle passed Sunfire, she smirked. "Seems you have uses after all."

"Oh, go and show off already like you want to." Castle left the room and headed for the lower levels.

Sunfire addressed the remaining knights. "This conversation continues on my return." She left the roundtable.

As Sunfire passed the doorway, she saw two bishops armored up and equipped with belvon rods. "You two. Follow me, and make sure no enemy annoys me."

They bowed as she passed and came to her two sides, slightly behind her.

Eventually, Sunfire and the two guards made it to the front gates and had them opened. They marched outside to the slime-tinted rock wasteland covered by a thick fog. A planet called Jöithamir; terrain ranging from murky swamps to harsh, barren rocks. Remote and uninviting, perpetually bathed in a moss-green mist, this planet lay in the Shipwreck System and was perfect for hiding.

Sunfire made her way down the many steps leading away from the front entrance and towards the surface of the planet. She reached the bottom, arms crossed and uninterested, striding through narrow paths between sharp boulders.

The sky was lit with color as plasma, large and small, rained from three star cruisers down on the planet. The shields generated around the area were the only defense to block the city-destroying amount of fire targeted at the Sanctuary. Sounds of battle were soon audible, plasma gunfire, echoes of screams of agony - none of omelic origin, but of Wersillian soldiers. The cries of battle were nothing to Sunfire. Insignificant in her mind. She had power unmatched in the galaxy and with a sole purpose to aim it towards. She had a prophecy to fulfill.

Kilometers away from Sanctuary, a dytirc jumped out at Sunfire and the two bishops. It fired its plasma rifle at Sunfire. A bishop intercepted the shot with quick reactionary speed, deflecting the shot with the emerald-colored, divisor inspired-weapon he carried. More shots and more deflects by the belven rod until one deflection hit the dytirc in the head. He dropped onto a sharp stone and was impaled, his body leaking away its thick blood.

A korkyran warrior came from in front, to the surprise of the bishops, and aimed a powerful jab at Sunfire. He bashed her in the face. A mere annoyance, as the punch packed all the power of a small insect behind it. Or it did to her anyway, and she didn't as much as slide backwards by the blow. The korkyra let his fist fall to his side in utter disbelief. Sunfire put her hand over his face and burned it to ash. The insignificant being dropped at her feet.

"I told you to keep the enemy from bothering me." Sunfire looked back at the bishops.

Now in a perfect spot, with a clear view of all the star cruisers, she breathed in. Her power let loose, and her right arm lit ablaze. She aimed at the closest ship and let loose an intense array of fire as strong as a solar flare. It burned a hole through the first starship, triggering it to explode into pieces of fire and metal. She moved her aim to the next ship and the next, until all the ships where blasted apart.

The scattered shards of the ships rained down against the shields. But it was of little importance to her. She was ready to move on to more important matters. She looked at one of the two bishops. "Time to reconvene the knights."

Chapter 32: Blood Shall Conquer
January 12, 2112

Catharine Darcrose

The light faded, but not all the way. Some remained tucked far away and around a corridor. Cathy's eyes adjusted. She saw something new. No longer was she burning from the claustrophobic underground ruins and the heat it stored. This new place was colder, with no wind, and far more open. She was definitely somewhere else, transported and maybe not even on the same planet, as if that were possible. From first glance, she figured it could be a storage warehouse, given the stacks of containers in front of her. However, they must be old, maybe even forgotten; webs and dust covered them like sheets.

Sighing, Cathy gazed at her cyberwatch, tinkering through the settings. She pulled up her location. "Error. Location unknown," it read. Dumb technology. Never helpful when you really need it to be. Even so, she messed around with the cyberwatch for another minute, knowing full well nothing helpful would come from it. She was right, per usual. Though she always wanted to be sure. Then something did catch her eye - the date. January 12, 2112. That couldn't be right, given it was December 31, 2111, only seconds ago, right? Leave it to technology to go haywire.

"I guess the adventure continues," Cathy whispered out loud and began walking past the containers through narrow alleys between each stack.

"That depends on you." A voice caught her off guard only moments after she started moving. She pulled her gun, light on, pointing it at a man, an omelic man, lounging against a seat-sized metal crate.

She didn't fire. "Not many can sneak up on me like that. Who are you?" Cathy hissed with impatience.

The omelic, with his hands up, was laughing. "Aren't you just a friendly one?"

"And you're too calm for comfort."

"Well, this is my home. I don't know about you, but in my place I like to relax, let my guard down. You know, have a few drinks and unwind."

His place? Cathy asked herself. *Why would I be teleported to his place?*

The man continued. "I got a splendid idea. Let's play carpenter. First we get hammered. Then we nail each other."

Cathy snorted at the crude remark. "Instead, how about you don't be an ass?"

He was uproarious with laugher. "You're right, that's me - the asshole. People that know me, know that my metaphorical verbal filter is nigh-nonexistent. But here we are, meeting for the first time. So maybe... just maybe you can let that one slide? No? Yes?" He squinted his eyes and bobbed his head from side to side. "Tell me I didn't push you away already."

She let out a breath. "You sound better with your mouth closed."

He was unaffected by her insult and laughed, even though she wasn't. "So you do have a few jokes in you. I was beginning to think you'd be boring. If only you knew how much of that I've had to deal with lately."

"And I thought you'd be less welcoming. Most omelics would be."

"You would know, wouldn't you?"

She shot him a sideways glare. "Excuse me?"

"You know, I feel that we got off on the wrong foot. I mean, not that you can really get on the right foot... you being an intruder, me being... you know. Sorry... I'm starting to ramble too much. Let's just start with your name. Is that cool with you, girl?"

With each sentence, this omelic became more irritating. Then again, she was trespassing, although unintentionally. "Catharine Darcrose. But you can just call me Cathy."

"Jeez. Not a last name that just rolls of the tongue," he chuckled, "though a very human first name. But me, I'm Castle."

"And what kind of name is Castle?"

"A code name meant to keep what I used to be concealed," he snickered, "and to make me feel all warm and special inside."

His joke did not land with Cathy. "If you say so."

Chapter 32

"Where do you think you are right now?" Castle, now more direct, stood up and paced around Cathy.

She didn't let him escape her sight, keeping her weapon ready and guard up. "You said *your home*, if I recall."

"I did, didn't I? Guess I really blew that one, huh?" He stopped and stretched his back. "Leave it to Castle to spoil the surprise."

"Not really. Only saying *your home* isn't exactly what I'd call precise coordinates. So, you want to tell me where on Omulice we are?"

"Omulice? Oh, you poor girl. You really are just a lost puppy."

Impatient, Cathy raised her weapon. "Where, then?"

Castle noticed but kept his cool, and his tone was calm. "You didn't stumble here on accident, did you? In spite of my previous comment about you being a lost puppy - which you still are - I can tell you're a woman who lives life with a plan. There's a reason you came through that portal."

"If you must know, I'm searching for the Brotherhood of Relics."

"Are you, now?" he chuckled. "Why would you be searching for a group that doesn't exist?"

"I have no doubt that they exist. It is my mission and duty to find them, and I will see it through."

"And what makes you so sure?"

She replied, "James Stone."

Castle reacted to the name with his eyes. Cathy knew he had heard that name before. He started to clap. "Congratulations are in order. As it happens, you succeeded in your mission."

"Wait a seco-- No! You're the cult known as the Brotherhood of Relics?"

"Yes... I'm the brotherhood, me... just me... by myself." He laughed at his sarcastic remark. "Look girl, let's get one thing clear, the brotherhood isn't a cult; it's a *creed*. And secondly, if you really knew anything about us, you would've recognized the markings on my gear. But you didn't."

"When I went through that starportal, I honestly didn't expect I'd be warped right into your lair. Hell, I didn't even think portals existed until just now. So how was I to know what to expect?"

"We wouldn't have that starportal lying around for no-odd reason."

"Then what is all this dust? It's like you have never been down here."

"I haven't really. Well, none of the brotherhood really has. It's where we keep old and unused tech."

"The teleported is unused?"

"I mean you... you were the first person to use it in, ah... a very long time. Still, we detected its activation, and they sent me to inspect the situation. You're lucky it was me. None of the others are as charismatic as I am... probably due to the whole we-like-to-stay-a-secret-thing that the brotherhood stands by. It's a whole thing, I guess."

"You don't seem to endorse that ideal so much."

"What can I say? I like the limelight."

Cathy let out a small laugh. "Look, this has been fun, but I came here with purpose. I have people to answer to."

"Most do. In the meantime, you should come with me."

Cathy was hesitant to follow. "How do I know I can trust you?"

Castle passed her by. "An outsider should never trust someone from the Brotherhood of Relics, much less myself. But you aren't an outsider. Anyone who was able to come through the starportal is someone truly special."

"Special? No. It isn't that. It was my mission to find you. All I did was my duty."

Castle gestured her along to his side. Cathy allowed herself to fall in by his side as they walked past the items and storage crates. Castle beamed. "I don't think you get what coming through that starportal entails... *human*. Then again, that wouldn't be entirely accurate, would it?" Castle stopped to face her.

Cathy's pulse increased. "Wait, I--"

Castle was cheerful. "Cathy, it's nothing to be ashamed of. I don't know why you would hide such a glorious part of yourself behind makeup. Omelics are the greatest species in the galaxy, so why would you pretend to be human?"

Cathy took a breath. "I'm human--"

"No use lying. Only omelics that descend from the brotherhood ancestors can go through the portal and come out the other side. All our technology requires you to have the right gene marker, which you most certainly do."

Chapter 32

"You didn't let me finish. You're right and wrong. My mom is human. My biological father... not so much."

Castle was silent for a moment, staring at her. His eyes looked her over from head to toe in disbelief. "The child of a human and omelic." His eyes widened. "I've heard such a thing is possible. Never... never had I actually seen someone of such a heritage. How interesting. Your dad... who was he? He must've been a descendant of our ancestors, lucky for you."

"He's no one to me. He forced himself on my mom, and I was the result. Can't complain much, since I now have a life to live."

Castle didn't stop staring. "I admit, you have my interest. When did this happen?"

"I was born October 3, 2082, so subtract nine months."

"That couldn't have been long after humans joined the ranks of interstellar species."

"About a year or so. My mom was a diplomat at the time and traveled to many worlds. I never cared to know all the details and put my mom through that memory again, but it would've happened during that time."

"So you mean to tell me you spent your entire life pretending to be human." Castle dropped his hands in awe.

"Only my mom and dad knew of my secret. My mom had skin makeup developed to hide my real skin color. My family was always home schooled, but I had special lessons to learn Omelic history and culture. You're the first person I've ever told that to."

Castle's hands went up, highlighting his smile. "Well, I'm just an approachable guy... someone you can put your confidence in." He hesitated. "I must say, you've got quite the family."

"Which I why I must finish this mission. I need to. Because then, and only then, will I be allowed to search for my lost sister."

Castle waved her on. "Come. Let's give you a guest-of-honor treatment, courtesy of a great brotherhood knight - me."

"A knight, huh," Cathy observed. "You aren't true knights like the knights on Omulice."

"You're right. We aren't. It's really just turned into a title at this point, and nothing more - a keepsake from our roots."

Castle led Cathy up a staircase of floating steps, glowing green over elegant silver. Spiraling up, the staircase took them up a tower, and soon windows were visible.

"You mentioned that you sought the brotherhood out. I'm curious as to why," said Castle.

"The chief admirals have requested me to give the Brotherhood of Relics a message."

"How about this: Upon our next meeting, I shall bring it up to the other knights."

Cathy hid a smile. "I would be very pleased."

A glow of red in the next window caught Cathy's attention. Drawn to it, she stopped to peer outside.

The air and sky lit up with a ray of fire, thick and focused. It impacted a Wersillian star cruiser and tore a crater directly through the hull. Seconds later, the ship exploded into pieces, sending heaps of flaming metal into the atmosphere. Then it moved to another and another, destroying every last ship attacking the place.

What are the Wersillian Legion doing here? Cathy thought. "That is one powerful defensive weapon the brotherhood has." Cathy marveled at the power.

"Yes, she is."

Cathy's heart jumped to her throat, and her eyes darted to Castle. *"She?"*

"She's an ace just like myself and another knight, Ghost."

Cathy was stone-faced. "That's no mere ace. That is a living god."

Glued to the window she watched as chunks of debris smashed into the shields of the sky. However, her mind was not on the scene, but on the revelation. Seeing such power chilled Cathy to the bone.

If that was ever released against the ARW, how would we ever hope to survive?

Chapter 33: The Roundtable
January 12, 2112

Sunfire

"I lent our honored guest a place to stay for the moment. She told me she has a message from her leaders to us," said Castle. He was the last of the five knights to gather around the roundtable. With the distraction of the enemy out of the way, the more important matter was this vote on the how to handle the war. Then they'd have to relocate to become a secret once more.

"First, we have a vote to get to. We can hear the guest out afterword." Sunfire stood at the head of the table. "Our vote will be to decide whether or not we stop the Wersillian War plaguing the galaxy. I leave the floor open for anyone who would like to speak on this matter before the vote."

Castle flicked his finger.

"Why am I not surprised?" Sunfire rolled her eyes.

Starlight shifted uncomfortably at the tension filling the air. Castle and Sunfire were about to go at it again, and Starlight looked like she wanted nothing to do with it.

Brawn glared at Sunfire. He spoke with words louder than need be, yet common for him. "Sunfire, you carry a certain weight when you speak, but remember, all our voices are equal." Like Castle was to Ghost, Brawn was quite opposite Starlight, the day to her night. He was loud and booming to her quiet and subtleness, brazen to her shyness, and reckless to her restraint.

Castle took the moment to say what he wanted. "The way I see it, this war is meaningless to us. We have no reason to get involved, and I see no benefit for our brotherhood. I'm all for the action, but it just seems pointless and time wasted against more important missions."

Ghost chimed in. "Castle. When we first met, you told me: *War is a gold mine filled with opportunity. Those who know where to look shall have power beyond that most others see in a lifetime.*"

"How is that relevant, Ghost? Sunfire means to end the war, not join it."

Ghost glowered. "You misunderstand. It's relevant because the longer the war goes on, the longer individuals engaged in the war have to explore that gold mine of opportunity. It is unpredictable what they may achieve or find, and that could be a threat to our brotherhood. Ending the war puts an end to those potential threats."

"True danger isn't in the threats you expect, but in threats you cannot see," agreed Starlight in her soothing, soft tone.

Sunfire looked to Brawn. "Anything to add, speak now."

"I've already made my decision," he boomed.

"Then all in favor of ending the war, raise your hand." All hands went to the air, and Sunfire was especially surprised to see Castle had come around. She smirked and gave a subtle nod to Castle. "I'm glad you came to your senses."

Brawn stretched back in his seat. "Now we come to the hard part. How do we end a war that has plagued the galaxy for nearly ten years?"

"We turn to our resident expert. Ghost, I've been told you have experience and intelligence with both sides of the war. This is your time to make yourself useful."

Castle let out a sarcastic laugh. "Hah. This won't be short."

"Time is a commodity we have," Starlight added.

Ghost stood up from his chair and walked to the head of the table towards Sunfire. "The floor is yours." Sunfire let him by and found a seat of her own.

Ghost activated the holographic aid and began. "To truly understand the war, we need to examine a key point in time, a moment in dytirc history known as the Great Amalgamation. It's exactly as it says, a great gathering of countless tribes to form a united Military Tribe. When they joined forces with the lycargans, they grew into a powerful galactic force in the rather short span of time. The Wersillian War first started with the Raid on Tathen. After years of tension, this attack on a resource rich moon was what pulled the ARW into conflict with the legion."

Sunfire put her finger out to stop Ghost. "Tell me why the ARW would care about a moon not within their territory."

"The ARW is of a standing principle that all worlds in the galaxy should be free and individual. The Wersillian Legion threatens that by attempting to conquer worlds to expand their empire and fix their issue of overpopulation. I will add that I do sense a secondary motive behind the Wersillian Legion's attacks."

"Origin of the knowledge?" Starlight's face sparkled with intrigue.

"The ARW is quite technologically focused and achieves near unending amounts of information stored within their military network. For us, even their best security measures are easily navigated. When I investigated James Stone, I got access to that network, and it had all the information I needed," Ghost answered Starlight.

"It seems to me that this war would end if the Wersillian Legion were to stop invading other planets." Brawn was loud enough to be shouting.

"I agree," Ghost confirmed. "If you track each battle, the statistics show that the ARW rarely makes attacks into Wersillian Legion territory and is on the defensive most of the time."

"Target the Wersillian Legion, and the war stops. Simple," said Sunfire. "Tell me about their leadership."

Ghost nodded. "Dytirc tribes traditionally held a hierarchy based on the strength of the tribes' warriors with the strongest alpha being the tribal chief. That never changed. In the beginning, the legion had eight alpha leaders, called warlords."

"Tell me what we know about them."

"That's where it gets tricky. I've met their head warlord, Airra, and once saw another trying to hide himself when I arrived at a meeting a while back - a male korkyra. I never witnessed his abilities and--"

Sunfire interrupted. "I'm going to stop you there. You said 'abilities.' Elaborate."

"Every known warlord has been an ace. This is why they are at the top. Airra has external skin made of hard bark and has the properties of a tree with freer manipulation. Even so far as to be able to regrow herself and duplicate herself."

"She sounds like she'd be a blast to battle." Castle smirked.

"Tell me about these other warlords," Sunfire pressed.

"The male korkyra I spoke of earlier was killed on Idor, I believe. Three other warlords were confirmed dead within the ARW records - named Cralo, Steion, and Eruvir Varzaac. If you include the two korkyran warlords that joined the legion later, six total warlords seem to be still alive, including Airra," Ghost informed.

"Nothing you know of these six?" Starlight asked.

"The warlords have often operated independently of each other and don't often contact one another. When they do, it is not easy to intercept. The Wersillian Legion are not like the ARW, not as technological, and they use old-fashioned, even unorthodox methods to communicate."

"A simple *no* would've been fine, bud," Castle jested.

"Our mission now is to find the warlords and destroy them." Sunfire stood up.

Ghost added, "That would cripple and crack their unity. From there, we would be able to put an end to their objective of attacking other planets with relative ease."

Sunfire made her way to the door. "Time to get to work, then."

Castle stood to grab her attention. "Ready to forget our guest already, aye Sunfire?"

Sunfire stopped. "Right. It slipped my mind. Call her in." Sunfire didn't bother to take a seat. She would rather wait by the door.

Castle called a bishop to bring in the guest. And they all waited until she arrived. Sunfire was surprised to see a human female enter the room. How is this possible? Has the starportal malfunctioned?

The human didn't venture far from the door and gazed around, taking in the room.

"On with it, human." Sunfire's patience was being tested.

"My name is Cathy--"

"I don't care. Give us the message you came to give."

Cathy looked to Castle with an unsatisfied look. Sunfire didn't really care about this human. She was under the impression that this was a person with their ancestral blood that used their sacred starportal. Now that it clearly wasn't the case, she had no time for her.

Cathy activated a message that played with use of holographic technology from her cyberwatch. A dor'o female appeared in the message. Her bright-red face and presence filled the room. She was elegant, polished as her stumps, and glowed with a radiant smile.

The message started. "I greet you members of the Brotherhood of Relics. My name is Day-Bringer, chief admiral representing the ARW, with this invitation to you. We've been made aware that it was with the brotherhood's aid that a vital message was delivered to one of our star cruisers - a message that saved the lives of thousands, including our own soldiers. We thank you for that. And we offer you an invitation to join our cause in stopping the Wersillian Legion from attacking free planets and killing many lives. It has been my pleasure to extend this offer to you. Feel free to consult with Catharine Darcrose should you have questions or should you like to meet with me." Day-Bringer bowed in respect before the message ended.

Sunfire stood on the message for a moment. "Human, your ARW is in luck. It was decided by us moments ago to end the war by stopping the Wersillian Legion."

Cathy stepped back and was aghast. "So you are going to join forces with the ARW?"

"I never said such a thing. We will stop the war, and we will do it ourselves. Come or stay, you decide." Her words were directed to Cathy. Sunfire pointed to Castle and Ghost. "You two are with me. Let's go."

"I can't go. I need to find my sister," Sunfire heard Cathy say from behind her.

"Come, and I'll help you find her myself," Castle reassured.

They all followed Sunfire out of the room. And it seemed Cathy made the decision to go with them.

Sunfire was moments from entering her personal starship with two knights and the human behind. The hatch was open, and she started up when a small buzz in her pocket stopped her in her tracks.

"What is it?" Ghost asked as the group stopped.

Sunfire pulled out a triangular device that glowed red. Even after all these years, that device never left her pocket. She had almost forgotten it was there.

Anighta, the name came to her head. She was the one who gave Sunfire the device. And it meant one thing - Anighta needed her.

"Yo, Firehead?" Castle snapped his fingers near her eyes to get her attention. "Don't let your mind wander too long. It's way too small to be outside by itself."

Sunfire looked up to them. "I know where we must go."

Chapter 34: Faith & Hope
January 14, 2112

James Stone

I woke up underwater, my back lying against bedrock. With haste, I sat up into the icy air of the room. Rubbing away the water from my eyes, I found myself in a pond at the center of an onyx and gold, domed cavern. Torches flickered against the rock covered in inscribed symbols. Brushed with the same hand, the aesthetic and design of the cyphers told me I was in yet another place of Precursor origin just like the Vault of the Seven. That was, of course, if these so-called Precursors truly existed in the first place.

Then Jeremiah popped out of the water next to me. He was as quick to recover as I was. "Did you get it?" he asked.

That's when it hit me - The Blade of Wrath. I had failed the last trial. I shook my head. "I didn't."

"Me neither. Worse yet, I no longer carry the Book of Sin." His voice was uncharacteristically dower.

There was a flicker of light, followed by a sudden voice. "Trial-takers whom awake in this district--" The voice seemed to echo throughout the cave, with no point of origin, almost as if the cave itself was speaking. "--Although unworthy of wrath, those whom awake here have proven worthy of commemoration. May those here shroud the light until extinguished."

Shroud the light? I wondered.

Jeremiah and I weren't pleased with ourselves. With no visible exit to take out of this cavern, we left the water and waited with our backs against the rock wall. Time ticked onward, and I could practically hear the clicks of a clock in my head. Yet nothing alerted my senses. Everything was still and quiet, like a soundless, underground cage left abandoned to the slow creep of time.

Many minutes passed, and I shifted around from my spot against the cave wall. I was beginning to fiddle with the idea that we may stay there until we were but skeletal remains. Still, nothing was happening. "Maybe you could ask God to throw us a bone," I said, with a small laugh.

"You could just as well as I. What's stopping you?" he asked.

"Don't think he cares for my voice."

"But because of his great love for us, God, who is rich in mercy, made us alive with Christ even when we were dead in transgressions—it is by grace you have been saved. Ephesians 2:4-5. He cares about all his children, James. You need only allow him into your life."

"There was a point in time that I believed, but that was long ago. Going down the path I have in life has led me to believe a controversial take on the subject... religion is all horseshivf aimed to control."

"Have you been hurt by it?" Jeremiah didn't take offense at all by my attacking words. His tone held a curiosity to it, a genuine interest in my story.

I shook my head. "No. See, my issue with religion is you got to do this and that... that and this. Live by these guidelines, or *thou shall be* forced to eternally suffer... all that shivf. And let me tell you what: That shivf just isn't me. I'm a man that lives by simple rules. People should be able to do whatever the hell they want with their life so long as they don't hinder the natural freedoms of others. If someone wants to live on pins and needles, fraken let them do it... let them self-destruct. If some dude wants to bail on a marriage or cheat, let him. It's only natural to want to spread the seed. Hell, if a man wants to be gay and gurgle on someone else's shaft, what's religion to say he can't enjoy himself?"

"Morality and belief are all he asks, James. Live under the ideal nature of a good, god-loving man who believes he is already saved by God. These restrictions that you allude to, what do you mean?"

"When I went to my local Sunday school, I remember tales of a lump-sum of things men are condemned for in the Bible. No eating rabbits, pigs, or camels... no short haircuts, requirement to have a beard... that stuff. I know there's more that I can't place."

Jeremiah's head rose in realization. "I understand. Leviticus - That is what you remember. That truly is a misunderstood book, and to appreciate it, you need to understand Leviticus in the context of the Bible. It represents a huge chunk of the Mosaic Law, which was a special covenant made between God and the Israelites. It is a strict, severe set of ordinances designed to separate the Jews from the Gentiles in every conceivable way. In other words, those laws were never made for Christians."

"You say that like you were there." I chuckled.

"When you've read it as my times as I have, you would be, too." He paused. "And besides, the Bible, although in inspiration of God himself, was written by men. Men's nature is to allow a certain margin for bias and personal beliefs to cloud what truly is the story of God. That is why there are many interpretations that led to different denominations."

"I admit, my attic has always been a little dusty when it came to religion. However, my stance is still my stance. Freedom and independence are core to the human condition to me."

"Very truly I tell you, whoever hears my word and believes him who sent me has eternal life and will not be judged but has crossed over from death to life. John 5:24. That is what I live by."

That sudden moment, a stone sank below the cave floor and gave way to the open sunlight. We went just outside the cave's entrance. Clouds roamed the sky, and I felt warmth upon seeing the beautiful sky once more. I looked at my cyberwatch. My eyes widened at the sight of the date.

"January 14, 2112," I shouted. "We were in the trial for a half a day tops. How can we go in on the twenty-second of December and come out on the fourteenth of January?" Though I already knew the answer. The question came more as a shock than anything else.

"Relativity," Jeremiah responded.

We both knew that meant the threat the corelinns spoke of would've already made it out of the forest. It was predicted to emerge and reach the Treasured City two days ago. In words put another way, we were two days late.

"James? James, come in." That was Valiic's voice on my cyberwatch.

"Valiic. Where are you?" I asked.

"We woke up in a cave."

"As did we."

"My cyberwatch says we are roughly three kilometers from the Treasured City."

I looked at mine and saw we were even closer than that. "Who's *we?*" I asked Valiic.

"Shadow-Walker and I woke in the same cave. However, a door gave way in our cave a bit ago, and we ended up finding Geariic and Frost. Based on what the voice told us, we believe that our group was separated based on how far we made it in the trial."

I looked to Jeremiah, who gave a nod in agreement. "It's just me and Jeremiah here."

The looming question was: *Where the frak did Brad go?*

I noticed someone else enter the voice chat. Speak of the devil, and he shall appear. "Where da hell y'all at?" The voice belonged to Brad.

"Holy shivf, Brad. Tell me you got it. Tell me you got the blade," I said.

"Fuck yeah, I did."

My face was about to explode with joy. "Son of a bitch! You did it, you goddamned bastard." I complimented him not with words, but with tone. Jeremiah tapped on his wrist and gave me wide eyes. I cleared my throat. "Alright, Brad, we'll have to celebrate with a beer on me later. For now, I need to know where you are at."

"Shit, I ain't far from where we started."

"That's the second best damn news I've heard today! Locate the shjarr threat and eliminate it."

"Consida it done, Stonewall." Brad closed his communication.

Valiic jumped in. "James, there's trouble."

"I just sent Brad--"

"Other trouble," he interrupted. "Alabon just finished speaking to Geariic over comm. It isn't good news."

"Alabon? Is he well?" My thoughts lingered on his well-being.

"He is. That wasn't the bad news. That head warlord we fought on Garatopia... well, she's here. And she brought an army."

"God help us all, then." My jaw clenched at the thought of Airra. As far as I was concerned, she was the embodiment of all that was wrong and evil in the galaxy.

Valiic continued. "It gets worse. Apparently, she released another Devisor bomb on the planet just a minute ago. According to Alabon, she wanted to *get our attention.*"

"So she knows we're here. Considering we now have two of those keys that she's after, I've a feeling she plans to royally frak us up the ass herself."

Jeremiah stood up and was now looming over me, listening in on the conversation. "Where was the bomb activated?" he asked.

"In a city south of the Treasured City called Lamnlair. Only thing is, it's moving through that city towards the Treasured City."

"Moving?" I asked.

"Whatever fuels it is beyond my knowledge, but it looks to be a tornado carrying a current of electricity."

Jeremiah nudged me on the shoulder. "Based on your map earlier, we are not even a kilometer away from Lamnlair," he said.

"So?"

"So, I know how to stop it."

I nodded to him. "Valiic, you guys head towards the Treasured City. Jeremiah has a plan to stop the Devisor bomb. Once we do, we'll meet you there."

"Warrior's haste, James." Valiic closed the chat.

I stood up. "What's this plan of yours?"

"No time. We need to move now before it picks up speed."

Still under the warmth of the sun, I pulled up a map on my cyberwatch. According to it, we had to go up the large hill that held the cave we left. We went to the side of the entrance and began our climb. Given the doom and gloom of our predicament, the slope was something out of a nightmare; every step was a struggle, as if I were pulling my feet out of ankle-deep mud. There were more rocky steps than I would have believed, a thousand-thousand steps, and horror waiting for Jeremiah and me at the end.

Still drained of energy from the trials, I was a near mess by the time I reached the top of the hill. Atop, the whole world spread out below us. I could see a great hermitage down the opposite side of the hill. Much further to the right was the fire-blackened ruins of some ancient civilization by the looks of it. To the west, one swollen red sun was half-hidden behind another hill and looked to be rising. Filling in the gaps was open country, farms, fields and forests, and beyond that, somewhere hidden was the city of Lamnlair.

Chapter 34

Jeremiah led us down the hill at a remarkable pace. In fact, I had trouble keeping up with him as we dodged and weaved through the forest. However, it wasn't dense, making the task more manageable.

Clearing the brush of the forest, which took less time than I thought, we made it to the outer parts of the city of Lamnlair. Already the buildings were ravaged beyond recognition. Piles of rubble and blocks were scattered everywhere, like a broken puzzle. Among the destruction were the bodies of deceased corelinns. Some were burnt to a crisp, some crushed, and others were pummeled to death – none of which were easy or deserved deaths.

Jeremiah went over to one of the corpses and crouched down by it. He stared for a brief moment, and I could see tears run down his check. He gave me a nod and led me down the street.

Further down, I could see some buildings still standing; architecturally like those we saw in the Treasured City. That was where we went. We rounded a street, and that was when I saw it. As big as the buildings itself, the tornado was rushing at us. Already a kilometer away, it ran through buildings as it zapped apart other buildings. You could see the very lightning bolts bouncing off the high-speed wind in a frenzy. And to make this already literally spinning disaster worse, it got bigger with every building it ran through.

The Devisor bomb came closer and closer.

"You said you know how to stop it. Now would be an excellent time to clue me in," I shouted over the winds.

Next to me, his eyes never left the cyclone. "I need to get to the core."

"How do we do that? This might come as a shock to you, but those winds are strong enough to push over buildings! Fighting through that is the same as wrestling a mountain!"

"You misunderstand. *I need* to get to the core, James. *I* do." Jeremiah took two steps forward before I grabbed him by the shoulder.

"I get wanting to sacrifice yourself to save the planet. But this is batshivf crazy! You'll die before you reach the center."

Jeremiah looked back. "It's our fault that weapons such as this exist. Finally, I know why God wanted me on this planet. I am the only one here who can destroy the bomb." I stared into the eyes of a man on a mission. He tilted his head sideways. "Tell me you didn't see it coming, James. Something inside you must've understood that I was never human," he said.

"Because you're an ace, like me." I was sure as day of the words coming out of my mouth.

"No, James. There are fewer than a hundred of us left, but we still exist. *Divisors still exist.*" I blinked, and my arm went limp at his statement. "Faith and hope. It's who I was, who I've *always* been." Like a kick in the nuts, the realization was sharp and quick. The piercing arrow hitting The Gatekeeper, the healing of Shadow-Walker, the burst of strength used to save Valiic and me – all of it tied to some latent gift of being a Devisor.

Before I had a chance to say anything, wings of pure radiant light erupted from his back. I was blinded and turned away. The image was burned into my brain. I couldn't see for seconds because of it. Finally, I shook away the daze just in time to see Jeremiah fly headfirst into the tornado. He was gone. And after a few more seconds, so was the tornado, dissolving into nothing.

My legs started moving. With a mind of their own, they took me to where the tornado had been. Down the street I ran, jumping over fallen debris and rubble.

There he was. On the street, motionless on his side. I almost made it to him when I noticed motion from the corners of my eyes. In the time it took me to get near Jeremiah, multiple enemies had enough time to set up an ambush. I was now surrounded by a dozen of them; lycargans, dytircs, and korkyras alike. Every single one emerged from holes in the ground dug under pieces of rubble. The tornado was just bait all along, swinging in the current. And my dumbass rose right to it, like an open-mouth fish.

I readied my gun as they readied theirs, though my weapon was converted to fight shjarrs and I had an aching hunch it wouldn't so much as give them a light sting. Might as well spit at them instead.

That sudden moment, there was a light hum in the wind. Soft, slow, each note dragged on, and it was altogether creepy. The tune was followed by something else. Call it a feeling in my stomach, but something was there. Something was about to happen.

Chapter 34

The foes surrounding me lost their breath. They grabbed at their chest as their eyes lost their color, then collapsed to their knees before falling completely over. All of them dead. Nothing over the top; just simple deaths. And that feeling around me kept growing. Getting bigger, *bigger*, until I felt surrounded by it.

Nothing prepared me for the sudden invisible force that had me on my knees. Air! My lungs couldn't breathe in enough of it.

What is that feeling? I thought. I was cold. My muscles felt frozen over.

I forced my head up, and my blurred vision saw movement. It was him again! It was the man I saw in the Ghost Town, and in Garatopia. *Why does his presence still haunt me?*

He bent down on one knee, over the body of Jeremiah. White light radiating from his figure. With one hand, he pushed back over bangs of his black hair. His soulless black eyes stared down at the dead priest, his expression calm and tranquil. Tall and thin, his bones were prominent behind his skin. He wore a dark suit jacket over a white undershirt; black tie; dress pants, shoes, he also wore a red tie pin.

"It's you," I struggled to say.

"Me. Me, me, me," he muttered. "What you're feeling is because of me. Living beings such as yourself feel as you do when subjected to this much of my presence."

"Who are you?"

"In due time, James. I'm not here for you, because you are not yet ready." He touched his palm to Jeremiah's cheek. "Rather, it is him that interests me. So few of them left."

"He said-- He told me that Devisors still live. Is he--?"

"Devisors. A rudimentary name befitting use by a primitive species such as yourself. How easy residents of this galaxy ignore that which is right in their face." The mysterious man didn't answer my ill attempt at a question.

He stood up and walked to me, his steps slow and light. He almost didn't look real due to how he walked as he approached me. Though my blurred vision could easily be the cause.

He put his hand on my back, and I felt even colder. I could even see my breath in front of my face. "Your place isn't here. You have somewhere else to be."

Vision left my eyes, and I was blind. I felt a choking sensation and loss of air. Then my body felt dense, as if submerged under deep water. All my senses were completely dulled, and I was fading away. Fading. Then nothing but blackness.

Chapter 35: Ultimate Sin
January 14, 2112

James Stone

"James. James, wake up!" My eyes opened to see Valiic holding my back up and calling down to me.

I was on a street, and just about everyone was there; Valiic, Shadow-Walker, Geariic, Alabon, Frost, and even the Prime Keeper of the Treasured City, Witna.

I stood up, with Valiic's help, and said, "We did it. Jeremiah and I stopped the bomb."

"Where is he?" Witna's eyes were shiny.

I shook my head. "He gave up his life to stop it." I intentionally held back my knowledge of him being a Devisor.

Grief weighted down the air. Shadow-Walker banged his hand on the nearby wall. "Damn. That punk was beginning to grow on me."

I nodded. "He truly was the type to grow on you, with his unending supply of optimism."

Frost signed a cross over his chest and raised his hand to the air. "Rest in peace, uzzo." He comforted Witna, who was beside him.

Geariic marched past Valiic and stood before me. "You know what we have to do now, right?"

I stared back. "If you're about to suggest that we go after--"

"*If* what? That's exactly what I think we should do. We need to go after Airra now. It's the right thing."

"She just used a Devisor bomb. Remember how weak that made her last time. She'll never be more weakened and vulnerable than she is right now," Valiic added.

"Let's not jump straight to go," I said. "After she kicked our asses straight to hell last time, going after Airra is chewing-the-cord dumb."

Geariic held taunt in stance and smirked. "Whatever happened to the old James? The man I heard about, the man I first met, *wouldn't* hesitate to go after a warlord," Geariic criticized.

"What happened? I lost people, Geariic. People I cared about took their last breath because of my hotheaded carelessness. When it was just my ass on the line, that was one thing. But it isn't just my ass anymore. I got family that needs me to have their best interests at heart. And frak, I wish I had understood that sooner. Maybe then Uslar, Malcolm, Vaalima, and Beverly would be alive."

Geariic snorted at the response. "So what? I said it once before: People die."

"You wouldn't say that if it was your brother," I countered.

Geariic's face was red with ire. I could tell he wanted to rip me a new one. He took a breath.

I took his silence as a cue to speak. "Most of us here have fought Airra. We know her. This *is* a trap... one as obvious as the day is bright. Regardless, we nearly all bit the bullet last time we took her on alone. So let's not go starting fires where there is no wood to burn."

"James. You have us this time. Trap or not, she has *no hope* against four aces," Alabon added as he neared us.

As stupid as it may seem, I really hadn't seen it like that. Here these two behemoths were ready to help my unit destroy Airra once and for all. In the best case scenario, an outcome like that could go as far as to end the war. Words didn't do justice to how appealing that was to me. To top off the cake, they already had killed another warlord, Cralo, a while back. They had experience few others had. Even with all the positives banging around in my mind, I just couldn't let myself repeat mistakes I had already made. It wasn't worth risking the lives of my family.

Valiic jumped in with his input. "James, we owe it to the people. Speaking for myself, one reason I joined this war was to protect those in need. The Wersillian Legion destroys lives every day. We can't let this be another place that falls because of them."

"Think of Narrisa," I implored.

"I do every day. There's a well-known maelkii saying: *Return with your shield or on it.* I'd rather never return to her than to return to her harboring the heavy weight of dishonor. Honor is everything. I won't let these people die knowing I could've done something about it."

I moved past Geariic and Valiic and called the attention of the rest. "Is that it, then? Is that what you all want?"

Chapter 35

Frost's veins popped thick in his neck, ice shelled over his arms. "Big Daddy's still got a score to settle with that ugly bitch!"

Shadow-Walker and Witna nodded in agreement. Of course, Witna wanted us to help. How could she not? Alabon was giddy and eager as ever. His body trembled with anticipation, and I knew in that moment he was on board.

I did not feel comfortable with this decision. Then again, I always preferred leading as a group over making the sole decision. If they wanted to try their hands at taking on Airra, I wasn't going to be the one to stop them.

"Fine, then. Looks like everyone's on board with Airra round two. Even still, there is still that matter of her army," I said.

"Leave that to us." Witna's expression changed from grief to anger. It was clear she wanted to avenge Jeremiah.

"Us?" asked Frost.

"Our species is quite good at coming together against a common threat. I'll send word immediately."

"Best go with her, Shadow. With your injuries, I don't want you near Airra."

"Not a problem with me." Shadow-Walker grinned. He followed Witna as she left.

The plan was set. The time to revisit our rivalry against the great head warlord Airra was about to reach another phase. My stomach was playing jump rope with my intestines at the mere thought to having do battle with her once more.

*****

The roars of battle raged on the outskirts of Pullentin, a city in-between Lamnlair and the Treasured City. At first glance, it would seem in this battle we'd lose right away, given the ability of the enemy to seemingly do as they wished. However, their being here was breaking an unwritten law that could hold severe consequences in the long run. So, they couldn't risk too many moves, and the corelinns had the weight of numbers. The battle where the corelinns took it to the Wersillian Legion today was on their terms, their land.

Using the distraction of the battle, my unit and I slipped into the city. It was Geariic, Alabon, Valiic, Frost, and myself on a mission to hopefully end the reign of terror left in the wake of Airra. We knew Airra was in the city somewhere, weakened and vulnerable. In the city streets, it became apparent fast this place was as quiet as a graveyard in a lone town. As we went deeper into the core, the screams of battle outside the city faded away. We were left with nothing but the howling wind.

As we passed the outsides of buildings, we saw they had already been scavenged, likely scavenged by the enemy in battle. Tents, restaurants, stands; all of it had been ransacked.

Deeper into the core of Pullentin we went until we found something egregious. Painted in blood on a few walls were words of a dytirc language. Translated, it read, *"Did you enjoy the present I sent you? Did you enjoy that bomb? I had to clone myself so I could activate it at that other city. All that effort and the corelinns... they were sooo unappreciative. I got them back, though. Yes, I did. Even a species as weak as they are can serve a purpose. So, just follow their bodies if you want to come play with me."* At the end of the last sentence was a grim smiley face painted in the same blood.

Just as she said in the message, a trail of bodies and bloody arrows told us where we needed to go.

"She's sick," Valiic gagged in disgust.

"You better believe we'll make her pay!" Frost assured Valiic.

I had no words for this massacre, this slaughter. All my instincts blared in my head and told me one thing: Airra was wicked and evil. This scene only reaffirmed that opinion.

Alabon was shaking with excitement. "Oh, oh, I wanna play. I wanna play with her." He tittered like a child seeing a pet for the first time.

Geariic was just as impatient. "Let's get a move on."

I led the way, following the bodies and keeping a firm mind of where I stepped. Those dead corelinns had already been through enough. They didn't need us stepping all over them.

As I saw more and more of the destruction that Airra had caused, I started to think about what Witna and Anighta told me. *A monster of the forest will bring destruction to this planet.* I was beginning to think that monster was Airra all along. Problem is, Brad was out of contact, so I had no way to confirm that thought. I was beginning to think there was never a massive shjarr monster at all and Brad was sent on a mission to kill something that didn't even exist. A real shame, too, because we sure could use him and the Blade of Wrath.

The dead took us inside a market. We passed the shattered doors and stepped inside a warehouse of food that wasn't all taken, like in the rest of the city. This warehouse wasn't ransacked. Some food was gone, but that was nothing unexpected in a market.

We found Airra sitting in the back on a chair next to a fruit cart, indulging herself. Behind her was a pile of horrors, bodies of corelinns stacked high. She was clearly drained of energy, else she wouldn't be eating as much as she was.

Beside her was someone new to me. The unknown lycargan held his weight with a cane in front of him. His eyes sagged, and age spots were all over his face. Even the sharp gleam of his claws had dulled, and the armored shell on his back had yellowed. On looks alone, he appeared to be of little threat.

"I see you got my message," Airra called to us.

I held up my hand to stop our unit and started to march forward. Geariic was of his own mind, since he followed close behind me while the others stayed put. "How much blood must be on your hands before you're satisfied?" I asked, with pumping fists.

"Killing and eating are the same for me. It's not about wanting to... it's about needing to," she retorted.

"Same monster as I remember," I growled.

She laughed with her wicked laugh that could stand hairs on end. "I'm touched you remember me."

"You nearly killed us the last time we met. None of us could forget that. You're powerful, elite even... but that's just it. The problem with being in the elite few – by definition, you are vastly outnumbered," I threatened. Then again, she was outnumbered last time, too, and still had the upper hand. But it's as Geariic said, we had the Bruising Brothers this time.

"Don't just stand there, then. Worst thing in the galaxy is a tease. Come, let's get on with it." She motioned at me with her arms.

I growled and pulled out my blade. "In your state, I wonder how many times it'll take before my blade pops its way into your brain." I started forward.

Geariic grabbed my shoulder. "James. Let's take her together." His grip was tighter than I would've been comfortable with.

I nodded to him and was just about to instruct everyone to surround her when I heard that laugh again. My spine spun in circles.

"Oohhh, Jamesssss," Airra sang. "Do you want to know how long Clover Landis lasted before telling us what we wanted to know?"

My blood ran to my head and all my muscles flexed at that name being spoken by such a foul mouth. "Shut your damn, dirty mouth!"

She continued with a glow in her eyes. "I can tell you exactly how many days and hours she lasted before giving in to Steion's hand. Would you like to hear?" Her mocking words were disguised as daggers, and the cut was deep.

I wanted to attack her right there, but Geariic held me back. "You really are the scab of the galaxy! Landis was a downright hero. Don't you dare soil her name."

"No, you're right. Her torture wouldn't interest you. But I know something about her that would. Oh... it really, *really* would." Airra let loose some unwholesome laughter.

"Geariic, take your hand off me. I'm going to shove my knife down her throat." I pulled forward, but he didn't relent.

"James? What are you two doing? What are we waiting for?" I heard Valiic ask as he started coming closer.

Airra stopped laughing. "Didn't you ever ask yourself *how* Steion knew your captain knew the location of that key?"

I felt a chill. Something was off. "What do you mean?"

"Ever find it odd that Steion knew just where your captain was when he took her?" She started to giggle. "In fact, I'm sure you feel like you have the upper hand right now. You probably feel you could kill me this very moment. I wonder what it was that has reassured you."

The old-timer next to Airra took a step forward. "I remember you, James Stone. I saw through Steion's eyes as you killed him. He warned you once that there are more warlords, some in places you'd never expect."

Chapter 35

"You?" I asked.

"I am a warlord - Yalfari Soodo. But I'm *not* the answer to Airra's questions."

Airra taunted us with her brazen eyes and ear-to-ear grin. "The answer, James... the answer is right behind you."

Geariic's grip tightened on my shoulder, and like a flash of light, I realized just what was happening. My body was locked in a cage of suffocating air at the thought, unable to move a muscle. My eyes were stuck staring into Airra's eyes; so confident, so evil.

She continued. "Did you really think I would roll over and die? Did you really think you were a step ahead of me? Dearie, you've never been on my level, not physically or mentally. You... *lose*... James. I will enjoy watching as you're torn apart by those two warlords."

"Frost! Move away from Alabon!" I turned and yelled backward.

Frost heard me and started to shell himself in ice armor. Alabon was already prepared before Frost was. His war-glaives already had electricity running through them, and he turned it on Frost. The bolts surged through the ice and lit him up.

It was no good, Frost didn't have a chance to react. He screamed in pain before passing out.

Just like that, it was Valiic and me versus Geariic and Alabon.

I was tossed to the ground by Geariic. "You Goddamn coward!" I spat up at him. He pulled off his warhammer, and I quickly rolled away, springing back up to my feet.

Valiic had already gained ground, and now he was rushing Geariic like a train. "Traitor!" He had a look in his eye I'd never seen before. There was hatred there. As wicked as Airra was, not even she received that look from Valiic.

The next moment, Valiic collided into Geariic before he could hit him with his warhammer. Geariic was sent sliding back. "You spit on everything maelkii hold dear! How could you fall so low?!"

Geariic growled. "I was getting real sick of you in that cave, but I had to hold myself back. Now I'm going to show you just how far that maelkii spirit will carry you."

"It isn't me you should worry about!" Valiic veins bulged from his neck. Alabon was closing in, but Valiic had noticed. Airra was hysterical in the background, enjoying every moment of the show.

"Wait for me. I want to play, too," Alabon cheered.

As he came close to Valiic, weapon ready to strike, Valiic spun with his shield in hand. It crashed into the side of Alabon and forced him to the ground. Valiic almost lost his footing from Alabon's heavier weight and stronger momentum.

"No sin is worse than betrayal by our laws! It is the *ultimate* sin in our culture!" Valiic screamed at Geariic. "You are no kin of mine!"

"You're fraken right we aren't kin. We've never been kin! The maelkii abandoned us. They left us on the street because we were different."

"Shove that pity shivf straight up your shiny ass!" I yelled. "Plenty of other soldiers were dealt worse cards in life than you two! And where are they? Where is their betrayal? They still fight proudly for the side of right." I ran at Geariic. "You two are cowards."

Alabon was up and attacked Valiic. He blocked the electric war-glaives with his shield. Forcidion doesn't conduct electricity, so he was able to fight off Alabon for the moment. Alabon pulled back one of the blades and went for Valiic's legs, but Valiic managed to disengage and dodge.

My senses flared! I ducked under Geariic's swing. He was slower than I was, which played right into my hands. From the other side, I pulled my weapon from my back and fired. It was no use at all. The corelinn weapon did jackshivf to Geariic. Instead, I tossed it at his eye, and that caused him to flinch.

"Landis died because of you." I had a tear in my eye.

"She wasn't the only one. We killed that idiotic captain and his crew on Idor before coming here. See, we had orders to try and obtain the Weapons of Sin so they wouldn't be used against the legion. I want you to know that before I kill you."

His next hammer swing was wild, and I dodged it as it came down. The explosion sent shrapnel into me, and I took cuts to the skin. I ignored the sting and forced myself close to Geariic once more. He was still recovering, and I went directly for his eyes with my fingers. He closed them, and I hit nothing but metal.

"Stop that, you fraker!" Geariic cursed.

That move allowed me to kick his hammer-wielding wrist and dislodge his weapon. I scooped it up with straining muscles. I forgot just how heavy it was. Like a batter, I swung with all my might, weight, and ass behind it and hit Geariic dead on. Even with the explosion, he came out unharmed, barely even knocked back.

"How's the medicine taste, backstabber?" I spat at him.

Just then, Valiic came charging in and tackled Geariic, colliding with him in the gut. Alabon was right behind him.

"Think twice," I said as I spun into another swing. The warhammer hit Alabon's back. That move sent him flying into crates of food left of Geariic and Valiic.

I wasn't about to waste the chance. "Can you handle Geariic?" I asked as I passed Valiic.

"Go. This one's mine." There was an intensity in Valiic's deep voice.

Geariic growled, "Give me everything you have, Valiic. At the end of this, I want you to know, without any doubt, that I was the better warrior."

"You are no warrior!" Valiic pounded his shield into Geariic's chest.

I turned my attention back to finding Alabon. I pushed away the crates of food blocking my path and followed a trail of smeared fruit on the ground. I turned into an aisle and barely managed to dodge Alabon's attack. His blade sliced into the shelves, and he came at me again with his second war-glaive.

I blocked with the handle of the warhammer and kicked him in the gut. He didn't even flinch. And before I could react, he snagged me by the arm and tossed my body through the shelves like a rag doll.

I landed hard. "Shivf," I put my hand over my side. There was some blood and a lot of bruising. Wobbly, I barely managed to stand. And to throw more misfortune my way, I no longer had the warhammer.

Alabon was coming, with a lot of momentum. *Think, think.*

On reaction alone, I grabbed a piece fruit beside me and tossed it at Alabon, hitting him in the eyes. He winced and shouted with pain, clawing it away. As durable as these two were, they had one exploitable weakness: They had zero protection for their eyes. So, the strong acid of the fruit against Alabon's eyes worked, and I was able to dodge. Alabon wildly ran over the broken shelves, tripping and sliding through some more. Alabon lost one of his war-glaives at my feet.

"You don't have to do this, Alabon." I walked toward him. "Don't follow your brother's idiocy."

He pushed himself to his feet. "Where he goes, I go." Alabon was walking towards me. Excitement shone in his childlike eyes. It was no use. These two were too far gone. "It's time to play a little game, James. I've wanted to play with you for so long."

I waved him on as he picked up speed. I slid my foot just under the handle of the war-glaive. This next part was all about timing.

Alabon was getting closer, his hands raised as he prepared to strike with his blade.

Now!

I kicked up the war-glaive at my feet and snatched the handle. I activated the electric current and threw it at Alabon like a spear. All in one swift motion.

Alabon's eyes blazed, and he reacted faster than I expected. He moved just a hair, and the blade sliced into his shoulder, missing his chest where I aimed. Blood ran down him as he crashed to the floor and into shelves. But I knew it wasn't enough to kill him.

After hitting Alabon, the war-glaive ricocheted close to me, and I picked it up for another attack.

"James! Watch out!" Valiic called, with breathless words.

I turned to see the sight of Geariic only a meter away, with his warhammer in hand.

"Don't you dare touch Alabon!" His eyes nearly froze me in place.

I managed to dodge his swing, but he planted a foot and halted his momentum. I sliced my blade across his face before he could react, just missing his eye. He backhanded me, and I spun backward. He recovered, and I took a warhammer hit to the side. Luckily, I was able to brace. But wait--

Oh shivf! I thought.

Chapter 35

The explosion blasted me through carts of fruit before I went sliding far away across the floor. I was soaked in my own blood. I couldn't stop coughing it up.

Christ! Christ almighty, I think that explosion damaged one of my lungs among other things.

I could barely see past the blood covering my eyes. I had no idea where I was in the market. Before I was sent there, I saw Valiic barely standing. Geariic must've done a number on him. Even as intense as Valiic was, he couldn't overcome an ace as strong as Geariic; correction, a traitorous warlord as strong as him.

The half-destroyed crate of food in front of me exploded in a barrage of splinters and wood chips. Geariic had made his way over to me. In the end, I knew this would be the outcome. We were far too outclassed by the Bruising Brothers. I smiled, with blood soaking my teeth. "Suck my balls, you traitor," I cursed him.

Geariic hovered over me, lifting his warhammer and preparing to land the final blow.

All of a sudden, a massive blast of light and heat came from Valiic's direction. My heart throbbed, and I wondered if he was okay. Just then, Geariic bolted and left me there. Why? That was his chance to finish me.

"Alabon!" I heard a screech of pain in Geariic voice.

There was only a second of silence.

"You've seen better days," said a voice. Wait a damn second. I knew that voice.

I felt a prick in my side, and my wounds started to recover at a hyper-accelerated rate. The pain eased up, and I could breathe much easier.

I was helped up by Ghost, who had spoken just a moment before. "It's you," I said. I could feel my veins begin to pop. "You here to kick my lily-white ass again?"

"You were a target. Nothing more. And now you're not."

"Don't go thinking we no longer have a score to settle. You still need to answer for Uslar's death."

His eyes held nothing back. They showed me that he accepted my words and even gave me a sense of calm. "Agreed. Given the current situation, it can wait. You'd best come with me."

Ghost led me over to the scene. Airra was no longer laughing. Her face was full of something I had yet to see in her - fear. And about time she felt that. Behind her was a human woman with two sidearms pointed - one at Airra, and one at the elderly lycargan with the cane. Her eyes met mine for a second, and she gave me a glare. My heart rejoiced when I saw Valiic leaning on his shield; injured, but alive.

Geariic had arrived only a few seconds before me. He fell to his knees next to a pile of ash and melted liquid. I was clueless as to what was happening.

"Alabon," he sobbed. Rivers of tears were flowing down his cheeks. Next to Geariic was one other omelic I'd never seen before. "All we wanted was to be great. That's what we were promised," Geariic whined. "When the war was all over, we were going to mean something... warlords leading over a united galaxy." Geariic ran his fingers through the ash like grains of sand.

The unknown omelic marched up to Geariic and put her hand outward and close to his forehead. "You're a warlord, too?" she asked.

Geariic cried, "You killed my brother. Why?"

The omelic unleashed an intense beam of fire meters thick. I turned away so as not to burn my eyes, and, when I looked back, I saw Geariic was nothing but ash and melted metal. I was stunned. More so when I now realized his brother must've met the same fate.

"That's Sunfire. She's a brotherhood knight, as I am," Ghost informed.

Sunfire made her way over to Airra, who didn't move. I don't think she could've, even if she wanted to. Her eyes fell low when she couldn't match the gaze of Sunfire.

"You look just as Ghost described you, head warlord Airra," Sunfire said.

"I've never seen you before," Airra responded.

"I'm called Sunfire. I'm here for a single purpose, a destiny entrusted to me to fulfill. I'm driven only to accomplish this goal. No adversary nor any obstacle will deny me my destiny. By this promise I live, and for it my resolve is unrelenting."

Chapter 35

"Calm down. All I said was, I didn't know who you were. No need to tell me your life story," Airra mocked. Her tone was lower, and she wasn't in the mood to laugh anymore.

"Fitting final words, I suppose." Sunfire raised her hand to Airra.

"Final words?" Airra's eyes flared, and she started to shift on her seat. "Wait, wait. Don't!" She realized in that moment Sunfire was no being of mercy.

Just then, my mind and body were overrun by a sudden, overwhelming pain. There was a ringing in my head, and I couldn't move. It hurt, but I couldn't scream. I wasn't the only one. All of us were stunned in place, save Airra and the old--

Wait! It was that old lycargan. The one called Yalfari. His hands were up, and he was focused on all of us.

"Run, Airra!" Yalfari shouted. Airra fell out of her chair before getting up. She was still weakened and could hardly move on her own accord. "This one is very strong! I can't hold her long!" His eyes were locked on Sunfire.

Airra picked up the pace and rushed out of sight. The nose and ears of the lycargan started to leak blood. Just then, I could see Sunfire take a step forward. But I couldn't move a centimeter.

Struggling, she was able to inch forward again. Then again, and again. Some blood now leaked from Yalfari's eyes. After fifteen minutes of pain-induced ringing in my head, the lycargan fell over, coughing up blood.

Sunfire picked him up and sat him in Airra's old chair. "You must be a warlord, too."

The old lycargan looked to be barely alive. His eyes were completely lost of color. "I am," he muttered in a voice that was hardly audible.

"Tell me what that was that you did just now," Sunfire pressed.

"My ability... I can link my mind to others. I did this to the other warlords so that we could always keep tabs on everyone." His head slowly turned to me. "That's how--" He coughed and his words were getting slower, "--I knew you killed Steion. But I had to sever those links... to buy Airra time to escape... from you." More blood poured out of his mouth as he coughed again. "I really hope... she does.

Otherwise... all this... stalling I've done is meaningless--" His head fell down, and the words stopped coming. He was dead.

"Well, that's just fraken great. Airra's probably leaving the planet this very moment," I spat.

Sunfire turned to me, with confidence on her face. "Nothing could be better for us. You see, Castle was tasked with planting a tracking device on her starship. With luck, she'll fly back to wherever it is she goes and gather the other warlords to face me. It is then we will track them down and end the war."

End the war. I couldn't believe what I was hearing. Did the Brotherhood of Relics really intend on killing all the warlords? What does that mean for the ARW? I had so many questions, and I didn't know what to ask first.

I felt a shove at my side, and I took a step backward. "You're James Stone, aren't you? I could tell the moment I saw you." It was that human girl from earlier who gave me a glare. "What are you doing here? No, never mind. That isn't important. Where's my sister?"

"Your sister? I don't even know who you are."

"Catharine Darcrose," she said.

My eyes went black at the mention of her last name. She was Beverly's sister, and she was here in my face. How could I begin to tell her what happened? How could I tell her that her sister was dead and it was my fault?

I was silent. She shoved me harder. "Where's my sister?"

I gulped and couldn't bear to speak. A tear fell from my eye. No doubt she saw.

"James, where is my sister?" She punched me in the chest and sniffled. I felt water on her fist. "Where is she, James? Where is my sister?" Her voice went quieter with each word. She punched me again, only softer. Her face fell on my chest, and I could feel the water soak through my shirt as she cried.

The others seemed to pick up on what was happening.

Her expression changed. There was anger, a lot of it. "You let her die, didn't you?!"

"It was my fault," I choked.

Using her leg, she tripped me as she pushed me. "You're the captain. How could you let her die? It was your responsibility to bring her back!"

On the ground, she had me pinned, and she pounded punch after punch into my face. She was strong, and I took them all. My body screamed in pain, and my brain begged me to stop her. But I didn't. Who was I to take that away from her?

It wasn't long before Ghost caught her arm mid-strike. She looked up at him, tears and hate in her eyes.

"Enough," Ghost said. "Enough," he repeated, softer. Cathy fell into him and sobbed. Ghost held her but had a look of discomfort on his face.

Sunfire was now over me. "James Stone. Ghost mentioned you on the way here."

I was massaging my face. "He did?"

"I'm told you have experience with warlords. Come with me, and help me put an end to them."

I nodded. "One condition: Make sure my unit gets back to the ARW safely. There are four left in my unit."

Sunfire gave a slight tip of her head. "It's a deal. Tell Ghost the specifics." She left my view.

After helping Cathy find a spot to grieve, Ghost came over and helped me to my feet again. "You're on the ground often." His humor was not apparent by his tone. "Four left, you say?"

"Valiic over there." I pointed. "Shadow-Walker and Brad Swift are currently elsewhere on the planet."

"I remember Damon. You'll have to elaborate on the other."

I nodded. "Lastly, Frost over there." I pointed to him. He was still passed out and looked badly injured. "And please help him. Use that stuff you used on me."

"It won't work on him as well as it did on you."

Sunfire was back to interject herself in the conversation. "Castle reported back. He was successful." She looked at me, then at Ghost again. "Continue your conversation as we move. It's time to leave."

Sunfire started to leave.

"James--" Valiic called to me, his voice weak. He was still bent over his shield and hadn't moved at all.

"Valiic, go be with Narrisa. I'll be fine with these two as allies," I commanded.

He gave a hesitant nod, and I could tell he understood. That was it. It was time to put an end to the war, to the warlords, everything. I felt like this was a dream, like this entire moment could be pulled out from under me. After all we had been through, was this really the beginning of the end?

Chapter 36: Purpose of a God
January 20, 2112

James Stone

We were outside the door to ending the war. Behind it was Airra. This was a fact we knew. For almost a week, the three knights of the brotherhood, Cathy, and I tailed Airra's starship as we kept tabs on Airra, and she never suspected it. Now here Airra was trying to hide at some Wersillian Legion safe house at the bottom of the Draynought System. Ghost had pinpointed a distress signal sent from this safe house to who knows who or where about two days ago and a starship had landed in response. It was what Sunfire hoped for, and all the pieces of her plan were falling right into place.

Present company included Sunfire, Ghost, Cathy, and myself. All of us had a burning taste for a fight. For each of us had a bone to pick with Airra.

Within the halls of the safe house, Sunfire burst through a door, to the surprise of Airra. She jumped backward and fell over herself. The room was completely devoid of any kind of décor or furnishings.

"You!" Airra nearly cried out the words.

In desperation, she duplicated into six of herself. Sunfire signaled for all of us to wait at the door. Ghost put a stasis shield down at the entrance.

All six clones of Airra surrounded Sunfire and lashed out vines and thorns. An entire storm of it, looking like a tornado was unleashed in there. Then there was a flash of fire, which incinerated it all. Even the stasis shield in front of us busted.

In a swift motion, Airra, trying to save herself, managed to use one of her clone bodies to jump in front of herself to lessen the blast against her. Still, she was launched to the other end of the room, partially on fire.

She broke off the parts that were on ablaze and regrew. Then she cloned again, but Sunfire blasted it apart in a mere second with a burst of flames.

Airra lay weak and battered in the corner of the room. There was no begging, no mercy to be had. She had fought and given all she had. It wasn't enough. Her efforts did nothing to stop the threat before her. Sunfire was too much. And I felt happiness that she was going to die, here, right before my eyes.

Ghost led us inside and closer to the scene.

Sunfire pointed her palm towards Airra, who let herself relax, appearing to accept her fate. "How 'bout a story?" Airra groaned.

"I don't think so," Sunfire countered immediately.

"You remind me of my dad. I killed my dad."

"A threat from a cornered rat is nothing to me." Sunfire stared down at Airra.

"So I get no last words, huh? Just like that?" Airra sighed. "I just want to tell you why I wear this jacket."

Sunfire nodded. I felt like Airra was just trying to buy time for herself. Even still, was it right for Sunfire to let her speak?

Airra started her story, which was to be her last, and spoke with slow words. "Within the tribe I was born into... they had this unorthodox way of living. I had an identical twin, a sister, born a minute after I was. By our tribe's law, I was firstborn and given the opportunity to be a great warrior. But my sister... she was born stronger than I at the time. All I needed to do was complete a test to claim my heritage. Hours prior to it, my sister... my beloved sister, betrayed me. She ambushed me and took my place and got everything I was supposed to. I was shamed when I went to our elders-- See, my sister claimed I was not myself and she was me. I was cast out... tossed away like garbage. Never had I felt so lonely and defeated. That was the moment I told myself nobody would ever hold dominance over me again."

"Too bad you had to face me." Sunfire's eyes lit ablaze. Her palm followed, and a stream of red hot fire engulfed Airra. The heat radiated throughout the room, warming my face and body.

The moment was so surreal. Can it be? Could we have finally won? With the head of the snake finally cut, the legion would surely die off. The moment felt unreal. Like I was in a dream.

"We won." The words felt fake rolling off my tongue.

The fire was still ablaze in the corner. Sunfire, turning back to me, said, "Not yet. There are still two warlords to eliminate." She was right. Including the head warlord's death, we had killed four of the six left.

Ghost jumped in. "Last two are a mystery to us. It won't be easy to track them down."

"Sounds like a job for you, Ghost. You were one of the best at it before I went under and still are after I rose again," replied Sunfire.

"So she is capable of giving a compliment," Ghost nudged a little jab her way.

"I wouldn't get carried away. You may have the other knights convinced, but with me, you have a long way to go."

"Noted. And--" Ghost started.

I interrupted. "I hate to interrupt this little internal power struggle, but look." My eyes and finger were glued to the same location. The location of the corner, the location of Airra's would-be grave. But instead, there was a rock; harder and denser than any I'd ever seen. It protruded from the floor and created a prism over the spot where Airra had been. It folded back into the ground and revealed Airra; still alive. She was gleaming, now more than ever.

Sunfire snarled, "You! How? Answer me now!"

"I have powers you've never seen," Airra lied in a tone apparent to us all. Something was different about Airra. She no longer had the hint of fear in her tone.

The room was silent for a moment, and in that moment I heard footsteps from behind; loud and boisterous, similar to a boultha. I wasn't alone. We all turned back to see. The silhouette was massive!

"I think this conversation is long overdue," the voice boomed.

Sunfire stepped forward, heading the crowd of us. "Conversation? I don't even know who you are."

"A natural born leader... I like that. A quality we share. And--"

Sunfire interrupted. "Either you tell me who you are and why I should care, or you catch fire and burn. It is your choice, but choose fast. 'Cause sometimes I can be in the mood to fire first and ask questions later."

In the shadow the hall, the man, the beast of a man, smiled with charm at her threat. Still walking closer, he spoke. "Asserting dominance with speech. Don't think that will intimidate me. And nor should you feel the need to, as I come to you in peace... to talk. And I hope you would return the same courtesy to me." His tone softened. "Airra, dear, come to me." The man finally stepped out from the shadows and into the light of the room. And he was massive, easily larger than a maelkii. Crystal-rock, jagged skin, ice blue in color, with hints of smoky black deeper in the crystal skin. Similar to a maelkii, his feet were bull-like feet, and spikes followed his spine to the top of his head. Even the black abyss eyes were spot on, with only a pupil colored to match his skin visible.

The being raised his arm, palm toward the ceiling, and curled his arm toward his chest; his fingers motioned like he was squeezing an orange. The floor rose and formed into a chair made from dense rock and minerals.

I heard an audible gasp and looked to Cathy, whose eyes popped with shock and surprise. Before anyone could speak another word, she yelled, "Kaizerious! You! Y-you... what a-are you doing here? Are you with them?"

Airra was now at the being's side after creeping along the walls, making an extra effort to stay far from Sunfire. "Dearie, he is my stepfather," she responded to Cathy.

"Go, Airra. Leave this place," said Kaizerious.

Airra didn't hesitate to leave, and as she left, Sunfire let off another round of fire. Only this time, Kaizerious shielded Airra's escape with rock.

Kaizerious sprouted more chairs from the ground behind us. "I invite you all to sit. Each of you has had a long day of fighting. But now is the time to catch your breath...breathe...we are in peace talks."

"Peace," Sunfire echoed the word. She didn't bother sitting; only Ghost did. "There is that word again. Funny coming from you - father of the woman who started this war."

"No. That was me," he admitted.

"All the more fitting, then."

Cathy was still in shock, and even had a tear forming. "You are responsible for the state of this galaxy, the many that have died in the war or because of it, the planets now barren of life and resources to fuel this storm! *You!*" She was stuck, looking for words to say. And I was oblivious as to why this was or how she knew him for that matter. So many questions, and not enough time.

Kaizerious said, "I'm deeply sorry you had to see me in this light. And since you are here, you should know I was the reason behind the attack on the brotherhood. As you left, I snuck a tracking device on your leg. It went in the portal before you. Though it never made it to the other side, I was able to see its direction."

"You betrayed my trust!" There was heartbreak in her voice. Like she had been stabbed in the back by a dear friend. "I thought you didn't fight?" Cathy said.

"I don't," Kaizerious reaffirmed.

Sunfire continued. "Ironic. A man who will not fight yet started the greatest, longest, and largest intergalactic war known in the history of every species that inhabits this galaxy."

"Flaws were never something I claimed to lack. And yes, know that I see where you are coming from. I can see how, in your perspectives, I must look like a madman, a murderer, and worse." There was a pause.

Something about him was different than all the warlords. He didn't come out here throwing around insults. He shrugged off each of our threats, turning the other cheek. He didn't start throwing punches. In fact, he had only shown us respect.

Kaizerious began again. "I now sit here before you, ready to answer the questions you may have and hope to arrive at a conclusion we all can feel confident in."

Cathy began. "Are you just another warlord we have yet to meet?"

Kaizerious let out a quick chuckle before responding, "I am not. I am a father. Some have indeed called me an overlord, but the word doesn't fit my taste."

Sunfire, annoyed, raised her voice to Kaizerious, "Look. From now on, you will speak to me alone--"

Kaizerious raised his distinct voice over hers. Being the deep, powerful voice it was, her voice was no match. "I have invited *all* here to participate in this conversation. You do *not* have the privilege of setting the rules here. I expect more of a leader than to silence those whom she leads." It was clear Sunfire was not the only alpha-personality in the room. In the wild, situations like this never turn out well for one of the alphas. I like to think we are more civilized about such things.

"Gods don't concern themselves with the opinions of a peasant," Sunfire fired back. I turned to catch Ghost's reaction to this. He has never been much of an expressive individual, but I could see his distaste for that statement.

"Gods who feed on the worship of those peasants, yet fail to uphold that for which they are worshiped for, shall only fall to the ground that much harder," Kaizerious countered.

"So much for not fighting. Those are fighting words."

"A mere attempt at a joke. I apologize... I have never been good at them. All the same, don't misinterpret my attempt at shifting your frame as a threat. I mean only to be friendly with you. And I still offer you a seat."

Still she didn't sit, and by now she was the only one who remained upright. "I don't want your damn seat." Sunfire flared her lip.

"Frame?" I whispered back to Ghost, who was the closest to me.

"He is referring to the unstated beliefs that give context to interactions. Frames are what give meaning to the words we say, like the difference between me using 'Be silent' in one tone as opposed to using *'Be silent'* in this tone. Put yourself in his position for a moment. A highly capable and powerful fighter beat and nearly kill his daughter, yet he talks and treats her and us as his guests, even inviting us to come to peace. Sunfire still engages him as a hostile in each word she speaks to him, and he is trying to shift her frame into his much friendlier one. Quite good this one is at the art of language," he answered.

The thoughts rattled in my head. Give me a mission, a physical task to complete, I'm your guy. But this. This was nowhere near my area of expertise.

Kaizerious was still locked with Sunfire in words. He said, "Is that really how you see yourself? A god?"

"I was born into the Brotherhood of Relics, a legacy, destined to make my vision a reality. All my life, I was looked on to make this galaxy a better place. Then I got my powers, and the truth only became that much clearer. I was prophesized to be the light that would keep this galaxy in order. Your war puts it out of order. And from where I stand, I believe I'm the only one who can correct that mistake."

"For a *god*, you sure don't see the forest for the trees. I get that this war may seem like it is only hurting the galaxy, but down the line, I see a galaxy brought together in unison. I see the forest, the big picture. Does that not fit the order you seek?"

"Not if it means the Wersillian Legion holds all the cards in the end."

"Who says it has to?"

"You did when you brought them together and promised them everything."

"And whoever told you that misinterpreted my promise. After all, this is their war with the ARW, not mine. The outcome of who wins remains to be seen."

"You're saying you don't care who wins?" I jumped in. I caught a sour look from Sunfire. "And if that is the case, why start a war in the first place if the result makes no difference to you?"

"I appreciate your effort to get at the truth. I picture anyone in your position would do the same. But put yourself in my position for a moment. Would you want those who seek to do your family harm to know the means to do so? If I make my motivations clear, you will know my next move. That is something I can't afford."

"You said you were here to answer questions," Sunfire added.

"And to talk peace. We should focus on that. I gave the dytircs what they wanted when they sought leadership and land. I gave the lycargans what they wanted when they sought religion. I gave Cathy what she wanted when she sought you, the Brotherhood of Relics. I am here to give those what they want. And now I know what you want, an end to the war. I can give that to you."

"And what do you want in return?" Sunfire asked.

"This war will end the moment I have the remaining keys... and James Stone."

Kaizerious's words hit me like a brick. *Me? What would he want with me?"*

"Off the table!" I threw the words at him.

"The hell you can!" Cathy added.

Sunfire, also surprised, said, "I get the wanting of the keys, which is bad enough, but why Stone? He is just a man."

Kaizerious, dead serious, replied, "If he is only a man to you, what is the harm in making this deal? You want the war to be over, for all worlds to once again destine their own fates-- James... he is of no use to you, no use to the Brotherhood of Relics. He has not done anything for you and will likely never do anything for your benefit. This deal is a steal for you."

Sunfire paced around in thought. Ghost looked over at her. "I shall inform the knights that we need to vote," he said.

Sunfire stopped. "Wait!"

"Sunfire?"

"I know what the consensus will be, and this decision is far too important to be made wrongly."

"Sunfire, we vote on every--"

"Enough!" She intensified, and her eyes lit on fire, followed by the palm of her hand. But instead of using it to intimidate Ghost, she turned and marched to Kaizerious. She held her palm uncomfortably close to his chin and neck while her face was centimeters from his. Their eyes were locked, but Kaizerious hadn't flinched in the slightest. I sat on the edge of my seat. "Kaizerious, you almost had me for a fool. But I'm a god, and even you, with your silver tongue, can't fool a god." Sunfire moved her palm a bit closer until the now blue flames nibbled at his chin. "Do you feel the heat of intimidation?"

"You sure enjoy your fire puns," he smiled. "I really wanted to help you, Sunfire. Truly, I regret I was unable to satisfy your ambitions and desires. For they could've changed the galaxy for the better. But I understand now that you can't handle the idea of *not* being the most respected individual in the room. Even your own has witnessed you fall today."

I gazed over at Ghost, and what I saw made me believe in those words, however unlikely it seemed.

"When you're dead, when the warlords are nothing but dust and the galaxy is rid of the legion, all respect for you will've long been forgotten. And had you not shown to be the manipulative worm you proved to be, I may have taken your deal. But you manipulated Cathy, the dytircs," lycargans, and now you are trying to manipulate us. That is why I can't trust a word you say or a promise you give. There is only one way this ends, and that is with you dead. And I've never faced an obstacle I have not been able to conquer. No being in this universe can match my power!" shouted Sunfire.

"You act as an impulsive child who has never heard the word *no.* "

This was getting bad fast. I wasn't the only one to notice. Ghost motioned for me and Cathy to group with him, and we did. "Sunfire!" Ghost yelled. "He has seen what you are capable of and isn't afraid. Why isn't he afraid?"

Kaizerious grinned. "Because I've seen stronger."

Sunfire was done. She lit up her entire arms and fired blue flames straight towards Kaizerious's heart. The flames roared and split around his body. Nothing was burning, and Kaizerious stood up. He towered over everyone in the room. "I said I don't fight, but I *will* defend my family and myself."

Ghost gestured for us to leave, guiding us to the back wall. He planted a device on it, and it began to drill a hole round enough to walk upright through.

"The situation is dire. We don't want to be here as it escalates," said Ghost.

"What about Sunfire?" Cathy added.

"She's just getting started," Ghost assured, with his trademark brand of near-emotionless calm.

As the hole went deeper, I looked back to catch Sunfire punch Kaizerious in the jaw. He winced but barely took notice, and yet her hand was somehow not in pieces. *What are those two made of?* This time, Sunfire lit her entire body ablaze before taking it to him.

We were leaving in a hurry. In the tunnel, I was sweating bullets. Whatever was going on in there, it was getting hot!

"Almost there," Ghost insisted. Running, he was pressing a series of controls built into the cloth of his armor at a furious rate.

The drilling device burst through to the other side. A starship waited.

"I had this brought to us," said Ghost.

The hatch on the ship opened to a ramp, and Cathy and I jumped inside before the ramp touched the dirt. That's when I noticed Ghost was not among us. I looked back.

"You two have a duty to your ARW. Go. Return to your people. The bishop piloting the ship will see you there," said Ghost, and he headed in the other direction.

"What are you going to do?" I asked.

"Just as you have a duty to your people, I, too, have a pledge to mine." He then stopped and pulled out a small device shaped like a poker chip. He put it into the cloth on his wrist and then tossed it my way. I caught it. "I made that to work with your cyberwatch," Ghost said while looking over his shoulder.

"What is it?"

"You remember I looked into your past when I was assigned to hunt you?"

"Hard to forget," I mumbled.

"You deserve to know the truth." His words left me standing in my own confusion, but he gave me no more time to question him. He was gone, dashed off to rejoin his brotherhood.

Chapter 37: Cut off the Head
January 20, 2112

Airra

Tremendous rumbles shook the ground! The battle going on outside the safe house must've been extraordinary. Airra stumbled against the wall of the hallway as another ground-shaking tremor swept by. Still weakened from her battle with Sunfire, her body was stiff and low on energy. She was vulnerable and hated the feeling.

Wondering through the halls of the safe house, she found her way inside the hangar, only to find the ship she arrived in was a steaming pile of smoke. She wasn't going anywhere in that garbage fire.

"Oh, damn. Were you going to use that to escape?" A voice came from the corner. Airra looked to see an omelic. "Sorry. That's... that's on me." The omelic chuckled, with both hands touching his chest. Based on his mannerisms, he had not a care in the world.

"A ruddy irritable one, aren't you?" Airra growled. Last thing she needed right now was a fight.

"I believe you misspoke. Charming, right? That's what you meant to say," He laughed at his own jokes. "But you, lovely, can call me Castle. Nice to meet you, by the way, but it's even better for you to meet me." Castle cackled.

"You must have a death wish to disable my ship and wait for me *alone?*"

"*Wait for you alone* - how kinky. I admire your feisty attitude. But that is just about all I admire." Castle gestured to the entirety of Airra's body. "I mean, it's like I thought I knew the word 'ugly.' But seeing you up close, I realized I never truly understood the word until just now."

"Can't count how many times someone has called me ugly, and that was before my skin turned to bark. Insults no longer bother me."

"You took the whole thick skin metaphor literally." He laughed. "Good on you. Let those naysayers know."

Half a smile found her face. "You sure talk a lot."

His laughing hadn't subsided. "One of my best qualities."

Airra joined in. "I do admit. You do make me laugh."

"So the ladies tell me."

Still smiling, she asked, "So while I've got you in a favorable mood, you wouldn't mind just letting me leave? Or is that too much to ask?"

Castle shrugged. "Well... here's the thing. I know... there's always a thing, and I'm afraid this one you won't like. See, with Sunfire and Kaizerious having their battle of the millennium, I was kind of feeling a bit left out. Maybe we can help each other out there. What do you say?"

Airra maintained her smile, even allowing it to spread. Even though she was weakened, she had appearances to maintain. "You'll regret picking a fight with me."

Castle stood tall with confidence. "Let me tell you something about me. Battle is a bit of a hobby of mine, and I specialize in sticking it straight up the ass. I don't care who my opponent is or how many of them there are. I go in there regardless, bend them over, and spread their cheeks real wide. I get a nice view of the colon, prostate, and the coccyx, and I knuckle-frak them all the way up to the palm till they feel a burning sensation deep in the ass. Conquering my enemies until they are shells of their former selves is a way of life for me, and I take pride in my work. I never accept surrender, frak you. If at any point you wish to withdraw from the fight, I kindly suggest that you go frak yourself. I follow absolutely no mercy rules or laws of war. All I know how to do is get shivf on my dick from sticking it straight up the ass... metaphorically, of course. Have I made your situation clear?"

Airra chuckled. "You do know your little intimidation speech was riddled with anatomical inaccuracies, right? Dytirc anatomy is not the same as omelic anatomy."

He laughed. "I thought it gave it more flair. Did it work?"

"It's funny. Creative, too. It might even work on others, but not me. Still, I enjoyed listening to it. But I can tell you're faking it. I can tell because I'm the real deal. I'm the one who's hooked on the drug of war. I've always loved the feeling of a battle. Indiscernibly really - that feeling in the middle of a fight - it's like I can suddenly see for miles. Of the thousands I've fought with, I've met less than five who truly share this thirst... this... *desire* with me. You're out of your league coming here to face me."

Chapter 37

Airra didn't give the talkative omelic a chance to respond; she was going for the kill while his guard was down. He was only a few meters away, and she reached him in little time. Her fingers sharpened into thorns, and she thrust right at his heart. Castle didn't move.

Airra was stopped short of her mark, but how? She then noticed some sort of field of energy around him. What was it? A shield generator?

"Oh. Did I stop your big moment?" Castle laughed at her. "If that's the best the ever-so-great Airra is capable of--"

Airra interrupted, with a hiss, "Dearie-dearie... we've just begun."

She unleashed a few piercing vines at him, and all were deflected around the same energy. She then tried to wrap a few vines around him, but it was still there. Somehow, he seemed to be covered by it. Nothing annoyed Airra more than not being able to harm her opponents. It was like having a drug placed in a glass container that can't be broken.

Airra growled at Castle, "Stop hiding!"

"Who's hiding? I'm right in front of you, or did your fight with Sunfire earlier leave you simple?"

How did he know about that? Unless-- He must be with the brotherhood. Of course, how could she be so stupid? He was that omelic with Ghost that one time, following that mission on Xan'Ohmo the Brotherhood of Relics agreed to accept for some dumb crystal-things. She should've recognized him earlier.

"I know you," Airra said.

"I was wondering if you'd ever remember." Castle laughed, as if she had told him a joke.

His defense was strong. Basic attacks weren't going to work. Time to grow. And so she did. Airra's bark skin layered over itself over and over until she was twice as tall. She concentrated her growth in her hands and turned them into drills half a meter thick and spun them toward Castle.

"Oh... this fight may actually give me some entertainment." Castle pulled out two throwing knives.

Airra attacked with her spinning drills, but Castle leaped back, avoiding it altogether. As he did, he tossed out the knives, but they hardly pierced her skin. She then felt a shove; it was that same energy from earlier, only this time Castle used it offensively. She slid back just a bit from it and was blinded as two explosions originated from those knives he had thrown earlier.

Damnit. Airra shook her head from the daze.

"I brought those bad boys just for you, Airra. Not something I do for just anyone, so you'd better feel special," Castle teased.

In spite, she lashed out some thorns, followed by a swipe of a few vines. Using that same energy, Castle blocked the thorns while simultaneously flipping over the vines. His agility and athleticism had clearly been improved with training. But there was a way to stop that.

Airra used much of her remaining strength to build a wall and roof to surround Castle. Made of vines, they interlocked and penetrated into the hangar wall he was near. Now the only escape was past her.

Castle gazed around at his surroundings. "Smart plan," he praised her.

Airra gave him no time to think. She powered forward and charged into him. His field protected him as he took the hit, but she carried him into the wall. The field stopped that impact as well, but Airra grinned as she noticed a tiny crack form. Her eyes gleamed at Castle as she now realized she could get through.

Even still, Castle showed no worry. "It's been sometime since someone was able to crack my aura field."

Aura field, so that's what it's called. Airra wondered if that was some ace ability of his.

Castle continued. "You truly are strong. I'll give you the praise you desire, but I'm afraid you did get one thing wrong about me when we talked earlier."

"And what's that, dearie?" she growled.

"I'm not alone."

A sudden blast of air knocked her straight to the floor and away from Castle. Airra landed and pushed herself up in an instant. She turned, but he was already there!

"Ghost! It's you!" Airra shouted.

Ghost came in strong, with a flurry of strikes. Airra took them with little effort, her bark skin serving as a strong armor. She retaliated with multiple vines as sharps as needles straight at him. He jumped above her, and just then something smashed into her feet, sending her falling.

Chapter 37

It was Castle's annoying aura. Above her, Ghost used his gauntlets to blast air above himself, speeding him right into her. Airra smashed to the ground. That instant, Ghost unleashed multiple blades from his gauntlets into Airra's neck - her weakest spot!

He pulled them back with magnetic technology and repeated his attack.

"Get off!" Airra pulled the walls and ceiling of vines back into her body and unleashed a massive growth spurt. That knocked Ghost off.

Quickly, she spun like a tornado and released a barrage of thorns in all directions.

Ghost blasted himself towards Castle, who shielded them both with his aura.

Airra relented the attack and gazed at them. As strong as she was, if she kept going at this pace, especially after her run-in with Sunfire, she'd deplete herself dry. Then she'd be helpless against these two, who looked to kill her. To cut off the head of the legion, so to speak. She needed to escape, and fast.

Airra spat. "Your ability is that of a coward, Castle."

He laughed. "You're joking, right? You... who hides under a suit of bark armor."

Airra ignored his words. She split into two bodies and covered each side of Ghost and Castle, surrounding them. Right now, two bodies were about all she could handle.

"It appears she aims to split us up," Ghost told Castle.

Castle grinned. "You know what to do."

Ghost nodded and jumped to the wall behind them, boots attaching to it. Castle dispersed his aura up into small spots spread around the room. Ghost burst from the wall into one of the spots, then to another and another. He was fast, especially with the aid of Castle's ability. Airra maneuvered her two bodies back to back to cover herself better.

This wasn't going to be an easy fight. To put it mildly, these two knew how to fight alongside each other. Moreover, they covered each other's weakness quite well. Castle lacked powerful offense, which Ghost brought, and Castle supplied him with defensive capabilities he otherwise wouldn't have. This two-on-one scenario she was in could easily be the end of her if she didn't play things perfectly.

She had a sudden idea. To have the best chance for success, she needed to single them out. Fighting both at the same time would be exponentially more difficult. And since Castle had that aura spread throughout the room, he was vulnerable. That was her target.

Quickly, Airra went straight for Castle.

He smirked. "You poor, ignorant thing. You fell for it."

Just then, his aura returned to his body. From above, Ghost was attached to the ceiling of the hangar, high in the air. He tossed out multiple devices that exploded on the ground. Waves of liquid splashed out near her. That instant, it reached both her bodies and started to dissolve her outer layer of skin. It was some form of acid! Castle, of course, was unaffected due to the shielding of his aura.

Quickly, Airra used one body to raise the other one above the acid, stalling the process. She launched a few vines to the ceiling, but Ghost cut them with throwing knives.

Frustration began to blossom. The feeling was back - the feeling of utter helplessness. She swore she would never feel that way again, yet she had twice today.

"Give up, Airra. You cannot hope to defeat us both," Ghost said callously.

The acid continued to dissolve the body below her. She had little time left. Just then, another monstrous tremor ruptured throughout the entire building. Ghost fell, Castle tripped, and Airra barely managed to latch herself to the top of the broken starship in the hangar.

The shaking didn't stop, and the building started to rip apart. Cracks formed, sections of the ceiling fell. The shaking was so violent, it felt like the entire planet was being pulled apart.

"Ghost! We need to leave now!" she heard Castle shout.

"We cannot leave Airra alive," he responded.

"Forget her, and check your video feed!"

The fear in his voice was nothing to be taken lightly. Airra couldn't afford to pay attention to them anymore. She used this opportunity to slip herself behind some of the mechanical parts in the corner of the room. Luck had it, the acid was blocked by the parts. She slid away a panel in the wall and slipped into a tunnel. She was glad Maliv had suggested the idea of installing secret escape tunnels when this safe

Chapter 37

house was under construction. He was always a careful man, and it was paying off for her.

Soon, Airra found her way to her stepfather's starship. Hopefully, he didn't mind her borrowing it. She rushed in and made her escape off the collapsing planet.

Chapter 38: A Clash of Sun & Rock
January 20, 2112

Sunfire

Sunfire blasted rings of fire at Kaizerious, with no visible effect. His skin was unburned, uncharred, not even a scratch. He looked at her with a simple gaze - a gaze ready to meet her blow for blow. Sunfire was prepared to fulfill the prophecy given to her long ago, and she knew she had to step up. With Ghost and the others far from harm's way, she could really let loose.

Still in the same room as before, Kaizerious flexed his arm, and the ground below her shot up like a pillar into her chest. She gasped as the wind was knocked out of her lungs. The pillar took her through the celling at increasing speeds. She felt like she was on the outside of a starship. The pillar stopped, but momentum carried her into the planet's atmosphere. What goes up must come down, and those rules applied to her. She plummeted, falling faster and faster. As she neared the ground, she blasted fire from her feet and hands. This maneuver slowed her down until she landed on the ground, feet first, and softly.

She was alone, far from the structure. The surroundings were full of quite a few topographies. There was a lake only meters in front of her, kilometers long. Past the lake was a forest. Behind her were mountains, sharp and steep. She could see this despite the darkness. No sun in sight. She launched out shires of fire all around the area, over the lake, by the mountains, over the forest. The shires of fire flickered like torches, yet bright enough to simulate dawn.

There was a thunderous blast in the distance, and like a bullet, she watched as something launched from the ground many kilometers away. It originated from the safe house and had a trajectory that led it close to her. As it neared, she realized it wasn't an object at all. It was a being; it was Kaizerious. He landed across the lake and in front of the trees. The ground shook, and a shockwave knocked down trees, created waves meters tall, and sent a gust of wind strong enough to cause rocks to tumble free from the mountains behind her. But she withstood the force and managed to stay on her feet. This was nothing to a god like her.

Chapter 38

Kaizerious, previously crouching from the landing, stood tall and looked to her. Sunfire knew he wanted her to make the first move. She obliged. She squeezed her fists behind her and blasted out a stream of blue fire. The sound was as loud as a starship engine, and she flew at unnatural speeds right towards Kaizerious. She cleared the lake in less than a second and thrust her shoulder in the abdomen of Kaizerious. He wasn't fast enough to react. He grunted in pain and was sent tumbling through the trees, crashing through the forest like a meteor, sending destruction and debris up in thick smoke.

Sunfire reversed the position of her hands and used another stream of fire to slow down her momentum before she reached the forest. She halted.

"Nobody could survive that." Sunfire believed her words to be the truth. After all, they were the words of a god.

When the smoke cleared, she saw Kaizerious in the distance, dug into the ground, trees broken around and over him. He then moved.

"No way!" She was aghast.

He pushed himself up, clearing the trees off him, then jumped towards her with a force nearly as powerful as when she had shot out fire earlier. She was quick enough to dodge Kaizerious as he neared. Just as he flew past her, the ground below shook, and out popped a pillar of rock, which was angled toward him. Kaizerious spun himself and landed against the rock feet first. The rock slid backwards with the impact, but it was enough to slow down Kaizerious down. He leaped at her again, with much less force. Sunfire dodged and landed a series of punches to the gut of Kaizerious. Her fist was engulfed in fire.

The force wasn't enough to hurt him. He tried to grab her, but Sunfire sidestepped. Having to jump first, she round-house kicked Kaizerious. He lifted his arms to the side of his head to block. Using the opening, she flipped off the momentum and slammed her hands together midair and sent an explosion to the face of Kaizerious. He grunted and stepped back from the force. She landed meters in front of him.

While he was still taking a moment to recover, she came at him again. This time, she reached behind her and grabbed the handle that was holstered at her lower back. She extended her arm, and from the base of the handle, bits of metal extended into a sword almost a meter long. She then lit the sword on fire, handle and blade. As she neared Kaizerious, he stood up, and Sunfire sliced at his face. Kaizerious blocked with his arm. The blade chipped into his skin. Finally, she had cut him. A moment passed, but no blood had emerged.

"What?" Sunfire yelled in shock.

Kaizerious then nailed Sunfire right in the gut with a full punch. His fist was the size of her entire stomach! She blasted a stream of fire behind her, using her free hand to slow herself down as she was launched away. She halted twenty meters away from Kaizerious, then fell to her knee, clinching her stomach in pain. Worse yet, Kaizerious had barely put any momentum behind that punch, meaning it was far weaker than he was capable of.

Kaizerious stood up. "What's the matter? You were so sure of yourself a moment ago." He teased her.

Sunfire, who was hunched over, stopped gazing into the dirt and stood. She looked back at Kaizerious and laughed. Kaizerious's expression shifted from playful to curious. Sunfire, still laughing, grinned. "This is the kind of fight I've been waiting for. Even holding back, I've never once come across anyone able to withstand my power this long. That is, until you."

"I'm glad to be of amusement to you. Maybe you can then die with a smile," Kaizerious teased.

He pointed toward Sunfire, and a spike-shaped spear suddenly flew from the mountain at her. She held up her sword in a defensive stance and let a shield of fire extend from its center. It spun rapidly.

The strike was so fast, Sunfire could barely keep track of it. There was a moment of nothing, then blood, dark as night, spurted out from the side of Kaizerious's neck. It streamed down him and covered his right shoulder. Kaizerious covered it with his palm. Dirt from the ground crawled up his body and into his palm. When he removed his hand from the wound, it was sealed by the dirt.

"Surprised you, didn't I?" Sunfire grinned. "I can tell you weren't expecting my shield to completely reverse your attack back at you."

"Surprised? No. But it is interesting. You are formidable, but I can tell you are holding back."

Sunfire burst out laughing. "I suspect the same of you."

"I knew the day would come when I'd meet someone like you."

Sunfire took a small step towards Kaizerious, with her palm extended. "Would you like to hear a story?"

"If your aim is to catch me off-guard, I'd advise against it."

A peaceful glow came over Sunfire's face as she began her story. "A long time ago, I was told that when I'd awaken, the very galaxy would be under a dark shadow of war. That I'd be the light to cast the shadow from existence. You are the body that shadow extends from. And I am the light."

"I'm a man that believes that the future is a chain of innumerable rivers, with no end. It is my many years that have told me that."

"My destiny is what I make it. That prophecy will be fulfilled because I want it to be so."

"Your weakness is your desire for the galaxy you envision. You keep your head too high in the clouds and miss everything going on below you. It's not the shepherd who daydreams of bigger plains that thrives, but the shepherd that tends to the needs of his herd."

"I don't speak in riddles."

"All I'm saying is that you cannot get the future you want without tending to the present you are given. That is why I'm the answer this galaxy needs, and not you."

"Easy to claim with that durability you've got there. However, from that last attack, I can see that you are weaker around your joints."

"Making me bleed isn't enough to kill me."

"Making you bleed lets me know that you can be killed. But you, however, don't have the speed to strike me with any consistency. That is why I will outlast you."

Kaizerious lost his friendly expression, and it dipped towards gloom. He then clapped his hands together. The ground below Sunfire split upward from both her sides. She jumped away and saw the two flat boulders smash into each other. Kaizerious had tried to crush her. He wasn't done. He flexed his bicep, and spikes made from various materials found from the ground came from all directions. There were thousands. Sunfire crossed her arms and extended them just as fast. Rings of fire exploded from her body and cut through the spikes.

Sunfire followed this defensive maneuver with some offense. She placed her hand over her mouth in a circle and spat out balls of fire towards Kaizerious. She landed moments later and turned back to see a wall of sand covering Kaizerious. It had protected him.

Sunfire grunted in frustration. Had she known in advance she was going to face such a powerful god like him, she would have brought more tools than just a sword. Even still, she had noticed Kaizerious holding back as she was. But why? The extraordinary power of her ace ability was based on charging up. For all the great power she wielded, it came at a great sacrifice. When all charged up, Sunfire had more power and energy than most normal beings can comprehend. She fed on heat and solar energy, and her body ran on and utilized it. She didn't require other sustenance or sleep, since the energy present in her body was already more than enough. However, once she used all that energy, she entered a cocoon-like state, where it fed on all the heat and solar energy available. That process pulled in the energy far more efficiently than she did on her own until she recharged - a process that takes many years at a time. This was why she was currently holding back during the fight. She didn't want to expend all her energy and be idle for years. Seeing what she has seen so far, it appeared Kaizerious has been holding back all the same. It proved he must have a drawback of his own. If she were to win, discovering that drawback may be required.

One thing was for sure. He had some form of terrakinesis; the ability to control and manipulate geology, such as rocks, dust, sand, and minerals. To what extent, was the real question. The only way to find out was to keep attacking, keep testing.

No more holding back. She could not lose.

Still hovering in the air, Sunfire shot out fire from her legs, blasting herself towards Kaizerious. She holstered her sword. As she neared the shell of sand protecting him, she blasted out an explosion so hot, the fire was white, and some of the sand turned to glass. Kaizerious pulled metal from the ground to protect him. She was faster and hit him directly in the side with another blast like the previous! The blast let loose a force so strong, the ground blasted apart as if a meteor had hit it. Dust covered the vicinity.

Impossible!

He survived! No being could survive a blow that powerful. What was he even made of? His durability was unreal.

Kaizerious shouted in pain as he was blasted partly in the ground. Sunfire came at him again, just as fast. "Enough," Kaizerious shouted. Enraged, he pulled away the ground around him before sending it outward in all directions like a tidal wave of rock, sand, and more.

"That won't work." Sunfire prepared to blast through it, only this time the wave of ground exploded apart as it neared her, with an untold amount of shrapnel. Too late. Sunfire took the hits. Some pierced her skin, and others didn't. She fell to the ground. Before she could do anything else, metal vined out of the ground and shackled her in place. She was trapped! The ground held her in place. "What?" she shouted in surprise.

As Sunfire tried to force her way out, more minerals poured over her. She couldn't break through the weight.

Is this it?

Her question was answered without hesitation. Kaizerious clamped his hand together in a fist. With that motion, the terrain pulled together around her, suffocating her, crushing her. Her head was seconds from going under.

The sun then peeked over the horizon.

Energy. Sunfire could feel the heat over her face, and she was empowered by it. She fed off it.

Sunfire closed her eyes and reopened them. They were engulfed in fire hot enough to be white. Her entire body followed, then she exploded the energy outward and was free!

Intense fire lighting her way, she blasted herself at Kaizerious and pulled together a string of explosive bursts of flames.

"What are you made of?" Sunfire growled. "Each of these moves should be enough to kill you."

Moving so fast she appeared to be blinking from one location to another, Sunfire changed her tactic. She started to attack from a short distance with rays of fire each time she moved.

Kaizerious's eyes intensified, and she saw the focus. She blinked and was shocked when he caught her by the arm. He had predicted her movement. "It takes more than brute force and speed to kill something like me," he said.

Sunfire used her other arm and sent flames into the face of Kaizerious. He turned to protect his eyes, but his fist had time to gain power and momentum and crashed into her gut. He let go of her hand at the same time his fist connected, and Sunfire took a blow so strong, she was sent hurdling past the upper atmosphere.

Into space her body hurled at ridiculous speeds. Into the planet's sun she went, into its solar flames. That only made her stronger. The power flowed through her body, and she stopped herself, dead in the center of the gas giant.

Floating inside a sun brings a certain perspective of things. For Sunfire, it was just the clarity she needed to see this fight was going to take close to everything she had. No more half-steps. If she wanted the vision she saw for the galaxy to be actualized, and for the prophecy to be fulfilled, she couldn't worry about using all her energy.

With more resolve in the heat in her blood than ever, she shot herself back to the planet, back to Kaizerious. Her speed was so fast, she started to see rays of light beside her.

Seconds away, she plunged into the atmosphere. Kaizerious awaited and smashed his hands into the planet, pulling it in half by the seams. Sunfire couldn't stop in time and slipped into the crack in the planet. Kaizerious used his power to pull it all back together.

She refused to be crushed and drove herself to the core of the planet before the crust was thrown back together. The core of the planet was now in a turmoil, and by her best estimation, the planet would soon tear itself apart. Inside the core, Sunfire unleashed a beam of piercing fire to carve a hole towards the surface. She took her newly created path back to the surface.

Up top, she flew back towards her mortal enemy, her opposite in many ways; the rock to her sun.

The surface was shaking itself apart, and volcanic magma had begun to seep through newly formed fissures. The focus on what was below caused her not to see the mountain hurling towards her! It was launched at her by none other than Kaizerious.

Chapter 38

She blasted it in half with sharp fire and slammed herself into the gut of Kaizerious only a moment later. He was sent blistering back, and she refused to give him any time. At speeds faster than his, she caught up to him and roared as she spawned a sun flare of bursting energy below him. A tremendous, thunderous ring of fire sent Kaizerious into the sky, scorched. The same ring cut the planet in two.

Sunfire caught herself thinking about Castle and Ghost. In her mind, she hoped for their safety, which surprised even her.

That train of thought shattered as the two pieces of the planet changed trajectory and shape. Almost every bit of the planet followed the direction Kaizerious went and formed around his flying body.

Her eyes couldn't believe the sight before her. Every mountain, volcano, desert, and more, started to change. Down to every mineral, every grain of sand, a shell of armor formed over Kaizerious. Organic life was the one thing left out as the shell of armor turned into legs, then arms, until a titan the size of a planet was created over Kaizerious.

Sunfire couldn't believe he had the power to manipulate the entirety of a planet into a suit of armor. And she refused to be outdone. She extended her arm in the direction of the sun and called the fire to her. Like a black hole, she forced the sun apart and reformed it over herself. She became her own titan in a suit of fire.

Making the first move, she launched everything she had at Kaizerious. He hurled chucks of rock the size of asteroids from his feet so he could gain momentum towards her. Both of them smashed into each other. A fist of fire crushed into the head of rock, and the knee of a mountain caved into the gut of fire. Titans pounded their way through open space, ricocheting around different moons and different planets.

After hours of battling, a moment of weakness presented itself. The glue that held the mass of a planet together began to degrade. It was crumbling apart, and Kaizerious was losing his grip on everything. She could see him, many kilometers deep through a crack. Seizing the moment in her hands, she pulled her sword and gave it one last burst at him.

She connected! Her blade dug into the heart of Kaizerious! Momentum took them both crashing to the surface of a moon. Like a meteor, their impact shattered their surroundings, and she was left standing over Kaizerious. Blade clear through his heart, his life's blood as dark as his evil soul poured over him. He was still on a knee, one hand grasping her arm. His eyes stared into hers, and she watched as they lost their last spark. He succumbed to his wound, and Sunfire ripped away the blade.

That fight had taken almost all her power to see through. Weary, Sunfire let herself fall to a knee. She stared into the face of the man she'd just killed and was impressed to see a smile on his face.

It wasn't long before a starship landed close behind her. She could tell by sound alone it was of the Brotherhood of Relics. She waited until Castle and Ghost came to both her sides.

"He died still on a knee!" Castle said in awe.

"He fought true." Sunfire's respect for her opponent found its way through her tone.

"I've gotta say, that was the craziest, wildest, most badass fraken showcase this galaxy has ever seen." Castle was shaking with pumped adrenaline.

Sunfire turned to Ghost. "Tell me you two got Airra."

Ghost was silent for a moment. "The planet under destruction gave her a moment to escape. I promise, it is only temporary. We will finish the job."

Sunfire began to rise. "No, I'll--" She then fell back towards the ground. The extent of her drained energy was even more than she had realized.

Ghost caught her and eased her fall. "We can handle Airra. You've used too much of your power. You'll revert back to your cocoon state soon."

Sunfire wasn't even upset. She held a gleeful smile. "I may've only been awake for a short time, but that was all I needed to correct the course of the galaxy. When I awake again, it shall be in a galaxy in prosperity."

Ghost started to help her up when Castle burst out with, "Hey! Hey! Why is the dead man moving?!"

Their eyes flew back to Kaizerious. The spark of life once again surged in his eyes. His previous wound was seared shut, as if it were under a spell, and he stood tall once more.

Chapter 38

Sunfire surged as much power back into her limbs as she could but got little response. Her mind took a jolt of fear. And the knights looked upon this impossibility with frozen feet. "You were dead! I killed you! What black magic is this?!" Her words shot out in rapid succession from her mouth.

Kaizerious started to walk their direction.

She continued. "I was supposed to win. I was prophesized to. I was to be the light to snuff out the shadow - to snuff out *you*."

Kaizerious stopped. His words and voice were low and filled with gloom. A meter away, he looked down at her. "You did exactly what you said you would. I *did* die, and your prophecy was fulfilled."

"No, this can't--!" Her eyes darted up and down his body, and her face was jittery.

Kaizerious held his right hand out to the side, and metal pulled from the ground began to build within his palm. "If you run every possibility in your head, then nothing will surprise you. When planning, I find such a talent useful. My last advice to you." A metal spear formed in his hand. "I was prepared for this outcome, prepared in the event of my death. I just happened to know the *right* entity to bring me back."

Sunfire shouted, "Castle," snapping him out of shock.

"Ghost, use it!" Castle shouted.

"It's our last one!" he retorted.

"Use it!" Castle repeated. He stepped towards Kaizerious. "The things I do for this brotherhood." In that instant, he pushed his aura in front of Kaizerious.

Ghost reached for something in his pouch. Kaizerious was fast, and he bashed the aura with his free hand. It shattered like glass. Castle's eyes rolled back in his head, and he collapsed on the ground. Ghost noticed and reached for Castle, still clawing with his other hand in the pouch.

"I can't get him. Sunfire, grab us both."

Ghost pulled out a spherical ball of glowing green. He crushed it, and Sunfire felt her body start to dematerialize into atoms. There was something else, something sharp, a new feeling burning in her chest.

Light faded away, but not completely. She then realized she was at the foot of the starportal. Ghost used the one and only graviton sphere the brotherhood had left to teleport them back to the starportal. It was a one-time escape plan used under impossible circumstances.

Sunfire felt the burning in her chest intensify and looked down. Her trembling hand scraped below her breast, and her eyes focused on the red crimson that dyed her pinky and ring finger. She had been pierced. That spear Kaizerious had formed now lingered through her torso, and by the angle, it partially punctured into her heart.

Eyes weakening, she glanced to the comatose Castle, then to Ghost. Ghost's stare matched hers in gloom. The situation was clear, and Sunfire understood her death was unavoidable. She had failed in her vision but was not ready to leave without passing the torch. Her voice was weak. "Hope is not lost as long as our brotherhood is there to guide the galaxy." Her eyes fell towards the ground, and she struggled to hold on. "Falseblood or not, you are a knight, Ghost. You know what you have to do. Save our galaxy."

The injury got the best of her, and she lost her ability to move. Her thoughts flashed over in her head, like flipping pictures of what had been; until it didn't anymore.

Chapter 39: Homecoming
January 20, 2112

Catharine Darcrose

Kaizerious was dead! Before Cathy's eyes, playing over the screen of the living quarters of the starship, Cathy watched the final blow end the life of Kaizerious. Cathy saw this, and something inside her gave her a surprise. Was this sadness she felt? Kaizerious had a hand in starting a war that had claimed the lives of millions, the lives of her brother and sister, and yet she felt sad he had died. Was it because she saw him as a friend? After all, she had spent a significant amount of time with him in her search for the Brotherhood of Relics. Which, in light of all this, now made sense to her; it made sense why he was interested in the brotherhood in the first place.

Kaizerious even saved her once from a bullet. But why save her? She was a part of the ARW, an enemy to him. He knew that. His duty was to his alliance, yet she lived that day because of him. Even now, she couldn't figure out what he had to gain by saving her, if anything at all.

Why?! she shouted in her mind.

She hadn't realized the frustration she felt had forced her up from the couch. She turned back to see James Stone still sitting there. His eyes weren't engaged with the video of Kaizerious and Sunfire's fight that had been going on. He was looking at his cyberwatch.

She turned away. Why would she care what he was doing? He failed in his duty as a captain when he didn't bring her sister, Beverly, back alive. And she still held him partly to blame. At first, the pain was deep, and she wanted him dead. But she realized she herself had lost her entire unit, too. That's the realization it took to place her into his shoes. She couldn't imagine staring into the face of their loved ones and telling them she failed those under her. That was what James faced when she showed up. Yet he let her wail away on his face. Part of her might never forgive him, hate him even, and yet part of her admired him for what he did for her.

At least she would be home soon. Brotherhood of Relic starships are much faster than ARW starships, roughly eight times or more from what she heard. They would be back in an ARW controlled star systems well before the day was over.

A sudden shock from the video shook her right out of her thoughts. Kaizerious was alive and walking right towards those brotherhood knights. She watched, trapped by her own icy muscles. Her eyes couldn't leave the screen.

The knights then disappeared, leaving Kaizerious alone. The screen turned off, and Cathy was left with her mouth to the ground. She was sure she had watched him die. And everything that dies is supposed to stay that way. It's just the natural order of things. No one, save Jesus Christ, has ever come back, *ever*. And yet it happened. By some fluke in the galaxy, it happened. No, there had to be some reason. There always is.

*****

After being dropped off at an ARW outpost on a moon called Baurtenson, Cathy and James waited as an Order of Aegis starship landed. It was there to pick them up, and none other than Kalvin Keefe was the first to step out of the starship. It had been some time since Cathy had seen this man. It was almost surreal to see such an important man grace them with his presence, like seeing a celebrity in real life.

Kalvin walked up to meet James. "How are you feeling?"

"You seem to always make an appearance at the right times, don't you?" James ignored the question.

"I will always be here when you need me most."

"Touching." James pulled out two objects Cathy had never seen before. "Take these two keys, and make sure you don't lose any this time, Kalvin."

Kalvin was overzealous. "You never cease to astonish me. This is incredible. Actually, this is beyond incredible. You have no knowledge of this, but you just provided us an enormous victory, James. Day-Bringer has fashioned a plan - a plan involving these keys that may prove to save us." James gave a nod that was hardly noticeable and started past Kalvin. He headed for the ship. "Wait, what are you doing?" Kalvin asked.

Chapter 39

"Take me back to my squad. I need to say my goodbyes."

Kalvin held his head in confusion. "Goodbyes? I do not understand."

James turned for a moment. "I plan on taking a leave of duty. And they deserve to know why." He then went into the ship.

Kalvin stared as Cathy did. After composing himself, he came over to Cathy. "You were with him for a substantial amount of time. Do you know what brought that on?"

Ever since that brotherhood bishop dropped them off on this outpost, she had kept her distance from James. So lately, she had no idea what he was up to. "He seemed off after Ghost gave him something." That was the only thing that crossed her mind.

"Ghost?"

"A knight of the Brotherhood of Relics," Cathy clarified.

Kalvin's eyes jumped at the name, and he seemed distraught. "Please, follow me aboard. I want to know everything that you have learned."

Cathy nodded and followed him aboard, where she started to tell him everything from her mission to finding the brotherhood to Kaizerious. Every single detail she recalled.

Chapter 40: On Neutral Grounds
January 27, 2112

Airra

The last request for a parley between the ARW and Wersillian Legion was years ago. It was held only a few months after the start of the Wersillian War, and Airra foolishly trusted that idiot Eruvir Varzaac to take charge during that parley. It went south, and he lost his life in a battle that followed the parley. She wouldn't make that mistake again. This time, she would answer the call herself.

Sitting in the commander's chair, Airra watched from above as dytircs and lycargans worked the star cruiser's controls. A bit behind her chair, Kaizerious sat in a chair of his own.

They arrived at the designated location, near a hypergiant sun. From the viewing window, Airra saw just one ARW star cruiser. This was a meeting on neutral grounds.

"Scans show that their weapons are disabled," said one of the dytirc pilots.

"They're hailing us," said another.

"Make sure they are unable to see me," Kaizerious commanded.

Airra nodded. "Patch them through."

A projection screen illuminated. On the screen was a dor'o. She had an unusual glow to her, possibly due to her soft smile or gentle eyes. Her face was bright, highlighting her bright-red skin. And her stumps were elegant and polished.

"I'm Day-Bringer, chief admiral of the ARW. It pleases me so to see you have respected our wishes to engage in a parley. Please, to whom am I speaking?"

A chief admiral, Airra thought to herself, *this must be important for one of them to show up.*

"Airra, head warlord of the Wersillian Legion, of course." Airra grinned.

Day-Bringer had a pleasant expression. "So you're the legendary head warlord I've heard quite bit about recently."

"One and only." Airra shifted in her chair. "Now, enough with the introductions. I came here to negotiate."

"As you wish. The ARW knows the Wersillian Legion is looking for these." The video cut to two of the Quondam Keys. They were placed inside some container, but it was too dark to make out many details. Day-Bringer continued. "Our terms are this: Cease all hostilities within our galaxy, and I promise, these keys will not be destroyed."

"Destroyed?" Airra growled. "Those keys are almost pure forcidion. It would take nothing short of--" Airra stopped when she realized where they were located.

"--a sun. That's what you were going to say, right?" Day-Bringer gave Airra a taunting expression. "As it happens, those two keys are contained within a missile pointed directly at the sun next to us, which has temperatures rivaling a supernova."

Airra's jaw flexed. "You conniving, ruddy bitch."

"Is that any way to conduct a civilized negotiation?" Day-Bringer's voice was full of mockery.

"This isn't a negotiation... not anymore. This is blackmail."

"Since you understand your current situation, I shall restate our terms. The ARW wants the Wersillian Legion and all its supporters to cease war-related activities. No more colonizing or attacking other planets or civilizations of any kind. The ARW will allow the Wersillian Legion to keep all that it has currently conquered, so long as native species are allowed equal vote in laws, regulations, or policies of any kind that affect their home worlds. In conjunction, the ARW will take no hostile actions against the Wersillian Legion, and those two keys will not be destroyed. These terms are more than fair. And we'll give the Wersillian Legion a week to comply with these terms." She paused. "I shall give you a few minutes to make your decision. I eagerly await your response." The video cut out.

Airra was full of fury. So much so, she wouldn't be surprised if she set herself ablaze. She turned to Kaizerious. "Those ARW scumbags think they can just end the war like that?!"

"Calm down, Airra. Remember our endgame. If those keys are destroyed, the galaxy as a whole will be lost. We can't let such a thing happen. As for now, we will heed their demands. The Wersillian War will cease. I trust you to finalize the agreement with them." He got up and started to leave.

"Wait. This can't be it."

"Relax, daughter. Every great mind has a backup plan, and I assure you, I do, too. But it'll take time. So be patient. We will talk later." Kaizerious left the room.

Airra sighed. She knew what she had to do. She knew he was right; they had to bring in a new era of peace if they wanted to reach their goal in the long run. Even though Airra would miss the thrill of battle, she knew it would not last forever. In the meantime, she'd have to find another vice to ease that urge.

Airra signaled for a dytirc to reopen communications with Day-Bringer. It was time for the two of them to settle into peace talks.

Chapter 41: End of an Era
February 7, 2112

Kalvin Keefe

Kalvin was back at his center of operations, back within the safety of Station 51. With the war at a standstill, military operations would assuredly decrease in pace. Nevertheless, efforts at the Order of Aegis could not afford to make such adjustments. This peace would not last. There was no doubt in Kalvin's mind about that. Even so, this time of harmony would prove valuable. It would allot him more time to conjure up ways to win the war the ARW was losing.

There was a knock at his office door.

"Enter." Kalvin looked up from his chair. He had just finished taking his daily brown pills.

A lady in her late sixties entered. She was a tall, curvaceous woman with sky blue eyes, which tilted downwards in the center and were framed by a set of rather long eyelashes. She also had a small mole under her left eye, as well as red painted nails. Her hair was coal-black and plunged over her dress shirt. She wore a scarf, shaded with black and red roses - a pattern significant to the Darcrose family. It had been a while since Kalvin had seen Elizabeth Darcrose, chief admiral representing the humans.

"Kalvin. It's a pleasure," she started.

"Always nice to see the head of the Darcrose family. After all, where would the Order of Aegis be if your family had not helped create it all those years ago?" Kalvin paused. "And I give you my sincerest condolences over your loss. Beverly died far too young."

"As we speak, she is being brought home. Having to bear the loss of two of my children is agonizing. But I need to be strong for our alliance and my family. At least with her, we will be able to have an open casket funeral at our estate. And I can rest easy knowing that she's at peace."

"Truly, I am sorry to hear such a tragedy," Kalvin reemphasized.

Elizabeth took a seat on the opposite side of the desk. "I've heard you have a new apprentice. Jay Bridges, I believe his name is. I would like to meet him."

"With things as frenetic as they were over the last few months, I had not gotten around to it. Rest assured, though, I still consider it a priority which shall happen in the near future. However, I cannot say as to when he will be fully inaugurated. That remains to be seen."

"I'm glad to hear that you haven't pushed us out."

Kalvin leaned forward. "That would never happen. The Darcrose family is much too vital to the survival of the Order of Aegis."

Elizabeth nodded in acknowledgement. After a pause, she said, "I was in a meeting recently where Day-Bringer brought all the chief admirals up to speed. Her plan to buy our alliance time worked better than we hoped. But this only means that you have to work extra hard if we are to win in the long term. And with so few aces, we cannot afford to have another incident like we did with Geariic and Alabon."

"Those traitors got what they deserved. Only, since they were the ones who reported that they eliminated the warlord Cralo, I fear that he may not actually be deceased. Sunfire did us a favor by eliminating three warlords. But we still have a ways to go."

Elizabeth gleamed. "She sounds quite incredible. Prophesized to end the war. If it hadn't been for her, James would've died, and the enemy would have all four keys."

"Indeed. Because of her efforts, we have two keys and three, maybe four warlords left. I only wish I knew what these Devisor keys open."

Elizabeth adjusted herself. "Even so, I hope you are keeping tabs on our other aces. Like I said, we must make sure they are truly on our side."

"The aces led by Drayvan are still on a mission to handle that threat Day-Bringer reported on. I estimate they should return in March. Frost, for the near future, will work more closely with me. James and Makayla will be on Earth."

Elizabeth leaned back in the chair and chuckled. "After recent affairs, it seems James's legionnaires have gained quite a reputation. Their squad has almost become a legend among other ground units. Yet, I hear that Valiic is retiring for good and the rest are taking an absence from duty. Not that it matters at the moment, since we are at peace, but it would be a shame if they never come back." She put her legs forward.

Chapter 41

Kalvin pulled out some papers from a drawer and put them on the desk. "James spoke with them after his return, and they all decided to follow his lead and take a leave."

"I believe James will be key for our victory, and the best way to bring him back may be through his unit." She gave a subtle raise of her eyebrow.

"I agree, which is why I am keeping tabs on them to the best of my ability. Valiic is least likely to return. As we speak, he is on his way to his partner, Narrisa on Jaba-Qwayk. Shadow-Walker is going to rekindle his relationship with his mother on Dorrath. As far as I am aware, he was cast out twenty years ago when he brought shame to his community. After spending as many years as he has working with the ARW, he hopes to be accepted back. James has left for Earth, and I am not sure where he plans to go at the moment. Brad, being the man he is, managed to slip past our tails and is currently unaccounted for. Unfortunate, too. I am captivated by the new sword he brought back with him."

Elizabeth stood up, with apparent satisfaction from her meeting with Kalvin. "I'm glad to see you have things running ever so smoothly here."

"I always do, do I not?"

"Indeed." Elizabeth took a look at the door. "The galaxy is going to be very different than everyone is accustomed to. We'll see if that will be a good or bad thing." Elizabeth made her way to the door. "A pleasure, as always." She left.

Kalvin was alone with his own thoughts. She had one thing right: This galaxy is in for a rapid change. Even he could not be sure if it would be for the better or worse. Truly the end of an era.

Chapter 42: Cold Embrace
February 8, 2112

James Stone

I chose to take a leave of absence, but the war had been put on hold anyway. Nonetheless, it just meant more time away. Took quite some time before I was approved, but I finally made it back to Earth. I hadn't been here since training in the legionnaire program. And it didn't at all feel like home. After all, I got so used to living on a star cruiser with my team. That's what I'd miss the most. Chances were, I'd end up visiting them at some point.

The cab stopped and dropped me off at a walking street leading to a small neighborhood of no more than fifteen houses, each rather extravagant and unique. None were put together using some predetermined models used to sell people on the dream. In fact, each house in this neighborhood was custom-built. The neighborhood itself didn't officially have a name either. Just a single road that led straight down a secluded area.

As I walked down the street, I passed a few houses on the left and a few on the right, with many trees in-between each house and each residential lot laying claim to a lot of land. It was the kind of place my mom often wished to move to one day.

The road soon turned directly right, with one housing lot against the corner of both roads. Another lot was just across. Down this last road in the neighborhood was a tree that split the road into two lanes. Etched in a small oval of grass, this old tree held bark patterned as if carved by its own dedicated rain-born river. It stretched up, as if proud to stand there under the sun. Green bounty and earthy browns, the tree was a centerpiece that gave this neighborhood character.

Passing that tree, the first house to the right was my destination. I stopped at the empty driveway. At the end, it curved to the right into a garage with a shed at the far left end.

The house was a classic in architecture, as were all the houses there. Little modern tech decorated the outside. Bricks and fiber cement for siding, and fiberglass shingles, this tri-level house was something of the

Chapter 42

past. Ivy and ferns grew through the crevices of an old winding stone path that led directly from the driveway to the front door. Obsidian-tinted iron gates loomed proudly around the backyard, with a patio just peeking into view. Rows of trees, green as the grass, guarded the back edge of the back yard, swaying gently in the wind, with some more placed here and there for shade. At the center threshold of the front yard stood the delicate marble fountain, the soft gurgling of the clear water was melodic as it resonated in the surrounding silence.

I took a breath and headed to the end of the driveway. That's when I heard the sound of some blocks clacking together and a man under heavy breaths. It came from the backyard patio.

I took a peek around the corner and saw someone placing pavers together on the half-finished patio. I went up the two risers and started towards the man. "Excuse me," I called as I neared him.

He stopped, turned, and stood up. "And who might you be?" The man was older, looked to be in his nineties, with an over-average physique for his age. Current technology gave humans an average lifespan of almost a hundred and forty, so at ninety, this man probably felt like a healthy fifty-year-old. He had a full head of white hair, with a graying, thick mustache with few blonde hairs left, and he had a blue tint to his eyes. His skin tone was an olive complexion, which shined under his sweaty body and tank top shirt. He wore some torn work shorts and a cap marked with a commander's rank during World War III on the front. He seemed old to be Ben's father, but Ben did mention he participated in WWIII.

Back when I was still making my way into the world, back in boot camp, Ben was there. He was my first real friend I had and he once told me I could come here if I ever needed too. "You're Benjamin's dad, right? He told me to come here if I ever needed a place to stay. He, uh... he said to say, 'Ben gave trust.' And I promise, I plan to stay just until I can pull a place together to stay." I felt awkward asking him, but I had no residence of my own. I have the money, but getting a lease or mortgage would take time. I could've gone to a hotel, I suppose, but I'd rather have someone I knew would be friendly to chat with.

"You're a friend of Ben's, huh? In that case, you are always welcome here for as long as you need."

I shook his hand. "Thank you, sir. Name's James."

"Derrick. Call me Derrick." He greeted me with his smile. "So, you're in the military?"

"I am. And it's an honor to meet a veteran such as yourself. Without you, our world may've been completely different."

"Please." He put up his hand. "I just did what anyone else would've done for their country."

"I know the feeling." I rubbed the back of my neck. "Anyway, you look like you could use some help."

"I wasn't going to ask, but I'm glad you offered. You look well-muscled. Any good at carrying things?"

"Sure. What do you need?"

"See that pallet of pavers in the yard?" He pointed. "Bring those over as I need them."

"Easy enough." I headed over to the pallet of pavers, while he went back to work. The pallet was almost full of pavers; each was four different shades of gray. Derrick was placing them over sand to finish the patio. I bent my knees and grabbed each side of the pallet. I heaved it up and carried all the pavers up to the patio, placing them on the finished side.

Derrick was in awe. "That's some gift you got there. Come to think of it, I believe I remember Ben mentioning you, but I'm pretty sure he might've downplayed what you can actually do."

I picked a few of the pavers off the top and brought them to him. "Yeah. It's part of my abilities as an ace."

"Ace, huh? Some soldier you must be."

I nodded at the compliment. "So is this what a retired war hero does for fun?"

His gut rose and fell with a few heavy laughs. "It's more of a project of mine. I always say, *I'll be done after this* or *this will be the last project.* But somehow, I always find myself working on another. This is just the latest one."

"Life's a grind," I responded.

"One project after another. I guess I like to stay busy." He continued to laugh.

Chapter 42

"So what do you do when the day's sun drops from the sky?" I asked.

"Not that much. But some of the guys around the nearby town like to go to a bar called the Hardware Store. I can give you directions if that is your vice."

"A bar called the Hardware Store?"

He chuckled. "Sure is creative, right? When their wives ask where they've been, the guys say the Hardware Store. As long as they don't get too hammered, it keeps suspicion off them. That bar even has a small selection of tools for those who really need to sell their story."

I handed him another paver as he finished placing the last one. "Sounds interesting. Might check it out tonight."

Derrick chuckled to himself. He used his cyberwatch and turned on the stereo system outside. "I hope you like classic rock." Rock music from the 1970s played.

"Is there any other kind of music?" I jested. "Surely not that new layered mumbo-jumbo." When I was young, all my mother listened to was classic rock, with some country mixed in. I guess the taste for that kind of music stuck with me.

We shared a good laugh and enjoyed each other's war stories as we worked an honest day's labor.

*****

Just as expected, I found myself in the bar called the Hardware Store. I find a bar the best place to gauge what the locals are like, and what to expect from the local culture. And I can enjoy a good ale while doing so.

The crowd was mostly human. Three qwayks, a dor'o, and a few others from allied species were sprinkled throughout the bar. Any species allied with the ARW are allowed residence just about anywhere in any planet under ARW control. However, if this bar was any indication, this town remained mostly under the touch of humans.

I pulled back a stool and took a seat at the bar table. The table twisted in an artistic way, curling around the edges, and was illuminated by the age-speckled bar lights. Along the back wall was every hue of amber liquid in their assorted bottles; every vice a man could want. I raised a firm finger to call the bartender. He didn't notice at first. He was scrubbing the glass of the chiller cabinet, recently re-stuffed with those stupid garish alcohol-pops all the young drinkers were slurping faster than soda.

He came around eventually. "Your drink?" the bartender, the only one serving tonight, asked.

"Woodstones," I responded.

He paused and looked me over. "I couldn't help but notice your cyberwatch. It's military grade, which means you must be a soldier, right?"

"Sure am. I can show you my identification card."

"No need. I trust you. Anyway, just want to let you know the first one's on the house."

"On the house?" I asked, a bit surprised at the generosity.

"Heroes get their first drink free." He placed the woodstone in front of me.

I lifted my drink and cheered to that. "You have my thanks."

The bartender left me to drink. I took just two sips before a woman took a seat next to me. A blonde beauty. She was one of a few in the bar, looking for someone to possibly take home.

"How come I've never seen you around here?" she asked. Her elbow was rested against the bar counter as she twirled her blonde hair with her finger.

"Been serving our great alliance." I took a drink.

"Military?"

"That's the one," I confirmed. In honesty, I wanted to be left alone, but I couldn't find it in me to be rude.

"Well, your hair looks nice. Never seen it naturally orange before. Did they... like, make you cut it that way?"

"Not at gunpoint," I joked.

"For real?" she asked, with such interest.

"No, I'm yanking your chain. Actually, most hairstyles are allowed these days."

"What's it like? Like... being under fire? Oh my God, did you, like, kill somebody?"

Chapter 42

I wanted to roll my eyes at her repeated dumb questions. But I contained myself. Instead, I opted for a different method of getting her to leave. "Oh shivf, I've killed so many, I lost count," I whispered in her ear. "This one time, a dytirc tried to ambush me. Only I had a grenade launcher and didn't have time to switch weapons. So I shot him and he just exploded everywhere. Arm there, legs over here, scrotum at my foot. Oh, and the blood--"

The lady spit out her drink. "I, ah." She cleared her throat. "I just came over to thank you for your service," she said awkwardly, then got up and left me to my drink. Mission accomplished.

The bartender came around to replace my drink. "Don't mind her. Some people don't know how to talk to soldiers."

I nodded in agreement.

After another full beer, I was getting close to calling it a night. My eyes were on my drink, and my thoughts were rustling around in my head. No matter how much I drank, I wouldn't get drunk, but that was never the reason I drank. For some reason, being alone drinking always helped my mind wander. At the moment, I couldn't shake what I had seen on that device Ghost gave me. I didn't want to believe it could be true. Before I determined anything, I would need to investigate myself. On leave, I would have the time. Only, where to start was the question.

The bartender came by to replace my drink. I lifted my hand. "I'm good." I then noticed it wasn't the same guy. He was different. I looked around and noticed I was the only one left in the bar. No way that should be the case. It wasn't even midnight yet.

"Are you sure?" the bartender asked me.

"Hey! What happened to the other guy? And where is everyone?" I asked the new bartender.

"What other guy? It's just me here. Just Grim."

Grim... what an odd name, I thought.

Grim continued. "I needed to make sure that it would just be us two left before my boss would meet you."

"Who?" My eyes darted around the room.

A sudden overwhelming feeling came over me. It was a familiar feeling, that familiar cold embrace that plagued me just after Jeremiah died. I dropped my drink, and it burst open, splashing beer all over the counter. My eyes dizzied, and my heart felt like it was skipping beats. It was the same feeling I felt before that man had showed up to inspect Jeremiah's motionless corpse.

I felt a hand touch my shoulder, then the feeling was lifted off me. I took in a deep breath and blinked the daze away. The hand lifted away, and I saw him again. He was sitting on the stool next to me. That mystery man who had followed me to so many locations. Soulless black eyes to match his expressionless face, tall and thin, bones prominent behind his skin, dark suit jacket, black tie, dress pants, shoes, a red tie pin, and a subtle glow to him; the whole nine yards.

"It's time we had a formal chat, James Stone." The suited man ushered over Grim, who handed me a glass of wine. "Drink. It'll help clear your mind." I took a sip and just stared. The man continued. "I took away the natural fear your soul has towards me just now. You should be able to focus more easily."

The fear was a near distant memory, just as he said. Even still, I could feel this man's presence. It didn't just emanate from where he sat. Instead, it felt like I was surrounded by it. I finally asked. "Who are you?"

His eyes were motionless as he stared into mine. "I've been meaning to talk with you. But I had to wait for you to see what you were up against before you were ready. You can see how aggravating that can be for me. Or maybe you can't. You are, after all, just one mere human. What would you know of what something like me has to burden himself with on a regular basis?" He didn't answer my question.

"You had to wait for me?" I asked.

"Yes. I needed you to see Kaizerious in person."

"Why?"

"You saw him die, yet he came back. Did you not question that as abnormal?"

"Of course I did. I'd never seen someone come back from the dead before except--" I stopped. "Except for when Uslar died. He came back... only for a short time, and--"

"Yes, James. Almost there." He egged me on.

"--and you were there just before he came back. You're...you're responsible for that...that evil man coming back!"

Chapter 42

The man gave me a mocking few claps. "Kaizerious came back because of me." He pointed to me. "Now, you James. *You* are going to be the one to stop him from coming back anymore."

"What? You just said that he came back because of you. So here's an idea, maybe don't bring him back." My eyes caught his, and I immediately regretted my words. I gulped as some of that fear from earlier crept back in.

"James, James, James." He moved his finger from side to side. "There are rules to this universe; constants. I am one of those constants. But every rule has exceptions or ways to circumvent them entirely. Kaizerious has done just that." His words were slow. "Kaizerious has created a blip in my otherwise perfect system. Those who die, stay dead. It's a system that makes sense. And it takes another to undo that blip. *You,* James. *You* are one of the few in the universe capable of such a task."

"How?"

"With my guidance, you will succeed. And I have much to show you."

"I meant how did Kaizerious come back from the dead? How could he escape the claws of death?" I reiterated my question.

He looked at his own fingers, then to me. "Funny you should reference such a thing. Let's just say, Kaizerious cheated Death a long time ago. He cheated *me.*"

END OF STORYARC ONE.

Thanks for joining the adventures James Stone and many others!

Enjoyed Book 3 of Galaxy at War? Here's what you can do next:

If you loved the book and have a moment to spare, I would really appreciate a short review. Your help in spreading the word is gratefully received.

More books to come in the future. Get your free short story (coming soon) plus news of the next books, giveaways, discounts, merchandise, and many more at: https://mailchi.mp/0542f8adf2f2/trey-deibel

Character Codex:

ARW Military

1112 Legionnaires (MIA):
- James Stone
    - Human, male, ace
    - Current captain, weapons specialist, formerly in Project Ace, missing in action
    - His mother [Sarah Stone], his father [Henry Stone]
- Shadow-Walker
    - Dor'o, male
    - Sniper, engineer, former mercenary, missing in action
- Valiic Bessile
    - Maelkii, male
    - Front line warrior, lieutenant, missing in action
    - His cohinla [Narrisa Bessile], his adopted dytirc children [Horana Bessile] & [Tielo Bessile]
- Brad Swift
    - Human, male
    - Explosives expert, weapons specialist, former assassin, tracking expert, former gang member, former lieutenant of the 51 Hunters, formerly in Project Glasshouse, missing in action
    - Ranked number one on the ARW's list of most dangerous ground troopers
    - Went by the name 'Damon Swift' for a time, nicknamed 'The Soulless Hitman'
- Narrisa Bessile
    - Maelkii, female
    - Front line warrior, retired from service
    - Her cohinla [Valiic Bessile], her adopted dytirc children [Horana Bessile] & [Tielo Bessile]
- Uslar Kip
    - Qwayk, male

- Field medic, rookie, killed in action
- Bremco Yahmar'liv
    - Qwayk, male
    - Former lieutenant, killed in action
- Clover Landis
    - Human, female
    - Former captain, explosives expert, killed by Steion after being captured
    - Her ex-husband [Malcolm Richardson], her deceased daughter [Alexx Richardson]
    - Formerly named 'Clover Richardson,' nicknamed 'Angel of Death'

707 Wolf-Pack:
- Catharine Darcrose
    - Human, female
    - Captain, tactician, pilot
    - Her mother [Elizabeth Darcrose], her younger brother [Alexander Darcrose], her younger sister [Beverly Darcrose]
- Kenny Morison
    - Human, male
    - First lieutenant, field medic
- Vayhara Lomia'dicia
    - Qwayk, female
    - Second lieutenant, engineer
- Edward McCollister
    - Human, male
    - Weapons specialist
- Tommlar Wloque
    - Qwayk, male
    - Navigations specialist
- Skolla
    - Warwolf, male

Chief Admirals:

- Day-Bringer
    - Dor'o, female
    - Chief admiral representing the dor'o species
    - Former manager of the Legionnaire Program
- Elizabeth Darcrose
    - Human, female
    - Chief admiral representing the human species
    - Her daughters [Beverly Darcrose] & [Catharine Darcrose], her son [Alexander Darcrose]
- (2 unnamed chief admirals)

Commanders:
- Sumillious Sizar
    - Qwayk, male
    - Commander of Tempest of Titans
- Dancing-Sky
    - Dor'o, female
    - Commander of Whispering Dragon
- Jeramiz Balthric
    - Maelkii, male
    - Commander of Leviathan II, went down with star cruiser
- Benjamin Cross
    - Human, male
    - Tracking and navigation expert, currently training in commander program
    - His older brothers [Isaac Cross] & [Samuel Cross], his father [Derrick Cross]
    - Called 'Ben'
- (Numerous others)

24434 Commandos:
- Wild-Heart
    - Dor'o, female
    - Captain, heavy machines operator
- Beverly Darcrose

- Human, female
- Recon, missing in action
- Her mother [Elizabeth Darcrose], her twin brother [Alexander Darcrose], her older sister [Catharine Darcrose]
  - (4 unnamed soldiers)

00942 Commandos:
- Francisco Reyes
  - Human, male
  - Captain
- (5 unnamed soldiers)

15661 Infiltrators (Former):
- Jujabar Yundor
  - Qwayk, male
  - Captain, killed in action
- (5 unnamed soldiers)

0920 Legionnaires (MIA):
- Shakti Waseem
  - Human, male
  - Captain, missing in action, likely killed in action
- (5 unnamed soldiers)

00844 Rangers:
- Alexander Darcrose
  - Human, male
  - His mother [Elizabeth Darcrose], his twin sister [Beverly Darcrose], his older sister [Catharine Darcrose]
  - Killed in action
  - Called 'Alex'
- (19 unnamed soldiers)

118 Achilles:

- Razaron Killemn
    - Maelkii, male
    - Captain, tactician
- (5 unnamed soldiers)

51 Hunters (Former):
- Malcolm Richardson
    - Human, male
    - Captain, tactician, killed after sacrificing himself to save others.
    - His ex-wife [Clover Landis], his deceased daughter [Alexx Richardson]
- Vaalima Stoox
    - Maelkii, female
    - Rookie, front line warrior, killed in action
    - Called 'Vaal'

Order of Aegis

Employment:
- Kalvin Keefe
    - Human, male
    - Director of Order of Aegis
- Jay Bridges
    - Human, male, ace
    - Apprentice to Kalvin Keefe, formerly in Project Ace, missing in action
    - Nicknamed 'Frost'
- Jean'ma Plow
    - Qwayk, female
    - Lead researcher at the Aegis Research Center
- Tarstbin Afuljack
    - Qwayk, male
    - Pilot
- Trevor Tarnish
    - Human, male
    - Engineer, technician

- (Numerous unnamed employees)

Bruising Brothers:
- Geariic Zserin
    - Maelkii, male, ace
    - Formerly in Project Ace, missing in action
    - His twin brother [Alabon Zserin]
- Alabon Zserin
    - Maelkii, male, ace
    - Formerly in Project Ace, missing in action
    - His twin brother [Geariic Zserin]

Project Aurum:
- Night-Shade
    - Dor'o, female, ace
    - Formerly in Project Ace, newest member to Project Aurum
- Ayeko Madoryia
    - Qwayk, male, ace
    - Formerly in Project Ace, training to be a field medic
    - Called 'Doctor Time'
- Drayvan Pryde
    - Maelkii, female, ace
    - Formerly in Project Ace, considered most powerful ace in ARW, current leader of Project Aurum
- Xavier 'Tank' Brockman
    - Human, male, ace, partially transformed into a mordazul
    - Formerly in Project Ace, formerly in 12560 Enforcers
    - Nicknamed 'Tank'
- Makayla Katakurry
    - Human, female, ace
    - Formerly in Project Ace, currently away on Earth

Wersillian Legion

Warlords:

Character Codex

- Airra
    - Dytirc, female, ace
    - Head of all warlords
    - Her stepbrother [Maliv Kuss]
- Yalfari Soodo
    - Lycargan, male, ace
    - Elderly
- Mara'Sane
    - Korkyra, female, ace
    - Chieftain of korkyras, warrior, has a form of dissociative identity disorder
    - Her bar'won [Dro'Zer]
- Maliv Kuss
    - Lycargan, male, ace
    - His stepsister [Airra]
- Dro'Zer
    - Korkyra, male, ace
    - Chieftain of korkyras, warrior, killed by Brad Swift
    - His bar'won [Mara'Sane]
- Steion
    - Dytirc, male, ace
    - Torturer, killed by James Stone
- Cralo
    - Dytirc, male, ace
    - Killed by Bruising Brothers, replaced by Dro'Zer
- Eruvir Varzaac
    - Lycargan, male, ace
    - Confirmed killed in the events after a parley, replaced by Mara'Sane
- (2 unknown warlords)

King Tribe:
- Larno
    - Dytirc, male
    - Tribal Chief
- (Numerous unnamed former or dead tribe members)

Planet Omulice

House Wolph:
- Kaydon Wolph
    - Omelic, male
    - King of Tolkran Kingdom
    - His father [Garrol Wolph], his mother [Cateron Wolph], his sister [Erryn Wolph], his uncle [Bearon Wolph]
    - Commander of his Royal Guard [Jeeryn Ghallows]
    - Master of Scrolls [Kaizerious]

House Lightbourne:
- Mauga Lightbourne
    - Omelic, male
    - Warden of Northpoint, First Under-Reign, third of his name
    - His younger brother [Wouren Lightbourne]
    - His squire [Heuw Podwin]
- Wouren Lightbourne
    - Omelic, male
    - Station Commander of a station of the Space Guard
    - His older brother [Mauga Lightbourne]

House Grimlock:
- Smyth Grimlock II
    - Omelic, male
    - Lord of Grimlock, second of his name

Knights:
- Gregor Mallister
    - Omelic, male
    - Knight of Dove's Ridge
- Qrow Jraxston
    - Omelic, male
    - Shadow knight of Direclaw

- Yarth Shooluck
  - Omelic, male
  - Knight of a rival kingdom to the Tolkran Kingdom

Brotherhood of Relics

Leadership:
- Castle
  - Omelic, male, ace
  - Knight of the brotherhood, worked undercover as a hired mercenary to fight against Allsung Socialists
- Ghost
  - Omelic, male, ace
  - Knight of the brotherhood, worked undercover as a hired mercenary to fight against Allsung Monarchy
- Sunfire
  - Omelic, female, ace
  - Knight of the brotherhood
- Starlight
  - Omelic, female
  - Knight of the brotherhood
- Brawn
  - Omelic, male
  - Knight of the brotherhood

Planet Coremoo

Occupants of Treasured City:
- Anighta Yin'Dahen
  - Corelinn, female, ace
  - Seer
- Witnamerrys Kekay'Hegar
  - Corelinn, female
  - Prime Keeper of the Treasured City
  - Called 'Witna'
- Jeremiah
  - Human, male

- - Last survivor of a group of humans and qwayks,
    formerly part of Project Outreach
  - Pastor
- Oyemar Kruh'Murta
  - Corelinn, male
  - Died after entering the Vault of the Seven

Vault Outpost:
- Momotashi Boo'Thuur
  - Corelinn, male
  - Outpost leader

Unallied

Mercenaries:
- Erryn Wolph
  - Omelic, female
  - Considered one of the best in the galaxy and
    commands a high price for her service
  - Her uncle [Bearon Wolph], her father [Garrol
    Wolph], her mother [Cateron Wolph], her brother
    [Kaydon Wolph]
- Ryben Bukkaro
  - Omelic, male
  - Called 'Scourge,' short for 'Scourge of the South'
- Patchface & Slackjaw
  - Omelics, males
  - True identities unknown, together they are
    nicknamed 'Clowned Fools'
- Bearon Wolph
  - Omelic, male
  - His niece [Erryn Wolph], his nephew [Kaydon
    Wolph], his older brother [Garrol Wolph]
  - Killed by Erryn Wolph
- (Numerous other unnamed mercenaries)

Character Codex

Unknown:
- The Broker
    - Species unknown, appears humanoid, male
    - Called many names [Rumpelstiltskin, Swallower of Millions, Sinnerman, Reality, Jyruckal, Undertaker, and more]

Planet Earth
- Derrick Cross
    - Human, male
    - Former commander during World War III, retired
    - His sons [Benjamin Cross] & [Isaac Cross] & [Samuel Cross]

Planet Xan'Ohmo
Allsung Monarchy:
- Ivinage-Hoi Tyim-Jointhajon
    - Allsung, female
    - Killed in battle
    - Called 'Ivinage'
- Frob-Guj Remse-Koallahoo
    - Allsung, male
    - Killed in battle
    - Called 'Frob'
- Evwei-Marashial Uef-Iexavozaj
    - Allsung, female
    - Called 'Evwei'
    - Leader of the Allsung Monarchy, killed in battle
- Gharah-Refacavezaro Oker-Umnazeex
    - Allsung, male
    - Called 'Gharah'
    - War prisoner, killed in prison
- (Numerous others)

Allsung Socialists:
- (Numerous unnamed)

Canon Fodder (Military Access - List View):

Login: 4hf84nw092niih1
Codename: SunRising027
Clearance: Level 10
Organization Type: List View - Custom Format - Custom Text Descriptions
Commands: <view type: hide errors>, <view type: hide unrecognized keywords>, <sort: alphabetically>
Logbook Description: Personal database. Does not include all within the Milky Way Galaxy.

2ⁿᵈ Big Bang of 2036	An unexplained supernatural event that occurred in the year 2036. This big bang released an unknown type of energy wave across the known galaxy at a speed far faster than light.
Alliance of Republic Worlds (ARW)	An alliance started by the maelkii and later added humans, qwayks, and dor'o to become the four founding species of the alliance. Other species later joined. Led by the ARW Senate and ARW Judicial Court.
Allsung Monarchy	One of two opposing sides of an ongoing civil war amongst the allsung species. This political regime seeks to create a world with one monarch at its head.
Allsung Socialists	One of two opposing sides of an ongoing civil war amongst the allsung species. This political regime seeks to create a system of government run and regulated by communities of people.
ARW Government	**ARW Judicial Court -** Official judges are voted into the court by the ARW Senate. The judicial court has the power to interpret laws and enforce laws on citizens under the ARW.

ARW Senate - Members of all species under the ARW have equal representation in this senate. The Senate has the power to vote on the creation, modification, or deletion of laws. In addition, the Senate can approve or deny treaties and manage ARW spending. However, only the four founding species can vote on military matters, which includes the election of the four chief admirals.

Chief Admirals - ARW's top-ranking military individuals that are appointed by the representatives of the four founding species. Each founding species under the ARW has one chief admiral to represent their interests.

ARW Military Programs

Achilles Program - One of many programs a part of the integrated ARW's military. This program is designed to create 119 independent squads, consisting of six individuals. Achilles are the most elite ground-based unit at the ARW's disposal. Due to being dropped straight into dire scenarios, achilles are diversely and extensively trained in all ground warfare. Achilles are dropped directly into combat and are equipped with some of the best resources the ARW has to offer, including veridium-plated armor.

Commander Program - One of many programs that is a part of the integrated ARW's military. This program initially required a significant amount of first-hand battle experience and additional training before applying. However, after 2108, this program's priorities changed. Instead, applicants were required to pass a series of tests, and the requirements for battle experience were drastically reduced. In the ARW, commanders are the second highest rank in the chain of command under the chief admirals.

Commando Program - One of many programs that is a part of the integrated ARW's military. This program is designed to create 26,500 independent squads, consisting of six individuals. Each squad is tasked with commanding the front line of an assault. Commandos are considered among the most elite squads on the front lines of combat.

Drop Pilot Program - One of many programs that are a part of the integrated ARW's military. This program is designed to train individual support pilots to pilot and transport ARW ground units.

Eagle Program - One of many programs that are a part of the integrated ARW's military. This program is designed to create 20,100 support units, consisting of ten individuals per unit. These support pilots are trained to aid ground assault missions where air coverage is required.

Executive Engineer Program - One of many programs that is a part of the integrated ARW's military. Within a star cruiser, the executive engineer is trained to perform maintenance on the ship and keep all functions running. Furthermore, the executive engineer is in charge of all maintenance crews aboard the ship.

First Officer Program - One of many programs that is a part of the integrated ARW's military. Within a star cruiser, first officers are trained in virtually the same manner as a commander. First officers are the second in charge of a star cruiser.

Helmsman Program - One of many programs that is a part of the integrated ARW's military. Within a star cruiser, helmsmen are trained to steer the ship as well as operate its onboard arsenal of weaponry.

Hunter Program - One of many programs that is a part of the integrated ARW's military. This program is designed to create 51 independent squads, consisting of three individuals. These units are tasked with detaining rogue ARW soldiers. With only 51 squads, hunters are the smallest program in the ARW but are second only to achilles in ground-based skill. Hunters are only one of two ARW programs with current access to power armor.

Infiltrator Program - One of many programs that is a part of the integrated ARW's military. This program is designed to create 17,125 independent squads, consisting of six individuals. Each squad is tasked with planning and initiating flanking maneuvers against enemy forces.

Legionnaire Program - One of many programs that are a part of the integrated ARW's military. This program is designed to create 1,112 independent squads, consisting of six individuals. Each squad is tasked with small but essential missions. Legionnaires are considered among the most elite squads at the ARW's disposal.

Navigator Program - One of many programs that is a part of the integrated ARW's military. Within a star cruiser, navigators are trained to chart viable paths from one location to another. Furthermore, they keep track of ally and enemy ship locations

Operations Assistant Program - One of many programs that is a part of the integrated ARW's military. Within a star cruiser, operations assistants are trained to assist the commander with various tasks to make their job more efficient.

Ranger Program - One of many programs that are a part of the integrated ARW's military. This program is designed to create 90,000 support units, consisting of twenty individuals per unit. These support units are basic infantry deployed on large-scale ground assault missions.

Recon Program - One of many programs that are a part of the integrated ARW's military. This program is designed to create 9,880 independent units, consisting of four individuals per unit. These independent units are trained for intelligence gathering during combat.

Science Advisor Program - One of many programs that is a part of the integrated ARW's military. Within a star cruiser, science advisors are knowledgeable in the fields of science. These advisors offer their expertise to the commander as needed.

Scout Program - One of many programs that is a part of the integrated ARW's military. This program is designed to create 14,880 independent units, consisting of four individuals per unit. These independent units are trained for intelligence gathering outside of combat, typically before an operation begins.

Shooting-Star Program - One of many programs that is a part of the integrated ARW's military. This program is designed to create 22,100 support units, consisting of ten individuals per unit. These support pilots are trained to fight off enemy forces in space.

Tactics Advisor Program - One of many programs that is a part of the integrated ARW's military. Within a star cruiser, tactics advisors are knowledgeable in the fields of war and military tactics. These advisors offer their expertise to the commander as needed. Sometimes, tactics advisors even coordinate with squads to assist the first officer and commander.

Watchmen Program - One of many programs that are a part of the integrated ARW's military. This program is designed to create 9,000 support squads, consisting of three individuals per unit. Watchmen are focused on tracking, navigation, and sniper support.

Wolf-Pack Program - One of many programs that is a part of the integrated ARW's military. This program is designed to create 707 independent squads, consisting of five individuals and a warwolf. Each squad is tasked with completing missions that take months or longer to finish, often behind enemy lines or in unknown territory. Wolf-packs are often geared with veridium armor and given access to a variety of equipment. Considered among the most elite and versatile ground-based squads.

ARW Military Terminology

Independent Squad - An ARW squad class that is designed for an independent chain of command. Each independent class squad contains a captain and lieutenant at all times. Any other individual roles, ranks, or layouts are left to the captain's digression.

Support Squad - An ARW squad class that is designed to support established independent squads or follow orders directly from a commander. Usually very large or drastically small in numbers, with hardly any middle ground.

ARW Time   The ARW uses a standardized dating system based on their capital, Grathefer-Qwayk. On Grathefer-Qwayk, a year is made up of 12 months, each month consisting of 31 days, spanning a period of 372 days of 24 hours each day, with no leap years.

With some help from qwayk technology, Earth's rotation around its sun was adjusted to match the same period of time as Grathefer-Qwayk.

Brotherhood   No first-hand knowledge of this group is available in
of Relics   the ARW database at this time. Considered a myth even by the omelics, the so-called founders of this cult or religious group.

Curse   **Frak** - Modern-day curse word that is often used to
Words   describe something ruined, damaged, or destroyed. Moreover, it can be used to describe sexual intercourse or as an exclamation of annoyance, anger, or contempt. Considered a more explicit variation of Frev.

Frev - Modern-day curse word that is often used to describe something ruined, damaged, or destroyed.

Shivf - A modern-day curse word that is often used to describe something or someone worthless. Moreover, it can be used to describe feces or as an exclamation of disgust or anger.

Snavo - A curse word that is used to describe an individual or a group of individuals as worthless fecal matter.

Derrium   A hologram display game. It involves building bases and troops. The objective of the game is to strategically use one's troops and resources to conquer your opponent(s).

Dor'o Allied under the ARW since 2080, the dor'o are known mostly for their famous tribal-like names and historic wars. Known to live within mountain cities, dor'o are very communal as a species and love activities such as dancing, drinking, and celebrating. The dor'o have no vow between males and females to live together indefinitely. Often, dor'o live among communities. And it isn't uncommon for dor'o children to be raised by an entire community.

These quick, agile creatures almost look like small devils. On the tops of their bald scalps, they have what is known as stumps, which resemble cut-off antlers, typically extending a few centimeters out of their scalps. Dor'o are the smallest species in the ARW, at almost half the size of a human, but their arms are just as long. Their skin and eyes can vary from brown to red-brown in color. Dor'o ears hang down the sides of their faces, and their nose and mouth protrude almost like small dogs. Although they are mammalian, vertebrate beings, they have a tendency to slouch just below their usually broad shoulders.

Dor'o Culture & History **Name Trials** - Dor'o system of naming their young. At a young age, dor'o are sent inside the Name Caves for two days. Using induced hallucinations, billions of possible outcomes can occur. A dor'o is named based on what he or she is seen doing inside.

Dor'o Weaponry **Arc Blaster** - A dor'o-created weapon. A short-range blaster capable of firing controlled lightning at enemies for massive damage. Fed by special electrical stasis rounds.

Buzzard-[series] Attack Choppers - Created by the Dor'o in 2101, these choppers use three rotator blades and thruster combinations for stability. Buzzard-[series] attack choppers are small aircraft containing a seat for one pilot and one mounted weapon device aimed at the ground. Countermeasures included suicide grenades.

C-[series] Scout Sentry Turret - A dor'o-designed sentry turret that is equipped with a scout rifle. C-[series] sentry turrets can automatically acquire and eliminate targets at long range using advanced figure analysis technology.

MULR War Machines - A dor'o-crafted drivable mechanized vehicle that can fit qwayks, humans, and dor'o. Fitted with stasis shielding and veridium plating, these machines are used to dominate the front lines.

Parlor-[series] Dropship - Dor'o dropship for space-to-atmosphere descents into hot zones. A Parlor-[series] dropship is equipped with emergence equipment and rapid cycle turrets for protection. Can hold two standard-sized units.

Rapid Cycle Turrets - A dor'o-designed mounted turret with four rotating barrels. Capable of firing off a thousand stasis rounds a minute, these powerhouse weapons can zap through a battlefield with ease.

Scout Rifle - The dor'o answer to the human sniper rifle. A long-range weapon class capable of firing a stasis beam at distances as far as three kilometers. Fed by stasis rounds.

Shock Grenade - A dor'o-designed grenade that releases a burst of electric energy to paralyze opponents for a long period of time instead of killing them. Became a standard amongst police forces in 2099.

Shock Rifle - A dor'o-designed weapon class that comes in large to small sizes. These rifles release a ball of electric energy to paralyze opponents for a long period of time instead of killing them. Became a standard amongst police forces in 2099.

Stasis Rounds - A dor'o-designed projectile for firing from a rifle, blaster, or other dor'o-based firearm that is typically made of hard light effused with electric energy. Its casings are cylindrical and butt-ended.

Suicide Grenade - A dor'o grenade that explodes into thirteen aerial sparks. Each spark explodes based on proximity. Considered a highly versatile area denial grenade in the ARW's arsenal.

Dytirc

First encountered in 2098, this alien species is from the Draynought System, where they inhabit nineteen planets and six moons. Dytircs are persistent, aggressive savages. Their society is focused on power and proving oneself. Before the war, the dytircs were split into many tribes with leaders who fought to remain the tribal chiefs of their respective tribes. Around the time before the Wersillian War, nearly every tribe merged into what the dytircs call the Military Tribe during an event known as the Great Amalgamation. Dytircs are a male-dominated society and are adept at various forms of hand-to-hand combat.

These four-armed, exoskeletal creatures are taller, faster, and roughly four times as strong as an average human. These mammalian, vertebrate beings normally have skin tones that range from dark to light gray. Their eyes, however, can be many colors but almost always have a black ring in their iris. Dytirc heads often look too large for their boney, rough bodies, and their skin is durable enough to travel through harsh terrain.

Dytirc Culture & History

Duel of Honor - In a time when dytircs believed in honor, this tradition where two individuals fight to the death in the name of one's honor was believed to gain favor in the eyes of their gods. The winner is granted their life. In the modern day, this tradition is often still considered a sin for dytircs to not uphold.

The Great Amalgamation - Historical dytirc event where nearly every tribe merged into one single Military Tribe. Believed to have occurred in 2097.

Dytirc Tribes

Fallen Tribe - A nearly extinct rebel tribe, its reminants are located on Delkeedo. Once great, the Fallen Tribe held notoriety and individuality at the highest honors. Before the war, they pursued knowledge of various cultural martial arts.

King Tribe - A nearly extinct tribe, its remanients are located on Delkeedo. The King Tribe held nobility and personal achievement at the highest honors. Before the Wersillian War, they perused knowledge of old arts and sculptures.

Military Tribe - A dytirc term used for their military. Believe in power and prosperity through numbers.

Feel the need to colonize and dominate other worlds as a means to spread peace and prosperity.

Extinct Species

These species are believed to no longer exist in the current galaxy.

Devisors - Dubbed the "Devisors," this mythological species isn't generally accepted as truth by most species in the Milky Way. For some who do accept this species' existence, they believe the Devisors to be the oldest known species in the galaxy. They are thought to have left monuments to aid in certain species' technological development.

Precursors - Within some known locations near the Inner Core, an ancient species is believed to have existed, dubbed the "Precursors." Almost no proof or record of them exists, convincing many to believe they are simply a myth.

Food & Drinks

Bammberry - Natural fruit that is found on Coremoo.

Pighmix - A strong energy drink created by the qwayk that doesn't lead to a crash. However, repeated use can be addicting and can lead to muscle fatigue.

Woodstones - Branded, popular beer made on Earth.

Global Department of Investigation (GDI)

Established in 2079 by the Earth's global senate as a worldwide investigation division for Earth. Fully cooperative with local police for maximum efficiency, the GDI uses physical evidence at the scene of a crime and uses deductive and inductive reasoning to gain knowledge of the events surrounding the crime. The GDI is also responsible for handling worldwide terrorist' acts and managing conspiracy cases.

Grabel	A jenjarian sport.
Hearon's Standard for Measuring Intelligent Beings Scale (Hearon's SMIB Scale)	With the aid of technological machinery, this scale measures an individual's capacity to learn and understand. Furthermore, this scale can measure a species potential for evolutionary development in terms of intelligence by analyzing groups of individuals within a species. It has become the standard scale for determining whether a species can or will be able to develop intergalactic travel. Those deemed to be able to hit that mark will score at least 100 on the scale. Species that can't hit 100 are deemed below the scale. Currently, the average human achieves a score of 132, while the average for qwayks is 139, the dor'o average is 120, and the maelkii average is 121.
Holy Triangle	Oteyk, Guardian of the Oceans; Saeona, Guardian of the Skies; and Moonikwaa, Guardian of the Surface. The most widely accepted religion of the corelinns.
Human Culture & History	**Selection of Communist Parties (SOCP) -** Established between the years 2061 and 2079, this alliance consisted of most of Earth's eastern hemisphere. Considered to be highly fascist, a single government consisting of a small group of individuals regulated all aspects of its economy, communication, and military.
	United Nations of Democracy (UNOD) - Established between the years 2062 and 2079 as a response to the establishment of the Selection of Communist Parties, this alliance consisted of the western hemisphere of Earth and some minor areas on the eastern hemisphere. A single senate and judicial branch governed this alliance as a type of democracy.

World War III - The last major war on Earth. A war between the UNOD and SOCP. It was a fight between the two super-nations for energy, resources, and land. Due to the destruction of the International Humanitarian Law, sixty percent of humanity perished in this harsh and cruel conflict. Lasted from 2067 to 2079 with the UNOD's victory.

Human Weaponry

Airjin Dust - A powder variation of airjin fuel, this compound is rarely used; it is mostly used in revolver rounds. Illegal for civilian use.

Airjin Fuel - Technologically advanced compound fuel that propels ballistic rounds faster than ever possible. Can send ballistic projectiles at speeds of three thousand meters per second. This compound is illegal for civilian use.

Annihilator - Massive turret with three separate, rotating chain guns. Often utilized by ARW soldiers in power armor.

Assault Rifle - Standard all-purpose weapon for humans. Typically, a rapid-fire, magazine-fed automatic rifle that is designed for infantry use. Assault rifles come in many designs, making them a highly versatile class of weapons. As of 2072, the ballistic rounds' explosive powder was replaced with airjin fuel, significantly increasing the speeds of bullets.

Ballistic Bullets - A human-designed projectile for firing from a rifle, revolver, or other firearm; typically made of metal, cylindrical, and pointed. As of 2072, the ballistic bullets' explosive powder was replaced with airjin fuel, significantly increasing the speeds of bullets.

EMP Grenade - Emits a burst that disables electronic-based weaponry and gadgets for a short time due to advanced circuit rejuvenating systems. Originally a human design.

Flamethrower - A large weapon that sprays out streams of burning fuel. Often utilized by ARW soldiers in power armor.

Frag Grenade - Standard human grenade that causes a single explosion, sending shards and shockwaves outward.

Grenade Launcher - A weapon that fires specially designed large-caliber projectiles, often with an explosive, smoke, or gas warhead. These human weapons come in many sizes, from belt feed to multi-tube and single-tube.

Hand Pistol - Standard, human-developed sidearms capable of firing single, powerful ballistic rounds. A small firearm designed to be held in one hand. As of 2072, the ballistic rounds' explosive powder was replaced with airjin fuel, significantly increasing the speeds of bullets.

J[series] Brutes - Approved for active duty in 2099, these heavy armored tanks are used as an anti-vehicular asset. Equipped with twin barreled, self-loading firing tubes and an additional fully rotatable turret at the front of the tank. Human designed.

Light Grenade - Created in 2051 by humans as a replacement for the flashbang grenade. The intensity of the flash, as well as its number and distance, can be manipulated before activation.

Raptor V[series] - Approved for active duty in 2099, these state-of-the art, lightweight infantry vehicles are idle for multipurpose situations. A human design, the Raptor V[series] is outfitted with all terrain tires, a protective cover for the driver and the turret operator, a fully rotatable, heavy-mounted gun, and an area for additional supplies.

Shotgun - Standard close-court combat weapons that were created by humans. A smoothbore gun for firing a small shot at short range. Shotguns typically fire a single slug shot or a scattering buckshot shell.

Sniper Rifle - Standard long-distance, human-developed weapon. An extremely powerful rifle developed for the military that is capable of destroying light armored vehicles and aircraft more than five kilometers away. As of 2072, the ballistic rounds' explosive powder was replaced with airjin fuel, significantly increasing the speeds of bullets.

V-Hawk Harrier Jets - Created by humans in 2103, these harrier jets were designed to impose maximum damage against enemy aircraft. Each jet comes equipped with twin grenade launchers with proximity projectiles and four mounted miniguns. Countermeasures included thruster technology and flares.

Hyperdagger A smaller version of a hypersword that can typically be carried in a pocket or similar small space. Almost always neutral (gray) based.

Hypershield Powered by similar technology to a hypersword, these shields can block the intense, rapidly rotating energy of a hypersword.

Hypersword   Powered by geminite, which focuses power and emotion to form a blade of intense, rapidly rotating energy. Primary weapon of choice for knights, lords, and kings. For most hyperswords, a bond with a scarlencoul is required to wield the power of non-neutral geminite.

Framing - The construction style of a hypersword. Many exist.

Geminite - The core source of power in hyper-weaponry. All of these gemstones can be found naturally throughout the planet of Omulice but cannot be created.

Shade/Base/Tint - Describes the color of the geminite and, as such, the energy flowing over a hypersword.

Stearth - The extendable spine of a hyper-based weapon, usually a hypersword, which gives structure to the weapon. Once extended completely out of the handle, the jurcabeyo gel covering the stearth helps the geminite focus and guide the energy around it.

8 Main Hypersword Combat Techniques:
➢   Technique I (Barriz)
➢   Technique II (Delfvii)
➢   Technique III (Toloum)
➢   Technique IV (Parmudo)
➢   Technique V (Jarrlinbar)
➢   Technique VI (Aargo)
➢   Technique VII (Svyn)
➢   Technique VIII (Dezzlow)

9 Blade Main Blade Shades:

> Silver-Base (Gray): Neutral, requires no scarlencouls.
> Sapphire-Base (Blue): Commitment & Loyalty.
> Citrine-Base (Yellow): Duty, Honor, & Justice.
> Amber-Base (Orange): Exhilaration & Enthusiasm.
> Ruby-Base (Red): Fury & Strength.
> Amethyst-Base (Violet): Gallantry & Courage.
> Emerald-Base (Green): Patience & Composure.
> Bronzine-Base (Brown): Valor & Empowerment.
> Bloominite-Base (Pink): Peace & Love.

Intelligent Species

These species' average intelligence is above Hearon's SMIB Scale, and either they have achieved space travel technology or are likely to in the future.

Allsung - A humanoid, mammalian species with impressive resistance to extreme cold. Currently under a civil war between two major governments many years long. Wherever they go, their war follows them.

Corelinn - As a species, they are not particularly tall, strong, or smart and have yet to achieve space travel technology. These amphibian species have large eyes, a gathered tangle of flexible tentacle-tresses extending from their heads, and are quite resistant to water. Corelinns are very peaceful and compassionate.

Gatero - Currently under the reign of the Wersillian Legion.

Jenjarian - A species with a taste for bugs, bright colors, sports, and warm temperatures. They are quite peaceful.

Laburtles - Bold allies of the ARW that openly mock the Wersillian Legion. Their planetary defenses and military strength are well known.

O'gark - They originated on a planet called Gorak. Currently, they support the ARW with funding and resources.

Plauranian - This species shares a similar vision of the galaxy as the Wersillian Legion and exchanges resources with the legion for military protection. As one of the first to support the legion, they are treated well.

Plowsu - They originated on a planet called Juster. This species is highly spiritual and works to preserve the natural beauty of their planet. Though they don't offer much in funding or resources to the ARW, they are supporters of the ARW's ideals.

Smokmorjorok - Species that are infamous for their drug organizations.

Valistares - A long-loyal species of ARW that provides funding and resources to fight the Wersillian Legion.

Yuerr - Inventors of the modern day, intergalactic currency known as jemns. This species is known for its greed, has the highest average wealth per person of any species in the galaxy, and typically lives in luxury. Since nearly all species depend on their currency systems, the yuerr government has heavy influence, and no other government dares make enemies of them.

Jemn Universally used as the galactic currency. Transferred in the form of credits or set-valued coins. Originally created and sponsored by the yuerr until they successfully overturned each and every old-world form of currency. As new species gain the technology to make use of intergalactic slip space travel, the yuerr are there to insist and aid their transition into the use of their created currency system.

Knoblelism Knoblelism is a masmormadic, monotheistic religion based on the lives and teachings of nine High Prophets and thirteen other prophets. Its adherents, known as Knobles, believe that these nine High Prophets were the hands and mouthpieces of the one true God sent to guide all to eternal light and life. All nine were prophesied in writings from ancient times that now make up the First Age section of the Book of Ancient Prophets. The following Second Age and Third Age chronicle the lives and teachings of those nine High Prophets, also called the Knoble Nine. The remaining thirteen prophets are chronicled in the last section, the Prodigals Addendum.

While Knobles across the galaxy share basic convictions, there are also differences in interpretations and opinions of the Book of Ancient Prophets and sacred traditions on which Knoblelism is based. Many of these differing opinions are the reason some maelkii houses were originally formed.

Knoblelism began to grow as a religion during the First Age, an age when maelkii written history began. A wandering monk named Rohanthius lost himself in a desert of sharpened rock. He collapsed after some time due to thirst and did not have the strength to beg for his life. "As I lay there on the ground, dying in the sun, the cold rock all around me, I spoke to the golden rock, not with my lips but with my mind. And the rock wept tears of fresh water, and my thirst was quenched. Rohanthius 12:3." He was saved later that day by a guide who found him. And that night, he had a vision. He was told to climb Mount Gaisma, an active volcano, and leap into the magma. Others called him a fool, but he leapt faithfully anyway. A year later, he returned with a tablet, predicting nine decades of prophecy.

Masmormadic - A collective of Masmormians who believe they are descendants of the light incarnate.

Korkyra

A species on the brink of extinction, this species originated from the Zellur System on a planet known as Corkeria. Korkyras are believed to have been governed and led by two alphas called chieftains and to have been split amongst packs. Due to little contact with this species, not much is known of their culture, past, or way of life.

Korkyras, on average, are said to weigh roughly three times the average weight of a human and grow nearly as tall as maelkii. They are roughly eight times stronger than a human, as intelligent as an average qwayk, and as agile as dor'o. Humanoids with bull-like heads, korkyras have a prominent muscle structure and are physically intimidating. Being that they have incredibly developed physiques and brawny frames, they're highly suitable for combat. Thick yet short and downy pelts cover the korkyran body, with manes growing along the chin and neck, the lengths of the arms, and the shins. Korkyran men and women almost always wear their hair long, and the males prefer braids to any other style. The coloration can range from solid gray to brown and even white, or mottled pelts with a range of spots and different colors. Horns are most prominent on males, although they are greater in number on females.

Korkyra Culture & History

Final War - The last civil war to take place on the korkyran home world, Corkeria, which left the korkyra nearly extinct and the planet completely unlivable, such that nothing but molten rock remains.

Korkyran Weaponry

Guardian Drones - Scout intelligence suggests these drones are utilized by the korkyran species as a means of aid during and out of combat.

Jumper - Scout intelligence suggests this particular vehicle, dubbed the "Jumper," to be the main source of transport for the korkyran species.

Pulse Rifle - Technology that is too complex for the ARW to currently make handheld. However, scout intelligence suggests this type of technology is the primary weaponry used by the korkyran species. In the case of the korkyras, these rifles are said to be biological in nature and use magnetically accelerated technology to fire pulse rounds that explode on impact.

Pulse Rods - A korkyran-designed projectile that is made to fire from various heavy pulse weapons and is typically made of metal, cylindrical, and blunted. Larger than pulse rounds, these projectiles are faster than ballistic rounds and create miniature quakes around them using vibrations.

Pulse Rounds - A korkyran-designed projectile that is made to fire from various handheld pulse weapons and is typically made of metal, cylindrical, and blunted. These rounds are faster than ballistic rounds and explode on impact.

Tectonic Pulse Driver - Scout intelligence suggests that this heavy-mounted turret is korkyran-made. Using pulse rods, this turret can tear through various armors and metals with ease.

Languages & Dialects

Jav'colo - One of the many languages originating from the dor'o that is widely used in many varieties throughout the world of Dorrath.

Quallic Dialect - Language and tongue spoken by maelkii of the Quallic House.

Umomah - An ancient, outdated omelic language once used primarily in the Tolkran Kingdom.

Locations & Monuments

Atlas - A decrypted legend says this monument is a "smoky window of keys." This rough translation came from a location on Maelkiin that is believed to be Devisor in origin.

Baurtenson - Mostly barren moon housing an Order of Aegis outpost. It is used primary for defense as it holds a key location against the Wersillian Legion.

Direclaw - The capital and largest stronghold of the Tolkran Kingdom. Surrounded by mountains, farmlands, and a treacherous sea. Being towards the south end of the Tolkran Kingdom, the weather is typically warm. Life here is luxurious for those who can afford it, although it is not without its slums.

Dove's Ridge - Small but beautiful, idyllic, and fruitful land, beloved by its inhabitants. Rich in agriculture. The landscape includes hills and woods similar to the countryside. A place inland, but near a river, located in the Tolkran Kingdom.

Garatopia - Also known as the Floating City, this was the first city built on the newly discovered planet of Idor. This jenjarian-created city was made with the intention of creating a beacon of luxury for the jenjarian species and acting as a gateway to expanding their territory.

Grando Military Prison - Dytirc military prison that is located on Delkeedo. Designed for information gathering purposes as opposed to holding.

Grim Ruins - A long abandoned place located at the edge of Grimlock. Much of its origin, past, and long-dead citizens are unknown.

Grimlock - Located on the northern edge of the current Tolkran Kingdom. A very old complex spanning several acres and protected by two massive walls. There is a village at one end, older than anything else in the complex, called the Grim Ruins. It is separated from the main town by a gate. Grimlock is located near an ancient forest that spreads over a natural hot spring. It is a place inhabited by mostly lowbloods.

Lamnlair - A city south of the Treasured City that benefits from its trade with the other rich nearby cities. Some call this city the little brother of the Treasured City due to its similar layout and architecture.

Pullentin - A city south of the Treasured City. It's well-known for its vast and plentiful markets and plentiful farmlands on the east end of the city.

Qurangmaar (Blood Forest) - More notably called the Blood Forest and located on the planet of Coremoo. An expansive forest thick with black and dark-gray trees and full of dangers. In its history, countless people have gone missing and died upon entering the forest, leading it to be called the Blood Forest. Corelinns have forbidden citizens from venturing inside.

Saulomon's Temple - Citadel that houses much of the knowledge, stories, and teachings of the Tolkran Kingdom's omelic ancestors. Contains many rooms, walls designed as bookshelves, and many floors.

Station 9 - Station 9 is the common name of a highly classified Order of Aegis facility. Its location is unknown and often speculated by civilians.

Station 51 - Station 51 is the common name of a highly classified Order of Aegis facility located on a remote, unnamed asteroid. Civilian access to this location is strictly forbidden by the ARW.

Surradimoor (Treasured City) - Though its official name is Surradimoor, this great city on Coremoo is known as the Treasured City. Of all the cities around the world of Coremoo, this is the most protected since it houses a building responsible for maintaining the weather in Coremoo. Should no prime hand be present to operate this tower, the weather would become unstable and Coremoo would be barren of life. As such, many have come and built around this tower, making the Treasured City the vast, lively place it is today.

Tegun Trade City - Located on the planet Grathefer-Qwayk, this legendary trade city is one of the most financially booming places in the Milky Way Galaxy. Countless shops and trademarked companies thrive in this great city.

The Galactic Hotel - Located on an asteroid orbiting the yuerr home planet, Yuerr-Olo, this ten-square-kilometer haven is a favorite meeting point for diplomats and tourists across the galaxy. This hotel is known for its one rule: *No life shall be taken by another on Galactic grounds.* It also offers complete, assured neutrality in any conflict.

The Narrways - A legendary forest that is located on the planet Juster has a mysterious mist flowing out of the trees. Entrance into this location is forbidden to this day by plowsu law.

The Underlevel - A series of entrances across Hondora that are all connected and go deep below the surface of the planet. The Underlevel is where the few inhabitants of this planet call home. However, these series of tunnels are mostly commercially run or used for the sole purpose of criminal mischief. Being in a hotspot in the galaxy, criminal activity thrives through these tunnels. The saying goes, "The deeper down the level, the more dangerous the individuals."

Trinity Towers - Three innovative and beautiful skyscrapers that once stood at the center of Garatopia.

Wolph Castle - Located in the Tolkran Kingdom, Wolph Castle is the residence of the king of the Tolkran Kingdom, his family, his court, and the location of the government of the kingdom. It dominates the skyline of Direclaw and serves as the city's primary fortress and redoubt. Wolph Castle was built over the remains of Drayfus Den, and parts of the castle, especially the lower levels, connect to old portions of Drayfus Den. Saulomon's Temple was later added to Wolph Castle in an expansion project.

Lycargan

Encountered in 2098, this alien species is from the Draynought System, inhabiting two planets. Lycargans have been known to spend an unordinary amount of time inactive or in thought. They are religious extremists who justify any and all means as a necessity for their beliefs. Lycargans are known for taking long periods of time before acting on situations but can make quick decisions if necessary. They enjoy causing emotional or physical distress to other species for sport. Though, little more is known about lycargan culture or history.

Lycargans are naturally armored around many vital areas of the body and have scaled skin elsewhere. Reptilian vertebrates, these beings are not as strong but have far superior durability than humans. Their feet resemble hooves and are mostly flat. Although bumpy and rough, their heads are round. Lycargans have an enormous, stubby bump extended out of their backs. Their skin and eyes are various shades of brown and are spotted all around. Lycargans also have the strange ability to roll into an armored ball and control the direction in which they roll.

Maelkii

Founded the ARW in 2061, this species is from the planet Maelkiin and is the only ARW founding species that originates outside of the Qwayk System. Other than the possible mythological species that may or may not have existed, Maelkii are believed to be the oldest known intelligent species in the Milky Way Galaxy. Maelkii value companionship, loyalty, and self-sacrifice. Warriors are considered to be one of the most valued positions in their society. Society, traditions, and culture can vary depending on the sub-communal houses that maelkii are born into or married into. For example, traditionalist houses believe that lifetime partnerships lead to powerful armies, and they encourage families to fight side by side with each other. Maelkii are the only species in the ARW to choose not to colonize other worlds, preferring to stay on their home planet.

Maelkii, on average, weigh roughly four times the average weight of a human and grow a few heads taller. They are nearly nine times stronger than humans and have skin that can be more durable than lycargan natural armor. Their eyes are like black abysses with a glowing center pupil, and they have upside-down triangular mouths. Their heads look too small for their bodies. Maelkii skin and eye color consist of shades of red, orange, and yellow. They have bull-like feet and small spikes that follow their spine to the top of their heads.

Maelkii Culture & History

Book of Ancient Prophets - The most studied and read religious book among the maelkii culture. Religious book for all Knobles.

Cohinlation - A sacred day in maelkii culture where male and female maelkii become one mended soul, partners in life and death for all eternity. The day an unbreakable bond is formed.

Maelkii Honor Pledge - Official document that allows maelkii to fight alongside loved ones.

Rowakii Robe - Traditional formal attire that maelkii wears. It comes in various colors.

Maelkii Houses

Escanorinn House - A maelkii house with a reputation due to their unusual beliefs and take on honor. This house believes honor is achieved through superiority and glory - a belief in oneself above all other things. This belief derives from their interpretation of one of the nine High Prophets in Knoblelism, Seurtasaron the Proud. One of the major five houses.

Quallic House - A maelkii house that roots themselves strong in ancient maelkii traditions. One of the major five houses, this community thrives on its strong values and beliefs.

Maelkii Weaponry

Plasma Cannon - Used by maelkii in the form of arm-covering weapons. These powerful weapons fire a concentrated burst of plasma energy instead of a mere shot.

Plasma Cells - A maelkii created casing of plasma energy focused into a tight space. Releases a burst of plasma at a time.

Type-2 Rover - More notably called Rovers, these maelkii-designed one-man transport vehicles have been in use since 2018 by the maelkii. Rovers use reverse gravity technology to hover in all directions at the same speed. Rovers are very small in size and typically made for base maneuvering.

Type-7 Carriage - More notably called Carriages, these maelkii-designed infantry vehicles have been in use since 2021 by the maelkii. Carriages use reverse gravity technology to hover in all directions at the same speed. They carry a sharp, dangerous-looking design signature to maelkii weaponry. Carriages offer a driver seat, a passenger seat, and multiple seats in the back for maximum transportation. This vehicle is often modified by other species to be used in new worlds without roads due to its adaptability in many climates.

Type-8 Cruisers - More notably called Cruisers, these maelkii-designed infantry vehicles have been in use since 2022. Cruisers use reverse gravity technology to hover in all directions at the same speed. Their sharp, dangerous-looking design inspires fear in enemies. Cruisers offer a driver seat, a passenger seat, and an open area in the back for the maelkii to station themselves and fire their plasma cannons at enemies.

Mordazul

An ancient species whose history goes back much further than most species. Very little is known about them or their culture due to the fact that they live in remote and hidden locations in the Enchanted System. Some believe they have hidden underground communities.

As a species, they have unique sound and vibration manipulation abilities. The palms, backs, and feet of a mordazul are very responsive to vibrations of all kinds. Adults are seen with large totems that grow and attach to their backs. When this process begins is still unknown. Their skin tone is typically shades of violet with a wavy texture that seems to layer over itself, similar to scales, yet still has a fleshy texture. Their totems have a similar appearance to a rocky pillar and are often colored like their skin, with natural and decorative lines and symbols throughout.

Mythical

Book of Sin - A mythical, one-of-a kind book shrouded in legend and mystery.

Foremoth - Mythical creature deriving from omelic culture as a moth with omelic features such as legs, arms, and a head that have the magical powers of foresight and prophecy.

Quondam Keys - Of the legends written about these keys, only one word has ever been decrypted: Light.

Shield of Sin - Mythical, one-of-a kind device shrouded in legend and mystery.

Vault of the Seven - Mythical location shrouded in legend and mystery.

Weapons of Sin - Mythical, one-of-a kind weapons shrouded in legend and mystery.

Non-Intelligent Species

These species' average intelligence falls below Hearon's SMIB Scale and makes them extremely unlikely to ever develop space travel technology.

Borjer - These creatures are found on a few planets in the Zellur System. Aggressive and territorial, these beasts have thick, long claws, brown-colored fur, and natural armor on their backs and scalps. Often, these creatures live in caves and can dig out tunnels in soft dirt.

Boultha - Layered with nearly indestructible hard-granite skin, these goliaths fall below Hearon's SMIB

Scale. They love to ram through all obstacles using brute strength. Boulthas have the strength of about fifty human men, or six maelkii. Tamed and used by the Wersillian Legion for war purposes. Their weakest area is their head.

Grenjore - Also called stone giants, grenjores are strong and vicious creatures that roam the world of Omulice. These creatures do not act out of reason or judgment. They attack anything they see without fail, even other grenjores. Such is also their major weakness since you won't see two gernjores in one location unless they are attacking each other. Their stone-hardened hide is thick and nearly impervious to many forms of attack. If the blood of a creature makes contact with their skin, they turn to stone and eventually transform into a grenjore. The meaning of the glowing red symbol on their chest is often a topic of speculation among arkenlords.

Growllar - Growllars are powerful and furry bipedal mammals that roam the snowy wastelands of Xan'Ohmo. These hulking predators have razor-sharp fangs and claws yet move with surprising stealth, relying on their white fur for camouflage while hunting prey in the show.

Scarlencoul - A symbiotic creature that is found on the world of Omulice. The creature feeds off the energy created by its host. In turn, the host can wield a non-neutral geminite and, by extension, many forms of hyper-weaponry. Therefore, before an omelic is knighted, they must go through the bonding process with a scarlencoul.

Shjarr - These machine, hive-minded creatures of various architypes appear in an ancient maelkii story that is not well-known. Architypes include: priests, fanatics, apostles, zealots, and sandren.

Spiasaurs - Giant spider creatures are found on a few planets in the Enchanted System. Hunt in packs and carry deadly venom to paralyze their prey.

Ungie - Large dog-like beasts with six legs and shark-like, sharp teeth. Tamed and used by the Wersillian Legion for war purposes.

Warwolf - Warwolves are genetically altered wolves: Twice as strong, twice as large, and smart enough to understand ARW soldiers on a basic level. In 2062, the Order of Aegis first began experimentation on genetic therapies and manipulation. Decades later, the process of breeding warwolves was perfected. However, it was a process that was slow and took years to complete. Once warwolves are bred, they are placed in training simulations with their designated wolf-pack unit.

Xyphins - These are man-sized bird-like beasts with two heads and fangs for talons. They are even strong enough to carry individuals for a short distance. Tamed and used by the Wersillian Legion for war purposes.

Omelic

Omelics were first encountered in 2082. Omelics typically keep to themselves and out of galaxy-wide conflicts and are considered among the strongest neutral societies. Due to their home world's vastly dangerous conditions and wildlife, omelics have built vast kingdoms and still remain divided as a species.

Their society is male-dominated, where women are treated more like objects than people. Though, it is rumored that some kingdoms are heading to a more cultured viewpoint.

As mammalian, vertebrate beings, these beings resemble humans in unexplained ways, even having the ability to breed with humans. Omelics are twice as strong as the average human. Though, they display less self-control. Their skin can vary in shades of purple, while their eyes can be any color a human eye can be, along with being yellow or purple. Like qwayks, omelics' hair is commonly white. However, unlike the qwayk, their hair can be shades of gray. Omelics grow to be, on average, slightly taller and slightly heavier than average humans.

Omelic Culture, History, & Titles

Arkenlord - Also seen as knights of the mind, arkenlords are a title given to accredited intellectuals such as scholars, healers, professors, engineers, and other learned individuals.

Grand Thirteen Kingdoms - Of the many kingdoms in the enormous world of Omulice, thirteen hold most of the land and power.

Master of Scrolls - Title granted in some kingdoms to the adviser in matters of intelligence and information gathering to a king.

Royal Guard - Military order of royal bodyguards, sometimes called royal knights, of a king or queen. Usually seen as the finest knights of their kingdom. They are sworn to protect the royal family with their own lives, to obey their commands, and to keep their secrets. Laws vary by kingdom but can sometimes even forbid royal guards from owning land, taking a spouse, or having children.

Ser - Knighthood in omelic culture is a rank given to warriors by their king who perform exemplary service. Its members are known as knights and use the title "Ser," though this may be superseded by other titles such as "lord," "prince," or "king."

Shadow Knight - Unique knights trained for covert or clandestine operations by order of their king. Typically highly skilled in survival, espionage, and swordsmanship.

Space Guard - The Space Guard is a military order that holds and guards the perimeter of Omulice within stations built into orbiting asteroids. They regulate who and what goes in and out of Omulice. Each station is led by a Station Commander, and members of this order mostly consist of volunteers taking tours of duty.

Omelic Houses

House Drayfus - An ancient omelic house of the Tolkran Kingdom that is no longer in power. Fell in the Battle of the Half-Brothers. Sigil is a two-headed snake with yellow eyes on a field of sharp ice.

House Lightbourne - An honorable omelic house within the Tolkran Kingdom. A house that is said to date back to the very beginning of omelic history. They've always been around and held land and power, but only became great a few decades ago. It is said to have started when a maiden lady adopted two homeless brothers and raised them until adulthood. Their sigil is a golden sun with a halo ring around it in the night sky. The current head of the house is Lord Mauga Lightbourne.

House Wolph - An omelic house many centuries old. This house has held kingship over the Tolkran Kingdom ever since they overtook it from House Drayfus a long time ago. Its founder, Aulton Wolph, grandfather of King Kaylob Wolph, was rumored to be the bastard brother of the current king of the time, King Aydon Drayfus. Their sigil is a red-eyed direwolf with white fur over a snowed field. The current head of the house is King Kaydon Wolph, son of Garrol and Cateron.

Order of Aegis

Established at an unknown date. Began to gain notoriety during World War III. Officially became the lead ARW military weapon supplier and research division in 2099. Their mission states: "A privately subsidized organization tasked with the development and research of technology and artifacts in order to support the well-being of the Alliance of Republic Worlds." Only members of high rank in the ARW's military are permitted to know about many of the classified projects created by the Order of Aegis. Public confidence in this company is at an all-time high due to their high turnout and standards for new technology.

Order of Aegis Projects

Project Ace - Official statement released by the Order of Aegis: "Project Ace offers aces a place to stay, learn about their abilities and gifts, and positively impact the future of the galaxy."

Project Aurum - Official statement released by the Order of Aegis: "The project that will end the war and defeat the Wersillian Legion."

Project Glasshouse - Official statement released by the Order of Aegis: "In times of war, greatness is born. Glasshouse aims to perfect those great individuals."

Project Outreach - Official statement released by the Order of Aegis: "In a galaxy vastly unexplored, Outreach seeks to explore strange new worlds. To find new life and new civilizations. To boldly venture into the deep emptiness of space. And to expand our knowledge of our galaxy."

Order of Aegis Signature Technology

Advanced Figure Analysis Technology - Originally designed by the qwayks in 2078 for their vehicles. Later adopted by the Order of Aegis to manufacture sentry turret weaponry and attachment sights. This technology uses advanced algorithms to identify species by measuring their figures.

Hythool - Created by the Order of Aegis, this optional poison is hidden inside the cyberwatches of captain-ranked or higher individuals. This poison can override the nano-immunal bots within an individual's body and give them a quick and painless death.

Magnetic Lock- More notable called mag locks; these devices were created by the Order of Aegis in 2096. These devices use a compound called magnetifer to hold an ARW-issued weapon in place for easy access. All ARW-issued weapons were fitted with a strip of magnetifer to attract to the mag locks.

Model-1 Battle Technoids - These are the first class of field-tested battle technoid models. Created by the Order of Aegis in 2109, these technoids come equipped with standard weaponry mounted to one arm. With artificial intelligence technology, these technoids can problem-solve and think just under Hearon's SMIB Scale. Because of fears, the Order of Aegis has a strict policy against creating intelligence on or above the level of Hearon's SMIB Scale.

Model-2[series] Battle Technoids - The second class of field-tested battle technoid models. Created by the Order of Aegis in 2111, these technoids are outfitted with stronger armor and heavier weaponry than the model-1 technoids; depending on the subclass, the heavy weapon can vary. With artificial intelligence technology, these technoids can problem-solve and think just under Hearon's SMIB Scale. Because of fears, the Order of Aegis has a strict policy against creating intelligence on or above the level of Hearon's SMIB Scale.

Multi-Purpose Tracking Pads - Officially went into use in 2111. An Order of Aegis created device used for tracking. Made to detect motion, scan for footprints and disturbances in the brush, and identify the path of a target.

One-Way Stasis Shield Technology - Recently, the Order of Aegis took stasis shield technology and improved the design to allow projectiles through one direction while maintaining its deflective properties on the other side.

Power Cuffs - Created by the Order of Aegis in 2100, these restraints combine veridium plating and stasis shielding technology to restrain even the strongest individuals. Can resist the strength of four maelkii.

Prototype-2 Power Armor - Approved for active duty in 2108, this expensive, full-body armor replaced the

Prototype-1 series. Created by the Order of Aegis, this sleeker, slimmer design was an overall improvement over its predecessor. The Prototype-2 series is powered by a fusion core located at the back of the armor. Includes a rechargeable shielding layer as a primary line of defense, veridium plating as a secondary defense, and a lightweight titanium plus caringhick-gem in-layered weave to keep the occupant safe and comfortable. It is currently only designed to be used by humans or qwayks.

SHRDR Air Fortress - Special Order of Aegis multipurpose hovercraft. This massive hovercraft can support an area singlehandedly. Due to its size and weight, it is far slower than standard aircraft or hovercraft.

V[series] Zappers - Recently developed by the Order of Aegis, this series of dropships is able to use slip space and stealth technology. This allows them to make quick drops into designated areas of interest.

Waterdrills - Originally created by the Order of Aegis, these small handheld machines use propellers to rapidly maneuver soldiers through water.

Other Weaponry

Endothermic Rifle - A corelinn weapon that fires crystallized water projectiles using an endothermic process.

Endothermic Grenade - A small explosive thrown by hand that was created by the corelinns. Upon exploding, it releases a blast of crystallized water.

Lava Bomb - Infiltration bombs that are used to melt surfaces before cooling rapidly. Can stick to services and detonate with a secondary device. First created by the allsung species.

Sticky Launcher - Small handheld weapon that can launch a single bomb at a time. First created by the allsung species.

Planets & Moons

Corkeria - Once the home world of the korkyras. Now a barren wasteland of molten rock as a result of the Final War.

Delkeedo - One of six dytirc-inhabited moons, the dytircs use this moon mostly for war prisons. However, some rebel tribes are reported to still inhabit this destination. Being terraformed back when the technology was fairly new, this moon has little to offer in terms of diversity and ecosystems. Most of the moon is muddy and hilly, with occasional mud ponds scattered around. Wildlife is scarce and is best described as foul and ugly. The climate consists mostly of pop-up rainstorms.

Dorrath - The home planet of the dor'o, this planet is covered almost entirely in cloud-touching mountains with underwater stream networks. Without much diversity in ecosystems, the variety of wildlife is low, most of which resides in the underwater stream networks. Some consider it a miracle that the evolution of a mammal-based, intelligent species such as the dor'o even came to be on this planet. The climate here is on the colder side, with long winters and a plethora of blizzards.

Gorak - Home planet of the o'gark, this planet is covered by vast amounts of deserts, mountains, and dusty valleys. Gorak is famous for its strangely shaped mountains that are great at collecting and preserving large amounts of water from the few times it rains on this planet. Being a mostly barren planet, wildlife and ecosystems are low. Most wildlife lives around the edges of mountains to shield themselves from the long and harsh dust storms. Water is scarce on this planet, where most reside in the poles or locked away in the mountains.

Grathefer-Qwayk - Home planet of the qwayk and capitol of the ARW, this planet is considered one of the most beautiful places to visit. Large cities, mountain-high tropical forests, mushroom kingdoms, and many other biomes give the planet a distinctive wonder. With such diversity in ecosystems and biomes, this planet has one of the largest varieties of complex wildlife. Furthermore, the climate across this planet varies greatly and is heavily dependent on the biomes.

Hondora - A small planet terraformed to be a neutral gathering place for industrial boom. This planet is famous for The Underlevel, which is a series of entrances across the planet that are all connected and go deep below the surface of the planet. The climate here is hazardous due to the dense amount of smoke, and because of that, all buildings are required to use atmospheric doors to keep the toxic air from reaching their citizens. All water is transported to this planet from a nearby ice asteroid, and the few animals that do exist on this planet came from outside this planet.

Idor - A newly discovered inhabitable planet, this once tropical place is no longer suited for life after a Devisor bomb rendered the planet unlivable and intolerably cold.

Jaba-Qwayk - One of the three worlds originally colonized by the qwayks before they joined the ARW, this planet is a world teeming with fungal-based biomes and an immense amount of primitive plants. Much of the planet has a fetid, humid landscape overgrown by forests of bizarre wilderness. Various natural springs and glowing biomes contribute to giving the wildlife here a distinctive look. Furthermore, climates across this planet vary greatly and are heavily dependent on the biomes.

Juster - Home planet of the plowsu, this planet is covered in mostly forests and winding rivers of fresh water. This planet, however, is beloved for its natural beauty since the plowsu consider it unholy to unnecessarily tamper with nature. Being covered in such vast amounts of fresh water rivers and forests has made the variety of ecosystems and wildlife low. Yet, the amount of wildlife is unusually high. Climate here varies from light rainfalls, to thunderstorms, to tornados. However, the temperature rarely comes close to freezing. For a short time, the Wersillian Legion took occupancy of Juster, but they have recently been forced away by the ARW.

Kuval - The location of Station 9 and is known only to certain individuals of the Order of Aegis and ARW Military.

Laloth - A great mining planet that is at the edge of the Parth System. It is well known for its abundance of mineral resources and various ores. The surface of Laloth is covered in endless sand, sandstone caverns, and desert forests full of vegetation that thrives on low water and lots of sun. Currently owed and inhabited by the species of laburtles. The climate here is dry, with various sandstorms and dust tornadoes.

Maelkiin - The home planet of the maelkii, this planet is too hazardous and toxic for most species to visit or live on without the use of special equipment. Some theorize that it is due to the harsh conditions on this planet that the local wildlife and the maelkii evolved to be as durable and large as they did. The ecosystems and biomes most prominent are volcanic or hot spring-based. The weather is harsh, and the temperature is typically hot. This planet is also nicknamed "The Lonely Planet" due to it being practically in the middle of nowhere at the edge of the known Milky Way Galaxy in the Maelkiin System.

Omulice - Omulice is a bountiful planet in the Enchanted System. It is the home world of the omelic species and the mordazul species. Much of the wildlife, ecosystems, climate, and typography of Omulice are similar to those of Earth; only the planet itself is roughly three times the size of Earth, giving it the nickname Earth's Big Brother. Another name it has been referred to is the World Unknowing Peace due to the many rival kingdoms occupying the planet. Unlike most other worlds, this ancient planet lacks a molten core and instead is comprised of a conglomerate of large, rocky bodies that make up a network of tunnels and caves, many of which are flooded. It is believed that the mordazul have built their homes hidden in the deep depths of these tunnels, since they are a rare sight to see. Omelics typically do not venture into these tunnels and caves, especially the ones that lead deep to the core, fearing the ravenous beasts that reside inside. Omulice's innermost core is rich with dense plasma, a naturally occurring energy unique to the planet, and this, coupled with its lack of molten core, gives this planet a reputation as an enigma to astrophysicists, who regard the world's structure as an extremely uncommon phenomenon in the galaxy. Furthermore, the planet itself is surrounded by motionless asteroids netted together in thousands of defensive energy lines like a web. The technology, believed by some to be Devisor in origin, protects the planet from threats.

Tathen - Small moon in the Parth System. Once ripe with resources and filled with villages of civilian life, this moon was taken over by the Wersillian Legion. They left almost no one alive and mined nearly all of this moon's natural resources, leaving it barren. The Raid on Tathen is the attack that is said to have officially started the Wersillian War.

Xan'Ohmo - Due to the dense snow and ice covering most of this planet's surface, it appears as a blue ball from space. Although some of the many treacherous mountains spread throughout the planet are rich with stardust, the climate forces many species to avoid colonizing this planet altogether. Few species can live comfortably on this very cold planet. Most of this planet's biomes and ecosystems are polar-based. The climate here is hazardous, with frequent blizzards and snowstorms.

Yuerr-Olo - The home planet of the yuerr, this planet is known for its vast oceans and many luxurious islands. Most of this planet's biomes and ecosystems are ocean-based, but they are some of the galaxy's most diverse and extensive in this regard. In ancient times, this place had much more land-based ecosystems and wildlife. However, due to the low amount of land, the yuerr species killed off much of those old ecosystems so they could compensate for their own growth. The climate here is mild, with occasional hurricanes and tsunamis. However, the yuerr have extensive safety measures to prevent such natural disasters.

Priority Code 199 Rederick   Known by captains of the ARW as the "drop everything and follow these orders" code. According to protocol, only a rank of commander or higher is authorized to use this code. Certain persons of interest have been cleared to use this code as well.

Prospects for Peace Act   In 2084, after the founding members of the ARW were set in stone, the ARW Senate passed the Prospects for Peace Act, which opened the door for other species to join the ARW in an effort to establish peace and democracy across the galaxy.

Qwayk   Allied under ARW in 2068, qwayks were the first official alien life to reveal themselves to humans after humans made their first jump to Mars with slip space technology. When the qwayks first contacted Earth, they offered humans a chance to join the ARW, which the worldwide senate on Earth voted to accept. This species is from the Qwayk System, where they inhabit three planets, with Grathefer-Qwayk being their home planet. Qwayks pride themselves on a high-class society and consider themselves very technologically focused. Furthermore, qwayk society is focused on pleasure, and, as such, there is next to no discrimination against race, sex, or orientation. Nor is it uncommon to find qwayks with multiple spouses. Qwayk architecture is considered nothing short of beautiful and genius.

Qwayks have white, flowing hair and light-gray to pale white skin. On the face of a qwayk, they have wrinkle-like waves that start from the base of their eyes and finish at their chins, which the qwayks call vantors. As mammalian, vertebrate beings, qwayks are one of the most humanoid species known. They have typically nimble builds, making them not as strong as humans. However, they have longer foreheads than humans, giving them larger brains. Females are usually smaller in size and either have green or yellow-green eyes. Males have either teal or blue eyes.

Qwayk Culture & History

Illumination Ceremony - A common qwayk ceremony to celebrate and mourn the passing of a loved one. It consists of pouring a substance over the body of the deceased that dissolves the corpse and turns it into a gas-like state in an array of colors. This signifies the dead becoming one with the universe.

Qwayk Weaponry

Designated Laser Rifle (DLR) - Standard all-purpose support weapon created by the qwayks. Each trigger pull unleashes an unrelenting laser that doesn't stop unless the trigger is released or the laser cell is depleted. Laser cells are reloadable.

High Intensity Laser (HIL) Cannon - A qwayk-designed weapon used on star cruisers. This massive weapon charges up and fires a massive stream of intensely focused solar energy to burn through enemy vessels.

Laser Cells - A qwayk-designed small casing of solar energy focused into a tight space. Reloadable and multipurposed for all qwayk-based weaponry.

Reciprocating Laser Rifle (RLR) - Standard multipurpose support weapon for qwayks. Each trigger pull unleashes a barrage of lasers at a rate of fire similar to a standard assault rifle. Due to their more compact size and overall slower depletion of energy, RLRs are typically more favorable for longer operations. Laser cells are reloadable.

Riot Grenade - A timed detonation device that emits a steady stream of lasers in all directions for a short time. Qwayk designed.

Resources & Materials

Brightstone - Translucent rock that is found on many asteroids around the galaxy. Its light-absorbing and emitting properties make it a sought-after resource for lighting. Abundance and ease of use make it a favorite among cultures.

Carringhick-Gem - Carringhick-Gem is a natural material found all over the galaxy. Once melted, this gel-like substance can be used to regulate temperature, change density, and absorb moisture.

Deepstone - Naturally occurring stone that is found in underwater caverns and does not decay from water corrosion. Typically located on planets near the Inner Core.

Durrinium - Nonconductive alloy that mimics the properties of other metals to a degree. Found mostly on planets, asteroids, and moons in the Maelkiin System.

Forcidion - The rarest known natural metal in the galaxy. This metal is only found on the home planet of the maelkii, Maelkiin. Forcidion is one of the heaviest metals and the only metal ever to be deemed unbreakable; the only way to wield this metal is at temperatures as hot as supernovas. In the year 1989, the maelkii used up all of this metal for their shields and have since passed down the shields from generation to generation.

Jurcabeyo Gel - Plentiful substance where the key ingredient, jurcabeyo sap, comes from the jurcabeyo trees that are found all over Omulice.

Magnetifer - A special compound that was created by the qwayks in 2065 to attract and repel only itself. Additionally, it is very easy to adjust the magnetic intensity.

Stardust - Stardust is one of the most sought-after resources in the known galaxy due to its being an essential substance in the creation of wormholes. Yet, because of the unexplainable way that stardust allows for the creation of negative mass to balance out the implosive pressure of a wormhole, stardust cannot fully be understood by modern science.

Veridium - A lightweight, nonconductive, vibration dispersant metal with extreme durability. This rare metal is a favorite resource for species able to afford its production.

Silent Dagger	Legendary, one-of-a-kind weapon custom-crafted by Shadow-Walker. Scout rifle capable of firing off special ricocheting stasis beams at a precise and rapid pace. Equipped with an adjustable zoom scope and thermal detection systems.

Slaag   A poisonous chemical that is classified as one of the top three deadliest poisons in the known galaxy. Can be used in a gas or liquid state and is powerful enough to overcome the nano-immunal bots used in various species across the Milky Way.

Slang   **Boney -** A degrading and derogatory term that is used to describe a dytirc.

Bowlhead - A degrading and derogatory term that is used to describe a lycargan.

Uzzo - A slang word that is used to describe a buddy or friend.

Star Cruisers   **Drifting Cloud -** A star cruiser made by the Order of Aegis. Exploration class. This ship has few weapons and defenses but is agile and has a large engine system for fast travel through open space.

Leviathan II - In 2092, the successor to the Leviathan I finished construction. This historical ship is only the second star cruiser created by humans. Its original purpose was for long-term exploration, but it was later modified for war purposes.

Tempest of Titans - In 2107, construction on the Tempest of Titans was finished. This massive ship ranks as one of the biggest ships in the ARW's fleet. The Tempest of Titans is designed for aggressive attacking due to its powerful haul and shields capable of soaking up and dispersing plasma energy. Mostly human-designed.

Whispering Dragon - In 2109, construction on the Whispering Dragon was finished. This massive ship was designed to jump in and out of combat using versatile mobility technology. Mostly dor'o-designed.

Technology **Atmospheric Doors -** The first models hit the mainstream in 2078 as a new standard public door frame. These devices were first created by the yuerr to use for the Galactic Hotel but were later picked up by various independent companies. Atmospheric doors use energy field technology to create a barrier between the air on either side of the door frame while allowing solid mass to pass through.

Atmospheric Masks - These are masks used as a way to breathe in unbreathable atmospheres. Use highly condensed storage devices to hold breathable air.

Coolant Pads - Universal pads that are produced by various independent companies for the medical purposes of cooling down an individual's body.

Cyberwatch Technology - The first models hit the mainstream in 2064 as a replacement for human cell phones. When humans entered the ARW, their creation was adapted by many independent companies across the galaxy. Cyberwatches became the standard, multi-tool devices used by nearly every intelligent species in the galaxy. Cyberwatches use chain web tools to connect through other cyberwatches or to signal arrays, allowing for service almost anywhere in the known galaxy. Specially designed cyberwatches can be made to connect to independent networks.

Ice Spray - Standard medical device used to treat plasma burns. Caution: It causes extreme pain when first applied.

Landscape Scanner - Simple device that can detect large structures through trees and vegetation. Originally manufactured by the qwayk and later adapted for military use.

Lifepack - A device that can be attached to knightly armor to be used in duels on the world of Omulice. If one is cut, the wearer loses the duel.

Magic Meal - Invented by the qwayks in 2077, this machine materializes different types of food and drinks on demand, mostly through the use of rapid stem cell technology. Furthermore, foods and drinks can be stored in a hyper-condensed state and can be restocked by buying meal pods. Cannot cook items.

Nano-immunal Technology - Universally used by many species as an antibody system given to individuals at childbirth. Nano-immunal technology is programmed to specific species' bodies for maximum efficiency.

Navigation Computer Technology - Qwayks installed this technology in all vehicular automobiles after the year 2067 as a means of transportation on their three occupied planets. Using satellites, the navigation computers can direct cars from one location to another while taking into account other vehicles and the environment. Later programmed to work with nearly all planets or moons occupied by species under the ARW.

Night Vision Visors - A device that is used to detect visible and infrared energy and provide a visual image. Can come in the form of eyewear, glasses, and high-tech versions that can even be displayed holographically.

Overshield - Uses stasis field technology to create an overhead shield that protects the individuals below it.

Peric Fiber - Flexible, durable fiber placed over wounds. Ointments inlayed in the material fight disease and infection as the wound heals.

Recon Beacon - A small beacon that is used to mark a location for scouting purposes.

Refractive Drive - Scout intelligence believes this to be a technology more advanced than stealth drives. Utilized primarily by the korkyran species, this technology can mask the visual image of the starship it is equipped with.

Render Chip - Universally used as communication chips implanted in an individual's ears to translate all known galactic languages into one's native language.

Reverse Gravity Technology - A technology that is commonly used in maelkii and qwayk vehicles. This technology allows vehicles to hover over the ground at a set height. Vehicles with this design can typically hover in all directions at the same speed.

Scaling Bolts - Bolt used to grapple from one place to another via a high-tech cord. Typically fired from a crossbow.

Slip Space (SS) Technology - Humans first developed this technology in 2072, with the first successful trial in 2081, where humans jumped to Mars. Upon entering the ARW, the other species helped humans push the technology to their level. Slip space technology creates a wormhole in space to shorten the distance between two pre-charted parts of space.

Stasis Field Technology - Originally designed by the dor'o in 2082, this technology uses stasis technology to create visible, hard-light fields for maximum protection.

Stasis Shield Technology - Originally designed by the dor'o in 2082, this technology uses stasis technology to create hard-light surfaces that can deflect momentum back at itself.

Stealth Drive - Creates an image mimicking field over a starship to disguise it from view. In addition, these drives offer additional tracking device blockage.

Tissue Spike - An emergency medical device that is used to rapidly grow back cell tissue in case of a major injury. Must be specifically designed for each species.

Tractor Beam - Originally created by the Lycargans in 2102 to hold starships against the underbelly of star cruisers. Later, this technology was adapted by both the ARW and Wersillian Legions to prevent enemy ship takeoffs. These devices use a technology similar to stasis field technology to hold an object in one spot.

WindMaker - Invented in 2099 by a private company that originated in Grathefer-Qwayk as a means to generate wind currents and manage the wind flow of a room. This device was later adopted by many other companies across the galaxy and is often a common household device.

Terminology   **Ace -** The official term used to describe an individual born with exceptional gifts that exceed a species' norm. Aces' gifts have been discovered to stem from the 2nd Big Bang of 2036 and are believed to be solely linked to a DNA mutation. With the exception of two twins, no ace has ever manifested the same abilities or properties as another ace.

Bar'won - Due to an organ called a barwa near the brain of a korkyra, two korkyras are compelled to one another. They can then share an intellectual bond with each other for life where they can share thoughts, feelings, and ideas. A korkyra's bar'won refers to the intellectual partner of that korkyra.

Behemoth-Class - Classification used to describe star cruisers of massive size, which exceed 4000+ meters (4 kilometers) long and 750+ meters in width.
Cohinla - Maelkii term for a lifelong partner or spouse. A bond deemed unbreakable in Maelkii society.

Forlorn - A place inside a dytirc prison where the occupants are subjected to starvation and dehydration for all other prisoners to witness. The goal of a forlorn is to drive the occupants crazy until they fight each other for the rewards offered to the last standing individual.

Lift - A modern drug that is supposed to take your head into the clouds and away from stresses. Currently, Lift is the most popular recreational drug in the galaxy.

Lowblood - A term used in omelic culture to describe a person of low social status, typically born into it.

Majaray - A spiritual room that is used to bring tranquility and peace to the mind. Typical characteristics include waterfalls, tempoed waves, sand, and sometimes soft music.

Mortan Sepulcher - Locations dedicated to the Immortals gang members who have fallen. It consists of a structure and a cave system. The cave houses tombs and other memorials for dead Immortal gang members, while the structure keeps records of all their achievements while in the gang.

Ocean-River: Large bodies of water that path and flow around continents like chains of rivers.

Parasibling - Siblings within polygamous households that are not blood related. Polygamous households are commonplace in qwayk culture.

Prime Hand - Operator of a sacred tower in the Treasured City that maintains the weather. Should no prime hand be present to operate this tower, the weather would become unstable and Coremoo would be barren of life. This sacred role has been filled for all of the corelinns history.

Prime Keeper - Leader of the Treasured City.

Sandren - A religious extremist who lives by a convert-or-kill philosophy. A sandren lives only to convert others to their beliefs, and if that individual won't convert, the extremist kills them, typically in a ritualist manner.

Smithhouse - Workshop that specializes in repairing, creating, and modifying a vast variety of weaponry.

Star Cruisers - A relatively massive starship that can carry large amounts of people within it and is typically manned by a crew. Sometimes it can be large enough to carry other starships.

Starships - Any manned vehicle that can be used to travel in space.

Stumps - Half-horn-like bumps at the top of a dor'o's scalp. Can vary in thickness, length, circumference, and even number.

Supply Crates - Large crates dropped from dropships, which typically contain equipment and weaponry.

Supply Pods - Small pods dropped from either star cruisers or dropships, which can contain equipment or deploy technoids.

Vantors - Wave-like wrinkles that extend from the eyes to the chin on qwayk beings. Can vary in color, tint, width, and distance between each individual wave.

The Immortals	Notorious, organized, intergalactic gang. Not much is known about this group.
Theoretical Technology	**Graviton Sphere -** Theoretical. Some believe graviton particles may be a component of quantum teleportation.
	Quantum Fabricator - A device that could theoretically materialize matter from another, preset location.

Unfortunately, the technology is too advanced to develop successfully.

Quantum-Materialization (QM) Crystal - A decrypted legend says these Devisor crystals created by matter-antimatter reactions are the greatest source of energy potentially available.

Refractor Fields - If it were possible to take the refractive drive technology of the korkyras made for starships and make it smaller, it could theoretically be possible to mask the visual image of an individual.

War-glaive
War-glaives are one-handed, edged weapons with two blades protruding from a center handle. Alabon Zserin is known to use two war-glaives created by the Order of Aegis. His mythical, custom versions can run currents of electricity through the blades.

Warhammer
Warhammers have a bulky head at the end with a large handle for two-handed use. Geariic Zserin is known to use one warhammer created by the Order of Aegis. His mythical, custom version can create explosions on impact.

Wersillian Legion
Alliance between the dytircs and lycargans, led by the 8 Warlords of Virtue.

Wersillian Legion Military Terminology
8 Warlords of Virtue - Legendary status generals of the Wersillian Legion that wield great power. Considered the most feared enemies, these individuals have the highest rank achievable in the Wersillian Legion. Four have been confirmed to be killed. However, two joined later, leaving a current total of six left.

Dytirc Honor Guard - Formidably trained individuals who protect high-ranking Wersillian Legion personnel. Often, wear heavy and durable red armor.

Korkyran Chieftain - Based on korkyran history, scout intelligence believes that korkyran chieftains are the leaders of a pack.

Korkyran Warchief - Scout intelligence suggests that korkyran warchiefs are a new rank amongst the Wersillian Legion. Taking precedence over an Ultra-ranked individual, korkyran warchiefs always come in pairs.

Major - This Wersillian Legion rank has command over all Minors during an operation.

Minor - Similar to an ARW captain, this Wersillian Legion rank has command over a small group of soldiers at a time.

Ultra - This Wersillian Legion rank has command over all Majors during an operation. Typically, only two or three Ultras are present in a battle.

Wersillian Legion Weaponry

Bow Caster - Wersillian Legion grenade launcher capable of firing off five mortar grenades in a rapid session.

Destroyer - Dubbed the "Destroyer" by the ARW, this all-terrain ground vehicle is designed to be multipurpose and adaptable. Its spiky yet lightweight design makes it almost as fast as a Raptor. Armed with a plasma cannon at the back, it is exceptional against armored vehicles.

Hauler - Dubbed the "Hauler" by the ARW, this transport vehicle can carry around forty individuals. Its small design, yet ability to carry slip space technology, makes it a favorite transport vehicle for the Wersillian Legion.

Mortar Grenade - Explosive device that unleashes a primary explosion followed by multiple smaller explosions. Designed by the Wersillian Legion.

Mortar Launcher - Shoulder-mounted Wersillian Legion anti-vehicular and area-denial explosive weapon. Fires a single mortar projectile that explodes in a circular outward explosion, with the secondary explosions reaching farther than the first.

Nitrex Grenade - Powered by nitrex, these grenades release self-containing, black flames that don't spread. With incredibly high temperatures, these flames can consume and melt just about anything. A Wersillian Legion design.

Plasma Bomb - A plasma-based bomb that can stick to surfaces and explode with a secondary device. First created by the allsung species. Used more regularly by the Wersillian Legion.

Plasma Cannon - The Wersillian Legion uses them in the form of mounted cannons on vehicles. These powerful weapons fire a concentrated burst of plasma energy instead of a mere shot.

Plasma Cells - A casing of plasma energy focused into a tight space. Adapted by the Wersillian Legion and modified to use less plasma per shot but last longer.

Plasma Handgun - Standard sidearm used by the Wersillian Legion. These single-shot, plasma-fed handguns run on reloadable plasma cells. A small firearm designed to be held in one hand.

Plasma Rifle - Standard all-purpose rifle used by the dytircs and lycargans. These rapid-fire, plasma-fed weapons run on reloadable plasma cells.

Plasma Vortex - Massive weapon used by Wersillian Legion star cruisers. Although slow, it unleashes a massive shot of plasma that can cause severe damage to other star cruisers.

Pursuer - Dubbed the "Pursuer" by the ARW, this vehicle is the dytirc and lycargan's primary aerial attack vehicle. Recognized by their platform atop the ship and twin plasma guns at the front, these vehicles are used for anti-infantry and anti-vehicular situations.

Wersillian War

Beginning in 2102, the ARW and the Wersillian Legion have entered into an intergalactic war where the ARW is trying to prevent the Wersillian Legion from colonizing other species' planets.

Appendix:

A Man Who Dreamt Hell (Scroll I):

The worst part about Hell is the brew. Don't get me wrong, it's not like the countless brew house conglomerates up in the land of the living that were producing anything of particular quality; once people get addicted to the stuff, you can sell them whatever overpriced garbage you want and make easy income. But once you've made it down here, bartenders just don't care anymore. In fact, everyone has stopped caring. We are all aware that eternal rapture is forever out of our reach, and nihilism and despair thrive in this cesspit.

"You there!"

I jolt out of my egocentric rumination at the sound of me being called. It was the bartender; a sixteen something with acne and braces, with a rim of silver hair coming out from underneath his dirty hat. I don't know why I keep drinking this over-sweetened swill. Probably because I care as little about the quality of my brew as I do everything else in this literal hellhole. This place is the closest one to my house, and it is just as nasty and overpriced as all the ones I frequented when I was alive.

You'd expect that a brew house in the Netherworld would be full of the screams of the damned or have walls made of the flesh of heretics, at least a hint of fire and brimstone. But no, it has the same as upstairs - same misery to deal with, and the same soulless atmosphere. If I didn't know any better, I'd think I was alive.

Sometimes I wonder if I really am in the Netherworld or just plain insane. I start to think that the slow descent of common decency in society has corrupted my mind to the point where I started suffering from some fringe form of mental breakdowns and believed I'm living in some ecclesiastical locality. But then I look up into what I hope is the sky and see nothing but an endless roof of bedrock located too high up to reach, all surrounding a small scarlet star that is the source of light for this underworld. And the village streets are painted in a constant red tint, as if in a state of permanent dusk.

The worst part of it all is living a meager existence for all eternity. There is no fulfillment, no passion. Life was one depression after another. Being dead is more of the same--

-- Arkenlord Mozaru Vox

A Man Who Dreamt Hell (Scroll II):

I've been dead for longer than I remember living; I played with electricity and lost. I was ready to die; I wanted to close my eyes and eat dandelions by the roots for all eternity. Imagine my surprise when I woke up in the middle of a trash-filled street with all the same lowblood clothes I wore when I was alive. I was barefoot because I was never able to afford shoes. I was soaked to the brine, and my body was covered in electrical burns. Now, my imagination didn't jump immediately to being in the Netherworld, even with the red ceiling looming above me. It was only after my second attempt at death via throwing myself off the roof of a tall building that I realized this was my new existence.

I had to learn a lot of these rules on my own, because unlike what most denominations will preach to you, there are no hellcats or hellhounds to torment you for all eternity. Hell was never about that. It was always just other people--

-- Arkenlord Mozaru Vox

Acknowledgments:

Here's to my mother, Debbie, my grandfather, Robert, my grandmother, Donna, and my uncle, David. I thank you for all your adventurous efforts into the uncharted waters that were my early copies. With your support, time, and advice, I was able to go the length and publish. I'll forever cherish your kindness.

Here's to my brother, Andrew, and my best friend, Khari. Thanks for your creative insight and conceptual ideas in the creation of the personas of Castle and Ghost. Without both your initial pushes, I wouldn't have a core piece of the puzzle that is this series.

Here's to my family and friends who gave their support and love towards me when I undertook this project. Without you all, my passion may never have gained any substance.

About the Author:

Writing is a dream and passion, an outlet of unencumbered creativity for Trey Deibel, and he dreams of a day when others can share in his love for storytelling. Trey, also known as Bruce Deibel III, is most passionate about creating enduring and intriguing worlds filled with unique and lively characters. A certified scuba diver and trained in wakeboarding, water skiing, and slalom, Trey is an adventurer at heart and enjoyer of the outdoors. By trade, he works as a licensed home inspector. By day, he enjoys movies, games, and music. He has a large interest in sci-fi, fantasy, and superhero movies, his favorite game is Overwatch, and the music he most enjoys is metal and rock, his favorite bands being Linkin Park, Slipknot, and Three Days Grace.

Follow Trey Deibel on Twitter: @bedeibel.

Credits:

Cover Art by Humbert Glaffo

Interior Concept Art by Indra Budistyawan

Edited by Karen Boston

Copyright:

First Printing, 2020

ISBN 978-1-950938-10-0

Book 3

Published by Trey Deibel

www.ingramcontent.com/pod-product-compliance
Lightning Source LLC
Chambersburg PA
CBHW022237020726
47496CB00004B/940